Clutching at Straws

Charles P. Sharkey

RINGWOOD PUBLISHING
GLASGOW

First published in Great Britain in 2021 by
Ringwood Publishing, Glasgow.
www.ringwoodpublishing.com
mail@ringwoodpublishing.com

ISBN 978-1-901514-72-8

British Library Cataloguing-in-Publication Data
A catalogue record for this book is available from the
British Library

Printed and bound in the UK by
Lonsdale Direct Solutions

Prologue

The graffiti-sprawled apartment block was in a state of terminal decay and earmarked for demolition. Most of the tenants had long since moved out as the area became notorious for crime and drug abuse. On the third floor there was one flat still occupied, and from below only the flicker of light from a television gave any indication that someone still lived there.

Inside the shabby flat the smell of nicotine and cheap alcohol permeated, but still failed to mask the musty smell of dampness. Empty wine and beer bottles litter the floor of the living room, while the remnants of an Indian takeaway were dumped in the filthy kitchen sink.

It was late, and a male in his mid-to-late twenties lay in a stupor on a threadbare couch, struggling to keep his eyes open when a porn film that he'd been watching began to lose his interest. He shivered, feeling the cold for the first time as the drugs began to wear off. He considered having another fix, but changed his mind, deciding to have a smoke instead. He then heard the front door opening. 'Did ye get them?' he shouted, sitting up and lifting a packet of cigarettes from the clutter on the coffee table.

There was no response.

'Did ye fucking get them?' he demanded, while looking for a lighter he had dropped at his feet. There was still no answer. A sudden coldness rushed into the room. He looked up. The living room door was open.

'What the fuck …'

Norman Watson had been lucky to get served; the shutter was already halfway down and the shop was in darkness. He ducked under it and banged on the glass door, before persuading the reluctant owner to fetch a bottle of cider and a packet of cigarettes if he wanted to get rid of him.

The icy wind that was at his back on the way to the off-sales was now biting at his face and the hand that held the bottle was soon numb.

When he finally got back to the apartment block, he unscrewed the bottle top and took a long, greedy drink, before peeing in the corner of the stairwell. Cursing the broken lift that had not left the ground floor in months, he climbed the badly-lit concrete stairs. *Ah hope that lazy bastard's no' fucking sleeping.*

Watson was almost halfway along the corridor when he heard what sounded like a gunshot. Torn between fear and bravado, he was rooted to the spot. The drugs and alcohol in his veins urged him on but he began walking slowly back towards the stairwell. Looking back he saw a stranger emerge from the flat. The bottle slipped from his hand and smashed. He ran for his life ...

Chapter 1

It had already been dark for a couple of hours. Winter had already set in and the rain that fell in the afternoon was now turning to sleet as the temperature dropped. Frank Dorsey was glad to be out of the cold. The pub was quiet and he stood at the bar watching the evening news while waiting for his second pint to be poured. The mobile phone in his coat pocket began to vibrate again, and this time he decided to answer it. He took it out, looked at the name that was flashing, and shook his head. It was DC Mitchell.

'What's up, George?' he asked. 'Fuck … Okay, can you pick me up … The Barkley?' He looked at the pint he had just paid for and let out a sigh. 'Joe, I'm going to pass on this one. Can you see if one of the boys on the corner wants it?'

'No problem, Frank. Something come up?' 'Aye, I guess there's no rest for the wicked.'

Dorsey was having a cigarette outside the pub when Mitchell pulled up, bumping the car on to the edge of the pavement.

'It's fucking freezing,' he moaned, getting into the passenger seat. 'What do we know about it?'

'Not much, just what I've told you. Strachan is already there with the scenes of crime team.'

'Strachan?'

'I did phone you three times, Frank …'

3

'It was on silent.'

Their destination was on the other side of the river from The Barkley, and it took them a while to get through the slow-moving rush hour traffic, which was not helped by the miserable weather. When they reached the locus, Mitchell parked the car on a piece of waste ground beside four other police cars. They walked over the frozen mud, causing small pockets of ice to crunch under their feet.

A young constable lifted up the blue and white cordon tape to let the two detectives through the outer cordon. The scenes of crime team had already erected portable lights around the building. The high-intensity LED lamps gave the place an eerie atmosphere, as though those who once worked there still haunted its skeletal ruins.

The factory had been derelict for years, and part of the roof had caved in on the main workshop. It had been a paper mill in its prime, and the concrete floor was peppered with bore holes where the heavy machinery had once been secured. At the other end of the building, on a mezzanine, were the remains of the managers' offices, with their gaping holes where the windows had been, but otherwise still intact. Another constable was standing outside one of the offices. He stopped shivering and straightened up when he saw the detectives carefully walking through the detritus of broken red bricks and twisted metal. Dorsey stood in the middle of the factory and looked up through the huge hole in the roof. The sleet had stopped and he could see a few stars flickering in a transient break in the clouds.

'There's Strachan,' said Mitchell, as the DS walked towards them.

'Watch you don't slip,' shouted Strachan. 'This place is like a fucking ice rink.'

'What's the story, Charlie?' asked Dorsey, lighting up and offering a cigarette to Strachan.

4

'No thanks, I've just put one out. We got a call just after five; a couple of youngsters were playing in here and found it. Jenkins is here already, I need to find somewhere to take a leak. I don't want my DNA turning up in a forensic report.'

'Do we know anything about the victim?'

'No, but he looks like a junkie … Sorry, Frank, I really need to piss,' insisted Strachan, walking off towards a dark corner of the building that had escaped the light from the LED lamps.

After getting Strachan's dismissive appraisal of the deceased, the two detectives cautiously climbed the shaky iron staircase to the office where the body had been discovered.

'Good evening, Inspector,' said Professor Jenkins, who was kneeling beside the head of the victim and carefully removing something from the gaping wound with a pair of tweezers. 'Give me a few minutes. I'm nearly finished here.'

'Take your time, Professor,' replied Dorsey, putting on a pair of rubber gloves that Mitchell handed him.

This was one time Dorsey did not need to ask the cause of death. He could work that out easy enough for himself. The nature of the head wound and the blood and brain splatter on the wall above the victim was enough. He watched one of the scenes of crime officers remove what he assumed was a bullet from the wall and place it in a production bag. He could not make out much about the victim other than he was a young, white male with dark hair and looked very thin. 'Do we have an I.D. yet?'

'There's nothing on him with his name and address, Inspector, if that's what you mean,' said Jenkins, getting to his feet. 'We'll just have to find out who he is the hard way … I'll no doubt see you in the morning, Inspector, with your usual questions,' said Jenkins, before doffing his hat and carefully making his way down the shaky staircase.

Dorsey slowly cast his eyes around the room as the scenes of crime team continued in their painstaking forensic search for evidence. Wary not to stand in the large pool of congealed blood around the victim's head, he kneeled down to take a closer look at what was left of the face. 'Do you recognise him, George?'

'No, but I don't think his own mother would recognise him in that state.'

Dorsey took another look around the room then nodded to Mitchell; he had seen enough. He ordered the body to be bagged. 'George, can you drop me off at the pub?'

It was almost midnight before Dorsey staggered out of The Barkley and got into a taxi. Once in his second floor flat, he poured himself a large whisky and drank it while watching the late news. There was no mention of the murder, but that would soon change. He shook his head and looked around the untidy living room. Dirty dishes were piled up on the coffee table. He made a promise that he would wash them first thing in the morning, but knew he wouldn't.

Staggering to the bathroom, he relieved himself before brushing his teeth. The late nights were starting to take their toll. His eyes were bloodshot and he had not shaved for a couple of days. Now forty years old and feeling it, he touched a few grey hairs he hadn't noticed before. The reflection in the mirror could have been his late father staring back at him. Dorsey just hoped he had his mother's genes when it came to longevity.

The bedroom was freezing cold. He put on the electric heater, which buzzed energetically before the bars began to turn bright orange. It wasn't much of a heater, but at least it would take the chill out of the air. He had to get the landlord to fix the central heating. He wasn't paying eight hundred pounds a month to live in a fridge! His thoughts turned to the murder as he emptied his pockets and put his change and keys onto the dresser. A couple of unruly coins rolled off and disappeared under the bed. He ignored them and undid his tie.

Now trying to get the image of the dead man out of his head, he undressed and got into bed. He was under the covers for only a few minutes when the midnight mail train rattled past the building, screeching, wailing, and casting its ephemeral shadows on the bedroom ceiling. The vibrations danced a chess piece from the board on the dresser; it landed on one of his discarded socks. He got up and put the fallen knight back on the vacant square. The noise of the train slowly faded into the distance. He turned the fire off and got back into bed with a shiver. It began to snow outside.

It was times like this that he missed Helen the most. He thought about her for a while. He could hear footsteps from the flat above; someone else was having trouble sleeping. His thoughts quickly turned to the murder victim again. He sat up and switched on the bedside lamp and lit a cigarette. The snow was now falling heavily.

Chapter 2

While Claire got the two older children ready for school, Mitchell tried his best to get one-year-old Becky to eat her food. With the hands on the kitchen clock seemingly moving faster at breakfast-time, both parents' tempers were often frayed.

'George, do you have to make such a mess?' complained Claire.

'Me? I'm only spooning it into her mouth, it's Becky that's spitting it back out. I need to have a shower and get ready for work ... Sophie, can you finish feeding your sister.'

'Oh, Dad, I haven't got time.'

'I thought you weren't going in until ten this morning, I was hoping you could take the kids to school this morning.' 'I can't, Frank's asked me to pick him up. We've got a post-mortem this morning. I need to leave early.'

'Frank! It's always bloody Frank with you. Why can't he get to work himself?'

'He's my boss, what do you want me to do?'

'I ask you to do me one little favour ...'

'Claire! Enough ... I'll be ready in fifteen minutes, if the girls are ready to leave when I get downstairs I'll take them to school ... anything for a bit of peace. But I'm not hanging about waiting for them like the last time.'

The primary school was only a short drive from the Mitchell's modest end-terrace house in Giffnock, but at this time in the morning the narrow roads around the school were like mini car parks for SUVs. Mitchell got the car as near as he could to the front gate before dropping off his two daughters, who ignored his usual advice about paying attention to the teacher and ran into the playground to find their friends. 'Thanks for the lift, Daddy … Goodbye, Daddy,' he mumbled sarcastically to himself, before driving off.

Mitchell eventually turned on to Kilmarnock Road after escaping from the maze of narrow streets around the school. He rang Dorsey.

'Frank, I'll be there in twenty minutes.'

'Don't rush, I'm just up. Oh, George, can you get me a packet of cigarettes?'

With the smell of whisky still on his breath, Frank Dorsey held a handkerchief to his mouth, while listening to Jenkins narrating the conclusions of the post-mortem. He was now feeling a little nauseous as Mitchell religiously noted down the details.

'He was a young male, no more than twenty-five years old. As you can see, he's been shot in the head at close range, the bullet passing through the skull and taking a part of the brain with it. There were no other wounds, apart from some minor cuts to the palm of his hands and knees. He was obviously facing the killer when shot,' said the Professor, before removing more of the sheet to expose the Y-shaped incision that ran from each shoulder to the sternum and then all the way down to the pelvic bone. The ruptured bowels emitted a rank smell through the yellow flaps of the cut skin that was difficult for Dorsey to endure.

In spite of the gut-wrenching stench, Mitchell continued

to note the details of the Professor's narration, including the fading tattoo of King Billy on the victim's left pectoral muscle, and the letters RFC, crudely scribed in Indian ink on the right forearm. The veins on the arms were clearly visible through the thin, almost translucent skin. Jenkins pointed out the needle marks that confirmed the deceased was a heroin addict, which surprised no one. 'I think you've heard all that I can tell you at the moment,' he concluded, opening his white coat and taking a gold watch from his waistcoat pocket. 'Good God, is that the time already? I've a lecture at ten o'clock this morning.'

'Talking of time, Professor, how long has he been dead?'

'Well, Inspector, the decomposition indicates somewhere between four and six days. It may be slightly longer due to the fact it was well below freezing the last few nights.'

'Was he under the influence of anything when he was killed?'

'I've taken samples for toxicology tests. I won't be able to tell you the results until tomorrow, but I can tell you that he had a curry, maybe two or three hours before he was killed,' said Jenkins, showing the detectives a tin bowl with the stomach contents.

'Jesus,' retched Dorsey, taking a step away from the smiling pathologist, 'how the hell can you tell that's a curry?'

'If you look in that bag over there, you'll find his shirt. It's not only covered in blood, but there's also a large stain down the front with the unmistakable smell of curry. It seems our friend was a messy eater. I'll have the stomach contents analysed just to be sure, but I can smell the spices, he definitely had a curry of some kind.'

'Was there anything found to help us identify him?'

'No, there was no wallet or anything…just a few pounds in small change found in his trouser pockets and a gold sovereign ring, which I removed from the right index finger.

It's with his other belongings. Oh, I also found this in his back pocket.'

'A tenner bag,' said Mitchell, looking at the small knot of cellophane.

'Yes, but hardly a tenner's worth. It looks like it's been cut with brick dust, Satan's cut,' said the Professor, shaking his head and pulling the sheet back over the body. 'The drugs are bad enough, but some of the rubbish they use to mix them is even more dangerous.'

'Thanks, Professor.'

'Don't mention it, Inspector. You look a bit pale, are you alright?'

'I'm fine.'

'Good, I'll have my secretary email the preliminary report sometime later this morning,' said Jenkins, taking off his white coat and hanging it behind the door.

Chapter 3

Before heading back to the station, Dorsey decided to make another visit to the locus. He would now be able to have a better look at the crime scene without disturbing potential evidence. He was also still feeling a little queasy and not keen to go to the station with the smell of whisky still on his breath.

Mitchell took the motorway this time to avoid going through the city centre and they were there within twenty minutes. The derelict factory looked very different in daylight. The scenes of crime team had moved their search to the general area around the building. Mitchell parked beside their mobile unit.

Once in the ruins of the factory, the only sound they could hear, apart from the distant noise of cars passing on the motorway, was the cooing of pigeons in what remained of the top floor. They climbed up the iron stairs, which officers had re-bolted to the wall to make more stable.

'Good morning, sir,' greeted a uniformed officer, who was standing outside the office, which now had tape across the entrance. Mitchell took a penknife from his back pocket and cut the tape. The floor was covered in labels left by the scenes of crime officers, indicating the position where the body was found and the blood splatter. There were still small bits of brain and bone fragments stuck to the opposite wall around where the bullet was removed. The two detectives carefully moved around the room which, without the body, was empty apart from rubble. Dorsey considered the large blood stain and kneeled down to take a closer look. He slowly cast his eyes around the room again to see if there was anything that might have been missed by the forensic team. He noticed a cigarette butt lying between two bricks and picked it up. He was surprised to find that the tip was still warm.

'Constable! Come in here!' 'Yes, sir.'

'Have you been smoking?'

'Yes, sir, I just had a couple to keep warm.'

'I don't mind you having a cigarette, but why the fuck did you throw it in here … this is a fucking crime scene,' scolded Dorsey, handing the constable the butt.

'I'm sorry sir, I wasn't thinking.' 'Get this doorway taped up again.'

'Yes, sir.'

Dorsey took another look around the room then nodded to Mitchell. He had seen enough; the real clues would already be in the lab. The constable stood aside as the two detectives made their way back out of the office and downstairs.

When they got back to the station, Barney Collins, a freelance hack for the local newspapers, was sitting in the waiting room. Collins could smell a murder before the police even knew there was one to investigate. Dorsey was sure that he was getting tip-offs from someone at the station, but who was anyone's guess. Barney was a dapper man, and always dressed in one of his made-to-measure suits and black fedora. He doffed his hat when Dorsey and Mitchell entered the reception. 'Morning, Inspector, I hear you've got a gangland murder case on your hands.'

Dorsey smiled, but ignored him and went behind the charge bar and into the main CID operations room.

DS Strachan was already at his desk.

'Norman Watson,' said Strachan, handing the Inspector a morgue photograph he had downloaded from Jenkins's email. 'A couple of the guys in the drug squad recognised him straight away. That's a mug shot from a few months back when they arrested him for possession of a couple of tenner bags. The lab is still to confirm a match with his fingerprints and DNA, but it's Watson alright.'

'What do we know about him?'

'I've checked his previous; he's a drug dealer with a heroin habit. The last address we have for him is care of his girlfriend, Morag Burns, in the Glenview flats. Watson was one of Moffat's street dealers, mainly heroin … near the bottom of the food chain.'

Dorsey read the preliminary report that Strachan handed him. It was the same man, although there would have to be a formal identification before the press were told anything. He looked at the photograph, but did not recognise him, then the address; 16/3 Glenview. This he did recognise. Glenview was one of four high-rise flats in a rundown area of the East End controlled by the Moffats.

'What do you think?' asked Mitchell.

'A drug deal gone wrong, or maybe he was ripping off the Moffats?' suggested Strachan.

'He was a brave man if he was.' 'Brave? Stupid more like …'

'Get your coat, George,' interrupted Dorsey, lifting the file from the desk. 'We'll have to speak to his girlfriend first, before our friend Barney gets what he's looking for … who told him anyway?' he added, directing his question to Strachan.

'You know Barney; he's got friends in high places.'

'Let's go, George.'

Chapter 4

Outside, the snow was already melting to slush and as they got into the car Mitchell immediately switched on the heater to clear the windscreen before pulling out onto the main road. Dorsey turned on the radio.

When they reached the Gallowgate, the local news channel made a matter-of-fact statement about the murder, keeping within the remit Superintendent Knox had given them. The identity of the man would only be passed to the press when the next of kin was informed. The cause of death was to remain under wraps in the meantime. Dorsey switched off the radio. 'Take the next left at the corner.'

'Some slums about here,' said Mitchell, looking at the boarded-up tenements covered in graffiti. 'You'd think they'd knock these junkie warrens down before they fall down.'

'They'll be gone soon enough. The council is going to clear this area.'

'The sooner the better,' said Mitchell, pulling up outside a row of tower blocks that looked like they had landed there from another planet.

They got out of the car and walked towards the front entrance of the second tower-block of four. Like the others, it had an optimistic name: The Glenview, which to the original occupants in the sixties promised a home of beautiful vistas away from the tenement slums they had left behind. The ground was slippery, and Dorsey stopped for a moment to look up at the grey concrete high-rise flats. A monument to modernity—*or was it stupidity?*—he thought, as Mitchell waited for him at the lift. The flat was on the sixteenth floor, a long way up in a metal box that stank of urine. The lift closed and slowly began to screech its way past each landing. Dorsey looked at some of the scribbled bravado, and recognised one of the nicknames: *Tuna*, a well-known character he had arrested a few times, and who died a couple of months back of a drug overdose. *Poor bastard; more sad than bad,* thought Dorsey. He smiled when he recalled Tuna's real name, John West. It wasn't too difficult to go from that to something fishy, but Salmon did not have the same ring to it. The lift finally shuddered to a halt on the top floor.

Dorsey dreaded having to tell family members that their loved ones had been murdered. Each time it was different. Some would respond in stunned silence, while others would break down in uncontrollable grief. He was never sure what to expect. 'Press it again,' he said, when the bell failed to get a response. Mitchell pressed the plastic button, stepping back when he heard the sound of chains and locks rattling on the other side of the door.

'Who is it?'

'Miss Burns?' said Mitchell.

'Aye, who are ye?' she asked aggressively, still unwilling to open the door more than a few inches.

'Police officers,' said Dorsey, producing his warrant card. 'Can we come in?'

'I've no' done nothing,' she said, reluctantly letting them into her narrow hallway.

The two police officers followed Miss Burns in through the cold, damp flat, which had the smell of poverty about it. It was only when they were in the living room that they realised that they were almost in the clouds as a panoramic view of Glasgow stretched out in front of them. The city skyline had a frosty look to it, and the Campsie Hills in the distance were covered in snow. Dorsey thought how much more stunning the view would be if someone had bothered to wash the windows. Mitchell took out his notebook, immediately writing down a description of the woman; mid to late twenties, five foot six, thin to the point of anorexic, with shoulder-length mousey-brown hair. She also had swelling above her left eye, which she tried to cover with her hair as she picked up a half-smoked cigarette from a large glass ashtray on the floor.

'Miss Burns, is your boyfriend called Norman Watson?'

'Ma ex-partner ye mean … the bastard … what's he been up tae now … that's his wean,' she replied, nodding to the cot in the recess corner. 'Is he in the fucking jail again?'

'Well, no … I'm afraid a body fitting his description …'

'A body … Oh fuck, no' Norrie …'

'It's not a hundred percent confirmed yet, but it looks like him from the photographs. He was wearing a sovereign ring and has a tattoo of King Billy on his upper chest and RFC on his right forearm.'

'Oh God, no' Norrie,' she began to sob, lifting a packet of cigarettes from the glass coffee table and lighting another cigarette from the one she had been smoking.

'I take it that he has these tattoos?'

'Aye, he loved the Rangers and King Billy more than his ain wean.'

'We might need you to make a formal identification.'

'What happened?'

'We believe he was murdered. Did he have any enemies?'

'Fuck's sake, murdered … How?'

'We can't say at the moment. Did he have any enemies?'

'No. Who'd want tae murder Norrie?' she asked through distorted tears and sobs that woke up the baby. While Morag got up and lifted the crying child from the cot, Dorsey took a moment to look around the living room, which was sparsely furnished and poorly decorated. The cheap black leather settee had seen better days and was torn in a number of places exposing the discoloured foam inside. He noticed the fungal stains on the wallpaper, which was hanging loose behind a large television set that dominated the room. The smell of damp was nothing to the stench of faeces that came from the cot. He pressed on, eager to get the interview over as quickly as possible. 'Did Norrie live with you?'

'Aye, sometimes … he's no' supposed tae be here … he's been oot oan bail fur battering fuck oot o' me when he was oot his face oan smack … but ah let him stay sometimes if he wasn't using … am oan a meth script, and the social work were threatening tae take the wean if ah let him stay here. He told me he wasn't using and was going tae go in tae a rehab. But he's a fucking liar at the best a times. There Kylie, stop crying pet … ah know, yer da's been murdered.'

'When was the last time you saw Norrie?'

'About one on Saturday afternoon, he went fur a few pints before going tae the game. He didn't even say cheerio tae the wean.'

'Which pub did he go to?'

'Probably the Royal, that's where he gets the supporters' bus.'

'The Ranger's game was at Parkhead on Saturday,' said Mitchell, still noting everything down diligently.

'How dae ah know?' she said, taking another long draw from the cigarette as though her life depended on it.

The two men tried to keep their minds on their questions as Morag sat back down on the settee and began to remove the child's soiled nappy. The smell was now overwhelming. Dorsey continued to ask questions, which were answered through sobs and the occasional desperate cry to God, followed by a string of curses.

'Did he phone you at anytime after he left on Saturday?'

'Phone me? Norrie never phones ... no, ah tell a lie, he phoned me a couple o' weeks ago tae find oot if ah videoed the Rangers game fur him. He only started going tae the games last month. One o' his mates stopped using his season ticket and gave it tae Norrie.'

'Did he get in contact with you at any time since he left to go to the game?'

'That's what ah said. He never fucking phones me ... There Kylie, yer arse is clean now,' she said, putting the child back into the cot.

'How'd he pay for his habit?'

'He was selling tenner bags fur ...'

'For who ... for the Moffats?'

'Am no' saying.'

'You've a bad bruise above your eye, how'd that happen?'

'Ah banged maself oan the edge o' the table when ah slipped oan her sick. She's always fucking sick.'

'When'd that happen?'

'A couple o' days ago ... it wasn't Norrie, if that's what yer thinking.'

'Do you know where Norrie stayed when he wasn't staying here?'

'Fuck knows. Norrie could get a piece at anybody's door. He just stayed wi' anybody that'd put him up, but he uses his mate, Willie Tucker's address fur his dole money.'

'Where does Tucker live?'

'Fuck knows, somewhere oan the other side o' the scheme. He's another fucking smack heid ... will ah get any compensation?'

'For what?

'Fur Norrie ... criminal injuries ... Kylie's his wean

19

remember. It's no' fur me, it's fur her?' 'You should go and see a lawyer; he'll be able to tell you.'

Once the questioning was over, they were both glad to get out of the flat. The smell of urine in the lift seemed even more offensive on the way down and they were soon relieved to be out in the brisk morning air. 'Criminal injuries, it's the first thing they think of,' said Mitchell. Dorsey did not answer at first but turned to look up at the high-rise flats.

'If I lived in that place, I'd be thinking of criminal injuries to try and get to hell out of it.'

'But that's it. If she gets criminal injuries, it'll go on drugs and booze. I've seen it all before.'

'You might even take drugs yourself, if you were stuck in that fucking place watching the clouds and life floating by your window day after day,' said Dorsey, stealing another look up at the block, before getting into the car. Mitchell turned on the engine and waited for the heater to start clearing the windscreen.

'So what have we got?' asked Dorsey.

'A twenty-five year old junkie, who sold heroin for the Moffats in return for a few tenner bags of the stuff,' summarised Mitchell from what he put into his notebook. 'It sounds like he was ripping them off.'

'But he couldn't have been selling that much to deserve a bullet in the head. There must be something else … maybe he tried to set up his own operation.'

'What if it's got nothing to do with drugs? Maybe she got sick of getting beaten up with Watson and got someone to put a bullet in him … she was hardly the grieving widow.'

'A crime of passion in the heart of the East End … I think it's more likely to be about drugs … don't you?' said Dorsey. 'Anyway, let's go and have a look at the factory.'

Chapter 5

Denis Moffat ordered the twins into the back study, the only room in the house that his wife would allow them to discuss business. He was a big man with a formidable physical presence and reputation that continued to intimidate his rivals. His face was hard, like weathered mahogany and his cold, dark eyes like ebony. Those that thought they could take him on in the past found to their cost the brutality of the man. At least half a dozen of his enemies had ended up in the city morgue. As the bodies began to mount up, he began to dispose of his victims with more care, and one motorway flyover was said to contain at least two of his former adversaries. The problem for the police, when this rumour found its way into the press, was finding out which flyover. Many thought it was just another urban myth about Denis Moffat, one in which he no doubt revelled. The one thing that had become something of a trademark was the cigars he chain-smoked like cigarettes. Anyone wanting the Big Man's favour always knew the way to his heart was a box of expensive cigars, and now he had so many that one of the attic rooms in his house was turned into a humidor where his collection was kept in prime condition.

Denis lived with his staunchly loyal wife, Irene, whom he married in his early twenties. Their house was a detached villa with a ranch-style porch and a huge extension to the back. After a few attempts on his life in the late nineties, Denis installed the latest security systems. Every corner had CCTV cameras that gave the place the appearance of an impregnable fortress and was soon nicknamed Fort Knox by the locals.

His three sons were now running the illegal side of the family firm, while Denis posed as a legitimate businessman. He had numerous investments in a string of pubs, bookmakers, sauna parlours and a security firm that gave 'protection' to vulnerable building sites around the city. The sons still had to defer to their father in times of crisis and his word was always final, his strong Glaswegian accent now only surfacing when he lost his temper. Benny, the oldest, was in prison serving a five-year sentence for serious assault. However, being in Barlinnie Prison did not stop him from controlling drug deals through his younger, twin brothers, Billy and Eric, and other trusted associates, who carried out his orders on the outside. With a couple of smuggled mobile phones, Barlinnie was more of a place of business for Benny than a prison, and his cell had become his office. The only thing missing was the lifestyle that the profits of the business guaranteed on the outside.

Three years older than the twins, Benny was now thirty six. Before being jailed, he dressed in imported Italian suits and wore handmade shoes that would cost the average Glaswegian a month's wages to buy. Unlike the twins, who had inherited their father's dark, stoic eyes and thin, wispy brown hair, Benny was handsome, with blue eyes and thick, dark hair like his mother. Everyone knew Benny as a ladies man who liked flash cars and fine wines. Prison was hell for him, but the custodial element of his five-year sentence was coming to an end. A month before his release date, he received a call from one of his associates that would put his previous drug deals in the shade. A consignment of cocaine was already on its way to Scotland that would make him a rich man. He decided that this was a deal that neither his father nor his brothers should know about.

The twins had a reputation for extreme violence that bordered on the psychopathic and had always managed to escape prison due to the fear they instilled in potential witnesses. Billy was the older of the twins by twenty minutes, and his temples were permanently scared by the claws of the forceps that were used to drag him reluctantly into the world.

His younger twin, Eric did not escape completely unscathed from the protracted birth and was left with a squint in his left eye that was blamed by the doctors on the lack of oxygen he received in the womb. Their birth defects helped others to distinguish them and added to their sinister appearance. Although Denis had his reservations as to how his boys turned out, his daughter Ashley, the youngest in the family, was the one that reminded him most of himself. Everyone said she had her father's brains and, like Benny, her mother's looks. Ashley was still in her late teens, an unplanned pregnancy that stunned the whole family, none more than Irene who had thought she was long past having children.

As far as Denis was concerned, his daughter was a gift from God that softened some of his hardness over the years. He made it clear to his sons that the family business was not for her; the boys were under strict instructions from an early age never to mention their activities to their sister. Every manner of subterfuge was used to make Ashley believe they all worked in the family's legitimate businesses and that her brother Benny was a victim of a miscarriage of justice. Unabashed by the irony, that summer, Denis threw a lavish party to celebrate Ashley's matriculation at Aberdeen University, where she was due to start her first year as a law student. Keeping her in the dark about the family's illegal activities was less of a problem after she moved to the University's halls of residence that autumn and was now only home for the occasional weekend.

Denis sat behind his oak desk and lit a cigar, staring at his sons through a cloud of grey smoke, as he listened to Eric, the more talkative of the two brothers. 'We don't know where he is. He disappeared last week with the money and what was left o' the gear. We've got people searching everywhere for him, but nobody knows where he is … even that stupid bird o' his doesn't know where he is.' Denis flicked a knob of ash into a large ashtray on the desk before speaking. 'You'll no' find Watson no matter how hard you try … he's lying in the morgue.'

'What? He's dead?' asked Eric, looking at his brother.

'Well, he's no' there on work experience. Somebody put a bullet in his head,' said Denis, taking another draw from his cigar before asking. 'So, who'd want to kill Watson?'

'What about Tucker and Tamburini, they sell most o' the gear for him?' Billy suggested.

'Those fuckers … I'll kill them if they've stole that fucking gear,' declared Eric.

'What have ah told you, don't swear in here son, you're no' out on the street now. Get back out there and find out what you can. If it was them, and they get away with this, then you're both going to be seen as weak. When you find them, take them to the lockups. I want to have a word first before you two start on them. Remember we don't want any more dead bodies on our hands. There's enough polis hanging about the area already. It's bad for business.'

Chapter 6

Morag Burns left Kylie with a downstairs neighbour and hurried across the scheme towards the Lomond Maisonettes, hoping to find out what Willie Tucker knew about Norrie's murder. She was careful to avoid going through the shopping arcade, where the Moffat twins were often seen hanging around the bookies. There was a bitter wind blowing through the wide-open concrete spaces between the maisonettes and high-rise flats. Her thin body shivered violently as she pulled the collar of her coat tightly around her neck. A dog ran out barking from the side of one of the maisonettes. It gave her a fright. She stopped and stared in defiance at it. The dog turned on its heels and ran back to wherever it came from. She hurried on, with her hair blowing wildly in the wind, until she reached a block of five-storey apartments.

She ignored the graffiti-smeared lift and hurried up the stairs to the third floor. Most of the windows along the corridor were boarded up and she stopped for a moment to light a cigarette, her hand shaking with the cold and tension. She chapped Tucker's kitchen window with the large sovereign ring that jutted out from her clenched fist, before rattling the letterbox. After a few minutes she bent down and shouted into the dark hallway, but there was no sign of Tucker. Frustrated she kicked the door, and turned the doorknob. She was surprised to find it unlocked. She shouted on Tucker again before going into the gloomy, cold flat, the soles of her shoes sticking to the tacky grime on the hall carpet. She was struck by the fetid smell that greeted her when opening the living room door. 'Oh fuck,' she gasped, raising her hand to her mouth and staring at Tucker's body, which was lying in the middle of the room in a pool of congealed blood. In her panic, she rushed back out the flat and along the corridor, her mind numb.

When she got to within a few steps from the bottom concourse she heard voices cursing the broken lift: It was the Moffat twins. She took off her shoes and began to walk back up towards the first floor landing, her pace quickening. The Moffats entered the stairwell still cursing the broken lift, while Morag stood in the shadows and held her breath. She listened as they passed onto the next flight of stairs towards the second floor. Her heart was thumping so hard it made her breathing erratic as she tried to catch her breath. She hurried down the stairs and out of the front exit, before putting her shoes back on and scampering along the side of the building. She was careful to stay close to the outside wall in case she was seen from above. Then, sure she was out of sight, scurried across the concourse, too frightened to look back. Morag Burns was in a state of complete terror when she entered London Road Police Station to report the demise of Willie Tucker, while demanding twenty-four-hour police protection. Dorsey had a female police constable go and pick up her baby from the neighbour's house, while he and Mitchell made their way over to the Lomond Maisonettes with the scenes of crime team not far behind.

Not wanting to disturb any evidence, Dorsey surveyed the murder scene from the hall for a few moments before the forensic team went about their work. The similarities to the Watson murder were obvious. Dorsey went back out to the corridor where Mitchell was on the phone to Professor Jenkins.

'He'll be here in half an hour … What do you think?' asked Mitchell.

'Shot in the head like Watson … executed … Maybe some other outfit is moving into Moffat's patch and took

26

these two out to show they mean business.' Within the hour, Professor Jenkins arrived at the flat and confirmed that the wound to the deceased's head was caused by the same calibre handgun as the one that had almost decapitated Watson. The Professor also thought they were killed within a few hours of each other, but he was unable to say which of the two met his Maker first. He was convinced that the same killer or killers were at work.

'It looks like you have a gangland feud on your hands, Inspector,' said Jenkins, as he handed the bullet retrieved from the skull to Dorsey, before removing his rubber gloves. 'I wouldn't be surprised if more bodies turn up in the near future. Whoever shot Watson and this guy, knew what they were doing.'

'Contract killings?'

'Maybe, and unless Mr Tucker was a very untidy man, whoever killed him was looking for something. Every cupboard and drawer in the house had been ransacked. No doubt the killer was looking for one of the nefarious evils of modern life, money or drugs.'

'Or both ... Let's hope whoever it was left prints.'

'I'd be surprised if you find the prints of the killer, Inspector. This was a professional hit ... if that doesn't sound too dramatic. Whoever killed Mr Tucker had planned the murder in advance and would almost certainly have been wearing gloves.'

'So you think it was just the one killer?'

'It's just a gut feeling, nothing more, so don't quote me. Executions like these are often the work of a sole operator. Too many cooks spoil the broth, so to speak ... Oh, before I go, I got the results of Watson's toxicology tests back this morning.'

'Anything interesting?'

'Yes, apart from the fact that he was HIV-positive, it was indeed a curry he had in his stomach, a beef curry to be precise. It takes a lot of gastric activity to break down the components of your average vindaloo. The lab estimates that its consumption was around three hours before Watson met his death. If you have a look in Tucker's kitchen you'll find three take away cartons, two with the remnants of what looks like beef curry and one with what's left of a chicken bhuna.'

'You know your curries, Professor.'

'When I first started this job, the most common content of the average Glaswegian stomach at time of death, apart from booze of course, was a fish supper. Now it's an Indian curry. The lab has become expert in the art of Asian cuisine and can almost identify the actual recipe that was used from the herbs and spices. It looks like Tucker and Watson had their last supper in this flat together.'

'With a third person?'

'Yes, unless one of them had two curries, which seems unlikely. I think there was someone else here, possibly another victim you haven't found yet.'

'Could it be the killer?'

'Improbable, I wouldn't expect the perpetrator to be the kind of person to sit down to supper with his victims before blowing their brains out. This was a premeditated murder, not a drunken brawl between friends that went too far.'

'That's interesting, but why was one body found here and the other in a derelict factory half a mile away?'

'Well, that's what you get paid for, Inspector. I'm not the detective.'

'Anything else?' asked Dorsey, ignoring Jenkins sarcasm.

'Yes, the tests also confirmed that Watson had recently injected heroin, probably just a few hours before his death. It looks like Tucker was also using heroin and they likely injected the drug either before or after their meal. The needles they used may be lying in the flat somewhere, but I'll leave them for you to find. Good day, Inspector … Oh, I better take that, don't want you losing it,' he added, taking the bullet from Dorsey and placing it in a production bag.

As the curious locals watched the area being cordoned off, two mortuary attendants, who Jenkins had summoned to remove the body, made their way into the building along with DS Charlie Strachan. The Professor stopped for a moment to let them pass and to light his pipe. He had a dislike for Strachan going back years, and was not a man for repeating himself to underlings. He simply acknowledged the DS with a forced smile and a nod of the head, before hurrying downstairs and out the building.

As Dorsey watched Tucker being zipped into the black body bag, he gave Strachan a summary of Jenkins's findings. 'What do you think?' Dorsey asked when he had told all there was to know.

'If there was someone else with them, we should get his prints and DNA from the flat, and so long as he's got a record then we should be able to trace him … But *you* don't think it's the killer?'

'No, but we need to find him, if he's still alive.' 'It might not be a he,' said Strachan.

'You're right, Charlie, it might be a woman, but I doubt it … What about the killer?'

'Frank, I'm not convinced we're looking for a lone hit man, Jenkins is just bumping his gums; the Moffat twins are more than capable of doing their own dirty work. I've seen this all before, dealers trying to punch above their weight, and getting a bullet in their heads for their troubles. Look on the bright side; we've got two less junkie drug dealers on the streets to worry about … Don't give me that look, Frank, I'm only stating the obvious.'

'We treat them like any other murder victims, is that clear?'

'Of course, Frank … I'll check with my informants, one of them will know what's behind this.'

'Okay, Charlie,' said Dorsey, before turning to DC Kate Harper and the other CID officers, who were waiting to get into the flat. 'Kate, once forensic are finished, I want this place searched from top to bottom. There may be drugs or money stashed somewhere, so lift the carpets and the floorboards if you have to.'

'There are no floorboards in these flats, sir,' said Harper.
'What?'

'Sorry, Inspector,' said Harper, wishing she had kept her mouth shut. 'My cousin used to live in one of these blocks. The floors are made of concrete.'

'Thanks, Kate, but it was just a figure of speech.'

In spite of the cold, Harper's face managed to burn red. Dorsey ignored her embarrassment and turned to one of the uniformed officers, 'Sergeant, will you arrange for door-to-door enquiries to be carried out immediately. I want every occupant still living in this block and the blocks opposite to be questioned. Someone must've heard the shot being fired, who knows, they might even be prepared to give a statement. I want any CCTV cameras in the general area checked.'

'Yes, sir, that won't take long. There's only a few tenants still living on the ground floor, the rest of this block is empty. I've spent the last twenty years dealing with this scheme, it's all "heard nothing, seen nothing" and "I'm saying fuck all to you bastards."'

'Well, we've a job to do. You never know, not everyone's heard of your three wise monkeys,' said Dorsey, before taking Mitchell aside. 'George, I think we better get back to the station to see if Burns knows what Watson and Tucker were up to, and maybe we'll find out who else was with them that night. Let

Strachan get on with things here, the less he knows the better.'

At London Road Police Station, Miss Burns was less agitated now she had her daughter with her. The desk sergeant had already arranged for the child's social worker to attend to look after Kylie, while her mother was taken into one of the interview rooms. Dorsey decided to keep the interview informal for the time being; the use of the tape recorder would only hinder his need to get her talking. 'Miss Burns, I'm going to ask you a few questions just to clear up what you know about the deaths of Norman Watson and William Tucker and their dealing with the Moffats.'

'Ah don't know anything?'

'You obviously know more than you told us this morning. You knew fine well where Willie Tucker lived, but you lied and told us you didn't. Before today, have you ever been in Mr Tucker's flat?'

No response.

'Miss Burns, this is a double murder enquiry and one of the victims was the father of your daughter. I've reason to believe that you were in that flat on the same evening your boyfriend, Norman Watson, and his friend, Willie Tucker were murdered. Were you in that flat?'

Again, there was no response, just a defiant look that implied the old well-worn retort *Prove it*. So Dorsey repeated the question with slightly more force in his voice. 'Were you in that flat?'

'Ah want ma lawyer.'

'Why do you need a lawyer? We are not accusing you of anything. You're only here as a potential witness.'

'Witness tae what? Ah didn't see anything … Ah want ma lawyer.'

'You can demand one all you want. You're not a suspect in these crimes and as a witness you've no right to have a lawyer present. The sooner you answer our questions, the sooner you can go home with your daughter. If you were there, then you are better telling us now, before we get the forensic results back and find your DNA and fingerprints all over Tucker's flat. If you wait until then, you *will* need your lawyer, because you *will* be charged with attempting to pervert the course of justice, and with your record you'll end up in prison.'

'And Kylie will end up in care,' added Mitchell.

There was silence for a moment as Morag stared down at the table in front of her and began playing with her hair, twisting the long, dishevelled strands between her nicotine-stained fingers. She began sobbing. Dorsey looked at

Mitchell, who shrugged his shoulders.

'Miss Burns, why did you ask for twenty-four-hour protection … what are you afraid of?'

'They murdered Norrie and Willie, what dae ye think am afraid o',' she responded, wiping the tears from her face with the back of her hands.

'Who murdered them?'

'Ah don't know, but ah was only in the flat in the afternoon.'

'What time were you there?'

'About one, only long enough tae …'

'To get a fix,' interrupted Mitchell.

She nodded in the affirmative. 'Am no' saying anything else unless ye promise that ye won't get Kylie taken off me again. Ah didn't get ma meth script oan Friday because ah wasn't well and couldn't get tae the chemist. Ah was rattling fur fuck's sake. Ah haven't used it since.'

'If you tell us everything you know, I promise that you and Kylie can go home after this interview, and, if you need police protection then you'll get it. Who are you afraid of?'

'Whoever killed Norrie and Willie.'

'But who was that?'

'Ah don't know, but somebody sent a text tae me and Norrie, about a couple o' months ago, threatening tae kill us if we didn't stop selling drugs.'

'A text? Did you both get one?' 'Aye, oan the same day.'

'Have you still got the message on your phone?'

'No, we just deleted them. Norrie thought it was just some weirdo trying tae wind us up.'

'What did it say?'

'It said something about God, and that he knows we're selling drugs, and if we didn't stop we're going tae end up in Hell. Ah can't remember the exact words.'

'So, it didn't actually say anyone was going to kill you.'

'If ye end up in hell, ye have tae die first.' 'Was there a number with it?'

'No, it came up *Sender Unknown.*'

'Who do you think might have sent it?' asked Dorsey, turning briefly towards Mitchell to make sure he wasn't going too fast for the diligent DC's note taking.

'How should ah know?'

'How'd they get both your numbers?'

'Ah don't know. Ye tell me.'

'Have you still got the phones?'

'Ah've got mine,' she said taking the phone from her pocket and handing it to Dorsey. 'Fuck knows where Norrie's is.'

'We'll have to get this checked, we might be able to retrieve the text and find out who sent it,' said Dorsey, handing the phone to Mitchell.

'Ye can't take ma phone, Ah need ma phone.'

'We'll get you another phone; this is a production in your boyfriend's murder.'

'What about aw ma numbers?'

'We'll get them copied on to another phone for you. Did either of you get any more of these text messages?'

'No, but we found out a few days later that Tucker got one.'

'Did you see what Tucker got?'

'No, he deleted it as well, but it said the same thing. He thought it was the Mormons or somebody like that trying tae fuck wi' our heids.'

'Did anyone else you know get one of these messages?'

'Ah don't know, we didn't think it was a big deal.'

'But you do now?'

'What dae ye think … they've both ended up fucking deid?'

'How did you get the bruise above your eye?'

'Am no' saying.'

'Were you selling drugs for the Moffats?'

'Am no' saying.'

'Okay, was Norrie or Willie selling drugs for the Moffats?'

'Am no' saying.'

'But you're no' saying they weren't either.'

'Am no' saying.'

'Okay, just a few more questions and then you can go home. Who was in Tucker's flat when you left on Saturday?'

'Just Tucker and Norrie, they were going tae have a few beers before going tae the Rangers game. Ah went back tae ma ain flat.'

'Did they go to the Rangers game?'

'Ah don't know … Can ah go?'

'I'll let you go if you tell me who gave you the black eye. You don't have to make a formal statement, just tell me who hit you.'

'Will ye let me go?'

'Aye, so who hit you, Morag?'

'It was Billy Moffat. He wanted tae know where Norrie was staying.'

'When was this?'

'Tuesday night. When ah told him that ah didn't know, he went fucking mental and smacked me o'er the face. But I'm no' making a complaint against him, he's a fucking psycho.'

'Last Tuesday, so Norrie was already dead when Billy was looking for him,' reflected Dorsey, turning to Mitchell who was still busy scribbling down her answer.

'Can ah go now?'

'Okay, I will send a police officer to keep an eye on you,' said Dorsey as he brought the interview to an end and Morag was taken home.

'George, what the fuck are we dealing with here?'

'They're low level, Frank. I can't see why someone would want to kill a pair of losers like them,' said Mitchell, putting his notebook away. 'According to the guys in the drug squad, Watson gets the heroin directly from the Moffats and then he divides it up with the other dealers further down the food chain.'

'Do you think the McGowans are trying to take on the Moffats?'

'I don't think Hughie McGowan's got the stomach for another feud with Big Denis after the last time they crossed swords.'

'What about Jackie Dempsey?'

'Jackie is not in their league, he spends most of his time

35

in his villa in Spain these days. These three are too old for any more aggro; they've made their peace a long time ago. They all know it's bad for business to be fighting with each other over drugs.'

'What about these texts?'

'I don't know what to make of them, Frank. I've never heard of drug gangs giving other drug gangs a written warning before taking over their patch, especially a warning that sounds like it came out of the Old Testament. It might be just some religious nut that sent them.'

'If it was, then it's a bit of a coincidence.'

'Not if they were sent to half the drug dealers in Glasgow.'

'True, but how'd someone get their phone numbers? It's not like they advertise them in the Yellow Pages.'

'Good point, Frank. Anyway, it'll be interesting to see how the Moffats deal with this. They're not going to sit back and watch their dealers being murdered. It doesn't look good.'

That evening, instead of going home, Dorsey walked down to The Barkley, convincing himself that getting to sleep would be easier after a few whiskies. The pub was quiet and he was tempted to walk back out when he saw Barney Collins sitting at the far end of the bar, laughing and joking with a couple of girls, who were obviously easily flattered. Barney excused himself to the girls, before lifting his fedora from the bar and approaching Dorsey.

'How're you, Frank. I hoped you'd be in tonight.'

'Why?'

'Just a chat, where's Mitchell?'

'Home with his wife and kids,' said Dorsey, drinking his whisky in a hurry before ordering another double.

'Well, it will soon be Christmas, I'm sure he's got plenty to do.'

'Enough of the small talk Barney, what do you want?'

'I hear there's been a second body found with its head blown off; another one of the Moffats' street dealers by the sounds of it.'

'I don't talk about my work in here. I come here for a bit of peace and quiet. You've obviously got your own sources, anyway, so there's nothing I can tell you that you probably don't already know.'

'Was that a double negative or are you just playing hard to get? Do you fancy another whisky?'

'Was that a bribe or are you just being a twat?' said Dorsey, downing his whisky in one. 'I'll see you around, Barney ... I think the two girls are missing your company.'

'Goodnight, Inspector, no hard feelings,' replied Barney. *How the fuck did he know about this one?* Dorsey cursed to himself, while walking back to his flat with the heat of the whisky still on his chest. He noticed for the first time the number of Christmas trees that seemed to have appeared overnight in the tenement windows on both sides of the street. The double whiskies had gone straight to his head, and he stopped to admire one tree that stood out from the rest. He tried to think of something that his son would like for Christmas.

Once in his flat, he poured himself a large whisky, and knocked it back with a grimace, before taking the bottle with him into the bedroom. Turning on the electric fire, he began to undress in the bitter cold. The breath from his mouth was clearly visible in the semi-darkness. The electric fire crackled before settling down to its usual droning noise; its three thin bars turning bright orange. He bemoaned the cold as he got into bed and pulled the duvet over his head with a convulsive shiver. It did not take him long before he reached for the whisky.

Chapter 7

Feeling like he had been hit by a train, Dorsey woke with a thumping headache. He looked at the bedside alarm clock which had failed to wake him at seven; late for work again. In spite of the cold, he quickly showered and shaved, before dressing in the same suit he had been wearing all week. Sitting by the kitchen window and smoking his first cigarette of the day, he was considering bringing in Hughie McGowan for questioning. He quickly changed his mind, knowing fine well that McGowan would refuse to answer any questions, and his lawyer would make it difficult to hold him for any length of time, without showing some evidence that he was involved in the murders. He stubbed the cigarette out and finished his cup of lukewarm coffee.

Superintendent Knox was at the charge bar when Dorsey got to the station. The two men nodded to each other, but said nothing. Dorsey was sure his time keeping would be the subject of another dressing down the next time they had a disagreement, which was now becoming a regular occurrence. Knox was not a bad boss to have, but he was not someone to treat lightly either, and Dorsey had pushed their friendship to the limit. *Thin ice* … those were the words the Super used the last time Dorsey was in the boss's office for being on duty under the influence. Now he had to virtually hold his breath in the morning when Knox was about; whisky had a way of hanging around long after it was good for anything.

'Morning, Frank,' said Mitchell as Dorsey took off his raincoat and shook the wet onto the floor. 'I got the preliminary forensic report in from Jenkins this morning.'

'Anything?'

'Like Jenkins said, they both had a beef curry a few hours before they were shot with the same gun.'

'That's interesting, we just have to find the gun and who had the chicken bhuna,' said Dorsey, not meaning his response to sound as sarcastic as it came across.

'We've already checked all the local restaurants and takeaways in the East End in relation to Watson, nobody remembered seeing him or delivering to that address. I'll ask two of the beat cops to take Tucker's mug shot and check them out again … who knows, maybe he went for them.'

Although Dorsey had his own office on the first floor, he decided it would be better if he also had a desk beside the other detectives now investigating the two murders. With Mitchell's help, he rearranged a few tables so they formed a mini operations area that faced the incident boards Harper had set up that morning. 'I'll take this desk for now, save me having to run up and down those bloody stairs every time we need to discuss something. George, can you put up what we've got while I have a look at what Jenkins is saying.'

Dorsey took the pathologist's report from Mitchell's desk and began reading, skimming over much of it until he reached the ballistics findings. The report confirmed that the bullets recovered from both crimes scenes came from the same weapon, a 9mm Browning pistol, one of the most widely used military pistols in history. The Professor had obviously done his homework on the gun, which was the standard issue handgun for most security services around the world; even the British Army had used it for over forty years. It did not help that over a million of these guns had been manufactured. The main thing the ballistics confirmed was the fact that he was looking for the same killer or killers for both murders. The cause of death was obvious; the similarities were undeniable, but there were no clues as to who might have put these two in the morgue. While pondering the possible culprits, who might have had the audacity to take out two of Moffat's dealers, the duty sergeant interrupted his thoughts.

'Sir, there's someone in the cells asking to speak to you.'

'What does he want, Harry?'

'I don't know, he wouldn't tell me anything. He'll only speak to you.'

'Who is it?'

'Massimo Tamburini, he was stopped last night in a stolen car with an offensive weapon under the driver's seat. I think he's looking for a deal.'

Tamburini was well known to Dorsey. He was from a decent Italian family, but decided there was more money in selling drugs than fish and chips and became involved with the Moffats, dealing tenner bags of smack to feed his own habit … until he got caught with half a kilo of heroin. After serving a three-year sentence, he returned to working in his father's chip shop, until the Moffats tempted him back into dealing for them with a few free tenner bags to get him hooked again.

Tamburini was now a recidivist criminal and his convictions for possessing drugs and housebreaking were beginning to mount up. He had cut deals with Dorsey in the past to get charges dropped and to try and reduce his sentence; but he would never finger the Moffats, he only grassed up other low level operators like himself. Mitchell, notebook in hand, followed his boss into the detention area, and waited as the sergeant went down the row of cells to fetch Tamburini. The first thing that Dorsey noticed was the fear in Tamburini's eyes as the sergeant ushered him towards the interview room.

'How are you, Massimo?' asked Dorsey.

'Have ye got a fag? Am dying fur a smoke.'

'You know you're not allowed to smoke in here.'

'Fuck the smoking ban, Ah need a fag or am going back tae ma cell.'

'You'll get one in a minute, take a seat,' said Mitchell, as he closed the door and sat beside Dorsey, who had already placed a tape into the recorder.

'Am no' going on tape before Ah get a deal,' said Massimo, beads of sweat appearing on his forehead.

'Don't worry, I'm only setting it up,' said Dorsey, taking an open packet of cigarettes from his shirt pocket and handing one to Tamburini. 'You'll get a light in a minute. What's it you want to tell us?'

'Give me a light first.'

Dorsey nodded to Mitchell, who grudgingly lit the cigarette. Tamburini took a long draw, blowing the smoke towards the ceiling as though he had just quenched a raging thirst. 'It's about Watson and Tucker. Ah was wi' them last Saturday at Tucker's flat ... but Ah want a deal before Ah tell ye anything else.'

Both Dorsey and Mitchell looked at one another, but tried not to let what they were feeling show. Dorsey quickly turned back to Tamburini, who was shaking all over, as he drew the life out of the cigarette like a condemned man. 'The sergeant tells me you were arrested last night in a stolen car with a butterfly knife.' said Dorsey. 'With your record you're looking at two years at least. What do you know that's going to make that go away?'

'Well, am telling ye nothing unless Ah get a deal,' insisted Tamburini, blowing a cloud of smoke into Dorsey's face.

Mitchell pulled the cigarette from Tamburini's mouth and stubbed it out.

'What the fuck did ye do that fur?' Tamburini complained, getting up abruptly from the chair and holding out his hands, while shrugging his shoulders like an Italian defender, who had just fouled another player in the box.

'Sit down, Massimo,' said Dorsey in a controlled tone, taking out another cigarette from his packet and handing it to Tamburini, who took his seat and the cigarette with a contemptuous sneer towards Mitchell. 'Did the three of you have a curry on Saturday night?'

'What?' The question obviously unnerved Tamburini, who put the unlit cigarette in the ashtray and look quizzically at the two detectives. 'How'd ye know that?'

'Never mind how we know, just answer the question,' interrupted Mitchell.

'We were in Tucker's flat watching the game. Celtic was two up at half-time and Ah bet Watson that if the Huns won then I'd buy the curries. The fuckers scored three in the second half, another doggy penalty in the last minute. Ye know what these fucking refs are like ... cheating Orange bastards.'

'There was nothing wrong with that penalty,' said Mitchell, drawing a raised eyebrow from his boss.

'So Watson never went to the game?' asked Dorsey.

'No, we got a few bottles o' Buckie and went tae Tucker's flat tae watch it.'

'Was there anyone else there?'

'No, just the three o' us.'

'Was Morag Burns there?'

'Fuck,' grunted Tamburini, wondering if he had anything to give that they didn't already know.

'Aye, but that was earlier on, she fucked off before the

game started.'

'Did you all take heroin?'

'No, just a few swallies, that's all.'

'Massimo, if you want a deal you have to tell us the truth. We know that Watson, Tucker and Burns all took heroin.'

'Alright, fuck. We aw had a tenner bag each. Morag got her fix and fucked off, that's when Norrie told her we were going tae the game … just tae get rid o' her. We then had a few cans and watched the game on the telly.'

'While you were out your tits,' interrupted Mitchell.

'We weren't out our tits; it was just enough tae take the edge off. Anyway the Huns won and Ah had tae get the curries in.'

'What time did you go for them?' asked Dorsey.

'Ah went down tae the Taj about half seven, and got three curries and a bottle o' *Irn-Bru*. Because Celtic got beat the two o' them were taking the piss. Ah got fucked off and went up the road after ah had finished ma curry.'

'Was it a chicken curry, by any chance?' asked Mitchell.

'Aye, Ah had a chicken bhuna; they had a beef vindaloo … what the fuck does that matter?'

'When'd you leave?' asked Dorsey.

'About half eight … maybe nearer nine … Ah just went up the road and had a few joints and went tae ma bed.'

'Were the other two still in the flat when you left?'

'Aye, they were just chilling out in front o' the telly.'

'Do you know what happened to your two mates?'

'Well, Ah know they were whacked.'

'Whacked? Have you been watching the Sopranos again,' mocked Mitchell.

'Ye know what Ah mean. Some bastard killed them.'

43

'Who?' asked Dorsey forcibly, half expecting an answer to be blurted out that would solve the case.

'How the fuck should Ah know? All Ah know is what Ah heard on the news.'

'So you've got nothing to tell us other than you were the last person to see these two alive and that they'd pissed you off over a game of football. That makes you our prime suspect,' said Mitchell with a degree of relish in his voice.

'Fuck off, Ah want ma lawyer … you're no' pinning this on me. They were ma fucking mates.'

'Calm down,' said Dorsey, offering Tamburini a light for the cigarette he had nervously lifted from the ashtray. 'We know you were not involved … you said you wanted a deal, but you've only told us what we already know.'

'There's something else … ditch the offensive weapon charge. Ah didn't know it was in the motor, fur fuck's sake. I'll do the time fur stealing the motor.'

'I'll tell you what, Massimo, if what you have is any use to us then I'll let you out on a bail undertaking. Your lawyer will have to fight the offensive weapon charge for you, but at least you'll be out in the meantime,' said Dorsey, well aware that Tamburini was showing the first signs of withdrawal. 'But you have to tell us first what you know about your friends' murders. You know you can trust me.'

'Aye, but Ah don't trust him.'

'It's me that you're making the deal with. So what do you know, and not just what you've read in *The Digger*.'

'Ah don't read that shit … You'll let me out today?'

'If what you say is any use to us, so spit it out.'

'If ye get ma mobile phone that they took off me last night, you'll find a text message Ah got a few months ago. It was threatening me if Ah continued tae sell drugs. At the time Ah didn't think much about it, but Tucker and Watson got the same text and look what happened tae them.'

'Who sent it?' asked Mitchell.

'How should Ah know, but Watson and Tucker both got one, and they're fucking deid!'

'What's your pin number?'

'10-11-96.'

Mitchell left the room and attended at the charge bar where the production officer was ordered to retrieve Tamburini's belongings. In the prisoner's property bag he found the mobile phone. Mitchell made a note on the production schedule that the phone was being removed from the bag on the orders of the Inspector. He then pressed the power button, bringing the phone to life. He entered Tamburini's pin number and quickly scrolled down the saved messages.On the twenty-first of October he found the text. It was similar to the one described by Morag Burns:

God knows that you are selling drugs and if you continue to sell them, then you will suffer the flames of Hell for eternity. The Lord, the God of the spirits of the Prophets, has sent his angel to show his servants what must soon take place. And behold, I am coming soon.

Mitchell returned to the interview room and handed the phone to Dorsey, who quickly read the message, and in turn, placed the mobile in front of Tamburini with the text message still open. 'Is this what you got sent a couple of months ago?'

'Aye, that's it.'

'Why'd you keep it on your phone?'

'No reason, but Ah bet your glad Ah did. Ah forgot all about it, until Norrie and Willie told me they got one.'

'Is it the same as the one that Watson and Tucker got?'

'Ah never seen theirs, but when a showed them this they said it was the same as the one they got.'

'Exactly the same?'

'Aye, Norrie said it was identical. He thought it was the Mormons or the Jehovah's Witnesses, or some other religious freak show that sent them.'

'But this text was sent to you?'

'Aye.'

'So whoever sent it must have known you were selling drugs.'

'Well, I've been done fur it a few times, big deal.'

'How do you think they got your number?' 'Don't know.'

'Were you dealing drugs for the Moffats when you got this?'

'What? No comment.'

'We know that you, Watson, Tucker and Burns were dealing for the Moffats, so don't deny it,' said Mitchell.

'So, if ye know, why ask? I've told ye everything Ah know, so am Ah getting out?'

'Answer the questions. Were you dealing for the Moffats?' insisted Dorsey.

'Aye, Norrie got a stash from them every couple o' months and he divvied it up between us tae sell.'

'Between who?'

'The four o' us … but if the Moffats find out Ah told ye, am a dead man. So am no' going tae court against them if that's what ye think.'

'I'm not interested in the drugs; I'm dealing with two murders. Who do you think sent these text messages?'

'No idea. Is that no' your job tae find out? Ah've told ye everything Ah know.'

'But you don't think it was some religious nut trying to

warn you about the evils of selling drugs.'

'What, someone trying tae save ma soul? No chance, no' after what happened tae Norrie and Willie.'

'Do you think it was the McGowans?'

'Ah told ye, Ah don't know … am Ah getting out, Ah've told ye everything Ah know.'

Dorsey ignored Tamburini's pleas to be liberated, and after a few more questions that did not reveal anything further, he was returned to his cell. Neither detective thought for a minute that Tamburini was the killer. They saw him as a petty criminal with a drug addiction, not the clinical killer they were after. At least now they knew who the owner of the chicken bhuna was, and they also had a phone with the text message still on it.

'Who do you think is behind it, the Mormons, the Jehovah Witnesses or the McGowans?' Mitchell asked, with a grin as he put Tamburini's phone back into the production bag.

'Your guess is as good as mine, George. Maybe it was the Moonies … before you bag the phone, can you copy the message and Google it?'

Mitchell typed the full text into his own phone. The response was almost instant. 'It's from the New Testament, the Book of Revelation.'

'Sounds like we may've a Bible thumping nut on our hands, who thinks he's an avenging angel. Print a copy of that out for me, along with the text from the phone and put it inside the folder with the forensic report. Just so you know, I've decided to let Tamburini sweat for a few more hours and then let him out on a bail undertaking tonight. Get someone to keep an eye on him to see what he's up to. Even if he's as scared as he acts, as soon as his methadone wears off he'll be back on the streets dealing again. Some things are worse than a bullet in the head, and one of them is coming off heroin.'

'So we're going to use him as bait?'

'Aye, something like that.

With the murder investigations still at an early stage, Dorsey was surprised to receive a memo from Superintendent Knox to attend a press conference that afternoon. This had been arranged by the Deputy Chief Constable to quell the growing media interest. Dorsey hated press conferences and thought they were more about giving the tabloids something to write about rather than helping their inquiries. He handed Mitchell the memo.

'This is the last thing I need.' 'Rather you than me.'

Dorsey went home at lunch time and changed into his best suit, and polished his shoes for the first time in weeks. He did not want to give Knox another excuse to criticise him about letting his appearance go. The press conference was an opportunity for Knox to wear his dress uniform, and to show his superiors that he was a very capable, confident public speaker, who should be considered for the Assistant Deputy Chief Constable's job, when the vacancy came up in the spring.

Most of the TV crews had already gathered in the foyer of the Riverside Hotel, when Dorsey arrived with Knox. On the way to the hotel, the two men had rehearsed the information that they would be prepared to disclose and what they wanted to keep under wraps. The obvious questions about drug deals gone wrong or turf wars were to be dismissed as speculative until further inquiries were made. They had no suspects, but they knew that would not stop some reporters suggesting certain East End gangsters were behind the murders. The drug gangs were all potential suspects, but they had to find hard evidence before they began accusing people in public, even if they were known gangsters. Dorsey, after some careful consideration, decided not to mention the text messages to Knox, fearing he would find it difficult not to share their existence with the press. Dorsey wanted to find out who else might have received one other than the four he already knew about. It was not inconceivable that hundreds, if not thousands of similar text messages were sent to known drug dealers in Glasgow; he did not want to start a panic by linking them with two recent murder victims.

The conference room was still being set up by the television crews when Dorsey entered. At the press desk, there were three chairs in front of a large screen displaying Police Scotland's logo. More chairs were being placed in rows facing the screens where the reporters would be sitting. The whole thing made Dorsey nervous, and while Knox was chatting to his PR assistant, he went back out to the street to have a cigarette.

One of the first hacks to arrive was Barney Collins, who doffed his fedora to Dorsey on the hotel steps. Barney knew there was no point asking the Inspector any questions about the murders, and simply maligned the weather as though he had been personally assaulted by it. Dorsey smiled and continued to smoke what was left of his cigarette before following Barney back into the hotel. Soon, other members of the press arrived, along with a couple of well-known faces from the BBC and STV news programmes. The stage was now set.

'Where the hell did you go?' asked Knox, now looking more nervous than Dorsey had seen him in a long time.

'I had to go to the toilet,' said Dorsey, taking a seat bedside his boss while the microphones were being tested by the audio technicians. It was soon clear to Dorsey why the Super was looking so anxious. Cullen, the Deputy Chief Constable, entered the room and took the remaining vacant seat.

After a few handshakes and contrived smiles, the conference was opened by Cullen. 'This conference has been called to reassure the public that they have nothing to fear, and that these murders have come about because of illegal drug dealing in this city, which is the scourge of our poorest communities. As long as drugs are allowed to be peddled by cynical gangsters, incidents like these are bound to occur from time to time. I will hand you over to Superintendent Knox who is in charge of this investigation.'

'Good afternoon, firstly we want to ask the public to provide us with any information that might help us with our inquiries into these two murders. We can confirm that both men knew each other and that they both had a history of drug dealing in the locality where they lived and died. The fact that they were known drug dealers will not in any way dilute our investigation or our resolve to bring the perpetrators to justice. We believe that both men were murdered sometime between nine and midnight on Saturday the tenth of December. If anyone has any knowledge of these crimes, or saw anything suspicious that night, please contact the police on the emergency number, which is now on your screen or call your local police station … Any questions?'

'Superintendent, is it true that both deceased worked as drug dealers for the same crime family, who are well known in the area?' asked the reporter from *The Daily Record*.

'I'm afraid we can't comment on this at the moment,' said Knox, looking at Dorsey, who nodded in agreement.

'Is this likely the start of a turf war?' the same reporter asked.

'We hope not,' said Dorsey. 'We're, at this moment, still investigating these killings as two related murders, but the motives are still unknown. We can't, at present, rule out the fact that drugs may be the catalyst for these crimes, but there's nothing at the moment to indicate that there's some drug feud, or "turf war," as you put it, going on.'

'And will the police investigating these murders be

armed?'

'The officers dealing with this case are all trained to use firearms, but these will only be issued if we deem it necessary to do so for the protection of our officers and the public. We have also specially trained firearms units who will be deployed if necessary.'

'Superintendent Knox,' asked Barney Collins, getting to his feet. 'Is it true that the police are investigating a possible vigilante, some kind of avenging angel who threatened the victims if they continued to sell drugs?'

'No, Barney, unless you know something we don't know.'

Dorsey could feel the blood rising in his face, considering whether or not to correct the Superintendent from misleading the press; he reached for a glass of water to clear his throat, but decided to say nothing. He was sure that Barney knew that the answer Knox gave was not true. His contact at the police station had gone too far this time in leaking that information before Dorsey had even shared it with his superiors. He instantly dismissed the notion that Mitchell was feeding Collins this information as incredulous. But he was the only other person who knew about the text message. His mind would not let it rest and gnawed at him as he tried to concentrate on further questions being asked by the insistent room of reporters … but who else would know about them? He could not bring himself to accept what seemed to be obvious … who else other than Mitchell? Still distracted, he watched Barney look at the roll of papers in his hand as though he was a canny lawyer considering his next crucial question in cross examination.

'Were both men shot in the head with a Browning handgun?'

'We're not prepared to disclose the modus operandi of these killings at present, suffice to say that we believe they were murdered by the same person or persons,' said Dorsey.

'We'll keep the public and the press advised of any further developments. In the meantime, this press conference is at an end.' Dorsey folded over his papers and got up, ignoring the bemused stare from Knox, who felt his position had been usurped by his subordinate. In spite of this, he pretended to be in agreement, and nodded to the press as he also closed his file. The Deputy Chief Constable shook Knox and Dorsey's hands again as the televising lights were switched off.

Dorsey drove Knox back to the station. The Super was reliving his television appearance, while Dorsey was still trying to come to terms with Mitchell leaking sensitive information about the murders to the press. It was Mitchell who had read the forensic report that morning and only he and Dorsey knew the murder weapon was a Browning. He was now convinced that Barney Collins' mole in the station was Mitchell. Had he been blinded by friendship not to see the obvious?

Unable to allay his suspicions, Dorsey waited for Knox to go upstairs before going into the main office to check the forensic report. It was no longer on his desk.

'Has anyone lifted a buff file from my desk?' he shouted across the office. The detectives muttered or shook their heads in the negative. 'Where's DC Mitchell?'

'He came in about ten minutes ago,' shouted one of the detectives from the other side of the room.

Before Dorsey could ask another question Mitchell entered the office carrying the buff file and a cup of coffee.

'Sorry, Inspector, I thought you were still at the press conference.'

'Sorry, about what?'

'I never got you a coffee.'

'I don't need a coffee. Is that the forensic you've got there?'

52

'Yes, I was just about to put it back on your desk.'

'Why is it off my desk?' demanded Dorsey in such a manner other officers stopped what they were doing and turned to listen. Mitchell did not answer, but looked at his boss in a confused vacuum. 'DC Mitchell, I asked you a question.'

'What do you think I was doing with it?'

'You tell me.'

'Open it and you'll find out,' challenged Mitchell, the anger in his voice only too obvious. The office was almost silent. Phone conversations were stopped in mid sentence and fingers hovered over expectant keyboards. The tension grew. Dorsey sensed that all eyes were on him, especially those of Mitchell. He opened the file and read a copy memo. The forensic report and a copy of the text message had been e-mailed to police headquarters at 11.30am.

'Who told you to send this?'

'Just after you left, I got a call from HQ; Cullen wanted an update before the press conference, so I sent them what we had.'

'You sent it to HQ?'

'That's where I was asked to send it to.'

'Brilliant,' said Dorsey, as though speaking to himself. He knew that half the CID in Glasgow could have read the email and its attachments before Cullen even got a look at it. 'The next time, ask me before you remove anything from my desk and send it to anyone!' snapped Dorsey, before walking out the office.

Mitchell looked in a state of bewilderment and turned to see the perplexed faces of his colleagues. 'What's that all about?' asked Harper.

'Fuck knows … your guess is as good as mine.'

'P.M.T,' shouted Strachan.

'What?' asked Harper.

'Post Media Tension ... they all get it.'

Dorsey stood outside the front door of the building, feeling rather foolish. He still had the buff folder in his hands. *So both Cullen and Knox must have already known about the text messages, and Knox knowingly lied to Barney Collins.* He was still none the wiser as to who would have told Collins. He knew he had not handled things well and would have to apologise to Mitchell once the dust had settled.

Chapter 8

His wife's voice was terse and to the point: 'You were late last week, don't be late again.' Dorsey listened to the message again before pressing the delete button and getting into his car. He looked anxiously at his watch and shook his head. He strangled a torrent of swear words at the petrol gauge as the car moved tentatively out into a line of slow-moving traffic. He had planned to go to the garage on the way home from work, but, as usual, the pub distracted him from his intentions. The petrol indicator remained at the bottom of the red empty mark and the engine was barely running on the last dregs of fuel in the tank. He did not have time to stop for petrol and willed the car along until it finally reached Newlands Road, and the former matrimonial home, as the lawyers called it. He was surprised to see Daniel standing at the front door, his face glum and holding his kit bag. Dorsey anxiously looked at his watch again, while switching off the ignition. 'Fuck.' he was nearly twenty minutes late. It was only then that he remembered promising to take Daniel swimming. He cursed again on realising he had forgotten to bring a towel and trunks.

'You're late,' said Daniel disparagingly.

'Sorry, son, I had to go into the office this morning … Why are you standing out here?'

'Mum had to go out and we couldn't find the spare keys.

She thinks you've still got them.'

'Where'd she go?' asked Dorsey, checking his pockets for the spare keys, but he had left them in the flat.

'She's gone to the lawyers,' he said, turning away abruptly and walking to the car.

'On a Sunday?' quizzed Dorsey, but Daniel was not in the mood to answer any more questions about his mother and walked to the car without answering.

'Do you still want to go swimming?'

'Why?'

'It's just that I've forgotten my trunks and towel.'

'You can hire them,' replied Daniel, getting into the back seat of the car, to make it clear that he had still not completely forgiven his father for cheating on his mother. There was nothing else for it, thought Dorsey, as he crunched the car into first gear and drove off. He would have to hire trunks and a towel at the baths. The car started to stutter, so he drove to the nearest petrol station while Daniel continued to sulk.

Once in the public baths they made their way to the changing room, which was cold and wet with only a couple of hardy-looking pensioners briskly drying themselves in a corner. Now undressed, Dorsey had another look at the blue trunks he hired and wondered how clean they were. The thought of finding another man's pubic hair in them made him think twice before putting them on, but there was no other choice. Daniel had already gone to the pool and was splashing about in the water by the time Dorsey rushed through the annoying hurdle of freezing antiseptic. Apart from Daniel, the pool was empty and he decided the only way to get out of his reluctance was to dive into the deep end and get the initial shock of the cold water over with.

He re-emerged on the other side of the pool, feeling his heart was about to give in. Daniel was now on his second length of the pool, changing from the crawl to the breaststroke. It was another way of ignoring and punishing his father's poor timekeeping, a fact that was not lost on Dorsey, who looked at the large Victorian clock above the changing rooms and willed it to get a move on; even sitting watching the latest mind-numbing blockbuster was better than this.

Harper had been phoning and leaving voicemails all morning, urgently trying to get hold of Dorsey. The discovery of another body, this time in the Calton area of Glasgow, had thrown up the possibility of an all-out drug war taking place in their division. This time the identity of the deceased was not a problem; he was Bob Devlin, a foot soldier in the McGowan clan.

The victim was found in his flat by his distraught mother. He was in his early thirties, seriously overweight; a rare example of a street dealer who was not also a user. Drink was Devlin's preferred poison. He was not married, but had a few kids to a couple of different women, and there were a few others he was not so sure about that insisted in calling him Dad. He was a minor dealer who sold directly to heroin addicts in the heart of Hughie McGowan's territory. The cause of death was as obvious as the other two victims, only this time Devlin had been tortured before being shot in the head. Once forensics had completed their work and the half-naked body was photographed from every possible angle, Strachan ordered it to be bagged and taken to the morgue. There was no sign of any mobile phone, and Devlin's mother, who had not spoken to her son in months didn't think he had one. Strachan had a reasonable idea of the time of death already. One of the neighbours had seen Devlin heading home with a carryout around seven o'clock the previous evening, and forensic were able to estimate that the body had been lying in its own urine for around 10 to 12 hours. Two unopened bottles of his favourite fortified wine were found in the flat, and clearly Devlin had been killed before he got a chance to drink any of it. Strachan assumed that whoever killed him was already waiting for him in the flat.

'Has Dorsey answered his fucking phone yet?' he shouted, pulling up his trousers that he could not keep from slipping down from around his waist.

'Not yet, sir,' replied Harper. 'I'll try him again.'

Outside the block of tenements a crowd had gathered around the police cordon to ghoul over the murder scene. Everybody in the area knew Devlin, and with his mother wailing in the street, the full horror of the murder was already common knowledge to the locals. Harper put her phone away, after another failed attempt to get a hold of the Inspector, when she saw the swaggering figure of Barney Collins appearing through the crowd.

'Another one,' shouted Collins over the heads of the crowd that were beginning to disperse now the body was on the way to the morgue.

'I'm sure you'll get all the information you need from the locals,' said Harper, getting into the police car with Strachan. En route to the police station, she turned on the radio in the middle of the news report about the recent murders. The justice minister was doing his best to reassure listeners that everything that could be done was being done to bring those responsible for the spate of drug related killings to justice.

'What're they all fucking flapping about? It's just one less fucking junkie on the streets, so long as they just keep killing each other, who gives a flying fuck!'

Harper continued to concentrate on her driving and said nothing. She did not know how to react when she was in the company of Charlie Strachan, she was never sure if he was serious or just trying to wind her up. She hated working with him.

When Dorsey finally got Harper's voice messages he had no option but to get back to the station as quickly as possible. He took Daniel straight home, which resulted in a verbal bawling match with his wife, before she slammed the front door in his face. It was with that on his mind that he entered the police station where Knox was already making one of his 'call to arms' speeches in the muster room. 'You finally got the call then,' said Knox, causing heads to turn in Dorsey's direction, before continuing with his overview of the recent murders. 'This has now become a major political matter; you all know that the press are already having a field day with the first two murders being drug related. This is the last thing the city needs.'

The muster was packed, and all the shifts had been called in, even those who had not long finished their nightshift. Dorsey smiled to himself, three murders and everyone in here's got a hard-on. He listened to Knox for about ten minutes before deciding he had heard enough and went out to the front of the station for a cigarette. The wind blew cold around the building, making him shiver a little. It was a typical grey December day; his hair was still damp and he could smell the chlorine on his hands. He thought about the argument with Helen again: how was it that she got to decide everything, while he had to pay the mortgage, his rent and Daniel's school fees. Of the three burdens on his monthly salary, the one he resented the most was the school fees. It was Helen who insisted that Daniel should have a private education; the local school was just not good enough for her son. She wanted Daniel to have every opportunity in life, even if it cost more than their monthly mortgage at the time. Dorsey remembered the arguments about the economic madness, but he eventually gave in, and was still paying the price. He now had a thirteen-year-old son who spoke to him in condescending tones, and who had aspirations to join the Tory Party.

'Fuck it,' he mumbled, crushing the cigarette butt with the heel of his shoe, before returning to the muster room.

Dorsey was surprised to see DC Sandy Cooper was now briefing the squad on the drug scene in the East End. He listened to Cooper for a few minutes before the DC brought his briefing to an end.

Knox approached and handed him an email from the Procurator Fiscal's Office. 'Frank, they want a meeting on Monday morning to go over the three cases and to decide on a joint approach with the media. You can meet with them, but don't let them dictate how we do our job; you know what they're like. No doubt the justice minister will be sticking his oar in next.'

'Why was Sandy Cooper here?'

'Sandy knows the drug scene in this division better than anyone. I asked him to give the squad a full briefing on all the players, from Denis Moffat down to the street dealers. We need every man we can get to stop these killings before we end up looking like a Mexican border town.'

'That's not why I asked. I thought he was still on compassionate leave.'

'I spoke to him this morning, his wife is out of hospital and he was desperate to get back to work.'

'What about his daughter?'

'No change. It's their only child; it must be hell for them … Anyway, I want Cooper on your team. If things get too much for him, let me know.'

'Sure, Andrew, Sandy's a good detective.' It was the first time in months they both spoke to each other using their first names.

'What about those text messages?'

'We still haven't traced who sent them and I think it's better for the investigation to keep them under wraps until we've more to go on. Don't want Collins writing some rubbish about an avenging angel,' explained Dorsey. 'I think

60

we should concentrate on the usual suspects.'

'Well, I'm sure I did the right thing lying to Collins about them yesterday, anyway, how'd he know about them?'

'How does he know about anything? Someone is giving him inside information.'

'Who?'

'I don't know, but I intend to find out … I better go and have a word with Sandy.'

Chapter 9

Denis Moffat was unusually concerned as he put the phone down and stubbed his cigar in the ashtray beside a picture of Irene and the kids. He lifted the picture for a moment; Saltcoats, late nineties, Ashley was still a baby. He wondered if he was imagining things, but it always seemed to be sunny in those days. He put the picture frame back down and began to drum his fingers on the table. He had not seen the twins for a couple of days, and could not get a hold of them on their mobile phones. He lifted his phone again and used the speed dial. His unmistakable voice rasped like sandpaper down the line. 'T-Bone.'

'Aye, boss.'

'I want you and Percy to meet me at the lockups, pronto!' Denis hung up without waiting for a reply and took a small key from his waistcoat pocket. He then went over to a large painting of a stag, which hung above a nineteen-seventies-styled cocktail cabinet, and removed it to reveal a Chubb wall safe. It had been that long since he opened the safe that it took him three attempts before he got the combination numbers in the right order and the dial finally clicked into place. Behind a bundle of envelopes and some jewellery, he removed a dated Beretta handgun and a box of 22 calibre shells. A black BMW was already parked in front of the lockups when Denis Moffat arrived in his silver Mercedes. He looked around for a moment before getting out of the car and kicking the bottom of the metal shutter, which rattled open almost on command. T-Bone let the shutter chain go as soon as Denis entered the dimly lit lockup, causing the metal to reverberate like a machine gun until it hit the ground with a thud.

'Do you have to make so much fucking noise?' snarled Denis.

'Sorry, boss.'

'He likes making a racket,' said Percy, who was sitting behind a workbench at the back of the lockup reading a newspaper. 'What's up, boss?'

'What's up ... you're the one reading the fucking newspaper. Two o' our men have been murdered and you're asking me what's up, boss. Like fucking Bugs Bunny!'

'They're only junkie dealers,' said Percy, who was never very complimentary when it came to dealers who used the stuff themselves.

'They still worked for us!'

'Who dae ye think bumped them off?' asked T-Bone, lifting a wheel brace from the floor and feeling it in his hands, as though planning his revenge in his mind.

'Put that thing down, stupid ... whoever it was is using guns,' said Denis as he bent down and removed a filthy rubber mat from the floor to reveal an oil-stained door hatch. He unlocked a small padlock and pulled the hatch up. 'Here, you two, get that out o' there, my back is knackered.'

T-Bone and Percy struggled to lift the heavy metal box from its confinement below the floor, and blamed each other as they caught their hands and fingers between the box and the side of the hatch. With Denis standing over them, they finally heaved it on to the floor with groans of relief.

'You two are getting too auld for this game,' said Denis, kneeling down to unlock the box, and taking out two handguns. 'Take these and a box o' ammo each, we've got a meeting wi' McGowan.'

'Why are we meeting him?' asked Percy, still looking at

the gun he had not used in years.

'One o' his dealers was found dead this morning. He wants to prevent a full-blown war. He's adamant that none o' his men killed Watson or Tucker.'

'Who killed his guy?' asked Percy, tucking the handgun into the waistband at the back of his trousers.

'Don't know, but he thinks it was us. He sounded scared, so I didn't tell him otherwise. Have any o' you two seen the twins?'

Both T-Bone and Percy shook their heads as Denis tried to phone his sons again. Both their mobile numbers simply rang out.

'Let's go, and remember this might be a set-up, so keep your wits about you. I don't trust that bastard McGowan.'

With the BMW following close behind, Denis slowed to negotiate a street bump at the entrance to the car park at the side of The Weaver's Tavern; Hughie McGowan's stronghold in the heart of the Calton. This was one part of the city, where even Denis Moffat never felt safe, and he looked around cautiously, before getting out of the car. It was years since he last stepped inside Hughie's pub. That was after their last feud, when Hughie's youngest son, Francis, ended up in intensive care, and Benny Moffat found himself in Barlinnie Prison for attempted murder, which was later dropped to serious assault.

After the trial, in which Benny got five years, Hughie and Denis shook hands and drew a line under the incident without further bloodshed. They knew that business was too important to ruin it in an all-out war.

This time was different. Both thought the war had already started. Big Denis was taking no chances; he put his hand inside his coat to feel the reassuring coldness of his Beretta. When the back door of the pub opened he signalled to Percy and T-Bone to stay back as he walked towards McGowan, who appeared with a nervous grin on his face.

'Thanks for coming over, Denis. The boys can come in as well, if they want. I just want to find out what's going on.'

Denis could see real fear in McGowan's eyes as he shook his hand.

'What the hell's up wi' you, Hughie?' asked Denis, turning to his own two men and waving them back. 'Wait wi' the motors.'

'Come in and have a drink wi' me,' said Hughie, with a plea in his voice. 'We need to get this sorted before it gets out o' hand.'

'I don't know what we've to sort out, 'cause I haven't done anything,' rasped Denis, following McGowan into the bar, which was empty apart from a young barmaid. 'Where's the rest o' your crew?'

'This is no' for their ears … what will you have?'

'I'll have a whisky,' said Denis, smiling at the young barmaid and taking off his hat. 'I've always liked this pub Hughie, apart from the Celtic pictures on the wall.'

'Well, it's a Celtic pub, but I don't give a damn about football. I'd rather play a game o' golf at the weekend than go and watch that rubbish every week … we should've a game sometime.'

'Whenever you like, but don't you think we should put a stop to this killing first?'

'Like I said on the phone, Denis, the first time I heard about your two lads was on the news. I would've phoned then, but I didn't think for a minute that you thought we were involved. I've got no interest in another battle over drugs.'

'What about your two boys, maybe they're trying to make a name for themselves.'

'Fuck, Denis, Rory and Francis are more interested in shagging birds. I can't get them to do fuck all. I swear. Denis, none o' my boys were involved in any of this.'

'Here, give me another whisky,' demanded Denis, handing the girl the empty glass. 'Make it a double.'

As the girl went back behind the bar, Denis turned to Hughie with a grin and whispered. 'She's a beauty. Are you shagging her, you dirty auld bastard?'

'I'd be a dirty auld bastard ... that's my youngest daughter, Emma.'

'Oh, hell, Hughie, I'm sorry.'

'It's alright, Denis, she can't help it if she's good looking.'

'Sorry, Hughie, I've got a daughter the same age myself.'

'I know, forget about it.'

'She's at Aberdeen studying law. It's hard to believe I'll soon have a lawyer in the family,' said Denis, trying to distance himself from his embarrassment.

'She must be a clever girl.'

'Your whisky, Mr Moffat,' said Emma when she returned with the drinks.

'Thank you, darling,' replied Denis rather sheepishly.

'Let's have a seat over there,' said Hughie, lifting his gin and tonic and moving to a table further from the bar.

Away from the distraction of Emma, Denis soon regained his composure. Ignoring the smoking ban, he lit up a cigar and stared through the clouds of smoke into Hughie's watery eyes. He could bluff him and get some territory in exchange for a truce, but felt a little sorry for McGowan, who at one time was his greatest rival. They had both grown old and quasi-respectable together. Why would either of them want to return to the past? The two old gangsters sat opposite each other like stoic chess players, waiting to see who would make the first move. Hughie showed less resolve and blinked first.

'What do we do about these killings?'

'If I give you my word, will ye accept it?'

'Of course, Denis, you've never gone back on your word in all the years I've known you.'

'Well, Hughie, whoever killed Devlin, it wasn't my doing. Like you, I've grown used to the quiet life. I don't want the polis at my door anymore than you do. What I think is going on here, is that someone is trying to get us into a war. While we're killing each other they'll just move in and take over the lot. They must think that we're too auld for this game.'

'But who?'

'Your guess is as good as mine, but I've never trusted that flash bastard Dempsey, or that son o' his for that matter.'

'No, Denis, I spoke to Jackie this morning after I phoned you. He's in Spain, and as worried as me about another bloodbath. He's only a few years younger than us and wants nothing more than to be able to go to his villa in Spain every other month. He doesn't want to spend anymore time in Glasgow than he has to.'

'Fuck him ... is he still shagging anything with a pulse?'

'Dempsey's okay. You and Jackie should patch things up. You were good mates once.'

'I'll never patch things up with that flash fucker, not after what he did ...'

'Another whisky, Mr Moffat,' asked Emma, lifting the empty glass from the table and replacing it with a double whisky.

'Thanks, darling, the service in here's great,' said Denis, unable to takes his eyes of Emma's tight fitting jeans, as she walked back to the bar. 'You're no' trying to get me drunk, Hughie?'

'You're safe in here, Denis ... you've got my word.'

'What's in a word if one o' your boys rushes in here wi' a shot-gun,' said Denis, half joking, but a little more on edge

67

than he was before he thought of it. It would be a fitting way to go for any crime lord, but Denis was not ready to die, not just yet when he could still piss straight. He loosened the top button on his coat just in case he had to get to his gun in a hurry. On seeing the other man's change of demeanour, Hughie moved uncomfortably on his chair, well aware of the legend of Denis Moffat's infamous Beretta.

'Denis, drink your whisky. Do you think for a minute I'd put my daughter's life at risk if I was planning anything other than a quiet chat?'

'Don't worry, Hughie. You know me, always ready for the unexpected, that's all. Drink your gin and tonic,' said Denis, lifting his own glass in salute to old times. The two men's glasses came together with a clink. 'To a peaceful time,' said Hughie.

'To peace in our time,' agreed Denis, showing no hint of recognition of the famous line. 'If I find out who's behind this, I'll let you know. We can take them on together.'

'Of course, Denis, I'll do the same … Let's hope no more bodies turn up.'

The two men shook hands and Denis drained the last of the whisky with a belch before making his way to the back door with an unaccustomed stagger, stealing another look at Emma, who was as unattainable to him as she was beautiful. 'Bye, darling, you must have got your good looks from your mother.'

Outside, Percy and T-Bone were still standing at the open doors of the BMW, vigilantly looking for any sign of trouble. A cold wind blew across the car park, which contrasted with the heat from the whisky that was giving Denis a touch of heartburn.

'Take the Merc up the road,' he said, handing Percy the keys and getting into the back of the BMW behind T-Bone. 'I don't want to get done for drink driving just before

68

Christmas.'

Feeling a little tipsy, Denis could not get Emma and her tight jeans out of his mind. The thought was too strong to dismiss and he could feel an erection growing under his coat as he struggled to get his breath. He began coughing in a fit that made T-Bone think he was having a heart attack.

'Ye alright, boss?' shouted T-Bone, adjusting the rear-view mirror to get a better look at Denis, who was now blowing his nose into his handkerchief.

'I'm fine, take me to Isobel's ... I need to unload my fucking sack somewhere.'

'Sure, boss,' said T-Bone. Without another word he turned the car in the direction of the city centre. It was now raining and getting dark when they drove across town to where Denis sought his solace. T-Bone turned on the window wipers as the rain splattered on the windscreen. Denis lit a cigar and rolled down one of the back windows. The wind and rain that rushed in cleared the flush from his face and he began to relax a little. The car then turned onto the street where Isobel's Sauna Parlour nestled between a pub on one side, and a chip shop on the other; a trilogy of Glaswegian culture.

T-Bone drove the car around the back of the building and parked at the fire exit.

'You can go to the bookies for a couple o' hours ... pick me up at six,' instructed Denis, getting out the back seat with some effort.

'Okay, boss, don't do anything that I wouldn't do.'

'Don't worry about that, I'm no' a fucking faggot like you.'

T-Bone was stumped; it's hard to have a bit of banter with someone like Denis Moffat. A joke to him was only funny if someone else was at the butt of it. The fire exit opened and T-Bone watched Denis being greeted by one of the girls.

'Fuck him,' he mumbled, 'it's not the size of his dick they're after, anyway.'

He then drove out the car park, eventually stopping outside the bookies on the Main Street, which was another of Denis Moffat's 'legitimate' businesses.

Isobel was in her forties and ran a couple of saunas for Denis. She made him so much money he even called this new shop after her. Always glad to make her boss happy, Isobel poured him a large malt whisky and flattered him like a spoiled child. Denis was putty in her hands. The smell of her perfume and the rush of nicotine made him heady with self-worth. Once he had finished the whisky, three scantly dressed girls came into the reception area to entice him into their beds.

'I'll take Julie first, and then you can send in the others,' he boasted; his mind with more ambition than this aging body was able to keep up with. The girls giggled as though to please him with their shallowness. He took Julie by the hand and led her into a backroom of candles and scent. As Julie danced her clothes off one by one, Denis became light-headed, and struggled to get his tie off. Defeated by the whisky that now ruled his tired mind, he lay on the bed and soon fell into a deep, drunken sleep.

Chapter 10

After Knox's 'call to arms' speech, Harper spent the rest of her shift in the incident room collating all the information she and Mitchell had on the three main crime families in the East End. Names, addresses, mug shots, profiles and previous convictions were checked to determine likely suspects. The whole exercise was confusing, because those likely to have been involved in the murders were also potential victims if the killings continued.

She decided the only way to make any sense of this mountain of material was to simply divide it into three separate entities, starting with the Moffats. The first, rather dated picture, she pinned to the incident board was of Denis Moffat, from a time when he still had a full head of hair. It did not take her long to get the board looking like a rogues' gallery of Glasgow's most notorious gangsters, with Denis's three sons taking pride of place below their father in the Moffat family tree, while Hughie McGowan and Jackie Dempsey headed their own criminal dynasties. Gruesome post-mortem photographs of the three victims were put on a separate board with the details of their deaths.

'What do you think?' she asked Mitchell, who stared from one board to another.

'Is that the best photo we've got of Denis Moffat?'

'I'll try and download a better one.'

'I thought he was off today,' he said to Harper when he saw Dorsey coming to the room.

'You two need to sort this out?' she said, handing Mitchell

an up-to-date photograph of Denis Moffat.

'That's up to him,' said Mitchell, replacing the old photograph of Denis with the new one.

Dorsey was still at the open door looking a little awkward.

'George, can I have word in my office, once you've finished what you're doing?'

'Sure,' replied Mitchell, putting down the photograph he was still holding.

Dorsey was already back upstairs and behind his desk by the time Mitchell entered his office. He nodded to the vacant chair at front of the desk, but Mitchell declined.

'About yesterday, George, I was wrong to speak to you that way, especially in front of the rest of the team. I don't know what I was thinking.'

'That's alright. We all lose it now and again.'

'Can we put it behind us?'

'I've already put it behind me. I just wish you hadn't done it in front of everyone else.'

'I know … that was bad … it must've been the press conference that stressed me out.'

'P.M.T.'

'What?'

'Post Media Tension.'

'Oh, maybe.'

'Is that all, sir?'

'What's with the sir?'

'Is that all, *Frank*?'

'No … I'm concerned about Barney Collins. He is starting to make us look foolish, and someone in this office is passing him information that he shouldn't be getting his hands on. He is compromising this whole investigation. I need you to keep an eye on what information we're holding back and who has been accessing it. It could be anyone.'

'Even me?'

'Of course not, George, You're like me ... beyond suspicion.'

'I don't think I was yesterday.'

'I was stressed out yesterday ... sometimes we say or suspect things because we're afraid they might be true. Again, George, all I can say is that I'm sorry. I've known you too long and trust you more than I sometimes trust myself. We'll leave it at that, will we?'

'Okay, Frank.'

'Anything new happening?'

'I've spoken to at least ten known dealers in the area, but none of them got or would admit to getting any threatening text messages. Forensics have managed to get the deleted message back on to Morag Burns' mobile, but they're only able to trace both texts to the same unregistered mobile. Anyone could've sent them from a doggy phone and sim card bought over the internet. They're still trying to trace where the texts were sent from. They think they might be able to trace it through the BT satellite signal in the general area, but that'll take time, maybe even weeks.'

'Let me know as soon as they trace the signal. It's early days, George; we've got to keep digging ...'

Heads turned when Mitchell and Dorsey came back into the main office smiling. The rest of the squad were glad to see that the two of them looked to have patched things up. The atmosphere that had hung over the office, lifted as quickly as it had descended.

'Inspector, I've got something,' shouted Harper, who was now viewing the hundreds of hours of CCTV collated from around the area where the first two victims were found. Dorsey made his way across the room to where Harper was sitting in front of a paused picture. 'This is the street that leads into the cul-de-sac where Tucker lived. The picture quality is shit, sir' said Harper as she pressed the play button. Dorsey and Mitchell watched in silence as a white van turned into the road leading to the Lomond apartment block. The grainy picture was not helped by the lack of light coming from the nearest streetlight, which was faulty and flicking on and off. Harper then fast forwarded the video, stopping it as the van re-emerged some fifteen minutes later.

Harper stopped the video again and turned to Dorsey. 'This is the same night that Massimo Tamburini said he was with Watson and Tucker. No other vehicle entered the cul-de-sac until seven o'clock the next morning.'

'And there's no other way into the flats?' asked Dorsey. 'Not by road. This is the only way in and out, unless you walk, then you can get there, probably half a dozen ways through the scheme.'

'What time did it arrive?'

'Just shortly after ten and stayed there for about fifteen minutes.'

'Is there no other camera angle that might show the registration on the van, or who's driving it?'

'No, there's another camera at the other side of the car park, but it wasn't working that night, probably still isn't. The flats are going to be demolished soon and the council probably don't think it's worth fixing.'

'Typical … have you got Watson and Tamburini leaving?'

'No, they must've walked back through the scheme.'

'I take it that's where the broken camera is?'

'Yes, Tucker's flat is halfway between both stairwells so it's as easy using one set of stairs as the other … Look, there seems to be some lettering on the side of the van, maybe the lab can enhance it.'

74

'Get the video over to them straight away and check all the CCTV on the roads around the scheme. This van must have been caught on one of them at least. We need to get that registration number … Kate, can you also check the CCTV for the following Friday, when Morag Burns found Tucker's body?'

'I'll check through these as soon as I can,' said Harper, pointing to a storage box full of DVDs and video tapes. 'I'll let you know as soon as I find it, sir.'

Dorsey went back upstairs to his office and phoned Daniel to apologise for cutting their day short, and to arrange what he wanted to do next week. After three attempts his son eventually answered. 'I'm busy, what do you want?'

'Daniel, do you have to be so rude? I'm only phoning to say sorry and …' Dorsey stared at the phone when he realised that his son had cut him off. He put his head in his hands and let out a deep sigh.

He got up and went back downstairs where Harper handed him the enhanced photo of the side of the van: *Caledonia Van Hire*. 'Contact them straight away and get details of all vans of this type that were on hire at the time of the murders. If the person driving that van killed Tucker, he must have also picked up Watson. Let's hope they haven't washed the van since then. We might finally get some forensics … if we're lucky.'

'I've also got the video of Morag Burns going towards the flats on the day she found the body. It also shows the Moffat twins crossing the concourse towards the same apartment block just after her,' said Harper, walking back to her desk. They both watched up to the point when Burns disappeared around the back of the block of high-rise flats. Within another five minutes the twins appeared on the screen.

'Stop it there,' ordered Dorsey. 'Which one of the twins is that?'

'Sorry, boss, even if I met them in the street, I wouldn't know which one was which … it looks like he's carrying some kind of blade,' said Harper.

'Good, we've got them carrying a weapon at least, George,' said Dorsey turning to Mitchell. 'Take Sandy with you and bring the two Moffats in for questioning. He knows them better than anyone.'

'Do you want them arrested?'

'No, just detain them. I want to let them sweat in the cells for a while, before we let them contact their lawyer.'

Chapter 11

Dorsey scanned a modest record of previous convictions, which were mainly for minor road traffic offences, before looking back through the glass at the solitary figure sitting in the interview room. It was nearly two hours since Eric Moffat had been brought in and Dorsey thought it was time to put a few well-chosen questions to him. He nodded to Mitchell, who opened the door with a smirk at the prospect of interviewing one of the Moffat twins. They took their seats, but Eric turned away and faced the wall. 'Am saying fuck all til my lawyer gets here.'

'Your lawyer's no' going to get you out of this one, son,' said Dorsey, as he opened a folder onto the table. 'We got evidence that will put you in jail for years. We've got you on video carrying a knife, but that's only the start of it.'

'No chance. You've no' got me on video carrying anything.'

'This is a still photograph taken from the CCTV near to the Lomond flats … what were you doing there?'

'Look at it,' shouted Mitchell.

'I want my lawyer … you've got nothing on me,' insisted Eric, still refusing to turn and face his accusers.

'You know Willie Tucker was murdered in one of those flats. This makes you and your brother prime suspects. So what were you doing there?'

'You think Ah murdered Tucker … well you're no' much o' a detective.'

'Why is that, you're there with a blade?'

'For fuck's sake, everybody knows he was shot in the head!'

'Don't get smart,' shouted Mitchell, getting up and pulling Eric around to face Dorsey.

'Get your hands off me! That's an assault.'

'Look at the picture,' insisted Mitchell, still holding Eric by the scruff of the neck.

'Alright, I'm looking, so what. That could be anybody carrying anything. Your CCTV is shit and you know it. You've got nothing on me.'

'How do you explain you and your brother's prints being found in Willie Tucker's flat?'

'We've known Willie Tucker for years. He's a mate and we've been in his flat hundreds o' times, you'll need to do better than that, Inspector.'

'If it wasn't you that killed Tucker, who was it?' asked Dorsey, as he continued to probe for a response that might lead somewhere.

'Is it no' your job to find out who killed him … detective?'

'Two dealers that worked for you were killed on the same night. Are the McGowans taking over your pitch?'

'Ha, ha, funny fucking ha, ha! You're a couple o' comedians … The McGowans, don't make me laugh.'

'Is that why Bob Devlin got killed … revenge?'

'Make up your mind, who have Ah killed … Watson and Tucker or Devlin?'

'So it's a turf war … Two of your guys get killed by the McGowans, and you and your brother take out one of their men.'

'You two are just making this up as you go along. I want my lawyer here; he'll kick all this shit in to touch.'

Dorsey struggled to think of something else to ask and turned to Mitchell. 'Is there anything you want to ask, George?'

'Yes,' replied Mitchell, who had the question already framed in his mind. 'Did you or your brother receive any strange text messages, to do with an avenging angel threatening you if you continued to deal in drugs?'

'What? What the fuck are you on about? I don't deal drugs.'

There was a sharp knock at the door. Mitchell got up and opened it only to be met with the duty sergeant and Philip Stanton, Eric's solicitor. 'I'd like a word with my client and anything he may've said in here without a lawyer present will be challenged in court.'

'Don't worry Mr Stanton, I said bugger-all about bugger-all,' intervened Eric, giving the two detectives a grin of triumph.

'We're only having a chat with him … the tape wasn't even on. You can take him with you,' said Dorsey, closing over the folder and getting to his feet. 'He's not been charged with anything.'

'Not yet,' added Mitchell as he exchanged a stare of mutual enmity when Eric passed him at the door.

'I want that bastard charged wi' assault,' shouted Eric, pointing in Mitchell's face.

His lawyer took him by the arm and pulled him away.

'We'll deal with that later Mr Moffat.'

'Bye the way, Inspector. I did get a text message a couple of months ago from some religious nut job. I just deleted it. No big deal.'

'Do you want to talk to us about it?'

'I've just told you. I deleted it.'

'My client is not answering any more of your questions.' Once Eric Moffat and his lawyer were gone, the two detectives looked at each other, before Mitchell finally broke the silence. 'Where'd that get us?'

'Absolutely nowhere, George, all we can prove is that he and his brother walked towards the Lomond flats after Morag Burns found Tucker's body. We don't even know if they went into his block, never mind Tucker's flat. They would hardly have gone back to the flat if they had already murdered Tucker.'

'What about the fingerprints?'

'What fingerprints? I just threw that at him to get a reaction. Even if we did find their prints, I don't doubt that he and his brother have been in the flat in the past. He was one of their dealers.'

'Why'd we not just charge him with the knife anyway?'

'What's the point? The Fiscal would throw it back at us. It looks like a knife, but it could be anything; looking like a knife isn't grounds to charge him. The quality of the CCTV is just not good enough.'

'So why'd we bring him in?'

'I wanted to see his reaction to the questions. At least he doesn't think the McGowans are big enough to try and muscle in on their drug operations. I don't think they are either. If it was the other way around then it would make more sense. Why would the McGowans start all this, what could they possibly gain out of it?'

'Well, he admitted getting a text message, at least that's something' said Mitchell, slightly annoyed that Dorsey seemed to be ignoring this.

'I'm not convinced the text messages are anything to do with the murders. If an avenging angel was going to kill anyone for selling drugs, you'd have thought the twins would be the first on his list. It all seems too weird to be true. A religious crackpot, who is also a professional hit man or is at least able to find one to do the killing for him? It's too much like something you'd get in one of those Rebus books.'

'I never knew you read crime novels, Frank.'

'Only when I was on holiday with Helen. She reads a new book every fucking day.'

'Anyway, we can't just ignore them, Frank. This is another drug dealer who has now admitted getting one. We need to chase up BT and find out if they've been able to find out the location they were sent from ...'

'I'm not ignoring them. It's still an important part of the investigation, but I think finding the white van is more important.'

'I wasn't saying it isn't, Frank, I just think the text messages are too strange to be simply a coincidence ... Do you still want us to lift the other twin if we see him?'

'No, just leave him until we've more to work with. If anything, Billy's less talkative then Eric when it comes to interviews.'

'If it wasn't for the squint in his left eye, it could've been Billy that was sitting there. God must have had an off day when he created two monsters like them?'

There was a timid knock before Harper put her head round the door. 'Sir, I thought you should know ... Tamburini's given the surveillance team the slip.'

'Fuck, thanks Kate. Get them to check all his usual haunts before *he* turns up dead next.'

Chapter 12

Denis sat in the backroom that was both his office and refuge. He poured himself a large whisky. He had only just received a call from the lawyer to tell him that Eric had been released without charge and was on his way home. He was still trying to figure out what was going on when the phone rang. It was Billy.

'Where've you been the last two days … do you know that your brother was lifted this morning?'

'I can't say anything over the phone, but I'll be back in a couple o' hours.'

'Make sure you are! I want to speak to you and your brother.' Denis hung up and swung around in his chair to look out the window at the back garden, which was in complete darkness. The only thing he could see was his own face sternly looking back, older than he liked to think. He could not get his mind to settle and was afraid that the twins may have been the reason Bob Devlin was lying in the morgue. At that moment, the thought of a murderous feud with the McGowans made him feel weary; there was nothing he could get out of it but grief. The Calton area was as Catholic as the Pope, and even with the McGowans out of the way, Denis would not be able to set up anything that would not be blown up within a week. He was too well known as a Protestant, with links to the royalists in Northern Ireland, to get very far in that part of Glasgow. The other thing that worried him was the swarms of police officers patrolling the streets in the East End since the three bodies were discovered. The police were already making it hard for business to continue and he did not want them to scare off some of his legitimate associates. He coughed a lungful of smoke and stubbed out his cigar in a moment's subdued rage. 'If those two idiots were involved in Devlin's killing … I'll smash their fucking heads together,' he promised in a hoarse, broken voice to his own indignant reflection, before getting up to see what Irene was making for dinner.

Irene laid the table with one eye on the clock and the other on her husband, who was sitting in front of the fire reading *The Evening Times*. 'I thought the twins were coming home for dinner tonight?'

'They'll be here soon. I spoke to Billy an hour ago and asked him to tell Eric to be here before eight … What are you making?'

'I told you already, there's a roast chicken in the oven.'

'Oh, right. I forgot … chicken.'

'Your memory is getting worse.'

'I'm just a bit tired, got a lot on my mind.'

'Well, I don't want to hear about it.'

'Do I ever burden you with my worries?'

'Yes, every night when you've got a drink in you.'

'There's someone at the door,' said Denis as the doorbell rang impatiently.

'Well, get up and get it. You're not crippled,' complained Irene, going back into the kitchen to baste the chicken. Denis threw down the newspaper and forced himself out of his favourite chair. The bell rang again and he could see the shadow of a man through the opaque glass panel as he walked down the hall towards the door. 'I'm coming, hold your horses,' he shouted, before carefully unlocking an array of locks and chains. 'Don't you have a set of keys?' he moaned, when the door opened to reveal Billy standing there impatiently.

'Aye, but you've got chains on, so I still can't open the door even wi' keys,' complained Billy, following his father into the warmth of the living room.

'Is that you, Billy?' shouted Irene from the kitchen as she continued to mix gravy in a pot.

'Aye, Ma … What's for dinner?'

'Chicken,' replied Irene, who had long given up on the twins when it came to their use of slang. 'It will be ready in ten minutes … where's that brother of yours?'

'He's probably down the pub celebrating getting out o' jail.'

'Jail! What are you talking about?' Irene shouted.

'For pity's sake, Billy, why'd you say that!' groaned Denis, shaking his head as Irene came rushing into the living room with a worried face looking for answers. 'What's this about the jail?'

'He's only joking; Eric hasn't been in the jail.'

'That's not a very funny joke, Billy!'

'Sorry Ma, I was only winding Da up.'

'I'll never get your sense of humour, son,' Irene rebuked, before going back into the kitchen to finish making the dinner.

With Irene out the way, Denis gave Billy a clip around the back of the head. 'I've told you a thousand times to think before you speak in front of your mother … where's your brother?'

'I don't know, like I said, probably in the pub.'

'Give him a phone and tell him I want him here for dinner, his mother is expecting him. I also want to have a word wi' the both o' you later.'

84

Chapter 13

The Moffat family had already sat down for dinner when Eric turned up half drunk. His mother, unlike most, was always pleased to see him and went back into the kitchen to plate up his dinner. Eric could see the stern look on his father's face as he took a seat beside his brother, who whispered in his ear. 'Don't tell Ma ye were in the police station today.'

'Why no', they'd nothing on me,' replied Eric.

'Eric!' said Denis, lifting a finger to his lips.

'Alright, I wasn't going tell her anyway … do you think am stupid?'

'Sometimes I do … I want to speak to both o' you after dinner.'

'What's going on?' asked Irene as she came back in with Eric's dinner. 'What are you all whispering about?'

'Nothing, Irene, I'm thinking of opening a new pub, it's under administration and is up for auction. I was just telling the boys.'

'Why do you need another pub? Have you not got enough on your plate?' she retorted, taking her seat.

'It's in the West End, a bit of class that serves decent food. It's somewhere I can take clients. You've got to impress people now to get any business.'

'Aye, well I don't know why you can be bothered with another place. Especially in the West End, who do we know out there?'

'That's it, I'm sick of all the halfwits that come into the

85

other pubs. I can't breathe in the East End without some loser waving at me from across the street because he's seen me in one of the pubs and thinks I'm his pal.'

'Where in the West End?' asked Billy, now convinced that his dad was serious about what he was saying and not trying to distract his mother from asking Eric where he had spent most of the day.

'On Byres Road, it's a smart looking place.'

'It can't be that great if it went bust,' interrupted Eric, still sulking after his father's remark on his intelligence or the lack of it.

'The owner had a few other businesses that took a nose dive, his trouble is our opportunity.'

'Right, enough!' interrupted Irene. 'I thought we agreed not to talk business at the dinner table. I'm not spending all day cooking a meal just to watch it going cold while you lot talk about things that can be discussed later.'

'Your mother's right … what did Brando say? *We don't discuss business at the dinner table.*'

'That wasn't Brando, it was Al Pacino in *Godfather II*,' said Eric.

'You're both wrong, it was James Caan in the original,' said Billy, who had watched the Godfather Trilogy at least once a year since he was ten.

'Whoever it was had more sense than you lot … now eat up, I've made a crème brûlée for dessert,' said Irene.

'I knew we shouldn't have got you that French cookbook last Christmas,' laughed Billy, dodging a slap on the back of the head from his mother.

'I'll need to start wearing a crash helmet in here,' moaned Billy, as his dad winked at him.

After Irene's crème brûlée, the twins followed their father into his office where they knew all the secrets were

86

kept. Like Romulus and Remus, they were each planning to build their own empires once the old man finally retired or shook off his mortal coil, which ever came sooner. Denis lit a cigar and sat back on his reinforced swivel chair to let the dinner in his corpulent stomach settle down. 'Why were you arrested today?'

'For nothing. They had CCTV o' us going to Tucker's flat, that's all. That was the day we found him wi' his head blown off.'

'Do they think we killed one o' our own dealers?' 'They don't know what to think. They're just clutching at straws.'

'Who interviewed you?'

'Dorsey and that other moron, Mitchell … they've got no idea who killed anybody.'

'Dorsey, he's been around a while. What about Mitchell, I don't know him?'

'He's a right bastard. He grabbed me by the neck and nearly strangled me. He tried to force me to answer Dorsey's stupid questions.'

'Where was Stanton when this was happening?'

'He was late as usual. They let me go without any charges as soon as he arrived.'

'And where've you been, Billy?'

'I'd to go and pick up some gear from Bristol.'

'You went down to Bristol yourself to pick a load o' drugs? Are you two as stupid as each other? How many times have I told you never to touch the gear yourself?'

'Cosgrove pulled out at the last minute, said he was sick. I couldn't get anybody else to do it.'

'That's no' the point … never means never. You should've phoned Bristol and told them to put the deal back a week 'til that piece o' shit Cosgrove got out o' his bed.'

'I tried, but they weren't interested. They said they had someone else looking to buy the gear.'

'So what, do you believe everything you're told? That's the last time I want to hear about you doing something as bloody stupid again. What do I explain to your mother when you get yourself ten years in Barlinnie for drug dealing?'

'Okay, I'll no' do it again.'

'Too right you'll no' … Anyway, I've been trying to get a hold o' you two for the last few days, why've your phones been off?'

'We got a tip off on Friday that the CID was tapping into our phones,' said Billy. 'We ditched them and bought new ones.'

'And you didn't bother to phone me or your mother to let us know you were alright!'

'Dad, we're big boys, we can look after ourselves,' said Eric, getting annoyed that his father referred to him as stupid for a second time, even though he wasn't with Billy in Bristol.

'Aye, you're a pair o' gangsters alright, but you'd both be nothing without my name and money to protect you every time you mess up,' shouted Denis, getting up to tower over his sons. 'From now on, all I want from you two is straight answers. What have you found out about these three murders?'

'Nothing,' said Eric as Billy shrugged his shoulders in agreement. 'Is that no' the polis's job?'

'Are you trying to be funny, son? You're no' too big for me to knock that grin onto the other side o' your face. If I find out that either o' you two were responsible for killing Devlin then you're both … ' Before he could finish his admonishment, Denis began a fit of coughing that turned his already red face a dangerous-looking shade of purple.

'Dad, are you alright?' shouted Billy as they rushed to help their father. Although Denis was in the throws of a fit, he pushed his two sons away and ordered them to get out of his office. 'The two o' you'll give me a heart attack yet!'

'What the hell's going on in here … are you alright, Denis?' shouted Irene, pushing past the twins to get to her husband.

'I'm fine,' he spluttered. 'It must've been that crème brûlée coming back on me.'

'Crème brûlée my arse … it's these bloody cigars, they're killing you.'

Chapter 14

Dorsey parked outside the Procurator Fiscal's office opposite the Central Mosque. It had been raining all night. He pulled up the collar of his raincoat and rushed into the building before he got soaked. Presenting his warrant card at reception, he took the lift to the second floor where the Fiscal was already waiting for him.

'Good morning, Inspector. The receptionist phoned to say you were on your way up. My name is Liz Baxter.'

'Morning, Miss Baxter,' responded Dorsey, shaking her hand, which was as warm as his was cold. He had already noticed that there was no wedding ring on her left hand and he was quite sure in his mind that he had addressed her properly; she did not correct him in any event.

Although they had never met, Dorsey was sure he had seen her before, maybe in court. She was a good-looking woman, probably in her early thirties, he thought, as he followed her along the long narrow corridor to her office. 'Take a seat, Inspector.'

'The superintendent told me you're taking a keen interest in the recent drug-related murders in the East End,' said Dorsey. She nodded, her dark brown eyes looking with such intensity he felt she was about to cross examine him. He opened his folder on his lap as though he had something to offer that would placate her.

'Yes, I've been asked to keep the Crown Office informed of any progress in the investigation. The Justice Minister is concerned that these types of killings give the country a bad name. You know what politicians are like; they don't care about anything until something makes them look bad in the papers. Are we dealing with a gangland drugs war?'

'That's what it looks like. This is everything we have at the minute,' he said handing her the folder. 'That's not a Glasgow accent?'

'No, I'm not from Glasgow.'

'Edinburgh?'

'Well, not quite, Linlithgow. I only moved through here a couple of months ago, so you'll have to excuse my ignorance when it comes to the names of these gangs.'

'It's not that difficult to get to grips with. The main ones are generally referred by the top man's surname, a bit like the Mafia, only more mince and tatties than pasta.'

'I'm sure I'll get to know them soon enough. So, what do you think kicked this whole thing off?'

'The obvious reason would be drugs.'

'So why are they able to operate if you know they're dealing drugs?'

'If it was up to me I would arrest the whole lot of them today and throw away the key, but it's not up to me. It's up to you guys in here. It's all about proving what we know in court. The few witnesses that did come forward in the past were soon too scared to give evidence when they realised that they might end up in the Clyde with a bullet in their heads. The only way to catch them is with police surveillance, and that takes time and manpower which we don't have enough of. We do what we can, but the top men, like Denis Moffat hide behind legitimate businesses, and leave the dirty work to others further down the food chain. He'll only get his hands dirty if he really needs to.'

'Like now, when someone's trying to take over his little empire.'

'Maybe … anyway, Miss Baxter, right now we don't have any clear suspect for these killings but we're following a few different leads and should get the forensic report about the Devlin murder from the lab later today … you never know, it might give us something. Unless there's anything else you want to know, everything's in this file,' he said, getting to his feet.

'No, there's nothing else. I'll read this and give you a call if I need to speak to you about anything. Thank you for coming in,' she said, smiling and getting up to walk him to the door. He followed her back along the corridor, catching the faint hint of perfume.

'I'll speak to you soon, Inspector. It was nice meeting you.'

'I hope the file will be helpful.'

'I'm sure it will.'

It had stopped raining, and when Dorsey crossed the road to his car, he could not help himself from looking back at the rows of windows. Sitting in his car, he tried to remember her first name, but it had slipped his cluttered mind and he raked his memory to no avail. He switched on the engine and stole another look in the direction of the building, scanning the second floor. What *was* her name?

Professor Jenkins had already carried out the post-mortem on Devlin and was in the process of stitching the abdomen when both Dorsey and Mitchell arrived at the morgue. 'You missed the best bit, detectives. All done,' said the Professor, cutting the surgical thread with a pair of scissors as though he had just finished tying a roast joint together.

'What have you got for us?' asked Dorsey, looking along the stitched wound that ran from the victim's throat to his groin.

'One bullet to the head as you can see. Just like the other two, only this time it was a different type of handgun used. The other two, you will remember, were shot by a 9mm Browning at close range. Our plump friend here, however, was not shot with the same handgun. We're probably looking for a Beretta semi-automatic, or something of that sort. I remember nearly thirty years ago we had a number of bodies turning up with bullets in their heads from such a gun. That was at the time Denis Moffat finally took over the East End. Although no one ever proved it was Big Denis that was behind the killings, it was common knowledge he used a Beretta.'

'But would he be daft enough to be using the same gun?'

'Of course not, he'd have got rid of that at the time. Guns are nearly always disposed of more carefully than the victims. Killers get used to the weight and feel of a particular gun and will generally stick to the same type. This looks like Denis may be back in the saddle, and it seems your initial idea of a drugs war was right … shall I expect more bodies soon?' asked the Professor, holding up a metal tray with the bullet he had retrieved earlier from Devlin's head.

'I'd be surprised if Denis Moffat carried out this killing, he's got plenty of other mugs to do that for him.'

'Maybe so, but he might've done it to re-establish his reputation. We older guys sometimes have to prove to ourselves that we're still as good as we were in our prime. Contrary to popular belief, vanity gets worse with age.'

'Is there anything else we should know, Professor?'

'Yes, and I'm sure you'll change your mind about Denis Moffat when I tell you. The unfortunate Mr Devlin was tied up and gagged for a time before his execution. Who ever killed him tortured him first. There are a large number of relatively superficial cuts on the body. Probably caused with

93

a Stanley blade, and these burn marks here, look like they were made with a large cigar …'

'What? Cigar burns?'

'Yes, but strangely enough these burns, unlike the cuts to the body are all post-mortem. Why would anyone want to do that? You can't get any answers or pleasure burning a corpse with a cigar, or have I missed something after all these years?'

'Are you sure the burns are from a cigar?' asked Dorsey as Mitchell turned to another page in his notebook and waited for the answer.

'A cigar or something of that type, what else can I say. I managed to extract some specks of ash that were left in the skin and sent them to the lab this morning. What they'll make of it is anyone's guess. I'd be surprised if they can't confirm it was from a cigar, but who knows these days, the wonders of science, they may even be able to tell us the brand … Now that would be clever.'

'And are you sure they were made after death?' 'Inspector, how long have I been doing this job, of course I'm sure. You don't have to note everything down I say, DC Mitchell. It will all be in the report. Unless there's anything else, I'm in a hurry today. I've a lunch date with a colleague from the toxicology department, and Mitchell, please don't write that down. Her husband doesn't know about our little rendezvous. All totally innocent, but you know what jealous husbands are like. I don't want to end up on one of my own slabs before my time.'

'What's your view on time of death? George thinks it was sometime between seven and nine on the Saturday evening.' 'That would be a reasonable estimate … but, at the moment, just to be on the safe side, I'd say sometime between seven and midnight. Good day, gentlemen.'

'We'll chat later, Professor,' said Dorsey, taking a closer

look at the burn marks on the deceased.

'Are you thinking what I'm thinking?' asked Mitchell, putting his notebook away.

'It's too good to be true. Big Denis always used a Beretta in the old days and no one smokes cigars like him. But he's been too careful all his life to do something as stupid as this.'

'If it's not Denis, then someone wants us to think it was him. We're back where we started: the McGowans. With Big Denis inside for murder and the twins running things, there would be chaos in no time. The McGowans would have their best chance to expand for years.'

'Do you think Hughie McGowan's got the bottle for something like this? Would he be so brutal to kill one of his own dealers just to fit up Denis Moffat?'

'Maybe one of his sons has finally stepped up to the mark or he's got the backing of Dempsey. Nobody hates Moffat more than Jackie Dempsey.'

'With what we've got already, I think we can at least have a chat with Big Denis. That'll be interesting.'

Chapter 15

They drove through the East End, towards the fortress that was Denis Moffats home. Both detectives were a little apprehensive when the car pulled up outside the large detached villa. It was years since Dorsey was last in the house, that time they had a warrant to search the premises for drugs that were suspected to be in the cellar. They found nothing, and left with Denis's words ringing in their ears. 'How stupid do you think I am?'

Dorsey knew what they had from the Devlin autopsy report proved nothing, but he could at least see Denis Moffat's reaction to the suggestion that he was suspected of being involved in the murder of one of Hughie McGowan's men. Before they left the vehicle, Mitchell took a couple of photographs of the house for the incident board, which he was now taking a professional pride in. 'He's got more surveillance cameras on the front of that building than the city chambers,' said Mitchell as they approached the front door. Dorsey knocked the opaque glass panel and took a step back.

Irene recognised Dorsey on the CCTV monitor from the kitchen. She took her time before opening the front door.

'Is your husband in?' asked Dorsey producing his police I.D. 'I'm Inspector Dorsey and this is …'

'I know who you are. What do you want him for?' 'We just want to speak to him, can we come in?'

'Do you have a warrant?'

'No, but we can get one,' interrupted Mitchell, impatiently.

'Well, we'll still be here when you get one,' she said, closing the door over.

The locks and chains were redeployed on the other side of the door with the same deliberate attention to security as a bank clerk in a safety deposit vault. The two detectives looked at each other for a moment before Dorsey knocked on the door again with a little more force. This time the door was opened by Denis, who was wearing a white vest and a pair of stripped pyjama bottoms. He had a small towel around his neck and shaving foam on one side of his face, which amused Dorsey a little.

'It's a bit late in the day for shaving, Denis.'

'It depends when you get out your bed, son. What do you want?'

'Can we come in?' asked Dorsey, showing his ID again.

'You're an Inspector now, son … Dorsey, isn't it?'

'And this is DC Mitchell. We have a few questions we want to ask you.'

'You better come in then or you'll catch your death out there and the newspapers will blame me for your untimely demise. You know what they're like when they're stuck for a story. Mind, wipe your shoes. The wife only got this carpet a couple of weeks ago.'

They followed Denis along the hall as he cleaned the shaving foam from his face and threw the towel into the bathroom. Unlike Dorsey, Mitchell ignored the request to wipe his shoes and left a trail of wet foot prints behind him. Denis let the two detectives into the living room and offered them a drink, which they both declined. He nonchalantly poured himself a whisky, as though it was an everyday occurrence to have two detectives in the house. 'What do you want to speak to me about?' he asked, maintaining his composure.

'I'm sure you're aware that we spoke to your son, Eric, about a number of murders in this area.'

'I hope he helped you wi' your enquiries. He's a good boy … sure you don't want a drink?'

'No thanks, we're interested in another killing … that of Bob Devlin. We believe he was killed sometime between seven pm and midnight on Saturday. Can you tell us where you were on 17th of December?'

'You think I killed him?'

'We've evidence which might suggest that.'

'What evidence?'

'I'm not prepared to disclose that at the moment,' said Dorsey, well aware he was on thin ice.

'You can't come in here accusing me, in my own home, with a murder and you won't even tell me why you think it was me! You've been reading too many stories written about me by that little weasel, Barney Collins. If a car backfires in the East End, he's on that computer of his writing shit about another gangland murder and implying that I'm behind it.'

'We only want to eliminate you from our inquires. That's if you've an alibi for that night.'

'You took my son in the other day without a shred of evidence against him. This could be seen as police harassment, but so that you get the picture, ask my wife where I was on Saturday night; she'll be able to tell you.'

'I'd like you to tell me first, and then we'll ask your wife. That's how it's done.'

'I know how it's done. If you must know I was here from about six in the evening and didn't leave until about nine the next morning. Ask her yourself, she's in the kitchen. Last Saturday was our wedding anniversary. Do you think I'd go out and murder someone on the night o' my wedding anniversary?'

'Well, most people wouldn't murder anyone on any night,' said Mitchell, drawing a sinister smile from Moffat that slightly unnerved him. Unable to maintain eye contact, he noted down the alibi before going into the kitchen to speak to Irene Moffat.

After speaking to Irene, the two detectives left with full details of their prime suspect's alibi in Mitchell's notebook. Dorsey was not surprised, even if Denis was the killer, he would have had plenty of time to agree an alibi with his wife. 'Why don't we get a warrant and search the place? He's got CCTV, that'll tell us if he was in the house or not,' suggested Mitchell as he switched on the ignition.

'He's not going to have any evidence in that house that's got anything to do with any crime, never mind murder. Any video tape that undermines his alibi will have been deleted long before now. Over the years that house has been raided umpteen times and absolutely nothing incriminating has ever been found. We had to pay compensation out the last couple of times, and Knox has made it clear that unless we can guarantee turning up evidence we're not to apply to the court for a warrant.'

'If Moffat knew that we were now too scared to get a search warrant, then the safest place for any evidence would be in his basement.'

'The gun and the cigar burns still don't add up to me. Barney Collins has created a legend around Denis Moffat's Beretta and everybody and their dog knows about his passion for cigars. He'd never be that obvious.'

'Maybe he's getting old and careless. He might even want everybody to think he did it, so long as he knows we can't prove it was him. That way he maintains his status as a hard man. Remember what Jenkins said about vanity and age.'

'Would he use his wife for a false alibi, and risk her going to prison if found out?'

'He's the type that'd use anyone for any reason so long as he got off the hook.'

'But she showed you their marriage certificate; Saturday *was* their wedding anniversary.'

'It doesn't prove he didn't do it.'

'But we can't prove he did.'

Chapter 16

Benny Moffat was no longer counting the months or weeks to his release date. The 24th December was not just Christmas Eve, but the day the Parole Board had agreed to his early liberation. No prison dinner for him this Christmas, and he could almost smell his mother's cooking. The time was dragging, but as everyone was keen to tell him, the first and the last few days of a prison sentence were the worst. In the last few months, with freedom on the horizon, he had become obsessed with keeping himself fit and even after a morning in the gym, he would still do press ups in his cell every couple of hours to maintain the muscles on his upper body. Before his sentence he had put on a bit of weight around his gut, but that was now long gone and he was as lean and fit as any amateur boxer.

With his father's name and reputation behind him, Benny did virtually as he pleased in prison, and if he needed something, including new SIM cards for his smuggled mobile phone, there were two screws in his father's payroll that would oblige. It was a standing joke among the other prisoners that Benny made more phone calls from Barlinnie than the Governor.

After another workout, Benny left the gym before his usual time to get washed and changed. He had a visit. It was Linda Boland, the girl he was seeing before he was arrested. Benny was glad of her weekly visit. She was good-looking and usually turned up wearing high heels and short skirts. She made the other prisoners' wives and girlfriends look drab. To please him she also left the top button of her blouse undone so he could see the top of her low-cut bra. On her last visit, as though preparing Benny for release, she told him that she was not wearing any knickers under her tight-fitting skirt, which had an instant result in Benny's baggy prison trousers.

Back in his cell, Benny took off his shirt, and admired his impressive build in the small shaving mirror above the tiny sink, before getting down on the floor and starting another gruelling round of press ups. Once he had wiped down the sweat from his upper body, he retrieved his mobile phone from under his pillow and phoned to make sure that the cocaine deal was still on.

Cooper and Harper were now at the last Caledonia Hire branch on their schedule. They had spent most of the day checking lists of names and addresses of customers that hired vans of the type seen in the video. Unfortunately, it was one of the hire company's most popular models and the two detectives had over twenty vehicles to check that were out for hire on the relevant night. Without the actual registration it was going to be a time-consuming investigation and they were still only checking hires from the Glasgow branches. As one of the managers annoyingly pointed out, the van could have been hired from any of their thirty branches across the whole country. The detectives thanked him for reminding them what they already knew but they had to start somewhere, and the Glasgow branches were the obvious choice. They finally left with another list of names and addresses to check.

'Thank God that's done,' moaned Harper as she slumped into the passenger seat and looked at the list again. 'We can start this lot tomorrow … Are you okay, Sandy? You've been quiet all day.'

'I'm fine. I've just got a lot on my mind at the minute,

Kate.'

'If you want to talk … about Hannah …'

'That's it, what's there to talk about. She just lies there day after day. Sometimes I wish she'd just die, at least then it would be over. The doctors have told us there's no hope of her recovering, but Rebecca won't give them permission to switch off the life support.'

'I'm so sorry, Sandy, life can be cruel sometimes,' was all Harper could think to say as they made their way back to the station.

After dropping Harper off to make a report of their day's work, Sandy Cooper drove back along London Road towards the Royal Infirmary. He parked on Cathedral Street outside the hospital and went straight to the intensive care ward on the third floor. He hated hospitals, with their clinical smells of iodine and disinfectant. The nurse at reception smiled at him. He went into the ward where his wife was sitting at the bedside holding Hannah's hand. It was a picture he'd had to endure every night for nearly three months and he could never get used to it. Rebecca looked up when she heard him approaching the bed. 'How's she been?' A question he always asked in hope rather in any expectation. 'She squeezed my hand a few times this morning but nothing since.'

'Well that's something,' he said, taking a chair on the other side of the bed. Hannah had been in a coma for two weeks before she first squeezed her mother's hand. At the time it was the sign of recognition they had been waiting for; the first step on the road to recovery. That was then, now it was no more than a reminder of that fading optimism. She had been on the ventilator and drip so long that her parents now had difficulty remembering what she looked like without being attached to them.

'I better go,' said Rebecca, putting on her coat and lifting a shopping bag from the floor. 'I got some mince for dinner, so don't stay too long.'

'No, I'll be home in an hour or so …'

'Well, I'll see you later then … Bye, darling,' she said in a low whisper as she bent over to kiss Hannah on the forehead. Once Rebecca was gone, he took the chair by the bedside and put Hannah's small hand in his, and said the Lord's Prayer.

It was after nine before he said his own goodbye to his daughter and returned to his car, only to find it hemmed in by a blue van with its hazard lights on and no driver in the cab. He got into his car anyway and turned on the engine to clear the frost that was already forming on the windscreen. He then pressed the horn and held it for a few minutes as it blared across the street. It took another couple of impatient blasts before the driver appeared and banged on the car window. 'Why all the fucking noise?'

Rolling down the window, Cooper barked back. 'You shouldn't have parked there you're blocking everybody else in!'

'Sorry if you had to wait a couple of minutes, you miserable git … I was dropping off a workmate who broke his arm.'

Cooper said nothing. He turned away as the man stormed off and got into this van. He then put his head down on the hub of the steering wheel and began to sob.

Chapter 17

Wednesday 21ˢᵗ December

With no more bodies turning up and little evidence to arrest anyone, Harper finally had a breakthrough when CCTV from a local garage produced their biggest clue as to who hired the white van on the night of the double murders. She played the video again for Strachan's benefit, and he watched in silence as the van pulled alongside a petrol pump just off the Springburn Road. One of the men got out and filled the tank, while a second man went into the shop. The video then switched to the camera inside the shop where the man approached the checkout counter. He looked to be in his mid-to-late thirties, dark complexion, probably eastern European, thought Strachan. The picture then switched back to the garage forecourt as both men got back into the van. The camera then switched to the other side of the forecourt. 'Shit, we still can't see the registration number,' moaned Strachan.

'Hold on, sir,' said Harper as she fast forwarded to another camera angle, covering the exit. She then zoomed into the number plate. 'I phoned the hire company ... this is the name and address of the guy who hired the van,' said Harper, handing Strachan a piece of note paper with the suspect's details. 'His name is Jan Bakowski—it sounds Polish.'

'Good work, Kate,' praised Strachan, staring at the name and address, while placing his hand on her shoulder. 'This might be the bit of luck we need. I want stills taken from the video and put on the incident boards. Once you've done that, get one of the local wooden tops to go to the petrol station and see if the guy paid by credit card or cash. If it was a credit card get the details and check who the owner of the card is with the credit company.'

'Yes, sir,' said Harper as she printed out the stills from the video, relieved that Strachan had finally lifted his sweaty hand away.

'We might have this wrapped up before Dorsey gets in,' said Strachan, turning to one of the detectives in his team and handing him the paper with the name and address on it. 'It looks like a team of Poles are muscling in on the Moffat patch. I want every officer available to be in the muster room in five minutes.'

'Should we not wait for the Inspector?' asked Harper. Strachan ignored her question and pinned up the photographs of the two suspects she had handed him. He turned to the assembled team of detectives. 'These are the guys we've been looking for. We've the address of the one that hired the van. So, be prepared, they'll be armed to the teeth.'

Strachan was not taking any chances. He waited for the rest of his armed unit to arrive outside the tenement flat on the north east of the city. There was no sign of the van and he ordered two armed officers to take up positions on the roof of a building opposite.

While he was briefing the officer in charge of the armed unit, Strachan got the intelligence he was looking for: the credit card used at the petrol station was a fake. When one of the officers on the opposite roof confirmed that there was movement within the flat, he gave the order to move in.

In a surge of adrenaline, the first of the armed units entered the close-mouth with battering rams and their weapons at the ready. Strachan followed with some of his own officers, and the order was given to put in the door and take the occupants by surprise and sheer force of numbers. Within seconds the door was battered off its hinges, and over a dozen armed officers flooded into the flat, screaming and making as much noise as possible to bewilder those inside into submission. Every door in the flat was kicked open and the rooms systematically searched for the occupants.

The all clear was soon shouted from every room except the kitchen where a woman was cowering on her knees in the corner with two terrified children in her arms. Strachan shook his head, and muttered a curse. He ordered everyone out of the kitchen, as he helped the woman to her feet. He could feel his own blood pressure rise when he realised she was heavily pregnant. 'Do you speak English?' he asked.

'Yes, of course … why have you come here?' She asked, the words trembling in her voice.

'We're looking for Jan Bakowski.'

'Jan? Why you looking for Jan? What's he done?'

'Is he your husband?'

'Yes.'

'Has he hired a white van recently?'

'A white van, I don't know. He has own van …What has he done?'

'I can't say at the moment, but we need to speak to him urgently. Is he working?'

'He has a small shop in the Trongate. He sells groceries, Polish food,' she said, getting up and taking down a business flyer that was held on the fridge with a large magnet with a picture of Pope John Paul II. 'Here.'

Strachan looked at the brochure. It looked genuine enough, *The Polish Delicatessen Shop*. But it could easily be a front for laundering drug money, he thought and hoped. However, he was now having serious doubts.

'Has your husband ever been involved in drugs?'

'Drugs? Jan ... no, never ... Is this why you're here ... Drugs?'

'Sir,' said Harper as she came into the kitchen and handed Strachan a photograph. 'We haven't found anything else, but we've still to search in here.'

'Leave it for a few minutes,' said Strachan, looking despondently at the wedding picture for a moment. The groom was smiling as he stared lovingly at his wife. He looked nothing like the two men they had caught on the CCTV. Strachan showed the photograph to the woman.' Is this your husband?'

'Yes.'

'I'll need to take this and have it copied,' he said, handing the framed picture back to Harper. The woman just nodded, as she continued to hold on to her two frightened children. 'Can you and the children sit in the living room? We have to search in here.'

Harper could see the tension on Strachan's red face as he checked the address on the leaflet again, before handing it back to her. After another cursory look at the address, Harper turned on the ignition and pulled away from the kerb as the armed response unit packed up and returned to the station. Over the noise of the traffic, Strachan continued to mutter curses of frustration at the picture on his lap of Jan Bakowski. 'Kate, are you sure you gave the Hire Company the right date?'

'Yes, sir, it was the right date. Maybe they've looked it up wrong.'

'Fuck ... if Bakowski's not involved then the fucking papers will have a field day with this.'

'Do you think she'll make a complaint?'

'I fucking hope not.'

It was raining when Harper pulled up outside the Polish

delicatessen. She followed Strachan into the shop, which was unattended. They waited for a few minutes before Strachan, banged on the counter and shouted. 'Shop! shop!'

'Alright, hold on. I'll be there in a minute.'

'Is your name Jan Bakowski?' asked Strachan abruptly, as a man in his early thirties appeared from the back shop.

'Is your name Jan Bakowski?' Strachan repeated.

'Yes, who are you?'

'Police,' said Harper, showing her warrant card. 'Is there somewhere we can talk?'

'What's this about?' asked Bakowski, lifting the counter latch and nodding for them to follow him into the back shop. 'I've done nothing wrong.'

'No one said you had,' said Harper, as she looked around the cramped room, which was stacked with all sorts of tins and jars, labelled in what she assumed was Polish.

'It's all legally imported,' said Bakowski, when he noticed her scanning the shelves.

'We're not interested in your shop or whatever you're selling. We want to know if you hired a van in the last couple of weeks?' asked Strachan, keeping the dates vague until he got some answers.

'Yes, so that's why you're here. Have you found it?'

'What do you mean?' asked Harper, before Strachan could react.

'Have you found the van? I reported it stolen a few days after I hired it. Is that not why you're here?'

'Where did you report it stolen?' asked Strachan, after he recovered from Bakowski's initial reply.

'I reported it to the hire company.'

'Not to the police?' asked Harper.

'No, they said they would report it to the police. I did not think I had to report it also.'

'When was it stolen?' asked Strachan.

'Excuse me for a moment,' said Bakowski as the phone in the front shop began to ring. While Bakowski left to answer the phone, Strachan turned to Harper. 'Did no one at the fucking hire company think to mention to you that the van had been stolen?'

'No, sir.'

'Christ, Kate, this is turning into a shambles, you should've checked your facts first. You need to find out which station the hire company reported it to. I hope it wasn't our station or Knox will have your arse in a sling.'

'My arse?' said Kate.

'Well, it's no' going to be fucking mine!' he whispered in a raised voice as Bakowski returned to the back shop, clearly annoyed.

'What the hell you do to my wife!'

'What do you mean?' demanded Strachan.

'Your policemen broke down the front door of my house and terrified her and the children … Why you do that?' he shouted.

'Calm down, Mr Bakowski, we had good reason to do what we did,' said Strachan with as much conviction as he could muster.

'What reason you have to terrorise my family … my wife say you looking for drugs. There are no drugs in my house.'

'Mr Bakowski, the van you hired was used in a double murder last week…'

'Murder?'

'Yes, a double murder, and we weren't told by the hire company that the van had been stolen after you'd hired it. They simply provided your name and address as the person

110

who'd hired it around the time of the murders. So if you've any problem with what happened at your home this morning, then take it up with them … If you don't mind we've a few more questions and we'll leave you in peace,' said Strachan, his face now flushed.

'Ask your questions and then go,' said Bakowski.

'Why did you hire the van?' asked Strachan, having regained control of himself.

'My own van was in the garage for a week, and I need van to pick up stock and make deliveries. I hired it for seven days, but it was stolen from the lane beside the shop.'

'What day was that?'

'Hold on a minute,' said Bakowski, turning to run his finger along a calendar pinned to the wall. 'Tuesday the sixth of December.'

'Did your wife not know you had to hire a van and that it was stolen?' asked Harper, much to Strachan's annoyance as he had forgotten the Mrs Bakowski had no idea that her husband had hired a van, never mind had it stolen.

'Why I need tell my wife? She has enough worry. I hire vans before, why I tell my wife … why she be interested?'

'Would she not be interested if she knew it had been stolen?' asked Strachan, trying to regain control of the interview.

'Maybe, why worry her … that my problem, not hers.'

'She must've noticed you'd a van one day and none the next,' suggested Harper, taking the stern look from Strachan in her stride.

'I don't take van home; I park in lane beside shop at night.'

'How do you get to and from your shop?'

'I have motorbike; it's outside … you want see it.'

111

The two detectives fell silent. They had run out of questions. 'No, that'll be okay, I saw it when we came in,' said Strachan. 'One final question Mr Bakowski, where were you on the tenth of December, between 7pm and 7am?' 'That was Saturday night,' considered Bakowski, looking again at the calendar before answering. 'At home with wife and children, I think you have already asked her? Now, if finished questions, I have work.'

Once back in the street, they took a closer look at the motorbike, but by now they both believed Bakowski was an innocent man.

Harper drove back along London Road in silence; she was feeling the pressure. She knew that Strachan was planning to put all the blame for the morning's fiasco onto her, and there was not much she could do about it.

That afternoon, Superintendent Knox slammed the phone down in a rage and immediately went down to the operations office and shouted for every one to be quiet. 'I've just had a lawyer on the phone on behalf of a Mr Bakowski. It seems we smashed into his house and terrorised his pregnant wife and two young children without any justification whatsoever. Where the hell is Inspector Dorsey?'

'He left a couple of minutes ago with Mitchell on a tip off,' said Cooper.

'What bloody tip off?'

'No idea, sir. He didn't say.'

'Tell him I want to speak to him as soon as he gets back in. That shambles this morning is going to end up in the morning papers and we're going to look like a bunch of amateurs.'

'That's a bit unfair,' complained Strachan. 'It was the hire company that failed to tell us that the van had been stolen.'

'I've just spoken to that man's lawyer. His wife got such

a fright she's now in hospital … and there's every chance she might lose her baby. Where's Inspector Dorsey? He's supposed to be in charge of this fucking investigation.'

Chapter 18

They had been driving for over an hour since Dorsey got the anonymous call about the location of the white van, but they were completely lost, somewhere in the middle of the countryside, miles from anywhere. Mitchell had turned off the satnav that was sending them around in circles. They had not passed another car for a while, and Dorsey was getting more and more frustrated as he tried to make sense of the map on his lap without any road directions to keep him right. After another couple of wrong turns, he was beginning to think the tip off was a hoax.

Tired of listening to Dorsey's moaning, Mitchell finally noticed a wooden sign pointing out the direction to the farmhouse. 'That's it,' agreed Dorsey, looking at the note he was holding. Mitchell turned the car off the main road and onto a narrow farm road that was only fit for tractors.

It was now dark and Mitchell dipped the headlights as they neared the farmhouse in the distance. Dorsey looked at the map again and then the directions the anonymous caller gave. It confirmed that they had found the right place.

'How'd anyone even know we're looking for it?' asked Mitchell, coming to a stop at a metal gate barring them from driving any further.

'Sometimes Barney Collins can be useful … he wrote another article about the murders this morning … and kindly informed the public that we're looking for a white, Caledonia Hire van,' said Dorsey. He got out of the car and checked the padlock on the gate. 'It's locked,' he said, turning on the small torch he was carrying.

The farmhouse was in darkness and they walked cautiously towards the outhouses. There was a full moon in the sky and the leafless trees cast shadows as their branches moved wildly in the gathering wind. Dorsey could hear himself breathing heavily while they crept ever nearer to the side of the house. He looked back towards Mitchell, who nodded in acknowledgement at the white van parked between the barn and the farmhouse.

'That's it,' whispered Mitchell, shinning his torch on the registration plate.

They rushed across the last few yards to the side of the building, the noise on the gravel breaking the silence. His back pressed against the building, Dorsey edged along the wall to one of the windows at the front of the farmhouse. The curtains were wide open, and, after straining to see through the darkness, he shone his torch into the empty room. Around the back of the building Mitchell carried out his own reconnaissance. They eventually checked out all of the downstairs windows and were now pretty certain that there was no one inside the building. 'What do you reckon?' asked Mitchell, with an anxious look as the moonlight cast a pale yellow hue across his face.

'See if there's any way of breaking in without causing too much damage. Remember, we don't have a warrant.'

'There's an upstairs window at the back which looks slightly open and there's a pair of ladders lying at the side of the barn.'

'Let's get them, and see what's in there.'

They lifted the ladders and placed them just under the open window. Mitchell began to climb, while Dorsey held the ladders to stop them moving from side to side. When Mitchell was half in and half out of the window, they heard the sound of a vehicle in the distance, coming nearer. 'Wait there!' shouted Dorsey, walking to the side of the house to see headlights coming along the road towards the gate. He rushed to the back of the house, but Mitchell was already inside.

'There's someone coming,' shouted Dorsey. 'Stay where you are.'

Dorsey could hear the car coming to a stop. He took the ladders and put them at the side of the house, and moved into the shadows of the barn where he could see a Land Rover stopping near to where they had left the police car. 'Shit … Shit,' he shouted, as he heard the spinning of wheels and watched the vehicle turning back on itself, before driving off at speed along the dirt track to the main road. 'We've fucked up,' he shouted.

Mitchell opened the front door of the farmhouse from inside to see Dorsey pointing at the headlights that were fleeing in the distance.

'George, phone and get a warrant so we can search this place and the van legally,' said Dorsey, relieving himself against the side of the barn. 'There must be fingerprints at least.'

'There's more than that in here,' said Mitchell holding up a polythene bag containing thousands of small blue tablets.

Within an hour of the phone call, the farmhouse was surrounded by police cars. Armed uniformed officers were posted at the gate, while those specialising in gathering evidence went about their work. In addition to the bag of tablets found by Mitchell, six bags, of what was believed to be cocaine, were found in a suitcase above a wardrobe. Fingerprint lifts were systematically recovered from every room in the house. In one of the rooms a dozen or so handguns and a semi-automatic rifle were recovered from under one of the beds. Outside, the white van was undergoing a forensic examination under external lights set up to allow the detectives to carry out their work.

'Well done, Frank,' said Knox, looking into the police van that was now loaded with the drugs and weapons. 'We'll get these bastards now.'

'Well, if we don't get prints or DNA from this lot then I'll be amazed. Nobody's that careful.'

'Do we know who owns this farm yet?'

'No, but George is trying to find out and bring them in for questioning. It's not a working farm any longer and must've been rented out.'

'After the debacle this morning at least this gives us something to go to the press with that might deflect from Strachan's fuck up. He had the cheek to try and blame Harper.'

'I heard about that, they were just unlucky, the rental company should've told us that the van had been stolen.'

'I suppose so; we'll have to put the best spin on it we can. Anyway, keep me posted if anything else comes up, I'm heading home. The wife's got a dinner party organised for tonight.'

'Enjoy your night; I'll get this wrapped up as quickly as I can.'

Chapter 19

The lockups were in semi-darkness with only a weak light coming from a single bulb, hanging from a twisted bare wire, under which sat Massimo Tamburini tied to a chair. His face was cut and bruised, with a trickle of blood running from his nose into the corner of his mouth. He moaned and wailed like a wounded animal waiting to be slaughtered.

Billy Moffat took a knife from his back pocket and held it before Massimo's terrified eyes. 'Where's our stuff, you thieving bastard.'

'Please, Billy, it's true, Ah don't know anything.'

'Liar, you were seen going into the flat … did you do-in Tucker and steal the gear?'

'No, he was already dead when ah got there …Ah just panicked and left … whoever killed him must've stolen the smack.'

'Ah still don't believe you.'

'Please, Billy, I've no' got your stuff … ye can search ma flat, there's nothing in it.'

'Don't worry, we already have, but you've stashed it somewhere,' insisted Billy, before coldly slicing off one of Massimo's earlobes. The screams only made Billy even more indifferent to the suffering he was causing, and he slapped Massimo hard across the mouth. 'Shut the fuck up!' Massimo swallowed his pain with the blood in his mouth, his screams turning to anguished sobs.

Patiently waiting for his turn to get his hands on Massimo, Eric sat in the shadows with his feet up on the workbench smoking, while he tried to find a radio station. The dated stack hi-fi, that had once been the Moffats' pride and joy before it was banished to the lockup, whistled and wailed as it struggled to pick up a strong enough signal. Beside Eric, stood the two men who had picked up Massimo that morning, Eddie Malone and Steve Cosgrove.

Eventually Eric found a country music station to his likening, which was conveniently playing *Your Cheating Heart*. With Hank Williams lamenting his unfaithful wife in the background, there was another sudden scream when Billy pressed the point of the blade into Massimo's left nasal cavity. 'Where's the fucking gear?'

'Please, Ah told you … Ah don't know,' shouted Massimo in terror, before the blade sliced through the skin of the nostril, causing the blood to spray over Billy's shirt.

'Look what you've done, you fucking idiot,' shouted Billy, giving Massimo a slap across the face. 'Turn the radio up … he's making too much fucking noise. Someone else take a turn, Am going for a piss.'

While Billy disappeared into the toilet at the back of the lockup, Eric handed a roll of gaffer tape to Malone. 'Here, put that on him to shut him up.' Malone went behind Massimo and tightly wrapped the tape around his bloody mouth. Now struggling to breathe, Massimo went into a convulsive fit, causing the chair to tip onto the concrete floor, almost knocking himself out cold. 'Get him up!' demanded Eric, flicking the butt of his cigarette at Cosgrove, who immediately took his hands out of his pockets and helped Malone to get Massimo back in the torture position.

'Are you lot fucking daft or what?' shouted Billy, coming back from the toilet, wiping his hands on his trousers. 'How's he going to talk wi' that wrapped 'round his fucking mouth?' By now Massimo was prepared to tell them anything to get his ordeal over with as Billy pulled off the gaffer tape with some of Massimo's two days' growth. 'Oh, shit,' he laughed, pointing to a damp stain spreading down Massimo's inside trouser leg. 'The bastard's pissed himself … Are you going to tell us what happened to the fucking smack now or do Ah cut your whole fucking nose off?'

'Please, Billy, Ah'll tell ye everything … but it wasn't ma idea, it was Tucker's. It was him and Watson that wanted tae bump ye fur the drugs. They were going tae sell them and fuck off tae London wi' the money.'

'So why'd you no' tell us that in the first place, you wee lying bastard!' shouted Billy, taking the knife from Massimo's face. 'You were in it wi' them, how else would you know what they were up to. The three o' you were trying to bump us, just tell me the truth and this will be all over.'

'No … Ah promise,' sobbed Massimo, his tears running with the blood onto his T-Shirt. 'Why don't we cut his balls off!' shouted Eric, getting to his feet, and taking out his own flick-knife from his back pocket.

'He'll probably shit himself,' laughed Billy. 'Please … Ah'll get ye the money.'

'We don't need your stinking money,' mocked Billy in an exaggerated Mexican accent, which made everyone in the lockup, except Massimo, laugh. 'This is no' about fucking money. We don't need your stinking money,' repeated Billy. 'Why don't we do what Mr White was going to do to the cop in *Reservoir Dogs*,' suggested Eric, who was as much a film buff as his brother. As soon as Massimo heard Eric's suggestion, he immediately forgot about his missing ear lobe and torn nostril and pleaded in utter terror. 'Ah'll get the money off ma Dad … Ah'll get it tonight … Please … Please!' he begged, knowing fine well that his father had long since disowned him and would give him nothing while he was still using drugs.

'Shut your mouth,' screamed Eric, wrapping a fresh piece

of gaffer tape around Massimo's battered and bloody face. 'I've wanted to do this for ages,' he said emptying a Gerry Can of petrol over Massimo's head.

Eric then teased his victim with the flame from his Zippo lighter, and achieved his desired affect. Massimo's bowels opened up.

'Oh, fuck he's shit himself,' shouted Billy, as he came between Eric and Massimo. 'Lets just dump him ... He's had enough. Remember what the auld man said about killing anyone for a few bags of heroin. Anyway, you'll burn the fucking lockup down.'

'Alright,' agreed Eric, turning to Malone and Cosgrove. 'You two brought him here. Now you can get rid o' him ... He's fucking stinking and making me feel sick!'

Chapter 20

Dorsey was taking a coffee break. He had spent most of the night at the farmhouse with Mitchell, who he sent home, exhausted, just before dawn. They had recovered so much evidence that it was not easy to know where to begin. He watched numerous production bags being carried into the main office, where they were logged and put into some kind of order. They would soon be on their way to the lab for analysis, but there was no doubt in anyone's mind the importance of the haul; they had stopped hundreds of thousands of pounds' worth of illegal drugs from flooding the streets of Glasgow. The productions included weapons, drugs and dozens of Romanian passports, driving licences, and credit cards, which added to the wealth of evidence being collated.

Harper noted that one of the Romanian passports had a picture of the van driver they had caught on CCTV. Even with the passport, the identity of the man was still a mystery. The name on the passport was different from the name on two driving licences and another passport, which all had the same photograph. The numerous passports, driving licenses and other forged documents threw up dozens of names, many with the same photograph. In all, Harper was only able to confirm the existence of three men behind this wealth of deception, each having numerous false names and forged documents to hide their true identities. The only thing she knew for certain was that the two of them were the same two men captured on CCTV at the petrol station. Dorsey ordered the photographs to be emailed to their counterparts in Romania for possible identification.

Whoever these characters were, thought Dorsey, they were as tough looking as any Glasgow gang he had come up against, and probably more ruthless. He was convinced that if they could track them down, then they would have the killers of Watson and Tucker, maybe even Devlin. The motive was simple: destroy the local infrastructure of the existing drugs gangs and fill the vacuum with their own drugs. Killing a few of those dealing at the bottom of the supply chain would soon destroy the Glasgow gangs' ability to get their own drugs to their customers. Their business plan did not have to be any more complicated than that, but it was ruthless none the less.

Exhausted, Dorsey went into his office and closed the door over for some peace and quiet. He rested his head on the desk to get a few minutes shuteye before the shift change. He was just about to doze off when the phone rang. Reluctantly he lifted the receiver. 'Oh, morning, sir,' he said, getting to his feet to shake off his tiredness. 'Thank you, sir ... Yes they are the likely suspects in at least two if not all three murders ... I'll get some sleep later; we're still sieving through all the evidence ... Yes, thank you, sir, I'll let the squad know you phoned.' Dorsey put the phone down thoughtfully; it wasn't often that the Chief Constable called to congratulate him. He went into the operations room as some of the day shift started to arrive. In need of some fresh air, he went outside for a moment. There was no point going home now. How could he sleep with all this going on in his head?

The brisk winter morning soon had him shivering, and he was just about to go back into the station when he noticed a stooped man, wearing a trilby and long black coat coming towards him in the early morning rain. There was an unmistakable smell of cooking oil as the man reached past him to open the door.

'Giuseppe?'

'Inspector, I didn't recognise you. Oh, a terrible thing has happened to one of my boys … thank God to see you here. It's terrible, Inspector, what those animals did to my boy.'

Dorsey had known Giuseppe Tamburini for nearly twenty years. He remembered feeling sorry for him the day the old man had to watch his son being sent down for three years for drug dealing. The father never held it against Dorsey, and told him at the time that Massimo deserved to go to prison for what he was doing.

Giuseppe was only a young boy when he came with his family to Scotland to escape the post-war poverty in Italy. The Tamburini family were hard-working people and built up their business with long hours serving the mainly working-class area of Dalmarnock, with what was once a great treat in the slums of the East End, a Tamburini fish supper. That was before the invasion of other more exotic cuisines gradually took most of their customers. Now a fish supper was an occasional option on a Friday night after the pub.

Once Massimo came out of prison, Giuseppe was prepared to let him run the fish shop with his older brother Dino. At first both sons grasped the opportunity. The shop was refurbished and soon selling pizzas, kebabs and even curries to keep up with the Glaswegian desire to soak up a good drink with spicy food. Although still unmistakably Italian, the chip shop had become multicultural and business began to improve. The family were even talking of opening another outlet, until Massimo's heroin addiction began to take control of his life and his interest in the family business gradually waned.

Massimo was soon missing shifts, leaving his brother to do all the work. His mother and father despaired. As the drug addiction took hold he was arrested time and time again for selling drugs and stealing to feed his ever growing habit. No matter how Giuseppe tried to save Massimo from his life of crime, the drugs had made the son a stranger to the father. When money started going missing from the shop, Giuseppe threw him out of the house to fend for himself. They had not seen or heard from him for over a year as Massimo sunk deeper into a life of crime and addiction.

Dorsey took the old man into his office and offered him a coffee, which Giuseppe declined.

'Take your time and tell me what's happened.'

Giuseppe ran his hands through his thinning hair, struggling not to cry. 'They've left him almost insane with fear ... the bastards, cowards ... my poor boy.'

'Massimo?' asked Dorsey, a feeling of dread, and the lack of sleep, making him light-headed.

'Yes, Inspector, I know he's no angel, but he was a good boy until he fell in with those Moffats ... bastards ... sorry for the language, Inspector, but they made him take drugs so they could use him like a fool. They're evil, worse than the bloody Mafia.'

'What did they do to him?'

'They tortured him, cut his face with a knife and beat him. His poor face ... even his mother wouldn't recognise him, if she was still alive ... God rest her soul. They then poured petrol over him and threatened to set him on fire. Cruel bastards, they're worse than animals.'

'Who did it?' asked Dorsey, grateful that Massimo was alive at least, but his mind racked with guilt.

'It was those devil twins, Eric and Billy. That's who did it to my boy ... all because of drugs someone else stole from them … Them and their damned drugs. Why they no' in prison, Inspector, they're no' fit to live wi' decent people … Why they no' in prison?'

'If Massimo is prepared to testify against them, then we'll be able to put them away for a long time. Will he give evidence against them?'

'He's terrified. I couldn't leave him in the hospital until his brother arrived. You speak to him, Inspector, make him give evidence or I swear I'll shoot those two swines myself.'

'I'll speak to him, but don't make threats about shooting anyone Giuseppe, that's a crime itself. Go home and get some rest. I'll send a couple of uniformed officers to the hospital to keep an eye on him.'

'Thank you, Inspector, you're a good man,' said Giuseppe, putting on his trilby and getting to his feet. 'I can't go home. I need to get the shop opened.'

From the window Dorsey watched Giuseppe walk back down the street towards his chip shop. He did not feel much like a good man at that moment, he had put Massimo back on the streets knowing he was in serious risk of harm. He also knew there was virtually no chance of getting the twins for what they did to him; even if Massimo agreed to testify, he would still need evidence to corroborate what happened. Dorsey took a pill from a bottle he kept his drawer and swallowed it with the residue of cold coffee. He had too much on his mind to go home and sleep. He went into the main office, which was now busy. The morning shift was being briefed by those now eager to get home to their beds.

Chapter 21

Denis Moffat had too much on his mind to get back to sleep. He received a call that morning from his source in London Road police station. The idea of a bunch of Romanians muscling in on his patch was not something to be taken lightly. He did not mind if they stuck to selling to their own kind, but now they've started to trade on his turf, something had to be done.

With a heavy sigh, he lay for a while looking at the Artex circles swirling into each other on the lowered ceiling. He hated that ceiling, and was determined to have the Artex removed before it drove him around the bend.

Once out of bed, the circles were safe for another while. For the moment he had more pressing matters to deal with. Irene was still sound asleep, oblivious to worries that got her husband out of bed before the postman had started his rounds.

Before leaving the house, Denis checked the magazine in his Beretta. Both T-Bone and Percy were sitting outside in the black BMW. They knew something big was up when they got the call that morning to come tooled-up. The boot of the car was full of knives, hammers, baseball bats, and a golf club that had cracked more skulls than had hit golf balls. Denis walked past his own car on the driveway and got into the back of the BMW.

'Let's show these fucking Romanian bastards who they're dealing wi'. They've got a whore house on Donald Street, lets shake them up a bit when they least expect it. I've phoned some o' the other boys; they'll meet us there in fifteen minutes. Remember no shooting unless we have to, this is just a warning to these fuckers.'

Chapter 22

Now feeling remarkably awake, Dorsey looked in the rear-view mirror to see if he looked out of sorts. His pupils were enormous and the lack of a shave made him look a little haggard, but he felt alert as he parked the car and crossed to the main entrance of the hospital. He showed his warrant card to the receptionist who did not look too convinced that he was police officer. She pointed down the corridor and gave him directions to the ward. After a few wrong turns, he saw the two uniformed officers he had sent earlier and nodded to them. He went into the ward.

There was another half dozen patients in the ward—all in different degrees of recovery—and not the best place to try and get a witness to give a statement against the most feared crime family in the city. Dino was sitting at his brother's bed. He got up when he saw Dorsey approaching.

'He's sleeping, come back some other time,' said Dino, blocking Dorsey from getting any closer to the bed.

'How is he?'

'Look at him, they scarred him for life, but cutting his face and beating him nearly to death wasn't enough. The bastards covered him wi' petrol and threatened to burn him alive.'

'You know as well as me who did this to him,' said Dorsey, taking Dino by the arm and leading him into the corridor where they could speak without fear of being overheard.

'Aye, but what can he do about it? If they think he's going to give evidence then he'll be killed next time and don't tell me you'll protect him.'

'That's why they're able to get away with this. If no one ever testifies then they'll just keep doing this to people. Is that what you want?'

'Is that what I want? What kind of question is that? It's no' up to me. It's up to Massimo; it's his life that'll be at stake, no' mine or yours.'

'It's what your father wants him to do. Will you at least try and persuade him to speak to me when he's ready. Here, take that number; it's my own mobile so no one at the station will even know if he phones. I can't make him testify, but he should at least tell me anything that might help me nail those two evil bastards.'

'Okay, Inspector, but I'll only give it to him if he wants to speak to you. Even if he agrees, it won't be for a while; he can barely speak he's in so much pain.'

When they went back into the ward the doctors were already beginning their morning rounds. Dorsey showed his warrant card to the more senior looking doctor, who looked at the card and then at Dorsey over the rim of his glasses. 'Is there a problem?'

'Yes. This man has to be moved to a room on his own, his life is in danger.'

'You'll have to speak with the ward administrators; I don't allocate beds to patients. Now if you'll excuse me I've my work to do.'

Dorsey turned to Dino, 'I'll get that organised this morning ... I'll speak to you later.'

Back at the reception, for the second time that morning, he met someone he had not seen in a long time, Sandy Cooper's wife. She looked much older, and her face was now dominated by the black bags under her eyes.

'Inspector, how are you?'

'I'm well, and you?' he responded, while trying to remember her first name.

'I'm fine, Sandy just phoned half an hour ago. Said you'd a busy night of it?'

'Yes, but that's the nature of the job. Are you up to visit your daughter?' he asked, now struggling to remember the daughter's name. He wasn't sure whether it was the lack of sleep, the amphetamine or just his poor memory when it came to names of people he only met occasionally.

'Yes, it's her birthday tomorrow, eighteen years of age and lying in a coma when she should be going to college with friends and enjoying life. I pray everyday for God to give her back to me … I'm sorry, Inspector; you've enough of your own worries.'

'No, no, don't be sorry. I can't even begin to imagine what you and Sandy are suffering.'

'Sandy always said you were a good man. I better go. It was nice meeting you again, Inspector.'

She smiled and turned away. It was only then he remembered her name.

Mentally drained, he got into his car and pulled out into the rush hour traffic. Before he had even got into third gear he received a call that a serious disturbance was taking place only a few miles from where he was stuck in traffic. All police vehicles in the area were being called to provide immediate assistance to two officers already at the scene.

When Dorsey finally got to the locus, whatever had taken place was over, but there were still a half dozen police cars scattered along the roads and pavement. He parked nearby and walked the last few hundred yards. The situation looked under control. He watched three half-naked women being placed in one of the police vehicles, their garish makeup looking harsh in the bright daylight. There was an ambulance on the other side of the road, where two wounded men sat quietly in the back. Dorsey noted that they both had jet black hair and sallow skin; Eastern Europeans, he assumed. None appeared too seriously injured, but all looked traumatised. There was a house in the middle terrace that was left without a window. Cheap floral curtains blew out from the bottom room as though a bomb had gone off inside.

Strachan was already in the house, trying to bully one of the male occupants into telling him what had happened.

'He doesn't speak English,' said Cooper, tending to the wound on a terrified man who had obviously been hit with something that left a lattice imprint on his bald head.

'He can speak English, but only when it suits him,' shouted Strachan. 'Take them out of here!'

'No understand … no understand,' the man continued to plead as he was taken away to be questioned further at the station.

'No one killed?' asked Dorsey, as Strachan noticed him for the first time.

'No, Frank; looks like they've just had their warning to saddle up and get out of town.'

'Still with the cowboy analogies, Charlie … Do we know who did it?'

'They were long gone by the time we got here. No one here's prepared to answer any questions. Either they don't speak English or they're just pretending they don't. They're mostly Romanians. That's the EU for you, the fucking free movement of gypsies, tramps and thieves.'

'Is that not a bit unfair for those that are here to work and make a better life for themselves?'

'But why do they let all these other lowlifes into the country. We've got enough of our own to deal with, without importing every other countries scumbags.'

'Don't let anyone else hear you talk like that. We don't

want to get branded as a bunch of racists. Anyway, I'll see you back at the station, Charlie.'

'Let's get the rest of them back to the station, and someone call the council and get this place boarded up,' shouted Strachan as Dorsey left them to it.

Chapter 23

Ashley Moffat was glad to get back to her room to pack her bags. Her roommate, Lucy was still lying in bed, having missed the morning lecture on property law.

'You're a lazy lump,' said Ashley, dumping her books and notes onto her own bed.

'How was it?'

'Just as boring as the last one you didn't go to.'

'It's typical of that old bore Mackay to have the last lecture at 9 o'clock on the last day of term. I bet you were the only one there this morning.'

'Well, you're wrong. Not everybody is as lazy as you.'

'Don't be mean. I'm just tired … Ashley, can you leave me your notes? I'll need to copy them over the holidays.'

'Over the holidays, why don't you just get out of bed and copy them now so I can take them with me to study at home.'

'My head's splitting … That was some party last night, too many tequilas. How come you never end up drunk?'

'I know when I've had enough.'

'At least I kept my knickers on unlike Mandy Becket.'

'Well, he is her boyfriend for God's sake. Anyway, just because they ended up in bed doesn't mean she had sex with him.'

'What else did they have?'

'Are you going to get up and at least walk with me to the station?'

'If you go to the library and get photocopies of your notes then I'll be ready when you get back, and I'll buy you lunch.'

Ashley sighed as she picked up her notes and left Lucy to get ready. She crossed the concourse to the library where she spent so many hours in the last few months studying. She was still not sure why she had decided to study law, however, it was such a big deal to everyone else when she was accepted by the faculty that she had no choice but to persevere with it, whether she liked it or not. Dropping out was not an option.

The library was all but deserted as most of the students were at home for the Christmas holidays. She copied her notes and went back to the halls of residence with mixed feelings about taking the train back to Glasgow. Lucy and her other friends were planning another night on the town before leaving. No matter how much they tried to persuade her to do likewise, Ashley was resolute that she had to leave that afternoon, and no amount of cajoling was going to change her mind. She obviously could not tell them it was because she had promised her father she would be home in time for her brother getting out of prison.

Lucy was up and dressed when Ashley got back to the room and helped her pack, still trying to persuade her to stay for one more night. 'Jerry Logan is going to be there tonight. You know how much you fancy him.'

'I don't fancy him, he's just a friend. Anyway I won't be there, my train leaves at two o'clock and my father will be at the station in Glasgow waiting to pick me up,' she said, locking her small suitcase and lifting it from the bed. 'Now, c'mon, Lucy, you promised to buy lunch and walk me to the station.'

Denis was sitting in his car outside Queen Street Station listening to Johnny Cash, *walking the line*. He had already chased off one traffic warden who tried to issue him with a ticket and was watching another making his way to the car with his ticket machine primed. Denis turned off his radio and rolled down the window. The warden approached the passenger door. 'You can't park here, sir.'

'Bugger off, son, if you want to keep your job,' said Denis, staring through the open window with menace.

'Is that a threat, sir?'

'Yes, it's a threat,' sneered Denis. 'Now bugger off, before you get yourself hurt, son.' The warden said nothing, and slowly backed off, only breathing again when the tinted window began to close. He turned and walked away from the car, more than a little shaken when he realised who he had tried to give a parking ticket to.

Denis turned up the CD player as Johnny Cash was *falling into a ring of fire*.

Ashley enjoyed the journey down the east coast of the country. She had spent her time reading lecture notes and occasionally looking out at the passing countryside until the winter darkness began to dominate. Now tired, she was glad when the train finally arrived in Glasgow.

Outside the station, her father's car stood out among the black hackneys queuing up at the rank. She could never understand how he could get away with just parking where he liked. Denis saw his daughter coming along the concourse and got out to meet her. After a few clumsy kisses on the cheeks, he took her suitcase and walked her back to the car. Like frost melting on concrete, a rare smile cracked across his face. Some of the taxi drivers recognised the *Big Man* and nodded to him as he put the suitcase in the boot.

Once in the car, Ashley turned down the CD player. Unlike the twins, she did not share her father's love of country music. Afraid of another one of his daughter's lectures on the dangers of smoking, Denis took a final draw from his cigar. He threw the large butt into the gutter with a shake of the head. Some dosser, he thought, will be smoking that tonight.

He put his seat belt on, his face still paralysed with his concrete grin and gently patted her on the leg, 'Your mother's going to be so happy to see you.'

'I can't wait to get home. I missed Glasgow,' she said, looking out at George Square, which was sparkling in Christmas lights and decorations.

'Now all we need is your brother home tomorrow and it will be the best Christmas ever,' said Denis.

'Dad, you've cut your hand?'

'It's nothing, I was doing a bit of work in the lockup this morning,' he replied, lifting his hand off the gear stick and looking at the raw laceration above his knuckles.

'You might need to get that stitched.'

'Never mind, it's only a wee nick. Here, put that on for your auld dad,' he said, handing her a CD of country classics that had seen better days.

It started to rain as Denis drove back through the busy city centre, failing to notice the blue Audi that was tailing him.

Chapter 24

Mitchell was surprised to see Dorsey standing studying the incident board when he arrived early for his back shift. He was even more surprised to discover that the Inspector had not been home for two days. It was bad enough working two straight shifts, but three. 'Have you not got a home to go to?' he said, handing Dorsey a cup of coffee.

'We've been too busy interviewing all day. After you left there was a raid on a Romanian sauna parlour on Donald Street, we've been wasting our time trying to find out who attacked the place. Even with interpreters, it's like trying to draw teeth just to get a straight answer from any of them. They don't know who or why they were attacked. We checked the males with the photographs found at the farmhouse. Not even close. I don't think they've got anything to do with the guys we're after. The girls are all over eighteen and took offence when asked if they were providing anything more than a massage. It was a complete waste of time, and when a couple of their lawyers turned up we had to let them go.'

'You look shattered.'

'Been worse, but there's so much evidence in here that it's just a matter of time before we identify the real names of these characters,' said Dorsey, looking at the new incident board with the pictures of the three suspects. 'These guys must've criminal records, have you heard back from the Romanian police?'

'Nothing yet, I'll send them another email.'

'Let me know as soon as they get back to you. What

about those text messages, have BT managed to trace where they were sent from?'

'I'll speak to Harper when she gets in, she was chasing that up yesterday. Not sure how they'd fit in with a gang of Romanians.'

'No, it doesn't make any sense. They might just be a red herring, but we still have to check it out.'

'Okay, but why don't you take a couple of hours out and get some sleep. I'll phone you if anything comes up.'

'Okay, but call me. I don't want that blowhard Strachan taking over everything and screwing up again.'

'Don't worry; he knows he is still in the doghouse with Knox.'

'Aye, but he'll be looking to get out of it.'

'Sir, there's a Miss Baxter at the reception asking to speak to you. She's from the PF's Office,' interrupted the duty sergeant.

'Thanks, Harry, send her up to my office.'

Dorsey straightened up his tie, before putting his hand through his dishevelled hair to at least keep it back from his forehead. He had not felt this nervous about meeting a woman for years and began to feel self-conscious. There was a knock at the door.

'Miss Baxter, sir,' said the duty sergeant, opening the door while Dorsey was still buttoning his jacket like a schoolboy waiting to see the headmaster.

'Come in, Miss Baxter … that'll be all, Harry.'

The sergeant gave his boss a wink before slowly closing the door, brazenly leering at Miss Baxter's rear. Dorsey shuffled papers and pretended to be preoccupied. 'Please take a seat, Miss Baxter. I was not expecting a visit from you today.'

'Well, I was on my way back from court when I thought

it might be worth my while getting an update. The Crown Office have been on at me to keep an eye on things since the press have taken such keen interest in what they're proclaiming to be a drugs war,' she said as she sat down and crossed her legs. 'Has there been any progress?'

'Yes, we recovered the van used by a gang of eastern Europeans suspected of being involved in at least two, if not all three of the murders.'

'And a substantial amount of drugs.'

'You've heard.'

'Yes, well, it's been on the news. Congratulations, Inspector.'

'There's nothing to congratulate me about, it was an anonymous call that led to the farmhouse, nothing that I did. It seems we've a gang of Romanians trying to set up a rival drug enterprise in the East End and that might be the motive for all three killings.'

'Why would that be a motive?'

'Well, to scare off those already dealing for the Moffats and the McGowans. These Romanians are heavy duty. We recovered a small arsenal and hundreds of fake documents that show they mean business. I'll send you over an up-to-date report as soon as we finish logging all the productions …' The phone rang. 'Excuse me.'

It was Mitchell giving him details of an email he had just received from the Romanian Police Headquarters in Bucharest. As he listened, he could not help but look at Miss Baxter, who was politely looking away, trying to show him, rather too obviously, that she was not listening to his telephone conversation. It gave him an opportunity to really look at her without having to constantly answer her questions. She was wearing a smart black suit and white blouse, the kind of thing you would expect a female lawyer to wear in a court room. Although she seemed to be fascinated with a picture of a Scottish mountain range that hung above his sparse bookcase, she was clearly not thinking about climbing any mountains in the near future.

'Sorry, Miss Baxter,' he said as he put down the receiver. 'Is there anything else?'

'What about these text messages that the victims are supposed to have got before they were murdered?'

'We've kind of hit a dead end with them at the minute.'

'Do you still think they've anything to do with the murders?'

'Not sure. We can't trace them to any phone that's registered in the UK. Whoever sent them could've used an untraceable sim card bought over the internet.'

'What about what was said at the press conference? Why did Superintendent Knox deny the existence of the text messages?'

'I don't think he was aware of them at the time.'

'But he should've been.'

'Miss Baxter, I feel like I'm being cross-examined here.'

'Sorry, Inspector, that's not what I intended. I just want to know as much as possible before I report back to the Lord Advocate. The Crown Office has had to answer some difficult questions in the media about how we deal with drug gangs in Glasgow.'

'It was my decision to keep any reference to the text messages under wraps until we found out more about their possible source. If hundreds were sent it would've just caused panic and hampered the investigation. You can tell the Lord Advocate that we're treating the text messages seriously, but at the moment that line of enquiry has come to a dead end. We have to find out who sent them before we know if they've anything to do with these murders.'

'Well, thank you, Inspector, I'm sorry if I was a bit

141

overzealous.'

'That's okay, Miss Baxter, you're only doing your job. I'll walk you out; it's a bit of a maze in here.'

Heads turned for the second time that day as Miss Baxter made her way through the busy front office. A few of the female officers shook their heads at their easily distracted male colleagues. At the front door, Dorsey shook her hand, and in spite of, or maybe because of the interrogation, he felt his pulse race when she smiled at him. He walked her to her car, a red sporty type that only added to her alluring appeal.

'Thank you again, Inspector,' she said, getting in to the car and turning the engine on.

'My pleasure,' said Dorsey, standing back as she drove towards the main road and waved. He felt a little silly when he instinctively returned her wave. He quickly put his hand down when he realised he was standing in the middle of the car park with his back to the station windows.

When he returned to the main office, Mitchell and Harper were in the middle of a conversation, which they both obviously thought funny.

'What's the joke?' asked Dorsey.

'Nothing,' said Mitchell, handing Dorsey a copy of the email he received from Bucharest. 'It's just that we don't see you walk many people to their car and wave goodbye to them.'

'She is the Procurator Fiscal.'

'And a good-looking woman,' said Harper, before turning back to her computer.

'Right enough, what about this email?'

'We've drawn a blank,' said Mitchell. 'Not one of the prints has come up on their data base, and no one in their drugs squad has been able to put a name to any of the photographs.'

'If all the passports and driving licences are fakes, then they might not even be Romanians,' said Harper, looking up from her keyboard.

'Never thought of that,' said Dorsey, suddenly realising how tired he was feeling.

'You've got a lot on your mind, sir,' said Harper, exchanging a knowing smile with Mitchell.

'George, send the prints and the photographs to Interpol. Let's see if they can shed any light on this gang, and you, Kate, stop the bullshit, we're not in the playground.'

'Sorry, sir,' she blushed.

'Kate, any luck with those text messages?'

'Yes, sir, BT has managed to narrow the signal area to their mast that covers the North East, mainly Bishopbriggs. They're still trying to narrow it down to a more precise location, but there have been no new messages sent recently. If the phone is used again they will be able to pinpoint the signal.'

'Well, keep on at them.'

'Yes, sir.'

Chapter 25

Saturday 24th December

Morag Burns froze when she answered the intercom. It was Billy Moffat demanding to get in. She rushed back into the living room and took a polythene bag of brown powder from her handbag. She tried desperately to find somewhere to hide it. She opened drawers and cupboards, but every hiding place seemed too obvious. She stood in the middle of the room in a state of near paralysis. The baby began to cry.

The hall door was lying open and she could hear the lift rumble and screech as it approached. Her heart was racing. The lift stopped with its usual shudder. She began to feel faint. She then heard voices echoing in the outside landing. The door was knocked hard. She was rooted to the spot with the bag of heroin still in her hand. The door was now being kicked. She ran to the cot and stuffed the bag inside the baby's nappy.

'Am coming,' she shouted, trying to control the feeling of absolute terror that gripped her. She took a deep, nervous breath and opened the door.

'Where's the fucking gear?' shouted Billy, grabbing Morag by the neck, and pushing her against the wall, while the rest of his gang rushed in and began to ransack the place. 'Ah don't know what yer talking about, honest, Billy,' she gasped as he let go of her throat and pulled her by the hair into the living room.

'Sit there,' he ordered, pushing her onto the settee. 'I've been told you've been dealing 'round the scheme. Where'd you get the smack?'

'It was just a few tenner bags that Willie had left in the flat. Ah needed the money fur the wee yin, that's aw, Billy, a few tenner bags tae get the wean something tae eat.'

'Your fucking boyfriend ripped us off, so what did he do wi' the rest o' the gear ... and our fucking money!'

'Honest, Billy, Ah told ye last week. Ah don't know what Willie got up tae. He told me nothing,' explained Morag, taking a cigarette from her handbag and nervously lighting it as she listened to her things being thrown about in the kitchen and bedroom.

'Where is it!' squealed Eric, grabbing Morag by the hair and pulling her almost over the back of the settee.

'Ah don't have any drugs ... Ah only had a few tenner bags,' she pleaded. Unmoved, Eric slapped her hard across the face and pushed her back down on the settee.

'If we find any drugs in here, you're fucking dead!'

Curled up in a ball with her hands over her head, Morag watched with terrified eyes as the living room was pulled apart. She did not care if they wrecked the flat so long as they did not find the drugs. She would give them the drugs in a minute if they would just take them and go, but she knew they would give her a beating anyway. She resolved to keep her mouth shut. The baby was crying louder than ever, but Morag was afraid to pick her up in case the drugs fell out of the nappy.

'Why don't you shut that fucking thing up,' shouted Billy, when the search came to a fruitless end and they stood about looking at each other. 'Maybe she is telling the truth,' said Cosgrove, pouring the contents of a drawer onto the floor. 'There's nothing here.'

145

'If you don't shut her up I'll throw it out the fucking window,' shouted Eric, coming back in from the cluttered veranda. He lifted the baby from the rank smelling cot. 'Fuck, don't you ever wipe her arse?'

'What are ye doing? No … no, please,' shouted Morag as Eric took the screaming child onto the freezing cold balcony. 'Tell me where the drugs are or your wean better learn to fly before she can walk,' he laughed, holding the wriggling child over the metal barrier.

'For fuck's sake, Eric,' shouted Billy. 'Don't drop the fucking thing!'

Eric ignored his brother and turned back to Morag.

'Where's our gear?'

'Ah don't know,' she sobbed, unable to look up at her tormentors. With no more response from her, other than whimpering, Eric took the child back into the living room and dumped her into the cot. 'Let's get out o' here, this place smells o' fucking shit.'

When the front door finally slammed closed, Morag slowly got to her feet. Exhausted and still trembling, she closed the veranda door, and lit a cigarette, trying to gather her thoughts. Did they believe her? Would they be back? Kylie had stopped crying and after her mother finally recovered her wits, the child was relieved of its soiled nappy and the bag of heroin.

The ordeal had left Morag weak and vulnerable. She now had to battle an old urge that was tempting her like never before. In a frenzy of desperation she soon had the bag of heroin open. She had promised Massimo she would not use it if he left it with her, but where was he now? Was he dead like Norrie and Tucker?

Her hands were still shaking when she took a small bottle of citric acid from the cupboard above the cooker, and recovered the rest of her drug paraphernalia from the mess scattered across the kitchen floor. With the certainty of practice, she added citric acid and a little water to a spoon of heroin and held it over the gas hob. The brew slowly merged together and turned into a brown liquid. The expectation caused her heart to beat faster. Once the heroin had cooled she drew it up through a cigarette filter and into the syringe in her trembling hand. Almost done, her heart was now thumping, her mind urging her to hurry. There were tears in her eyes. Tightening one of Norrie's old belts around her upper arm, she pressed the needle into a protruding vein and closed her eyes. The drug rushed through her body like wildfire.

Chapter 26

Benny Moffat shook hands with the two prison officers who escorted him to the gate. Although still on parole for the remainder of his five-year sentence, he was finally outside the gloomy Victorian prison and determined never to return. Now he would reap the rewards of the substantial drug deal he had masterminded from behind bars. Free, he planned to party like never before. His smile broadened when he saw his Porsche waiting for him and he smugly turned back to make sure the two prison officers were still watching as Linda got out the car and ran to meet him with open arms.

'How do you feel?' she gushed, after covering him in kisses and lipstick. He swung her around in his arms so the wardens could get a good look at her.

'Free at last, thank God I'm free at last,' he shouted, putting her down with a conceited grin. 'Get in,' he ordered, taking the keys from her manicured fingers, and throwing his bag into the boot. 'I've been dying to drive this beauty again,' he said, getting into the driver's seat, and taking his sunglasses from behind the visor. He looked at himself in the rear-view mirror for a moment, before turning on the ignition and letting the car roar *in situ*. 'Look at those two stupid bastards,' he sneered, turning back to wave at the two prison officers. They ignored him and pulled the gate back over.

Having seen the back of Benny Moffat, they went back to the cacophony of noise coming from the canteen in the main building. 'He'll be back,' said the older of the two officers. 'Mark my words, he'll be back.'

Instead of going straight to his parents' house as planned,

Linda tempted him to go back to their flat first by lifting her skirt so he could see that she was wearing suspenders. A smile on his lips, Benny turned towards the city centre. Linda, without much thought, unzipped his trousers and lowered her head onto his lap. The car swerved into the next lane for a moment as Benny struggled to concentrate on the road ahead.

He stopped her from going too far; the last thing he wanted was to get stopped by the police with trousers undone and a hard-on. Sitting back up, Linda brushed her hair aside. She then looked at herself in the vanity mirror, before putting on fresh lipstick. Benny zipped up his fly and put his foot down. He drove at speed along an empty bus lane that took him into the heart of the city in minutes. Glasgow looked strange to him after being away so long. He made the most of his ephemeral feeling of freedom by lapping George Square a couple of times before turning towards his luxury apartment on Albion Street.

He parked in the basement car park and groped Linda again, feeling between her legs, but stopping as quickly as he started, determined not to come in his trousers before he got her into the apartment. In the lift, she began teasing him again, by slowly lifting the hem of her skirt above her stocking top. He lit a cigarette and thought of how hard he was going to fuck her. The bell rang as the lift jolted to a stop and the doors opened on the fifth floor. When they got out, a middle-aged woman got in and exchanged a look of disapproval at the cloud of cigarette smoke that prompted her to cough. 'You're not supposed to be smoking in this lift,' she complained.

'Well, don't smoke then,' said Benny, taking another drag from his cigarette and blowing it into the lift as the door began to close. He then followed Linda to their apartment at the end of the narrow corridor. 'Stop it,' she giggled as she tried to open the front door while he fondled her breasts

149

from behind. 'There's a bottle of champagne on ice in the living room,' she said scurrying along the hall. 'I've got to go to the bathroom.'

'Alright, don't be long,' muttered Benny, opening the living room door, still flushed with lustful anticipation.

'What the hell!' He recoiled in stunned surprise. Suddenly streamers exploded over his head and everyone that had been holding their breath behind the living room door began cheering. The excitement in his trousers quickly subsided. Familiar faces appeared one after another, eager to welcome him home with a kiss or vigorous handshake. His mother touched his hair and cried. He was still her little boy. His father had lost none of his strength and Benny felt his hand buckle in the old man's vice like grip.

'Dad, enough, you'll break my fucking fingers.'

'No need to swear,' admonished his mother. 'Not in front of the family lawyer,' she added as Ashley came forward to embrace her brother.

'A lawyer, and where were you when I needed you, sis?'

'You know fine well I'm not a lawyer yet, and, anyway I want to do divorce law, *not criminal law,* when I qualify.'

'I'll keep that in mind for the future.'

'You're back together again?' asked Ashley, nodding discreetly in the direction of Linda, who was going around the guests with a salver of canapés.

'Aye, let's say she's been looking after things … Where's Pinkie and Perky?'

'They're on their way,' said Irene. 'I wish you didn't call them that son, it will only set them off.'

'I don't want them turning up drunk and making out they're a couple of hardmen.'

'Benny, don't start them when they get here.'

'Don't worry. I know what they're like. They slag

everybody else but can't take it themselves. I'll get them a couple o' bottles of cheap wine and let them drink it in the garage.'

'They're your brothers for God sake, why would you want to annoy them?'

'Leave it,' said Benny. 'I need to talk to some of the lads.'

Benny left his mother before they ended up arguing, and went over to a group of well-dressed men of his own age, who were drinking and laughing among themselves in the corner of the large open-plan living room. These were Benny's friends, nouveau riche from the drug money that was giving them a lifestyle that others their age could only dream of. The cocaine business looked like it had been good for them over the last few years, and as the champagne flutes clicked in celebration of Benny's return, he wondered just how much he had missed out on while behind bars. Two of them looked to be especially prosperous. Known simply to most as the Rankin brothers, Scott and Craig had recently taken over The Venue, one of the hottest night clubs in the city centre. They both dressed in expensive suits, and their girlfriends looked like they had just walked out of the glossy pages of *Vogue*. Benny knew the brothers when they did not have the price of a packet of cigarettes between them, but that was before they started robbing Post Offices around the country. They were soon making a name for themselves after bankrolling a large shipment of cocaine when there was a drought of the Class A drug in the country.

So long as they stayed out of the East End of Glasgow, Denis Moffat did not have a problem with the brothers and neither did Benny, who had already made plans to get away from the seedier heroin trade and into the more trendy cocaine market. At the moment, he was more interested in their beautiful girlfriends, who giggled like school girls as more champagne was poured. 'This is Sophie,' said Scott, putting his arm around the blonde to make sure everyone

151

knew who she belonged to. 'Nice to meet you,' said Benny taking her hand and looking straight into her stunning blue eyes.

'And you,' she replied, in a Polish accent. 'I've heard all about you.'

'Nothing too bad, I hope.'

'And this is Veronica,' said Craig. Benny repeated his courtesy, but was not as impressed with her as he was with Sophie, who he could not keep his eyes off as they all laughed and joked while Louis Armstrong sang *It's a Wonderful World* in the background.

Whether it was ogling Sophie or the champagne, Benny could not suppress *it* any longer, and he took Linda by the arm and headed for the bedroom. Putting the radio on to drown out Linda's tendency to over-dramatise her orgasm, Benny almost ripped her clothes off and threw her onto the bed. The frustration unleashed itself in only a few short minutes, and, after catching his breath, Benny turned to lie on his back still thinking of Scott Rankin's beautiful girlfriend.

'Is that it?' said Linda, sitting up and examining her torn dress. 'Look what you've done. I can't go back into the party wearing this.'

'Stop moaning, you've got a wardrobe full of dresses,' said Benny, sitting up and looking at himself in the mirror.

'Benny, I need to get some new clothes,' moaned Linda, searching for something to wear.

Benny got up and removed a picture of a Lamborghini from the opposite wall and opened the Chubb wall safe behind it, with a rather obvious code: 1690. He lifted out a ream of crisp new bank notes and threw them onto the bed.

'There, buy yourself a couple of new dresses, something classy like the one Scott's girlfriend's wearing.'

'What? You bastard! Do you think I'm not classy enough

for you? Keep your money, I'm not your whore,' she shouted, before slapping him across the face.

Benny grabbed her by the throat. 'Don't ever do that again,' he sneered, slowly releasing his grip. 'Now get changed.'

'You don't have to be so rough,' she sulked, lifting the money from the bed and putting it in her handbag. Benny shook his head, and went into the en-suite to put on some aftershave and comb his hair. He was still thinking about Sophie.

Chapter 27

The city centre was busy with last minute shoppers. Dorsey had spent over an hour looking for a Christmas present for Daniel. After walking from one shop to another without any clear idea what to buy, he found himself in the electrical department of Frasers, looking at a top of the range laptop that he wouldn't mind himself. He lifted it and was impressed how light it was, but still could not see a price label. He then turned to an assistant, who had floated towards him on seeing his obvious interest in the expensive piece of kit. 'How much is this?'

'It's one of the best we have, it has a very large hard drive,' said the assistant, now hovering beside him like a dragonfly above a stagnant pond. 'It also has the latest Intel processor and a bundle of free software, including an anti virus ...'

'How much?' Dorsey asked again, not interested in the technical detail.

'It's £650, but you won't get a better computer at that price.'

'Have you not got something for about half that price?'

'Well, we have cheaper models.'

'No, just give me it!' said Dorsey, changing his mind and now determined to buy Daniel something that he would not be able to turn his nose up at.

'That's only a display model. If you come with me to the counter, I'll get a new one for you ... Sir, are you paying by debit or credit card?'

Carrying the computer under his arm along Argyle Street,

Dorsey stopped for a moment outside the shop where he had bought Helen her favourite perfume the previous Christmas. He then talked himself into the shop and bought her another bottle of the same expensive scent. He reasoned with himself that he could not go around for dinner on Christmas day, and not give her anything ... what if she's bought him something, and he turns up empty-handed? Anyway, he wanted to buy her something. What was wrong with that? No one was arguing with him, but himself.

Just as he was paying for Helen's gift, his mobile phone rang and he went outside to take the call. 'Where? Okay, I'll be there in fifteen minutes, don't touch anything until I get there!'

Dorsey put the presents into the boot of the car and drove across town at speed to a tenement flat on London Road. The area was already cordoned off when he arrived, and he parked near Celtic Park and crossed the road to where he saw Sandy Cooper standing with two uniformed officers. 'Who is it this time?'

'Jamie Sylvester, he worked for the McGowans ... usually street dealing. Looks like the same *M.O.* as Devlin, shot to the head and cigar burns on his upper torso. He's been dead a while.'

'Who found him?'

'Couple of guys from the council, a neighbour reported a stink coming from the flat and was worried when she hadn't seen Sylvester around for a while.'

'Let's go and have a look at it. Has Jenkins been told?'
'Aye, he'll be here in an hour. He's on his way back from Edinburgh.'

The front door was hanging from its hinges having been forced open by the council workers. The two detectives

155

were met with a pungent smell of decay when they entered the tiny one-bedroom flat and saw the bloated, half-naked body lying on its side on the floor, still tied to a chair. The abdomen was burst open and the deceased's intestines were spilled onto the floor. The smell was beyond rancid. Dorsey, holding his hand to his nose and mouth, got as near as he wanted before backing off. 'I think we'll let Jenkins deal with this, the smell is fucking unbearable.'

'Look,' said Cooper, pointing to a cigar butt. 'Surely we've got whoever did this now. There must be DNA on this.'

'Would Denis Moffat be so careless or stupid to leave that behind?'

'Either that or it's been left on purpose. I've spoken to the mother, Sylvester only smoked rollups.'

'I want this place photographed straight away, don't bother to wait for Jenkins. Bag that cigar butt and get it down to the lab. If Moffat's DNA is on that then we've got him.'

'What about our Romanians?' asked Cooper as he carefully followed the inspector back out to the landing.

'Where do they fit in?'

'I'm pretty sure they were involved in the first two murders, but nothing else makes any sense. I don't get the cigar burns. Why would Denis Moffat be so obvious or careless?' said Dorsey, stepping aside to let the Scenes of crime officers enter the flat in their white overalls and rubber shoes.

'He's old school, maybe he doesn't know much about DNA.'

'He's not that old.'

On the way back to the station, Dorsey decided to pay Morag Burns another visit, sure she knew more than she was letting on. He was considering the conflicting evidence in his head as he turned into the car park outside the flats. The Romanians were the only fly in the ointment; if they were not seen driving into the cul-de-sac near the time Tucker was killed, then the evidence would point to a simple turf war between the Moffats and the McGowans.

'Why don't we threaten to get the social workers to take the kid off her if she doesn't tell us everything she knows,' suggested Mitchell, getting out of the car.

'Let's see what she's got to say for herself first. She probably wouldn't be all that bothered if the social workers took the baby.'

The wind was whistling around the high-rise building as they got out of the lift and crossed the landing. Mitchell banged the front door while Dorsey studied some of the graffiti scrolled on the abused walls. Looking around, he could understand why some people took heroin; the sense of hopelessness almost tangible. Mitchell banged the door with his fist again before shouting through the letter box. 'She's no' in,' said a woman who appeared at the door opposite. 'She went out this morning wi' the wean. Ah don't think she's coming back.'

'What makes you think that?' asked Dorsey.

'She put the keys through the letterbox.'

'Do you know where she went?'

'No, and Ah don't care either,' said the woman, closing over the door now she had said her piece.

The two detectives did not speak on the way back down in the lift. Dorsey was thinking about Helen and the text she sent asking him to come to the house early on Christmas morning, how early she did not say. He was tempted to phone her back, but decided it was better to keep the time as vague as possible, that way he couldn't be late. The lift shuddered to a halt and brought him out of his thoughts.

'Put a call out for her, she won't have gone too far,' he said, following Mitchell out to the car.

Mitchell sat for a moment before turning on the ignition. 'What are you doing tomorrow? You're welcome to come over for Christmas dinner?'

'Thanks George, but I'll have to go over and see Daniel and give him his present. I'm sure Helen won't begrudge me a place at her table, it's not like she's seeing anyone else.'

'Good, it was just if you were going to be on your own … it was Claire's idea, you know what women are like,' said Mitchell, switching on the ignition and reversing out the car park.

'Tell her thanks anyway. Are you sure you don't want to come in for a few pints.'

'It's not that I don't want to, Frank, but I promised Claire I would be home early to help her get things ready for tomorrow. With three kids, Christmas is a bit hectic.'

'Well, make the most of it; they won't be youngsters for very long. Daniel's already a teenager and it seems like only yesterday he was born.'

'You'll soon be able to go for a pint with him.'

'I don't know about that. Who knows what he's going to be like in another five years time. He speaks a different language from me already … just drop me off here.'

Chapter 28

In the back room of the Weaver's Tavern, Hughie McGowan was considering his options. He had just heard Jamie Sylvester's body was found. This changed everything. Hughie knew he had to do something now he was convinced that the Moffats were targeting his own dealers. If he did nothing then he would be seen as frightened and ready for a takeover.

The decision to murder Denis Moffat had not been taken lightly and it was only the insistence of Rory that forced Hughie to relent and order the hit. Eugene Docherty was ex-IRA, and the only man Hughie could rely on to do the job right. He could not risk a botched hit; a wounded Denis Moffat was the last thing Hughie wanted to deal with. Eugene's orders were clear: under no circumstances was he to even attempt to kill Denis Moffat unless he was sure he would be putting him in the morgue.

That night Hughie found in impossible to get to sleep. He lay in bed fretting, wondering if he should call off the hit. His nerve was always weak when he was alone at night. The mobile suddenly rang, causing him to jump out of bed in a panic. He stared at it. Eugene's name flashed on the screen. When he finally picked it up, he could not stop his hand from shaking. 'Hello.'

'It's me—Eugene.'

'Have you done it already?' he asked, unable to control his breathing as he waited for the answer.

'No, I was just wondering, like, do you want me to take

out his wife as well? They're always together.'

'No, for fuck's sake, Eugene, wait 'til you can get him alone. Don't kill his wife for fuck's sake; we're no' animals.'

'Suit yourself.'

'Is that it? You phone me at two in the fucking morning to ask me that!'

Hughie immediately cut the call. He was still shaken when he climbed back into bed, but was now unable to even close his eyes, never mind get to sleep.

Chapter 29

Dorsey woke to see the rooftops of the tenements opposite covered in a thick blanket of pristine snow. It was a long time since he last experienced a white Christmas, and it made him smile.

After a cup of coffee and a cigarette, he began wrapping Helen and Daniel's presents, while listening to the usual fare of Christmas songs on the radio. He hated wrapping presents, no matter how hard he tried the Christmas paper always looked like it had been stuck together by a five-year-old. They would have to do. With that chore done, he went into the bathroom and showered, before shaving and putting on his best suit; the one usually kept back for weddings or funerals.

With his car buried under a thick blanket of snow, he decided to walk rather than drive. The thought of walking through three or four inches of powdery snow on Christmas day appealed to him, and he put on the Dr Martens that had not been worn since his days on the beat. Checking everything for a second time, he put the Christmas presents into a large carrier bag before making his way downstairs and into the brisk morning air. He began walking, cautiously at first, until the virgin snow crunched reassuringly under his feet. There were already a few children out throwing snowballs at each other. One boy looked miserable, standing outside a close-mouth with his new bicycle lying redundant against

161

the wall, the desperation to get on and ride it etched on his disappointed face. Dorsey was now glad that he did not get Daniel a bike, which was his first thought, before deciding on something a little safer. It was such a wonderful morning that he took a diversion through the park, which was magical in its winter mantle. He watched some local children build a snowman while others raced down the slopes on sledges. This is how Christmas Day should look.

He was hoping that some time together as a family would make Helen reconsider the divorce and maybe they could even get back together, for the sake of Daniel, if nothing else. The payments towards the mortgage and his own rent were draining his monthly salary and he missed being a husband and a father. He lit a cigarette when he got to the other side of the park before turning towards the main road. The traffic moved slowly along the recently gritted surface. He noticed more children with sledges and decided it might be a good idea to take Daniel to the park while Helen was busy making dinner. The last thing on his mind that morning was work; it was not going to ruin another Christmas. Even so, as he was about to switch off his phone, he could not help himself from checking if there were any new voice messages. There *was* one, from Mitchell; it was short and to the point. *'Boss, just to let you know, that Knox thinks we should bring in Denis Moffat for questioning and try and get him to agree to giving a DNA sample to check it with the cigar butt ... We're going to bring him in tomorrow morning and Knox wants you to be there for the interview. Have a Merry Christmas.'*

Dorsey was elated. For the first time they might have enough evidence to put Denis Moffat behind bars for the rest of his life. He phoned Mitchell at home. 'It's me, I got your message. This is too good to be true ... George, don't let Strachan know about this or he'll bring in Moffat today. Just keep it under wraps 'til tomorrow. By the way, have a nice Christmas and I'll see you in the morning.' Dorsey could

162

scarcely get the smile off his face as he crossed the road at Shawlands Cross. This was going to be one interview he was going to enjoy.

When he reached the junction of Kilmarnock Road and Newlands Road, he looked over to see the Christmas tree that now dominated the living room window frame. It was covered in delicate white lights, and not the crass coloured ones he used to struggle to untangle each year. Daniel then appeared at the window in his pyjamas. They exchanged a wave.

When he got to the end of the path, Daniel was already waiting at the open door. 'Merry Christmas son. Here, you better take this.'

'What is it?'

'Open it and see,' urged Dorsey, closing the door as Helen appeared in the hall.

'You're here early, did you not get the message I sent you this morning?'

'No, what message?'

'Twelve o'clock, to give me time to get things ready.'

'Don't worry. I won't get in your way. I thought I'd take Daniel to the park for a while.'

'Brilliant, thanks Dad,' said Daniel as he opened the lid of the laptop.

'Hope you like it,' replied Dorsey, pleased with the first smile that he had brought to his son's face in a long time. 'Here … that's for you.'

'You shouldn't have,' said Helen, reluctantly taking the present. 'I haven't got you anything.'

'That's fine. I guess I don't deserve anything.'

'Thank you,' said Helen, unwrapping the perfume and placing it on the dresser. For a moment she moved towards him. He stared into her eyes and willed her to kiss him, but she turned away. 'Daniel, get your coat, your father is going to take you to the park for a while.'

'Oh, not now, I want to play with my computer first.'

'You can play with it when you get back, remember it's not a toy and you'll have to learn how to use it,' said his mother.

'I know how to use it. It's the same as the one we've got in school.'

'Well then, smart arse, let me see you use it,' said Dorsey, sitting down bedside his son on the floor. Helen left them to it and went into the kitchen to make preparations for Christmas dinner.

Once Daniel had finished exploring the capabilities of the computer, Dorsey managed to coax him into his coat to go for a walk in the park while Helen continued to prepare the dinner.

In spite of the goings-on around him in the park, Daniel was engrossed in his new mobile phone that his mother had got him, and followed his father around the frozen duck pond with little interest in anything else. Dorsey had given up trying to have a conversation with him, the nods and grunts from his son beginning to annoy the hell out of him. 'What are you doing on that thing that's so bloody important?' Dorsey demanded, when he finally lost patience with him.

'I'm looking at my Facebook page.'

'Put it away, you can look at it anytime.'

Daniel could see his father was serious, and he reluctantly put the mobile phone in his coat pocket. They stood together at the side of the pond. An old woman fed the swans, which were crammed into a corner that was not frozen. 'Has your mum said anything about me?' Dorsey asked, as two more swans flew over to join the feeding frenzy.

'What about?'

'About anything.'

'Well, she said that you'd be over today with my present.'

'Anything else?'

'About what?'

Dorsey let out a sigh and pulled up his coat collar, it was like drawing teeth. Years of experience interviewing hardened criminal failed to help him to get answers out of Daniel that amounted to anything. 'Has she been to see the lawyer again?'

'I don't know. I never asked.'

'Are you not interested if your parents are getting divorced or not?'

'It's none of my business.'

'It's none of your business? What kind of answer is that? Of course it's your business.'

'You'll both get a divorce whether I like it or not.'

'Do you care?'

'Can we go home now?'

'But, do you care?' Dorsey repeated, surprised at his son's apparent indifference.

'What does it matter what I care about, it's you who fucked everything up,' raged Daniel, sick of his father's interrogation, as he turned and stormed off back towards the park gate.

Dorsey had never heard his son swear before and had to stop himself running after him to give him lecture about showing some respect. He knew he had no right to be the arbiter of his son's morality when his own was so wanting. He lit a cigarette and followed Daniel back to the gate.

When they returned to the flat Daniel went straight into his room in spite of his mother's plea for him to keep his father company while she got dinner ready.

'It's alright, he probably wants to speak to his friends on that new phone you got him. Do you need a hand in the kitchen?'

'That's a first.'

'Well, I've had to learn to cook.'

'No, Frank, you'll just get in my way.'

'Well, you can't say I didn't offer,'

'Why don't you watch the TV. There must be something on worth watching.'

'I wouldn't bet on it. There's probably nothing but old films I've seen before.'

'Daniel!' she shouted. 'Will you come in and sit with your father for God's sake.'

'It's alright, Helen, leave him there. He'll come in when he's bored with all that technology,' said Dorsey, as he went into the living room. It was then he noticed that the dining table was set for four. He was expecting to have a quiet day with Helen and Daniel to give them a chance to try and rebuild some bridges.

'Who else is coming for dinner?' he asked, trying to sound unconcerned.

'Mum and Dad are coming over at three. It's as easy to cook a turkey for four as it is for two.' Dorsey was never top of his class at school when it came to arithmetic, but even he could do the maths. He suddenly felt foolish as he stood in the middle of the living room with the remote in his hand, his son ignoring him in his bedroom, while his wife was in the kitchen cooking a Christmas dinner that he would not be staying for. He looked at his watch, one-thirty. His in-laws could arrive at any time, and he did not want another shouting match with his mother-in-law, who made her feelings about him all too clear the last time they met.

'Is that the time?' he shouted through towards the kitchen.

'I better get going before your parents arrive. I don't think your mother will be too keen to see me,' he said, putting the remote back on top of the TV.

'You can stay and say hello,' said Helen as she came back into the living room to see him with his coat on.

'No, I don't think that's a good idea. I'll say goodbye to Daniel. I've got to be at George's at three anyway. Claire was good enough to invite me over for dinner.'

'Well, I'm glad you've got somewhere to go. I'd hate to think you were on your own at Christmas.'

'Don't worry about me. I can get a piece at anybody's door,' he said, immediately thinking how stupid he sounded. 'Well, Merry Christmas.'

'Daniel, will you come out and say goodbye to your father?' Helen shouted, hoping her son would act as a buffer as she resisted the temptation to ask her forlorn-looking husband to stay for dinner.

'Why are you going?' asked Daniel.

'I've got to go, son.'

'That's not an answer.'

'Daniel! Stop it, and say goodbye.'

'No, you say goodbye. It's you who doesn't want him here,' shouted Daniel as he went back into his room and slammed the door closed.

'He'll be alright,' said Dorsey. 'I better go.'

'He's been like that for a while, don't think he knows what he wants,' said Helen, as she held the front door open.

'Do any of us?' replied Dorsey. 'Goodbye.'

'Goodbye, Frank, and take care of yourself. You look very tired.'

The snow had turned to slush and had lost its earlier allure to him. He walked along the pavement, before crossing to the other side of the road. Unable to help himself, he looked back towards the living room window, half expecting to see Helen and Daniel standing there, but there was no one there. He turned onto Kilmarnock Road where a bitter wind was blowing. The usual busy thoroughfare was quiet, and, apart from an Indian restaurant, all the local businesses were closed.

Pulling up his collar, he walked back towards Shawlands Cross, not sure where to go, having already ruled out going back to an empty flat. He needed a drink, but The Corona Bar on the corner was already closed and Sweeney's on the Park was getting ready to pull down the shutters. He decided to cut through the park. The phone in his pocket buzzed, and he checked the text message box. It was from Daniel. *Merry Christmas, Dad ... Thank you for the computer.* He wondered if Helen had forced him to send the message. He decided not to reply—what was the point? He then noticed the text message he had missed earlier from Helen. *You can come around at twelve for a couple of hours and see Daniel, but my family will be here at three for Christmas dinner.* He pressed delete.

The park was now almost empty, and the snow was left to melt in the drizzle that was now falling in the thaw. He sat on a bench without wiping away the half inch of snow that still defied the rain.

Chapter 30

After the chaos of Christmas morning, Denis Moffat went into his office for a bit of peace and quiet, and to make a few phone calls. Ashley was in the kitchen with her mother, both busy preparing the dinner, leaving Billy and Eric to go down to the pub for a few pints.

'Mind, don't be coming back here drunk. I'm not wasting all this time making dinner for you two to throw it up in the toilet,' said Irene.

'Mum, that's disgusting,' said Ashley as she turned to rebuke her mother.

'Don't worry, we'll be back at half two. You know what Dad's like if we miss the Queen's speech,' shouted Billy from the hall. He put on the new coat that his mother had bought him for Christmas. It was a perfect fit. He then followed Eric into the snow-covered street, quickly making a snowball with only one target in mind. He threw it at his unsuspecting brother, hitting Eric on the back of the head.

'Fuck off, you moron,' shouted Eric, turning to confront Billy with an even larger snowball, which he threw with a vengeance. Billy ducked, and the snowball splattered against the living room window. The snowball fight continued all the way down the street before they called a truce outside the pub.

Denis had been watching his sons' antics from his office window and shook his head. 'Thank God Benny is out, they two are a pair o' halfwits,' he mumbled, lighting his first cigar of the day. He turned back to his desk when the phone rang. 'Aye, what is it?'

'They're going to bring you in tomorrow morning,' explained a cautious voice in a strained whisper.

'Bring me in for what?'

'They intend to question you about a murder.'

'Murder … Who've I supposed to have murdered this time?'

'Jamie Sylvester.'

'Who the hell's that? I've never even heard o' him, never mind murdered him.'

'He's one of McGowan's dealers. They found him the other day in his flat in the Calton. He'd been dead for nearly a week. There was a bullet in his head and cigar burns all over his body. Forensic think the bullet came from a Beretta.'

'What's that got to do wi' me?'

'They think your DNA is on a cigar butt that was found in the flat beside the body.'

'My DNA, how is that possible? Someone is trying to set me up. I want you to find out who's behind this shit.'

'I don't think anyone here thinks you're stupid enough to leave a cigar butt with your DNA on it, but I also don't think anyone cares if you did or not. They're happy if you take the fall for all the ones they think you got away with.'

'If they don't think it was me, then they must at least think I'm being framed, but by who?'

'Hughie McGowan is one theory; the other is the twins …'

'My boys! Are ye fucking mad!'

'That's what I've heard being suggested. They think that maybe the twins are tired of waiting for you to retire and are looking to take over while you're in prison … it's just one of a number of theories being mooted at the station.'

'Look, I pay you twice what you get from your job,'

coughed Denis, through a cloud of cigar smoke. 'I don't want theories, I want facts. Who's trying to frame me? Find out and get back to me or you'll be joining me in Barlinnie if I go down for this. You know what that place is like for bent cops.'

Flushed faced, Denis banged the phone down. He began to feel dizzy and beads of sweat gathered on his forehead. He stubbed out his half-smoked cigar and struggled for breath. A feeling of panic began to overwhelm him. He got up from the chair he was embedded in, but quickly lost his balance. The walls seemed to close in around him.

Irene heard the thud on the floor and was at her husband's side in minutes. Still coughing, Denis struggled to catch his breath.

'Ashley, phone for an ambulance, I think your father's having a heart attack,' Irene shouted, trying to control the panic in her voice. She took a cushion from one of the chairs and lifted his head onto it.

He forced a weak smile. 'I'll be fine in a minute.'

'Those bloody cigars,' she scolded. 'I've warned you, but will you listen to me?'

Denis could feel the weight of his own body pressing down on him as he tried to get up. He slumped back down again and groaned. Ashley came back into the room. 'I've phoned the ambulance,' she said, slowly approaching her mother, while staring at her father's ghostly white face and watery eyes. 'Is he alright?'

'I don't know. His breathing's erratic. Bring me his angina tablets—they're in the bathroom cabinet—and a glass of water.'

'Help me get up,' rasped Denis in a barely audible whisper, straining to lift his head from the cushion.

'Stay where you are,' insisted Irene as she gently rubbed

the sweat from his brow with her apron.

'Is that them?' asked Ashley, handing her mother a bottle of tablets.

'Aye … Here, Denis, try and swallow one of your pills.'

'Mum, that's the ambulance here.' shouted Ashley from the window as the blue lights flashed on the ceiling above Denis' head.

'I love you,' he whispered weakly. Irene held his hand tightly and tried not to cry.

Chapter 31

Denis felt a heavy weight on the left side of his body as he tried to focus on the faces that had gathered around his hospital bed. He could hear voices, but it was like they were in a tunnel. When he tried to speak he could not hear anything coming from his own mouth. *Where's Benny*, he mouthed in vain as the cacophony of voices echoed around his head without meaning. Irene's face came up close to his. It was stretched like a reflection on a bevelled glass; her eyes were huge as she said something which Denis could not understand. He asked for Benny again, but his words were silent ghosts that no one else could hear. When Irene moved away from the bed to speak to one of the doctors, his blurred focus then fell on the twins. *Bastards, he shouted in his void. Try and frame me, look at them. You pair o' fucking traitors.* He recoiled when Billy came close to the bed, head bowed and solemn, as though he was paying his last respects to a dying King. *Am no' dead yet*, mouthed Denis as he turned away only to see Eric staring at him from the other side of the bed. He tried to lift his arms to push them away, but he could not make his body do what he wanted. He felt like a soul trapped inside a dead, useless corpse.

'I think he recognises me,' said Eric, looking into the dark pupils of his father's eyes. 'Quiet, I think he's trying to say something.'

Denis was not just trying to say something, he was screaming. *Get them away from me ... Someone get these two bastards away from me.* But his pleas only reverberated in the echo chamber that was his own head.

'What's he saying?' asked Irene, rushing back to the bed. 'Denis, it's Irene, can you hear me? Say something.'

Denis was now feeling like a puppy being asked to give its paw for the umpteenth time, and again he tried to speak.

'Get me Benny, where's he?'

'I think he's trying to say something about Benny,' said Irene turning to Eric. 'Where is your brother, anyway? Has no one phoned him?'

'I phoned and left a message on his answering machine about ten minutes ago,' said Eric, shrugging his shoulders. 'He still hasn't phoned back.'

'Phone him again,' said Irene. 'Ashley, come over here and hold your father's hand. I need to go to the loo.'

The anger that consumed Denis began to ease when he saw Ashley looking at him with her sad brown eyes close to tears. *Princess, where's Benny?* he mouthed. She looked back at him and smiled as though she was trying to cheer up an unhappy child in a pram. He tried to speak again, but he could tell from her facial expression that she could not hear the words that he was so desperate for her to hear. Was this the nightmare end for him, left mute in a place somewhere between life and death? Was he to remain in this passive state forever? Trapped in this world of thoughts without deeds, and words without sounds; a wilderness where only he resided.

In his frustration, Denis closed his eyes. Exhausted, he soon fell into a deep sleep that overwhelmed him in seconds. Instead of the peace his mind sought, his conscience was now tormenting him with the past he had so conveniently blacked out over the years under a veneer of respectability. His mind had not forgotten its crimes of the past; it had merely stored them away never to be reopened in his lifetime. Now, against his wishes, his mind defied him, and the genie was out the bottle, and no matter how he tried, he could not stop the

174

victims of his reign of terror coming back to torment him. First to appear was his old boss, *The Badger*, his hair and beard now as white as snow, like some old man from the Bible. He turned the side of his head, revealing a gaping wound where Denis had unloaded his Beretta.

'How are you, Moffat? Remember me?'

'Aye, what do want? You're dead. I killed you. Why are you here?'

'I bet you never thought this day would come.' 'What day?'

'Your death of course. Your demise, your day of reckoning. When you shake off that mortal coil, kick the bucket, pass away, call it what you like. It all means the same thing … The day that you've to pay for your sins and we know that you've more than most to tally up. Don't we, Denis?'

'Get away from me. You don't exist, you're fucking dead.'

'Hell's not that bad, at least for some of us. I'll see you again on your way down. You've got further to go down than I did … Bye, Denis.'

He tried to wake up, but was unable to break from the paralysis his mind was in. He could feel someone squeeze his hand tightly. *Benny, is that you?* Then the darkness seemed to clear for a moment, but instead of his eldest son standing over him, it was another of his victims, Fred "The Fence" Wilson, who ended up in the foundations of a M8 motorway flyover, leaving Denis the sole partner in their pawn shop on Shettleston Road. Fred was now in the form of a snake, but he still wore his trademark porkpie hat, and smoked his usual French cigarettes. He grinned into Denis' face and hissed.

'Hello, Denis, nice to make your acquaintance once more and at such an auspicious occasion, *hiss*, on your descent into the bowels of Hell, *hiss*. Where I hear it's, oh, how'd I describe it, *hiss* … like Hell,' he laughed with a hissed intake of breath.

'Get away from me. Get away, you're no' real. Get away,' shouted Denis, as he again tried to wake from what was either a nightmare or his pending death, he was not sure which. Fred then removed his hat as though attending the deathbed of a dear friend, instead of the man who had murdered him.

'There are different levels of suffering down here, *hiss*, just like Dante's *Inferno*, *hiss*, and I hear that the devil is busy extending his basement dungeons for your pleasure, *hiss*, or should I say your pain, *hiss*. They're stoking up the furnaces as we speak, *hiss,* so that you'll get a warm welcome, *hiss.*'

'Get away, you bastard!' shouted Denis, his eyes suddenly open. He then began to cough and splutter back from the edge of darkness.

'Can someone get the doctor!' shouted Irene, while she tried to comfort Denis through his fit of coughing.

Chapter 32

Monday 26ᵗʰ December

The alarm clock rang for a second time. Dorsey hit the snooze button, giving himself the luxury of another nine minutes in bed before getting up to face another day. Feeling exhausted, and with a pounding headache, he was now paying the price of his over-indulgence. With only the sound of the wind and rain lashing against the window he tried to escape back into the sanctuary of his dreams until suddenly remembering that they were due to bring Denis Moffat in for questioning. He sat up, but a little too quickly. The whole room seemed to turn upside down. He fell back onto the pillow. The previous night was a blur. It took him a few moments before recalling taking a taxi into town and ending up at The Corinthian Bar on Ingram Street. His drunken attempts to chat up some girls nearly half his age came back to embarrass him. At forty he had crossed some kind of Rubicon. The alarm rang again, but this time he got up and turned it off.

The room was freezing. The central heating rattled and grunted before it settled down. It would take a while before it banished the cold air, but at least it was working again. He braced himself before going into the bathroom that was even colder than the bedroom. Eventually the warmth from the shower brought him out of his stupor.

He drove across the city, glad to see the rain was washing away the last of the snow. The slush on the side of the roads was all that was left of a rare white Christmas. The city centre was already busy with shoppers looking for bargains in the Boxing Day sales. The computer he bought Daniel would now be selling for half the price. He turned away from the busy Trongate, and drove along London Road towards the Loyalist enclave that was Bridgeton Cross. The names of the pubs were enough to confirm to most Glaswegians which side of the sectarian divide ruled here, but just to make sure that there was no misunderstanding, the publicans were kind enough to hang the Union Jack and Red Hand of Ulster flags outside.

At the station there were already a number of officers in the operations room standing around the Superintendent. 'Damn,' he muttered when realising Knox was giving one of his early morning briefings to the squad. Before going in, Dorsey cupped his hands to smell his breath. There was more than a hint of whisky, and he backed off, going to the toilet to give Knox time to finish.

There was an audible sigh as Knox conveyed the news that Denis Moffat was in hospital and not fit to be interviewed. 'Any questions?' he asked as he looked around the disappointed faces.

'When will we be able to question him, sir?' asked Mitchell, who could barely sleep the night before with the thought of accusing Denis Moffat of murder.

'Not until the doctors say so. They're not even sure if he's going to make it.'

'Well, that would be a result,' said Strachan. 'We can wrap this whole investigation up and pin all four murders on him.'

'I'll take that as a joke, Charlie. Now get back to work. There are other suspects in this case and we still haven't tracked down those Romanians. And what about those bloody text messages? Kate, have BT got anything?'

'No, sir, other than they originated somewhere in the

Bishopbriggs area … Until someone uses the phone again they can't give us an exact location.'

'Okay … George, can you tell Frank to come and see me as soon as he gets in?' said Knox, as he looked at his watch again.

Dorsey washed his face and combed his hair; as long as he did not look too bad then maybe Knox would not get close enough to smell the whisky. He took a deep breath and exhaled before making his way into the operations room.

'What's up?' he asked Mitchell, who had not noticed Dorsey coming up behind him.

'Frank, thank God you're here. Knox wants to speak to you. He checked his watch before he went back upstairs.'

'What was he briefing you lot about?'

'Denis Moffat was admitted into hospital yesterday with a suspected heart attack. We'll not be allowed to interview him until the doctors say so. It could be weeks, even months.'

'Shit, it could be never. The first time we get a chance to nail him in years and this happens.'

'We still don't know if it *was* a heart attack.'

'Well, whatever it was, it's given us a little more time to look at this again. I'm still not convinced that Moffat would be so stupid to leave a cigar butt when he knows his DNA would be on it.'

'We still don't know his DNA is on it, without a sample how are we going to check it?'

'We could get a court order and force his doctors to provide one.'

'I don't think the courts will grant an order. His lawyers will argue that without any other evidence we're just fishing.'

'We can try.'

'Frank, you better go and see what Knox wants.'

'To hell with him. Get your coat. Which hospital is Moffat in?'

'The Royal Infirmary … You're not thinking of going, Frank?'

'It's the same hospital that Massimo Tamburini is in. I've been meaning to go back and see if he's ready to give a statement against the twins. We can always pay Denis a courtesy visit; just see how bad he is.'

'What about Knox?' asked Mitchell, following his boss into the street.

'Just tell him you forgot to tell me,' said Dorsey, throwing Mitchell the car keys. 'You better drive; I had a few too many last night.'

'Hell, Frank, don't tell me you drove to work this morning!'

'Why … are you going to breathalyse me?'

'You're a nightmare sometimes.'

Massimo was sitting up when they entered the ward.

'How are you?' asked Dorsey, taking a seat beside the bed. Massimo looked at him through blood shot eyes.

'What do ye want?' he mumbled through his swollen mouth which barely moved.

'Who did this to you?'

After a moment's hesitation, Massimo turned to face Dorsey. 'Ah fell down the stairs … Ah was drunk.'

'How did you end up covered in petrol?'

'How should Ah know? Am no' answering any more questions.'

'Did the Moffats do this to you?'

'No comment … Am no' answering anymore questions … just leave me alone.'

'Did your brother Dino speak to you?'

'What about?'

'About giving evidence against the twins.'

'Aye, but Ah'm the one that would've to go to court, and as soon as they know Ah'm a witness, then Ah'm a dead man,' he whispered with great effort to get his words out of his broken mouth.

'So they did do it,' said Mitchell.

'Just leave me … am no' saying anything else,' insisted Massimo as he turned away.

'Well, if you change your mind you know where to get me,' said Dorsey getting up from the side of the bed and nodding to Mitchell. 'Let's go, George.'

In the corridor Dorsey saw the forlorn figure of Giuseppe Tamburini walking towards him. The old man looked worn out, but managed a smile when he saw Dorsey and Mitchell.

'How are you, Giuseppe?' asked Dorsey, while Mitchell went back to the reception to find out which ward Denis Moffat was in.

'You're here to speak to Massimo?'

'Aye, but he's not interested in speaking to us.'

'I'll give evidence against those bastards. I'm no' afraid what those Moffats do to me. I'm an old man, Inspector, what can they do?'

'I'm afraid it's Massimo that'll have to give evidence, what he told you about the twins is only hearsay. We can't use it in court. Can you have a word with him? Unless he gives a statement and is prepared to back it up in court then the twins will get off with what they did to him.'

'I've told him already … what can I do? He's terrified of those thugs, and who can blame him after what they did? Bloody animals.'

'If your son changes his mind, give me a call.'

Mitchell returned from the reception. 'What did he say?' he asked, as they both watched Giuseppe shuffle along the corridor.

'He can't get his son to give us a statement. Massimo is too afraid. But at least we know it was the twins. What ward is Moffat in?'

'Ward 2B.'

Irene was sitting at her husband's bedside with Benny, who was wearing a new Armani suit, looking like he had just returned from Marbella instead of finishing a stretch in the toughest prison in Scotland. Irene immediately got up and walked towards the two detectives. 'What do you want here?'

'We heard about Denis's heart attack, and we thought we'd visit to see how he is,' said Dorsey looking over at the bed where Moffat lay with a drip attached to his arm and an oxygen mask over his face.

'You mean you came to gloat over a sick man's misfortune, Inspector. I don't want you going anywhere near him. He's very ill—it was a stroke, not a heart attack.'

'Is he conscious?'

'He comes and goes.'

'How're you doing, Inspector?' asked Benny, getting up to stand with his mother.

'Hello, Benny. They finally let you out.'

'I've done my time, Inspector.'

'You've only done part of your time, remember you're still on parole,' interrupted Mitchell.

'I wasn't talking to you, Mitchell, I was taking to your boss' said Benny, with a scowl on his face. 'The last time I saw you, you were wearing a uniform and chasing wee boys for playing football in the street.'

'Don't get smart, son. I'll be keeping an eye on you. If

you step out of line you'll be back in Barlinnie before you know it, and you'll have to put your fancy suit back in the wardrobe for another few years.'

'You must be getting hard-up for detectives, Inspector, if you're promoting wooden-tops like him into the CID.'

'Go and sit with your father, Benny, and don't always be looking for trouble, son,' said Irene.

'That's it, Benny, do what your mammy tells you,' said Mitchell, with a mock laugh in his voice. Benny just smirked back, but it had the tinge of a threat that Mitchell would pay for that, but he still did what his mother told him and went back to sit with his father without another word.

'You're as bad as him, and you're supposed to be a detective,' said Irene, turning to Mitchell. 'If you'd wait outside then I can have an adult chat with your boss,' she added, folding her arms.

'Wait outside, George,' said Dorsey, nodding towards the door. Mitchell turned from Irene and stared at Dorsey, before shrugging his shoulders and heading for the door in a foul mood.

'Now we might be able to talk some sense, Inspector. Why are you here? And don't take me for a fool.'

'We need to speak to your husband about these drug-related murders.'

'He's told you that he's got nothing to do with what's going on. Whatever he did in the past is in the past. He's a businessman and the last thing he needs is trouble with the police.'

'When he's well enough tell him we need to speak to him. We've concrete evidence that ties him into at least one of these murders.'

'What evidence?'

'You know I can't tell you that. Let's put it this way, an

183

alibi won't be of much use to him this time.'

'Why are you telling me this?'

'Between you and me, Mrs Moffat, I think that someone is trying to frame him. The problem for your husband is that it doesn't matter what I think, if the evidence points to him then he'll have to take his chances in the High Court. If someone is trying to frame him, then whoever that is, must also be behind one or more of these murders. Your husband might've an idea who that is.'

'Inspector, how long have you been trying to put my husband in jail?'

'Nearly twenty years. But he still calls me son, even now.'

'He calls everyone son ... Even if someone is trying to frame Denis, do you think for a minute he's going to tell the police? My husband deals with his own problems, and he'll deal with this.'

'Not if we arrest him and put him in Barlinnie to wait for his trial.'

'Why'd you do that if you think he's innocent?'

'I only think he's being framed, but I could be wrong. It'll be up to a jury to decide if he's guilty or not. All I do is collect the evidence and submit it to the Procurator Fiscal.'

'And you're not going to tell me what the evidence is.'

'No, but I'll tell Denis as soon as he's well enough and willing to speak to me. If he can point me in another direction then I might let him recover at home until I've exhausted all other possibilities.'

'I'll speak to him when he's able, but don't think I'm taken in by all this. You probably don't have any evidence anyway. Denis is his own man, and he'll speak to you if he thinks it's in his interest, but don't hold your breath. The doctor thinks he'll be like this for a while ... and, Inspector, don't bring your poodle with you the next time.'

Feeling that the residue of the previous night's binge had now worn off, Dorsey decided to drive back to the station. Mitchell reluctantly handed him the car keys. On the way he explained the conversation he'd had with Irene, but Mitchell was still in a bad mood and listened in silence. They were almost back at the station, when Dorsey suddenly slammed on the brakes and turned and stared at Mitchell. 'What the hell's up with you?' he shouted.

'What are you on about?' responded Mitchell, more than a little startled at the ferocity of Dorsey's manner towards him.

'The silent treatment, that's what I'm on about. You're worse than a woman sometimes.'

'For God's sake, boss. You made me look like an idiot in front of that bitch. Making me stand out in the corridor like a naughty school boy,' bemoaned Mitchell.

'You always have to have your put downs, making it clear how much you hate these people. That's why they never want to tell you anything. Irene Moffat is no' daft, she knows all about corroboration and would never speak to two cops at the same time. It's just her way. You either work with me or you don't.'

'What's that supposed to mean?'

'Exactly what it means, you can work with Strachan and I'll take Harper.'

'Is that what you want?'

'No, but it's up to you.'

'Alright, I'm sorry about the silent treatment, it was a bit childish … Can we just move on?'

'Okay.'

185

Chapter 33

The superintendent was on the phone when Dorsey chapped loudly before letting himself in. Knox nodded towards the chair in front of his desk while listening intently to whoever was on the line, before eventually responding. 'Yes, sir we'll provide a complete update to the Procurator Fiscal tomorrow. Dorsey is with me and we'll work on it together … yes, sir. I'll tell him.'

Knox put the phone down in a slow and deliberate manner, allowing Dorsey the opportunity to speak first.

'You wanted to see me?'

'Yes, about three hours ago. Did Mitchell not tell you?'

'He forgot … he just remembered when we got back a few minutes ago.'

'Where have you been?'

'I didn't think I had to report to you every time I needed to piss.'

'Frank, don't speak to me like that. I'm still your boss.'

'Andrew, you were also once my best friend, now you act like all those other idiots who let a few pips on their jackets go to their heads.'

'Is that it? You're jealous of a bit of gold braiding? I thought you were bigger than that, Frank. I never wanted to have to say this, but if it wasn't for me and that bit of gold braiding that you're so contemptuous of, then you'd have been back on the fucking beat after that affair with Reynolds's wife …'

'They were separated at the time.'

'What the hell does that matter? They were still married and serving officers. You're lucky Reynolds wanted a divorce before he knew about you and his wife or he could've insisted on you being dismissed. If it was up to Cullen, you'd have been transferred to the Shetlands,' rattled Knox, his voice rising in anger. 'And you come in here this morning trying to wind me up as though it was my fault you messed up your marriage.'

'Alright, Andrew, I'm sorry. I've just had a few bad days, that's all … I didn't know you stood up for me back then.'

'What did you expect me to do?'

'But the dressing down you gave me in front of Cullen, what was that all about?'

'What did you expect, a commendation? That was the price you had to pay for me putting my own neck on the line for an ungrateful, selfish bastard like you.'

There was a moment's silence as Knox looked through some papers on his desk, while Dorsey squirmed in his chair. *First Mitchell and then Knox, what the hell was up with him,* he wondered, as he lined up the possible culprits for his rage, the Christmas dinner that never was, being the obvious one. 'Are you going to tell me where you were this morning, Frank?' asked Knox, suddenly looking up from his paperwork, and adopting a more conciliatory tone after venting his spleen.

'I went to speak to Massimo Tamburini, to see if he was ready to give us a statement.'

'And was he?'

'No, not yet, he's terrified of the Moffats, and who can blame him.'

'How do you know it was the Moffats?'

'He told his father it was the twins, and Massimo all but

confirmed it to us, but he declined to make a statement.'

'Was that it … you spent three hours speaking to someone who was not willing to give you a statement?'

'No, I also spoke to Irene Moffat, just to spook her a little and plant some seeds. Denis Moffat will not be fit for anything for weeks, maybe months.'

'But he's still our only suspect for the Devlin and Sylvester murders.'

'Looks that way, but we still don't have his DNA to test the cigar butt.'

'So we don't even have his DNA on the data base?'

'No, the last time he was arrested and charged with anything, DNA was just three letters in the alphabet.'

'Very droll, Frank … So we don't even know if it's his DNA that's on the cigar and there is no other evidence against him.'

'No.'

'So, even if you bring him in for questioning, he can refuse to provide a sample.'

'I'm afraid so, but I was hoping that you would be able to persuade a sheriff to grant us a court order to make him provide one.'

'You know as well as I do that without any other evidence then that's not going to happen. There's no way that his lawyers will let us get such a warrant with no other evidence to incriminate him. Without his DNA to match the cigar, where's your evidence to even question him without his lawyers objecting and accusing us of harassment again?'

'It's the only evidence we have.'

'But it's not enough. Without the DNA, where is the link to Denis Moffat? He's not the only person that smokes cigars in Glasgow. We can't even detain him for questioning on that evidence.'

'I agree, and for all I know we could be pissing up the wrong tree and find out it isn't Moffat. But the circumstantial evidence we have suggests it's him, and that's all I've got to work on at the moment.'

'So, let's assume we get the DNA and it is Moffat's cigar, do you think he killed both Devlin and Sylvester?'

'It would make compelling evidence.'

'That's not what I asked.'

'I'm not sure what to think. The *M.O.* is the same; it's the same calibre gun, both were tortured and the burns were all post-mortem. It has to be the same killer. With the cigar burns and the murder weapon being a Beretta, it all points to Denis Moffat. I also got confirmation from Professor Jenkins that the traces of ash left on both bodies came from a similar type of cigar. But that's all we've got to link Denis Moffat with the two killings, and without his DNA.'

'Okay, I'll speak to the Procurator Fiscal's office and let them decide if we've enough grounds to obtain a court order. Even with the DNA on the cigar, will it be enough to get a conviction? His lawyers will argue it was planted there by one of his enemies, or even the police. We'll need something else to get this into court.'

'I agree. Would Moffat be stupid enough to leave a cigar butt to be found. It doesn't make any sense. Not Denis Moffat.'

'A jury may have similar doubts. We don't want him walking out with another not proven verdict. Anyway, we can't question him until he's well enough. Maybe something else will turn up.'

'That's just what I was thinking. We've the statements from Burns and Tamburini confirming they were dealing for the twins. Even though they'll never give evidence against them, it still gives us grounds to get a warrant to search the Moffat house. I doubt if we'll find any drugs, but if Big

Denis is getting careless in his old age, maybe he never got rid of the Beretta. Get that gun, and he'll have to provide a DNA sample. Then we've nailed the bastard.'

'I'm sorry, Frank, you're too late.'

'What do you mean?'

'While you were at the hospital, I arranged for a warrant to search the Moffats' house, using the contents of those two statements. Strachan is already at the house.'

'Couldn't you have waited 'til you spoke to me before getting the warrant?'

'That's why I wanted to speak to you this morning. So don't blame me, Frank.'

'Well, I better go and do something useful.'

'Before you go, are there any developments with the other two murders?'

'No, we've drawn a blank with the text messages, the best BT can give us is that the messages were sent from somewhere in the Bishopbriggs area. They need someone to use the phone again to nail the exact location.'

'What about these Romanians, anything happening there?'

'No, I'm afraid not. They've gone to ground after we raided the farmhouse. We also drew a blank with the Romanian police. They've no record of these characters. Harper's sent their photographs and prints to Interpol,' explained Dorsey, still reeling that Strachan had outflanked him once again.

'And?'

'We're waiting to hear if they've managed to get a match on any of them.'

'Give them a phone later today; we need to let the PF know we're as keen to get them as we are to get Denis Moffat. Anything else I should know?'

190

'There was no forensic evidence to suggest that Watson was ever in the van we recovered from outside the farmhouse. Jenkins thinks if Watson was in it, then he'd have found something.'

'Where does that leave us?'

'They're still the main suspects for both killings, and there's still the drug haul we've got them on ... if we find them.'

'Yes, Cullen was on about that again this morning. You've given him something to crow about to the press. The street value has been estimated at half a million pounds,' said Knox, trying to coax Dorsey out of his obvious disappointment over the search warrant being given to Strachan.

'Exaggerated at a half a million, you mean.'

'You know how desperate he is for the top job when Dunbar retires.'

'And no doubt you'll be looking to get his job.'

'That's how it works, Frank. With your experience, there's nothing to stop you from applying and getting Chief Inspector. They're still taking applications.'

'I'm happy with the rank I've got. I couldn't spend every day in this office filling in forms like some bank clerk. It would drive me round the bend. Why do you think Bob took early retirement? Let someone else fill his boots.'

'That someone will be your immediate boss, and might not be as accommodating as Bob was when it comes to your unconventional ways of working. I hear Strachan's got a good chance of getting it.'

'Strachan? Let him get it, he probably needs it more than me.'

'You say that now, Frank, you might not say that if he's the one calling the shots. You two have never seen eye-to- eye.'

'He's not got the job yet. I'll deal with it when the time

191

comes. Okay, is that everything?'

'Oh, before I forget, you have a meeting tomorrow with the Fiscal, Elizabeth Baxter, who you've met before. The Crown Office wants a progress report on all four killings. The politicians need these murders to be wrapped up as soon as possible, they don't want the world press to start showing an interest in our drug wars as though we are turning into some sort of tin pot South American country. What's the point in the Council promoting Glasgow as a tourist destination, if people are too frightened to come in case they end up with a bullet in the head?'

'That's a bit over dramatic … the world cup was in Brazil a few years ago and there're hundreds of murders there every year because of drugs.'

'That's Brazil. We're not a third world country.'

'Fair enough. What time do I have to meet her?' asked Dorsey, getting to his feet.

'Phone her and arrange a time. But do that after you check with Interpol about these elusive Romanians. The more progress we're making, the less she'll be on my back, and the less I'll be on yours.'

Chapter 34

Irene Moffat was still in the hospital when she got the phone call from Ashley shortly after Dorsey and Mitchell left. 'So that's why those two bastards were here this morning,' she said to Benny, who was driving her back home.

'They were making sure there was no one at the house so they could wreck the place,' said Benny, weaving through the East End streets like a rally driver. 'You know what they're like.'

'Ashley said they put the door in without even checking there was anyone there to let them in. They obviously didn't think she was there.'

When they got there, Irene's blood pressure rose on seeing the front door almost split in half and hanging from its hinges. Benny drove off as soon as his mother got out of the car; he could not risk being near the house in case anything illegal was found and the police tried to pin it on him. Even though his father had always been careful over the years, Benny was not prepared to take any chances, especially while on parole.

Irene met Ashley at the door, she looked bewildered. 'Mum, I tried to get the door open, but they just smashed it in before I got a chance to undo the security chains. They said they had a warrant to search the house for drugs.'

'Don't worry, pet. There're no drugs in this house. Here, take this and get a taxi to the hospital. Someone needs to sit with your father ... I'll deal with these bastards.'

Strachan was impatiently waiting for a locksmith to

arrive to open the safe. Irene stood in the hall with her arms folded while half a dozen CID officers continued to go through every inch of the house. 'You'll find nothing in this house. This is nothing more than police harassment,' she complained bitterly. 'You waited until he was in hospital before you did this … you're nothing but a bunch of cowards.'

'We're just doing our job; this is not about your husband, it's to do with your two sons and their involvement in drugs,' said Strachan.

'So why are you searching my husband's office and trying to break into his safe?'

'Your sons live here, and the warrant is to search these premises. And that's what we're doing.'

'Search away, you'll find nothing.'

'Are you sure you don't know the combination to this safe? It'll save us from having it forced open.'

'No, and if I did, I wouldn't tell you.'

'Suit yourself. We'll get it open one way or another.'

When the locksmith finally arrived, the rest of the house had been searched from top to bottom. Nothing incriminating had been found, other than dozens of boxes of cigars recovered from an attic room.

'You're not going to charge him with smoking too much?' Irene mocked, as Strachan had a cursory look at the array of expensive cigars.

'Put them in the van.'

Bemused at the departure of her husband's cigar collection, Irene produced her TV licence and showed it to Strachan, just to further annoy him. 'And we've paid for our satellite dish as well.'

Strachan ignored her, he was still pinning his hopes on the contents of the wall-safe. Most of the other officers had now gathered in Denis' office to watch the locksmith at work. Expecting a long drawn-out procedure, Strachan was surprised when the locksmith turned to him and smiled. 'That was easy. These old safes are next to useless … child's play to open.'

'Well done,' said Strachan, going to the open safe and putting his hand into its secrets. Deflated, he pulled out a handful of documents, but no Beretta. He handed the documents to Harper, and put his hand back in desperately searching for a secret compartment at the back. He let out a groan, before turning back to the rest of his squad. 'That's all that's in it.'

'It just looks like a lot of legal documents, leases for his businesses and the title deeds to this place,' said Harper, perusing what Strachan had handed her.

'Satisfied,' said Irene, staring at the forlorn faces, none more disappointed than Strachan's. 'You'll be hearing from our lawyers,' she said holding the door and gesturing for the officers to get out of her house.

'Let's go,' said Strachan, after another look into the empty safe.

Outside a crowd had gathered on the opposite pavement, waiting to see who was going to follow the boxes of cigars in the back of the police van. Before Strachan reached his car, a familiar figure crossed the road to speak to him.

'Are you arresting cigars now, Charlie?' asked Barney Collins, unable to keep the smile off his face.

'Never you mind, Collins, this is police matter and a live investigation, so I don't want anything about this appearing in the newspapers that will compromise this investigation.'

'The public have a right to know, and until you have arrested anyone I can print what I like.'

'You do that.'

'Charlie,' shouted Cooper from the side of the house.

'You better come and have a look at this.'

Strachan brushed past Collins and walked back towards Cooper.

'What is it?'

'I found something in a black bag under a loose slab in the back garden. I didn't want to touch it.'

Strachan followed Cooper into the back garden where two uniform officers were standing beside the uplifted slab. 'Get the photographer in here,' he shouted over the garden fence.

Chapter 35

As though emerging from the depths of the ocean, Denis Moffat felt his mind rise up from the darkness it had been in. He gulped for breath. A nurse who had been checking the temperature of a patient in the opposite bed, rushed to his bedside. 'There, Mr Moffat, cough it up,' she said putting a bowl under his chin as he brought up some bile and blood. After a few convulsions and more bile, he finally fell back down onto his pillow, his eyes streaming and his mouth wide open. He continued to struggle for breath. 'Where … am … I?' he finally slurred in a weak voice as the nurse wiped around his mouth with a damp cloth.

'You're in hospital; you've had a mild stroke. I'll get the doctor.'

'Where's … my … wife?'

'She had to go home, but your daughter went downstairs for a coffee. She should be back up shortly.'

When the nurse went to fetch the doctor, Denis tried to remember what had happened to him, but his mind was blank. His peripheral vision was also blurred and he had to turn his head to see around him. There were another three beds in the small ward and he noticed the man in the bed opposite staring at him. He was about to say something when he saw Ashley coming into the ward, her face breaking into a broad smile. He tried to smile back, but he could only feel the right side of his face moving. His face was lopsided. He was unaware of the saliva that dribbled from his mouth. 'How're you, Dad?' she asked, taking his hand and sitting beside the bed.

'Ashley … what happened … to … me?' he asked with a struggle.

'You collapsed in your office yesterday; we thought you had a heart attack. The doctors have confirmed that you've had a stroke and should make a full recovery. Here's the doctor now,' she added as the nurse lifted the medical file from the bottom of the bed and handed it to a young doctor. 'Nurse, put the screen around until I carry out a few tests,' said the doctor. Ashley got up and moved away from the bed. She went into the corridor to check her phone for text messages. There was one from her mother. *How is he? Has there been any change?*

She immediately texted back: *He has come around, and the doctor is examining him. His speech is slurred.*

After about ten minutes the doctor reappeared in the corridor. 'Your father is out of any danger, the medication seems to be working well. I'll arrange for him to have a scan tomorrow.'

'Thank you, doctor,' said Ashley. Relieved, she text her mother again, before going back into the ward.

Denis was sitting up in bed.

'How do you feel, Dad?' she asked, taking his hand again. It felt cold and limp as though she had picked up something dead that was not even part of him.

'I'm … no' good … darling … why's your … mother … not here?'

'She'll be here shortly; she spent the whole night with you and had to go home for a few hours. The police had a warrant to search the house this morning.'

'A … warrant … what … where …' his mind became confused and the question lost any meaning to him as lay back down on the pillow and stared at the ceiling. He wanted his swirling circles and his mind back.

198

'That's it, rest for a while. Mum will be up soon.'

Denis did not have the strength to say any more and lay there with his eyes closed. He tried to remember what he had been doing before he ended up in hospital, but nothing made any sense. What were the police looking for? He was too weak to open his eyes again, and slipped into a deep sleep.

Chapter 36

There were cheers in the station when Strachan entered waving the black bag containing the Beretta. Knox was the first to congratulate Strachan, who was trying to be as modest as his professional vanity would allow. 'It was a team effort, sir.'

Dorsey waited for Knox to finish whatever he was saying and go back upstairs, before approaching Strachan.

'Well done, Charlie,' he said, offering his hand as though he had just lost a round of golf. 'Where was it found?'

'Sandy found it under a slab in the back garden.'

'A strange place to hide a murder weapon, in your own back garden,' said Dorsey.

'There's been plenty of murder victims found in the murderer's back gardens. So what's so strange about finding the murder weapon? Are you still a bit sore that you weren't in early enough to lead the search yourself?'

'No, who said I was sore?'

'Knox said you weren't too happy when he told you I was leading the search.'

'Never mind what he said. It's a team effort and the main thing is we got a result. But we should wait until we get the ballistics report back before we get too excited. That Beretta might've been under that slab for years.'

'I don't get you Dorsey; we've just found the most incriminating piece of evidence against Moffat in years and all you do is look for flaws.'

'But even you, Charlie, must think it's strange that Denis Moffat, of all people, would hide a murder weapon in his back garden. Why'd he not get rid of it?'

'Moffat is just like everyone else, he's getting old. Maybe he's got a touch of dementia.'

'Dementia? He's not even sixty yet.'

'Then maybe he's not as clever as everybody seems to think he is. With the evidence we have now, that evil bastard is going to prison for the rest of his life. Even Marcus Hepburn will have a hard time getting him off with these murders.'

'I hope so, Charlie, let me know as soon as you get the lab report. I've got a meeting with the PF tomorrow.'

'Sir, we've just had this emailed through from Interpol,' interrupted Harper, handing Dorsey a dozen sheets of A4. 'Their prints have all been confirmed from those found in the van and the farmhouse. The reason the Romanian police couldn't match what we'd sent them is that these guys aren't Romanian, they're Bosnian Serbs. They've identified the three suspects from the prints we sent them. This guy is definitely the man we've on video paying for the petrol. We have forged passports and driving licenses for all three of these guys that were found at the farmhouse.'

'Well done, Kate. Maybe now we can track these bastards down,' said Dorsey, looking at the pictures and personal details of the Serbs. They were all ex-members of the Serbian Delta Militia, responsible for some of the worst massacres of Bosnian Muslims during that country's civil war. Dorsey now realised what a lucky escape he and Mitchell had at the farmhouse. If these characters had been at the farm there was no way they would have given themselves up without a shootout. They were a band of brothers, or butchers more like, who had been through the most brutal war in Europe since the Second World War. All three served in the same fanatical VRS unit under General Ratko Mladić, who had been found guilty of war crimes in The Hague, including genocide and the Srebrenica massacre. Dorsey looked long and hard at the picture of Stephan Kovač, who was the leader of the gang. He had been a colonel in the Yugoslav army before the war that tore the country apart and left him and thousands of Serbians on the wrong side of the border. He had an international warrant outstanding for alleged war crimes committed in Bosnia. His lieutenant was his nephew, Miloš Petrović, a heavy-set man with cold staring eyes. Nikola Nedić was the youngest of the three, and the gang's driver. He had been a schoolteacher before the war. There was a picture of Nedić with his wife and two sons, with the date on the back, *1992*. He, like the rest of the men, had Bosnian warrants for armed robbery and drug trafficking attached to their papers. They were all classed as extremely dangerous by Interpol.

'Have a look at this lot,' said Dorsey, handing the Interpol dossier to Strachan.

It was late afternoon before Dorsey was handed an email of the fingerprint and ballistics reports he had been anxiously waiting for. He called the squad together to update everyone.

'You all know we had a major success today in finding the Beretta in Moffat's back garden. Well done to everyone involved in the search this morning. I've just received the fingerprint and ballistics reports from the lab. You'll not be surprised to discover that there are no prints on the weapon. That would've been too much to hope for ...' There were a few moans of disappointment, but most of the other detectives took the lack of fingerprints as only to be expected. 'However, there were fingerprints found on the plastic bag, but there's been no match on the national database. So, whoever those prints belong to doesn't have a criminal record. That leaves the mother and daughter. We'll have them brought in and their prints checked today. Now the really good news ... There is a ballistic match with both bullets recovered from Devlin's and Sylvester's heads ...' There was a cheer, as the detectives congratulated each other with handshakes and backslaps. 'Alright everyone, he's not convicted yet, but with the Beretta we can now charge Denis Moffat with both murders. He'll now have to provide a DNA sample, and if it matches the cigar butt we'll have a watertight case against him.' There were more cheers from the muster, which brought Knox downstairs. Dorsey continued with his briefing. 'That's two of the four murders that we can hand over to the Fiscal once Moffat is fit enough to be arrested and charged. As you know, the investigation into Watson and Tucker's murders had hit a bit of a brick wall. We still don't know who sent those religious text messages to the victims or if they are even relevant to their murders. But, and it's a big but ... we now have details of the drug gang. They're not Romanians, in spite of the passports we recovered, they're Bosnian Serbs, ex-militia.' There was an audible intake of breath from around the room. 'Kate will hand each of you copies of the information we received from Interpol. No one in this team is to pursue any of these characters unarmed or on their own. Is that understood?'

'Yes, sir,' came the collective response from all but Strachan, who was still reading the emails.

'These men are war-hardened killers, and will think nothing of shooting police officers. They're also wanted by the Bosnian authorities and Interpol for war crimes, robbery, and drug trafficking. So, no matter the circumstances, no one is to tackle these guys alone ... any questions?'

'Do we have any leads on where they might be?' asked Cooper.

'No, they may've already left the country for all we know.'

'Let's hope so,' shouted Harper from the back of the

room, breaking the tension for a moment.

The laughter quickly subsided when Knox entered. No one but Dorsey had noticed him standing at the open door. He took the dossier from Strachan and studied the papers for a moment. He then turned to the assembled room of detectives.

'There'll be a press conference later today in relation to the drug haul, I will make these pictures available to the media in order to warn the public and hopefully get their help in locating the whereabouts of these men. At the moment we're only seeking them in connection with the drugs found at the farmhouse and there'll be no mention of the murders at this press conference. We want to question them before they get their stories fixed. They don't know we've got them on video, but that is not enough to get a conviction for murder. Like Inspector Dorsey's just said, they're extremely dangerous and only armed officers should attempt to challenge and arrest them … Right, back to work.'

Chapter 37

The discovery of their safe-house and loss of a substantial shipment of drugs caused little disturbance to Stefan Kovač's plans to flood Glasgow with cocaine. He was not a man to be deterred by setbacks and had already found a new safe house in the wilderness of the Fenwick Moors, a large area of moor land between Kilmarnock and Glasgow. Kovač stood at the window of the cottage as the rain poured down outside. Petrović was sitting in front of the fire, quietly reading a book and smoking. Kovač took a semi-automatic pistol from under his black leather jacket and checked the magazine before putting it back into the holster. He had lost none of his military pride in keeping his weapon in perfect condition. He looked at his watch again when he heard the sound of a vehicle coming. 'He's here,' he shouted, letting the curtain fall back as Petrović got up and put his jacket on. Outside, a blue car pulled up with the rain battering off the roof. Nedić got out and greeted Kovač at the open cottage door. They shook hands and spoke in their own language, before Kovač ordered the car to be unloaded. The boot contained half a dozen boxes, which had travelled halfway around the world in a container of coffee beans. Nedić had met their suppliers at a secret rendezvous in Liverpool that morning and drove back with the drugs to Glasgow without incident.

They placed the boxes in the kitchen and Kovač proceeded to open one of them and take out a clear plastic bag containing cocaine. He weighed the bag on a set of kitchen scales; it was just under a kilo. He then carefully slit the top of the bag with a pen knife and removed a small amount of the powder on the blade. He placed a line of cocaine on the table, before snorting it up through a rolled bank note. Kovač nodded his head in appreciation as the others looked on. It was the pure undiluted cocaine they had been promised. The others took turns to test the drug for themselves, all agreeing that it was the best quality they had brought in so far. The boxes were then taken to a room at the back of the cottage where they were stored pending their distribution.

Nedić drove the Škoda to the back of the house to keep it out of sight. He stopped for a moment to look around the drenched moor land. The silence was eerie. Through the drizzle he could see the farm track meander for a couple of miles before it reached the B778, a minor road that very few ever travelled on. He went back into the farmhouse confident he had not been followed.

Chapter 38

The whole family was gathered around Denis's bed in the evening. He had recovered some of his strength and listened to his wife telling him that he would be fine in a few days time. Fearing that it might bring on another stroke, she had still not told him about the gun that was found in the back garden. She wiped the side of his mouth with a tissue as he tried to speak.

'Why … were the polis … at the house?'

'Don't worry about that,' said Irene, turning to look at Ashley, who mouthed that she was sorry.

'I need … to speak … to Benny … alone.'

'Mum, why don't you go down to the cafeteria with Ashley?' said Benny. 'You two wait downstairs in the car,' he said, turning to the twins. Irene gave Denis a kiss on the forehead. 'I'll be back up shortly.'

Denis waited until the others had left before turning towards Benny, nodding for him to sit down.

'Benny, go to the lockup … and hose it down … the whole place … you need to get rid of the strongbox. Make sure … you clean my Beretta and everything else in it … and dump them … in the Clyde.' said Denis, his speech slightly improved and more coherent than it had been.

'Okay, Dad, but the polis have already found your Beretta when they searched the house this morning.'

'My Beretta … found it where in the house?'

'It was under a slab in the back garden.'

'In the back garden? That's impossible.'

'They also took the CCTV tapes and all your cigars.'

Denis lay back down on his pillow, he tried to remember putting the gun under the slab, but his mind was blank. He began coughing and tried to sit up again to catch his breath. Benny looked around for a nurse.

By the time Denis had regained his composure Irene and Ashley came back into the ward. Benny got up to give his mother the chair he was sitting on. 'I better go,' he said, leaving his mother and sister to comfort his father.

Downstairs in the car park, the twins were sitting in their father's Mercedes; Billy was in the driver's seat, much to the annoyance of Eric. Billy turned the window down when he saw Benny approaching. 'What's he saying?'

'Not much, but he wants the lockup cleared and hosed down. I've got a meeting in town, so you two can do that tonight, make sure the strongbox is emptied and whatever's in it dumped in the Clyde. I'll meet you back at the house later.'

The twins spent most of the night hosing down the lockup and making sure there was nothing but old car parts left lying around. They had a good rummage through the strongbox before lifting it, with a struggle, into the boot of the car, and driving to the Clyde to dump it.

Billy parked on a path leading to a pedestrian bridge, which linked the East End with the playing fields on the Southside of the river. They waited a few minutes for an old man with his dog to pass before lifting the strongbox out of the boot.

'This weighs a fucking ton,' moaned Eric, struggling to keep a grip as they finally reached the middle of the bridge. 'We'll never get it over the fucking barrier.'

'Put it down,' said Billy. 'We'll need to take most of the

stuff out. Have you got the key?'

'No, you've got it!'

'I gave it to you, you fucking idiot,' shouted Billy, as he searched through his own pockets. 'It's alright, I've got it.'

'I told you, so don't call me a fucking idiot.'

Still arguing, they took out the guns, knives and a couple of boxes of bullets and threw them over the bridge. They then watched the empty strongbox disappear under the dark waters of the Clyde before walking back to the car satisfied they had followed their father's instructions to the letter. When they got to the car Billy's mobile phone began to buzz. It was Benny.

'Have you cleaned out the lockup yet?'

'Aye, we've dumped the stuff. I was tempted to keep the auld man's Beretta …'

'The Beretta, fuck, what've you done with it?'

'It's in the Clyde wi' the rest of the stuff, why?'

'Fucking hell …'

'That's what you told us to do! What's the problem?'

'Nothing, I cant' think straight at the minute.'

'Where are you?'

'Never mind … I'll speak to you later.' Benny hung up.

Chapter 39

Kovač and Petrović were wearing the suits they had bought that morning. Nedić smiled at his two comrades, neither of them looked very comfortable.

At six thirty, Nedić drove them into Glasgow with seven kilos of cocaine in the boot of the car. The drugs were stuffed into a briefcase. They had booked a room for the night in the Marriott Hotel, but they only planned to be there for as long as it took to hand over the drugs. Nedić parked in a lane near the hotel where he knew there were no CCTV cameras operating.

'Remember, if you see anything suspicious, phone me,' said Kovač, before taking the briefcase from the boot and nodding for Petrović to follow him.

While Kovač went to the reception, Petrović went straight to the lift, as though he was already a guest in the hotel.

'Do you have your passport, Mr Dubinsky?'

'Yes,' said Kovač, handing the girl a Polish passport.

'Can you fill in this form?' she asked with the smile. 'Is it just for the one night?'

'Yes.'

'Would you like a wakeup call and a newspaper?' she asked, preparing the terminal for the Visa card that Kovač handed her.

'No, thank you.'

'Room 122, on the sixth floor' she said, handing him the key. 'Would you like a porter to take your bag up?'

'No, it's fine, I only have this,' he said holding up the briefcase. 'My luggage is in the car, I'll get it later. Thank you.'

'Enjoy your stay,' she said as she watched him make his way to the lift before another customer attracted her attention.

Once in the room they waited for their customer to arrive. Kovač was always fearful of being set up, and knew very little about the man they were due to meet. His own contacts had confirmed that the Glaswegian would be good for the money, but they could never be too careful. Kovač checked his revolver, before pouring a drink from the mini-bar. He then went to the window and looked out at the Glasgow skyline, with its bridges over the Clyde lit up in a variety of colours.

The loss of the first shipment was a setback, but that was all it was to Kovač, who had factored in the possibility of at least one shipment being discovered. However, another loss would be unacceptable to those backing him.

There was a knock at the door. Kovač, with his hand reaching to the revolver inside his jacket, turned and signalled for Petrović to open it. When the door was opened, he was bemused to see a woman dressed in a United Arab Emirates air hostess uniform. She wore a hijab that covered her face with the exception of her eyes and forehead. Both men looked at each other. 'Who are you?' demanded, Kovač, his hand still on the revolver as she walked into the room pulling a trolley suitcase behind her.

'You don't have to know who I am,' she said, lifting the case onto the bed. Kovač took his hand away from inside his jacket.

'He uses a woman to do this for him,' he laughed.

'It's all there,' she said directly to Kovač, whom she immediately took to be the boss. 'If the stuff is good then

211

he'll want the same again next month.'

Kovač smiled and opened the suitcase. He nodded when he saw the money, lifting a wad of notes and throwing it for Petrović to catch.

In the downstairs lobby, the receptionist, who had checked Kovač in, went into the main public lounge to speak to the duty manager. There had been a double booking for the bridal suite that had left two newlyweds in tears at the front desk. The manager was busy talking to one of the guests and she stood at the door for him to finish. While waiting, she was still trying to remember if she was the one that had made the double booking when a picture of Kovač appeared on the lounge television. He was wearing a combat jacket with military insignia, as were two other men whose photographs appeared in quick succession. She moved over to the bar to listen to what was being reported. She felt a sudden panic when a senior police officer appeared on screen, warning the public that the men were armed and dangerous. Forgetting about the double booking, she made her way across the lounge.

'Mr Taylor, can I speak to you for a minute?' she asked, the blood draining from her face.

'What's wrong, Tracy? You look as though you've seen a ghost.'

'Can you come to the reception?' she asked, trying to get him away from the guest.

He followed her into the foyer, before taking her by the arm and stopping her. 'What's going on, Tracy?'

'Mr Taylor,' she said in a half whisper, looking around to ensure no one else was listening. 'I booked a man into Room 122, this evening. I've just seen him on the news. The police are looking for him and they said he is armed and dangerous. I saw him get into the lift with another man.'

Now Mr Taylor suddenly looked ashen faced as he tried

to take in what she was saying and more importantly, what he should do about it. 'Are you sure it's the same man?'

'I'm positive,' she replied, rubbing the goose bumps on her arm.

'Show me the booking.'

While Mr Taylor checked the booking, Tracy went into the back room of the reception and rewound the CCTV that covered the sixth-floor corridor. 'Mr Taylor, you better come in here,' she shouted, stopping the video.

'Look, I was right, the other man is with him,' she said, pressing the start button. 'I think we better phone the police,' said Tracy, looking up at Mr Taylor, who now wished he had not swapped shifts with the other duty manager that evening. Dorsey had been in the pub for about a half an hour when he got the call from Mitchell. He was glad he had only managed one pint and not the double whisky that he was tempted to have when he first came in.

'Can you pick me up?' he asked, smiling when Mitchell guessed he was in the pub. He hung up and left the empty pint tumbler on the bar.

It was freezing outside, and he buttoned up his coat and stamped his feet to keep warm. He lit a cigarette and tried to think of the best way to deal with the situation. They would have to get the other guests out of harm's way, but that would not be easy. As he finished his cigarette, Mitchell pulled up at the kerbside.

At that time of night, the Marriott Hotel was only a ten-minute drive, but it gave Mitchell enough time to tell Dorsey all he knew about the situation they were heading to. An armed unit was already on its way, but they had orders to wait in their vehicles until Knox got there. The Superintendent obviously wanted to take the glory.

They arrived to see Strachan and Cooper standing at the front entrance with someone Dorsey assumed was the hotel manager. Dorsey got out of the car and showed the manager his warrant card, before turning to Strachan. 'Is Knox here yet?'

'No, he's on his way ... this is Mr Taylor, the duty manger.'

'Mr Taylor, my name is Inspector Dorsey. What floor is the room on?'

'The sixth ... Room 122.'

'And are the two men still in the room?'

'I think so, but when we looked at the CCTV recording, a woman also went into the room about five minutes after them. She was dressed as an airhostess, and wearing a hijab. She also had a trolley-case with her. She looked like an airhostess from the Emirates or Gulf Air.'

'Mr Taylor, can you clear all the public areas of the hotel without causing a panic? Just tell them it's a fire drill and get them into the car park at the back of the hotel.'

'What about the guests still in their rooms?'

'Get your receptionist to phone them and tell them to stay there.'

'Inspector, there're over three hundred rooms in the hotel. It will take reception all night to phone every room ... it's impossible.'

'Okay, then get the reception to call all the rooms on the sixth floor, but be careful they don't phone 122.'

'What do they tell the guests?'

'Tell them the truth. There're armed men in the hotel and the police are here to arrest them. That'll keep them in their rooms. In the meantime, can you arrange to clear the public areas and get the guests and staff out as soon as possible? These two detectives will give you a hand ... George, you come with me.'

Having relayed Dorsey's instructions to the receptionists, the manager and his assistant began clearing the restaurants while Strachan and Cooper ushered those in the bars into the street. 'Hurry up, it's a fire drill, it will be over in twenty minutes,' shouted Cooper.

'It's freezing out there, why the hell are they having a fire drill at this time of night?' moaned one disgruntled guest, with an American accent.

'Take your coats,' shouted Strachan.

While the foyer was being cleared, Dorsey was viewing the CCTV. 'Can you wind that back?' he asked one of the receptionists.

'Yes, but not from here, you have to go into the backroom.'

'Has anyone been seen leaving this room in the last ten minutes?'

'I don't know, we've been too busy to watch it.'

'Shit, they're leaving,' said Dorsey as he watched Kovač and Petrović walking towards the lifts. In spite of their business-like appearance, he immediately knew he was looking at two ruthless killers.

'There's no woman with them,' said Mitchell.

'She's either left or is still in the room, but we'll have to deal with these two first. Everyone out of here and stay away from the front of the building,' shouted Dorsey, still watching the Serbs impatiently waiting for the lift to arrive. The two receptionists hurried out the building with the rest of the front of house staff, Dorsey and Mitchell drew their weapons and took up positions at either side of the lift. Strachan and Cooper joined them. They all watched the slow progress of the elevator as it passed each floor. 'Wait until they walk out and take them from behind. There may be other guests in the lift so be careful,' ordered Dorsey.

The lift bell rang. It stopped on the second floor. It then seemed to take forever before it moved again. There was an audible sigh from Cooper, when the lift bell rang again.

It stopped on the first floor. 'Fucking hell,' he mouthed, the sweat on the palms of his hands making it difficult for him to hold his gun straight. The tension grew when the lift finally reached the ground floor and the doors slowly opened.

'Police!' shouted Strachan, stepping forward with his firearm pointing into the lift. There were screams from within as two elderly women turned away from the gun that was pointing at them.

Dorsey stared at Strachan. 'I told you to wait until they came out, you stupid bastard … you and Sandy stay here.

We'll check the stairs.'

'What about them?' asked Cooper, pointing into the lift. 'Just get them out of there.'

Dorsey and Mitchell made their way to the stairs, but before they reached the first floor, the hotel fire alarm began to ring throughout the hotel. They looked at each other for a second, and without saying a word they turned and ran back down the stairs towards the basement. When they got there they found the fire exit lying wide open and could just about make out the sound of screeching wheels over the noisy fire alarm.

They returned to the reception and began viewing the CCTV again. There was something familiar about the woman wearing the hijab as he watched her walk along the corridor with the trolley-case in tow just minutes before the Serbians followed her out of the room. He zoomed into the gap around her eyes, but the picture became too blurred. 'George, can you get someone from forensics to have stills taken from this video. I want them enhanced around the woman's face.'

'Okay. What do you think was in the trolley case?' 'Either drugs or money, the Serbs' are more likely to be selling them wholesale than buying. I think she was acting for whoever was buying from these guys. But without the drugs or money we've nothing to prove why she was in that room. Have forensics found anything else?'

'Nothing, but they're still checking the lift for fingerprints. You can imagine how many prints are in a lift. Hundreds of guests must use it every day.'

'Get them to check the fire exit doors first; she might have also left that way.' Benny and Linda were already halfway across the city as a number of police cars raced by them at high speed. They had no idea how close Linda had been to being arrested in the hotel. Benny laughed at how easy it had been.

'I'm not doing it again,' exclaimed Linda, whose hands were still shaking as she lit a cigarette and put her right hand on Benny's crotch. 'But it does make you as horny as hell.'

He squeezed her thigh just above the top of her stocking top. 'Let's go and make some money.'

'Where are we going?' asked Linda, pouting in the vanity mirror in the sun-visor and fixing the fringe of her hair.

'We're going to be fucking rich,' shouted Benny, putting the Porsche into top gear.

Chapter 40

It was after 2 am before Dorsey got home. He was exhausted and still frustrated that the Serbians had escaped so easily. He lay on top of the bed, too tired to even take his suit off, and soon fell asleep. His mind was restless and he tossed and turned in a broken sleep that was giving him little peace.

His dreams were confused as his mind tried to make sense of the last few days. He saw himself at Helen's dinner table, carving a large turkey and serving it to her and Daniel, who were both happy and smiling in a way he had not seen for such a long time. He could even hear the sound of Christmas carols in his head as large flakes of snow fell past the window. With this feeling of contentment, he smiled in his sleep. This delusion of a happy family only lasted for a short time before the arguments started, with Helen screaming and shouting at him as Daniel cowered in the corner holding his ears. Like a fugitive from his own nightmare, Dorsey rushed from the wreckage of his marriage into the foyer of the Marriott Hotel, where Knox was berating Strachan. There were bodies lying everywhere. While Dorsey scanned the carnage; he suddenly saw the eyes of the woman in the headscarf staring at him from behind the reception. She removed her scarf. He woke up suddenly. 'Linda Boland,' he mouthed to himself. He tried to make sense of this sudden revelation. His heart beating hard, he got up and lit a cigarette. He remembered her from Benny's trial a few years earlier when she gave evidence in Benny's defence. Dorsey finished his cigarette and lay back down on the bed. His eyelids were heavy and they soon closed again.

When the alarm went off, Dorsey woke even more exhausted than he was before going to sleep. He had too much to do that morning to lie in bed for long and sat up to light his first cigarette of the day. He looked out at the cold grey sky that awaited and tried to recall the night before. The thought of how close they had come to arresting the Serbians gnawed at him. He took long draws on his cigarette, promising to give them up in the new year. Helen had always hated him smoking, a thought that prompted him to stub the half-finished cigarette in the ashtray at the side of the bed. He got up and took his crumpled suit off before going into the bathroom to get washed.

While in the shower, he remembered the weird dream and the unmasking of Linda Boland. He began to doubt himself, trying to remember the eyes in the video. Wishful thinking, he remonstrated with himself. If he told anyone of the dream at the station they would think he was losing his mind.

Washed and showered, he made a bowl of porridge and forced himself to eat. He knew that he would be in for a long day. While everyone else continued to enjoy the Christmas holidays, he had killers to catch—ruthless, professional killers.

The office was a hive of activity when he arrived. Already the incident board had the stills from the hotel video alongside the original photographs of the Serbian gang. The two Serbs were clearly identifiable from the photographs they had received from Interpol. The only one missing was Nedić, who it was assumed must have been waiting in the getaway car outside. Then there was an enlarged still of the mysterious woman in the hijab. Dorsey studied the photographs, transfixed on the eyes he had seen in his dream,

219

but were they the eyes of Linda Boland?

'What do you think?' asked Mitchell, handing his boss a cup of coffee.

'I don't know, George,' replied Dorsey, almost tempted to tell him about his dream. The more he looked into the eyes the more he was convinced he was looking at Benny Moffat's girlfriend. 'Does she remind you of anyone?'

'Marta Hari,' said Mitchell, with a rare grin.

'I'm serious, George.'

'It could be anyone under that garb, might even be a man. None of the reception staff remember seeing her. Harper's still checking all the other cameras to see how she got into the hotel.'

'Inspector,' shouted Harper from her desk. 'I think I've got something.'

Dorsey and Mitchell made their way across the office to where Harper was busy rewinding a video taken from a camera on Argyle Street. 'I think this might be the car the Serbs were driving,' said she, pressing the play button. The three detectives watched in silence as a blue Škoda Saloon drove along Argyle Street before turning into Oak Street. Harper stopped the video, and turned towards Dorsey. 'That was at seven thirty-five, which is only a few minutes before Kovač booked in at the reception.' Harper then turned back to the computer and pressed the fast forward button. It took only a few seconds before she stopped it again, and pressed the play button. They watched the same car drive back out of Oak Street and onto Argyle Street, only this time at speed. Harper again turned to Dorsey. 'This was around eight thirty, shortly after they were caught on the hotel CCTV leaving their room.'

'Can you make out the registration?' asked Dorsey, convinced beyond any doubt that they had the Serbian's car. Harper just turned back to the screen and clicked the mouse a couple of times. Dorsey turned and smiled at Mitchell. 'Get the number checked straight away, George … good work, Kate.'

'That's the car again on Clyde Street, before it turns onto Glasgow Bridge. It's heading for the Southside. We'll have to check the CCTV cameras on the other side of the river to see where it's headed,' she continued, now feeling elated. 'Good. Is there CCTV cameras on that side?'

'I'm not sure; there could be some on the main roads.'

'Get in touch with traffic control and see if they can follow where the car went. Contact me as soon we know its destination. Is there anything on the woman?'

'Nothing yet, there is CCTV at the front of the hotel, but there is no sign of her going in or leaving by the main door.'

'She probably used the same fire exit the Serbs used to get out,' said Mitchell.

'Then someone in the hotel must have let her in. George, check all the staff for anyone with a criminal record, especially drugs. I've got to go and see the Fiscal this morning to give her an update.'

'Lucky you,' said Mitchell.

Dorsey was glad to get out of the office before Knox made his morning appearance. He left Mitchell to brief the Superintendent and drove to the Procurator Fiscals' office. He was looking forward to seeing Miss Baxter. The last time he had very little to tell her. Now he was feeling confident with the progress he had made in the last few days. He parked at the back of the building and went into the foyer, where he confirmed his appointment.

'I'm afraid Miss Baxter's gone to the sheriff court this morning, she left about ten minutes ago,' explained the receptionist, with an apologetic look as though it was she who had left him in the lurch.

221

'Did she say when she'd be back?'

'No, but they never do.'

'Okay, thanks, can you let her know I was here?' he said, looking at his watch. It was still only ten to ten. Once outside, Dorsey looked over to the sheriff court building, which was only a two-minute walk away. He decided to take a stroll over and at least have a quick word with her.

There was a queue outside the main entrance as the public went through the usual security checks. Dorsey showed his warrant card and was allowed through a side door by one of the security staff. After checking the court list, the receptionist pointed to courtroom six, which was on the ground floor. The courtroom was open but not in session. Dorsey went in through the public entrance expecting to see a room full of lawyers. But, apart from the clerk, who was busy shifting through a pile of papers on his desk, the court was empty.

'I'm looking for Miss Baxter.'

'And who are you?' asked the clerk, looking up from his desk and peering over his glasses.

'Inspector Dorsey, I was told she was due to appear in here this morning?'

'She has a Proceeds of Crimes hearing before Sheriff Hammond, but it's not due to start for another half hour. You might find her in the canteen.'

The canteen was quiet, with a few lawyers getting their caffeine fix before their cases were due to call. Dorsey saw Miss Baxter sitting on her own drinking coffee, while looking through a substantial buff file. He ordered a coffee and approached her table. 'Morning, Miss Baxter.'

'Oh, Inspector,' she replied slightly startled to see him.

'Do you mind if I join you?'

'No, of course not. Are you here to give evidence today?'

222

'No, we had an appointment this morning at ten.'

'We had?'

'Yes, I was told you wanted an update on the investigation and confirmed the appointment with someone from your office yesterday.'

'No one told me. As you can see, I've got court this morning.'

'I've noticed,' said Dorsey, sipping his coffee as Miss Baxter closed the file in front of her. 'A Proceeds of Crimes case.'

'How did you know that?' she asked, fixing her gown that had slipped off her shoulders.

'I'm a detective,' he replied with a smile. 'You've probably not got time to listen to me at the moment. Will you be free later today?'

'I hope to have this finished for lunchtime. I could meet you at one, if that's any good to you.'

'I'll call in to your office at one. I might've more to tell you by then. I better go and let you prepare for your case. I'll see you at one.'

'Okay, Inspector … I'm sorry about the mix up this morning.'

'No problem, these things happen.'

Before Dorsey reached the car park he got a call from Mitchell. 'Frank, we think we know where the Serbs might be hiding out. The car was caught on a speed camera on the A77 near Kilmarnock, but not on the next camera, which was only one mile along the same road.'

'Maybe they just slowed down?'

'It's not that kind of speed camera. They have average speed cameras there, and the next camera would have picked up the registration number even if they had slowed down. The car must've turned off somewhere between the first and

223

second cameras. The only turn off is to Stewarton. By the way, the registration plates are false.'

'Okay, get someone to check any recently rented houses in that general area, and let me know what you come up with.'

Dorsey hung up and put the phone in his pocket; he had two and a half hours to kill before his meeting with Miss Baxter. He decided to drive to Stewarton on a reconnaissance mission. Once he had found the hideout then he could bring in every available armed officer in Glasgow and Kilmarnock to overwhelm the Serbs with sheer firepower. He could already feel the adrenaline pumping through his body as he rushed across the car park and got into the car.

It had started raining hard just before he turned onto the A77 and headed south. He put on the radio to drown out the sound of the window wipers swishing from side to side. He thought about Miss Baxter again.

He soon passed the Fenwick Hotel which was on the edge of the moors. It wasn't long before he passed the first speed camera and took the turn off to the remote town of Stewarton. The rain was now almost horizontal in the relentless wind that was sweeping across the moors. He was glad he had his old anorak in the boot.

He pulled into a parking bay on the High Street opposite the Millhouse Hotel. He looked at the parked cars on either side of the street. He could see only two blue cars, but neither of them was a Škoda. The town was quiet. There were only a few pedestrians braving the hellish weather. He lit a cigarette and watched a couple more cars passing down the rain-drenched street. His phone buzzed. It was Mitchell again.

'Frank, I think we've got the farmhouse. I've spoken to the local estate agents in Stewarton; they've confirmed that a Mr Dubinsky rented a farmhouse only last week.'

'Dubinsky ... That's the name Kovač used to book into the Marriott,' said Dorsey, throwing his half-smoked cigarette out the window, and taking a pen and notebook from inside his jacket. 'Where is it?'

'It's about two miles down the Kilwinning Road. The farm is just off to the left after a small bridge. Are you still with the PF?'

'No, I'm in Stewarton.'

'Fuck, Frank, don't go near that place until we get there.'

'Get as many armed officers down here a soon as possible, we don't want them slipping through our fingers again, and stop worrying, George.'

'Frank ... !'

Dorsey hung up and pulled back on to the High Street. He felt another rush of adrenaline. He was doing everything he had told his own men not to do, but could not stop himself. He drove slowly along the country road until he reached the bridge. To the left he could just about make out the farmhouse on the hillside through the grey sheets of rain.

Like a military operation being put into action, Strachan barked out orders as the armed units of London Road Police station mustered in the main office, eager to get going. 'Why don't we alert Kilmarnock, they can get an armed unit there in ten minutes,' suggested Mitchell.

'This is our fucking investigation, George. If Dorsey is stupid enough to go near that farmhouse on his own then hell mend him. If they don't kill him then Knox will,' barked Strachan, before turning to address the rest of the team. 'Remember, these guys are professional killers, so don't hesitate to use your firearms if they even look like going for theirs.'

Mitchell, still shaking his head, checked the magazine in his sidearm and followed the others to the waiting police

225

cars. He tried to phone Dorsey again, but there was no answer. 'Fuck, Frank, answer your phone,' he uttered to himself, getting into the backseat of one of the cars with Harper.

Dorsey turned onto the dirt track and drove up a steep slope for over a mile until he came to a fork in the road. The greyness was slashed by a streak of lightning, followed by a growl of thunder. He pulled over, parking the car on a grass verge, before going into the boot to get his waterproof jacket.

Battling the torrential rain, he gradually made his way along the hedgerow until he reached an iron gate. The gate was closed, but it was not padlocked. The words *Beware of the Dog* were painted on a piece of wood tied to the top bar. There in the grey rain was the farmhouse with the blue Škoda parked outside. He had gone as far as common sense would allow, and was just about to walk back to the car when he heard voices. Two men emerged from the house carrying a large storage box, which they put into the boot of the car. It was Petrović and Nedić. They were speaking in their own language and began arguing. Another man appeared at the front door carrying a briefcase, Kovač, mouthed Dorsey. Kovač shouted what sounded like orders to the two men. They stopped arguing. He handed the briefcase to Nedić to put in the boot.

Torn between common sense and stupidity, Dorsey watched them getting into the car. He heard the condescending voice of Knox in his head, 'So you let them slip through your fingers again, Frank.' The Škoda turned slowly towards the gate. Dorsey stood behind the hedgerow to let it pass. He was not feeling suicidal. The car suddenly stopped on the gravel path. Dorsey peered through the wet bushes. Kovač got out and walked back to the house. The Serb must have forgotten something, thought Dorsey, who now remembered his own car was blocking the road. He had to move it before he was discovered. He ran as fast as he could, trying desperately not to lose his footing. The path was muddy and slippery, and he had to jump over puddles in his frantic dash to get to the car. Out of breath, he reached the fork in the road where the car was parked. He couldn't find his keys. The constant rain was affecting his thinking. Where the hell are they? He searched his pockets again, cursing when realising he had left them in the ignition. There was another flash of lightning. He got into the car and turned the engine on. The sky roared.

In spite of the anorak, he was soaking wet and the rain was still running down his face from his saturated hair. He wiped the wet from his eyes. The exhaust coughed, as though the car had caught cold. He reversed, carefully avoiding the ditch to his right. When the car was at least twenty yards back, he stopped. The gears jerked a couple of times as he tried to hold it on the slippery slope. His phone on the passenger seat started buzzing. It was Mitchell. 'Not now, George,' he beseeched under his breath, his heart pounding. In the distance he could see a breach in the sky just above a church steeple, as if someone had torn a dirty piece of wallpaper away to expose another, brighter pattern underneath. He tried to stop his mind wandering. His phone was still buzzing. Then the sound of car doors being banged focused his mind.

From the vantage point of the slope, he could see the progress of the Škoda through the sparse winter hedgerow. He reversed back another few yards. His mind was made up. He put the car into second gear and slammed his foot down on the accelerator.

The impact propelled him forward as the airbag exploded into his face like a giant boxing glove. There was a sharp pain in his side where the seatbelt pulled him back from the steering wheel. He bit his tongue. The taste of blood filled his mouth. Dazed, his ears suddenly popped, as though coming out of water. It was then he heard the Škoda's horn blaring. He pushed the airbag aside, and saw the gaping hole in the hedgerow where he had forced the Serbs off the road. He forced himself out the car in spite of the pain in his ribs. Once outside, he spat a mouthful of blood into the wet grass. Through the gap in the hedgerow he could see the Škoda lying on its roof, with its wheels spinning and windows shattered. The horn was still sounding as though it was calling out for help. He climbed down the slippery grass embankment and into the field, cautiously approaching the driver's side first.

The only man in the car moving was the front seat passenger.

'Don't move!' shouted Dorsey, immediately recognising Kovač.

The Serb was like a fly caught in a spider's web as he tried to right himself and undo the seat belt that was holding him prisoner. Still watching Kovač, Dorsey put his hand inside the driver's coat pocket and removed an Alfa Combat pistol. Nedić groaned, but was too far gone to resist. Dorsey took a closer look into the back of the car, where Petrović was out cold, maybe even dead.

Now with a gun pointing at his head, Kovač soon gave up his struggle to get free. The Serb said something in his own language and smiled. Dorsey carefully checked him for weapons. There was a pistol in a holster under his jacket. Dorsey studied it for a moment, before throwing the Russian-made weapon into the hedgerow. He reached for his handcuffs, but they were gone, probably still in his car.

Exhausted, Dorsey sat on the wet grass verge beside the upturned car. It had suddenly stopped raining. He looked back down the road towards the turn off, but couldn't see very much through the greyness. What the hell was keeping them? He considered going back to look for his handcuffs but was afraid to take his eyes of Kovač in case he had another weapon in the car. He began to feel light-headed, and was fearful he might pass out. His eyes were suddenly tired. He wanted to lie back and close them for a moment.

Kovač was now staring at him with the intensity of a wild animal preparing to pounce on its prey. They kept their eyes on each other as the sky cracked open with another flash of lightening. The gun in Dorsey's hand was beginning to feel heavy.

Chapter 41

Strachan could not believe his eyes when they reached the dirt track and saw half a dozen police cars and two ambulances already parked along the grass verge. He got out of the car he was driving and approached Mitchell in the car behind. 'Did you fucking phone Kilmarnock? When I told you not to … '

'Aye, Charlie, and you can report me it you like.'

'I fucking will,' said Strachan, before walking towards Dorsey's car. The whole front of the passenger's side was crushed and the bonnet was open and bent back on itself. There was still smoke coming from the engine: a write-off. He turned to see the Škoda lying on its roof. Petrović was still being removed from the wreckage by paramedics as two armed officers from Prestwick Airport stood guard with their automatic rifles. Kovač and Nedić were already on their way to Crosshouse Hospital under armed guard.

'Where's Dorsey?' shouted Strachan.

'He's in the farmhouse,' replied one of the Kilmarnock CID officers, carrying bags of cocaine from the upturned car. 'He'll get a fucking medal for this. There's at least twenty kilos of cocaine in the boot of that car and a briefcase of cash that would choke a horse.'

'Was he injured?'

'A few bruised ribs. He was lucky; these guys were armed to the teeth.'

Strachan wiped his mouth; there was nothing he could think to say. He walked up the muddy road in the direction of the farmhouse. He passed another couple of Kilmarnock's finest and could barely acknowledge them as they passed with smiles on their faces. It was as if Dorsey had joined another gang and deprived his own mates of some of the glory. There were two uniformed officers at the front door with semiautomatic rifles nursing on their folded arms. They stood aside.

It was a typical Ayrshire farmhouse, dimly lit with the smell of tractor diesel hanging in the air. Dorsey was sitting on a large oak table in the middle of the room, while a young female paramedic was busy rolling a bandage around his torso.

'Well, well, if it isn't the fucking hero. No wonder you live in Battlefield.'

'I would've waited, Charlie, but they were making a run for it. I'm glad you contacted Kilmarnock; I was about to pass out when they arrived.'

'Don't thank me. Thank your guardian angel, Mitchell.'

'Anyway, Charlie, as they say, all's well that ends well.'

'Are they ours or Kilmarnock's arrests?'

'Ours, I had them under arrest before they got here.'

'Well, I have to hand it to you, Frank, you're something else.'

When the news of the arrests reached Knox, he punched the air, before calming down and telephoning Cullen, who took the news in his stride. 'Well done Andrew, this must be the biggest haul we've had in ten years. The Chief Constable will, no doubt, see this as justification for you taking over from me in the summer. It's a win, win situation for both of us. The one thing about Dorsey is he never fails to surprise me. One minute he's putting his career on the edge of a precipice and the next he's doing something like this. Give him my thanks on behalf of the entire force. We'll live on the publicity from this for months before he fucks up again, but don't tell him I said that.'

'I think we should have a press conference later today to reassure the public that we've these guys in custody.'

'Good idea, Andrew. We should milk this for everything it's worth. Can you make the usual arrangements?'

Dorsey got back to the station to a hero's welcome that he could have done without. His rib cage was hurting bad and he recoiled every time someone came near him to slap him on the back. 'George, tell them to back off,' he said as he deflected another unwelcome embrace. 'Sorry, boss, but you're a legend now,' said Mitchell.

'Right,' shouted Dorsey, as the excitement abated a little, 'The next one of you that slaps me on the back is fired. Now get back to work … Nancy, can you get someone to bring me a coffee?'

'Sir,' said one of the uniformed officers from the front desk. 'You've had three phone calls today from the Procurator Fiscal's office; Miss Baxter wants you to phone her back when you get a minute.'

Dorsey grimaced as he opened the door to his own office. He had forgotten all about their one o'clock appointment. He took a bottle of whisky from the bottom drawer of the only filing cabinet in the office he actually locked. The whisky went down with its usual kick and he felt a sudden pain in his rib cage. The phone on his desk rang.

'Inspector, it's Miss Baxter again.'

'Okay, put her through,' he said preparing his apology for missing their appointment.

'Hello, Inspector … '

'Before you give me a hard time, I'm sorry, Miss Baxter … '

'Don't be sorry, I was just phoning to congratulate you. I hope you're not too badly injured?'

232

'No, but how do you know I was injured?'

'It's all over the evening news. I can't believe that after leaving me this morning you ended up arresting a gang of armed Serbian drug dealers on your own. It's like something out of a comic book.'

'I was lucky, that's all. I just rammed their car off the road. Anyway, I'm surprised you're still working at this time, thought you lawyers were all nine to five.'

'I wish. We have to do unpaid overtime like everyone else these days. Can we meet tomorrow?'

'What time?'

'Let's say, 2 pm.'

'Okay, I'll be there unless anything turns up. I'll phone you if there's a problem, bye.'

'Bye, Inspector, hopefully see you tomorrow.'

Dorsey hung up and took another sip of whisky. The pain in his ribs that disappeared when he was speaking to Miss Baxter suddenly came back with a vengeance. He took some more of the pain killers that the paramedic gave him and washed them down with the whisky. Being the hero did not sit well with Dorsey, but he was glad that Miss Baxter seemed impressed. Apart from the drugs haul, he now had all the suspects for the four murders under armed guard. There was a knock on the door. He put the whisky bottle and empty glass on the floor at his feet. It was Knox, still wearing his full dress uniform.

'How're you, Frank? You look like you've been through the wars.'

'Just a bit sore,' replied Dorsey, putting his hands towards his ribs.

'Maybe you should've gone to hospital.'

'Apparently there's nothing they can do for bruised ribs. I've just got to take it easy for a while.'

'Well, you deserve a rest, Frank. I'm sure Strachan can deal with the investigation until you're fit again.'

'No way, Andrew, I'm in this until the investigation closes and we hand over the files to the Crown Office. There are still interviews to be done.'

'Denis Moffat is likely to make no comment and I'm sure the Serbs will be advised to do the same. You should let the rest of the team handle it.'

'I'm not taking time off 'til they are all charged.'

'Okay ... I've brought this down,' said Knox, producing a bottle of Glenfiddich and two glasses from behind his back.

'We're both off duty, and I thought you could use a drink.'

'You have one,' said Dorsey. 'I've never liked malt whisky. The reason they make blended whisky is because most malts taste awful.'

'Have a drink, Frank,' insisted Knox, opening the bottle and pouring two large measures. Dorsey nodded at the glass that Knox passed to him. 'I hope this is not a trick to get me sacked for drinking while on duty.'

'We're both off duty, Frank.'

'You know and I know that while we're in this station, we're always on duty ... anyway cheers,' said Dorsey, taking his first drink in Knox's company for over a year. 'It's not as bad as I thought.'

'That was a good bit of work you did today, Cullen asked me to pass on his regards. The press conference went well.'

'Another press conference, Andrew, you'll soon be asked to appear on *I'm a Celebrity, Get Me Out of Here!*'

'You're a cynical bastard, Frank; I've got a job to do like everyone else. The press conference was Cullen's idea. We had a responsibility to warn the public about these Serbians being on the loose, and we also have the same responsibility to let the public know that they're under arrest and no

234

longer a danger. Anyway, the media were only interested in your heroics; Cullen has put you forward for a bravery commendation. So cheer up, you miserable bastard,' said Knox, reaching over and clinking his glass against the one Dorsey had just taken from his lips. 'Remember, Frank, we're all in this together.'

'One for all and all for one,' said Dorsey, lifting his glass back to his lips, before emptying it and putting it back down on the table. He put his hand over the empty glass when Knox moved to refill it.

'Have another,' insisted Knox.

'Go on then.'

'Frank, I've a meeting with the Justice Minister tomorrow, he'll be looking for a complete update of the four murder investigations. So what do I tell him?'

'As you already know, we've enough evidence to charge Denis Moffat with the murders of Devlin and Sylvester, but not enough to charge the Serbs with the other two murders. None of the guns recovered is the murder weapon. The Serbs had all Russian-made firearms.'

'That's too bad, they must've got rid of it,' said Knox. 'So we only have them on the drugs and firearms charges?'

'Yes, unless one of the Serbs is prepared to make a deal and testify against the other two.'

'What kind of deal can any of them expect? Dropping a few charges will not make much of a difference to the sentence they'll get.'

'I'm thinking about dropping all charges, if one of them, except Kovač, is willing to give evidence against the other two for the murders of Watson and Tucker.'

'How can we justify that to Cullen? He'll never agree to such a deal.'

'We've done deals like this before, why not now? Without

a deal we don't have enough to charge any of them with the murders. We've no evidence against them other than the CCTV showing them entering and leaving the car park outside Tucker's apartment block on the night he was murdered. There are thirty apartments in that block. There is no proof that they were ever actually in Tucker's flat, never mind murdered him. We've nothing on any of them as far as Watson's murder is concerned. Their defence lawyers will get their own pathologist to dispute the time of death. You know how inconsistent times of death can be when a body has been lying for any length of time. So, unless we offer one of them a deal then both those murders will have to be stuck in the unresolved filing cabinet, because we'll not have enough to charge any of them. We don't have any other suspects, other than the McGowans, and there is absolutely no evidence against them.'

'What about those text messages, do we know anything more about them?'

'We haven't got anywhere with them. Whoever sent them has likely ditched the phone. They might have nothing to do with the case. Who knows?'

'Frank, police work is not a science, sometimes there are things that we just can't get to the bottom of. Even if we don't have enough to charge the Serbians with the two murders, they'll still face serious drug trafficking and firearms charges, no matter what they say in their interviews. They could get anything up to fifteen years each, more than they would probably get if convicted for the murders of Watson and Tucker, so justice will still prevail.'

'God, you sound like a politician,' interrupted Dorsey, with the whisky rising. 'Where's the justice for Watson and Tucker?'

'Sometimes we just have to do our best, and, unless these Serbs start incriminating each other for the murders then we just have to accept what we do have. There's no way Cullen will sanction letting one of them off completely when we have what is stonewall evidence of drug trafficking. Anyway, I better get going, my next train is in fifteen minutes,' said Knox, leaving the bottle of whisky on Dorsey's desk. 'You should get off home and rest, those ribs will be even more painful tomorrow. Remember, if you need to take a few days off; don't even bother to phone in. Strachan can take over 'til you get back. Goodnight, Frank, and well done.'

'Goodnight, Andrew. I'll be in tomorrow if it kills me.'

Now that Knox was gone, Dorsey poured himself another glass of whisky; he was already well over the limit and would have to leave the car, anyway. He opened the file on his desk, which contained the emails from Interpol. He read through the profiles of each of the three Serbians, again. None looked like they would be willing to make any deal to save their own skin. Only Nikola Nedić was actually married with a family back in Bosnia. Could he be the weak link? Even so, Dorsey knew that he would have to convince Knox that the deal was in the public interest. They could give him immunity from prosecution, and still keep him in custody until the trial of the others was over, then send him back to Bosnia to face the charges waiting for him there.

Dorsey got up and put his coat on; he might just have to go over Cullen's head on this one. Surely the Crown Office would see the sense of offering Nedić a deal. After putting the two bottles of whisky into the bottom filing cabinet, he went into the main office. The operations room was quiet for a change with only Harper and Cooper still at their desks. 'Where is everyone?' he asked, looking at his watch.

'Some people have a home to go to,' said Harper, regretting the words as soon as they left her mouth. Too late to retract them, she turned back to her computer.

'Sandy, do you think you could drop me off? I had a few

whiskies with Knox; I don't want to end the day back here in the cells for drink driving.'

'Sure, Frank, I'm finished here anyway.'

Dorsey followed Cooper into the car park. The cold wind caused him to brace himself, and immediately wished he hadn't. 'Ah, fuck,' he moaned.

'Ribs still sore, boss?' Cooper asked, opening the doors of the car with the remote and getting into the driver's side. 'Oh, it's murder, Sandy,' said Dorsey, carefully lowering himself into the passenger's side with a litany of curses on his lips.

'Where're you going, The Barkley or home?' asked Cooper, putting the car into reverse and manoeuvring it onto the side street.

'Home,' replied Dorsey, eventually, after considering the options; feeling a little annoyed that everyone in the station from the cat to the superintendent knew exactly where to find him when he was off duty, either at his flat or The Barkley. Maybe he should change his pub for a while. 'How's your daughter?' he asked hopefully, but with little expectation.

'Just the same, she's not going to come out of it,' replied Cooper, as he turned down High Street and headed towards the Southside. He passed the High Court buildings to his right and the arched entrance to the Green on his left, where Glasgow once hanged its criminals. 'The doctors have asked permission to switch off the respirator, I've agreed, but Rebecca is totally against it. We've had arguments every night about it.'

'I'm really sorry to hear that Sandy. It must be tough on both of you.'

'It's Rebecca I'm worried about; Hannah is gone and she's not coming back. Rebecca is fading away to nothing. I don't want to lose both of them. You know she had a breakdown a few months back?'

'Yes, I heard. It must be tough on you, Sandy, to have to deal with all this?'

'What else can I do?' said Cooper, unable to stop the tears running down his face.

'Pull over for a minute,' said Dorsey.

'Sorry, boss. I'm fine. It's just the constant worry.' 'Pull in here.'

Cooper stopped the car in a bus stop near to the back of The Brazen Head pub and turned off the engine. 'I'm sorry, Frank,' he said wiping the tears from his face. 'I can't bear to lose them both. They're all I've got.'

'Don't be sorry, Sandy' said Dorsey, putting his arm around him, in spite of the pain it caused him to lift it. 'You should take some time off. No one should have to work with what you've got hanging over you.'

'I'm fine, I'm just a bit tired. If I stop work then it'll just make everything worse. I need to take my mind off things, and that only happens when I'm working. The rest of the time I'm just waiting for Hannah to die. I'll take you home, Frank,' added Cooper, wiping his face, before turning the ignition back on. 'God will look after us.'

Chapter 42

Benny parked around the corner from the Venue nightclub on Sauchiehall Street. The head bouncer recognised Benny and nodded for him and Linda to go straight in. There were a few hostile comments from some of those queuing in the freezing cold, but that only made Linda smile.

The DJ was playing *Umbrella*, a song that clearly packed the dance floor. Through the flashing coloured lights Benny saw Scott Rankin at the bar, sipping a ridiculous looking cocktail.

'How are you, Scott?'

'You made it, Benny,' said Rankin, shaking his hand. 'That was top gear you got us. You must have a good source.'

'You know I do, Scott. It was good when I sold you it, but I bet it's now being mixed down to shit.'

'You know how it works, Benny, the stuff you get is already mixed, then you mix it again and we add our own ingredients. It's a bit like Coca Cola; no fucker knows the recipe, and when it reaches the mug in the street—who cares?'

'Hope you kept some of the good stuff for yourself, Scott.'

'Enough, but I'll want another lot by the end of the month. Are you good for it?'

'Sure. What does Craig think of it?'

'He's impressed. Thinks it's much better than the stuff we've been getting lately.'

'Is anybody going to buy me a drink?' moaned Linda,

240

a little annoyed at being ignored as much as not having a drink in her hand. Benny ordered a round of drinks, but Scott nodded to the barman. 'You don't spend a penny in here, Benny, remember that.'

'What if you're not here to tell the barman?'

'I'll let them all know that Benny Moffat's now one of the inner circle. They'll soon get used to you.'

'Cheers,' replied Benny, clicking his bottle of beer with Scott's mojito.

Linda just smiled and sipped her cosmopolitan; she was well aware this was boys talk and decided just to make the most of the free drinks.

'Come with me,' said Scott.

Linda proudly grabbed hold of Benny's left arm as they followed Scott into the piano lounge at the back of the club, where his brother Craig was sitting holding court. He saw Benny with Linda on his arm and got up to meet them. 'Hi, Benny, come and join us … Get up and give them a seat,' he barked at those sitting opposite him.

'It's okay, Craig. We're just having a few drinks.' 'Sit down, Benny. I want to talk to you.'

Benny sat down and Linda took the seat next to him. Craig looked at Linda and then back at Benny.

'Linda's sound, anything you to have to say to me you can say in front of her.'

'Okay, can you get more of this stuff in a few weeks time? We can offload what you gave us no problem.'

'Sure, Craig, same deal, forty grand a kilo,' said Benny, deciding that the 5 kilo he had left was going to turn into 10 as soon as he got back to T-Bone's flat where he stashed it. He was already kicking himself that he had not mixed down the first two kilos. Schoolboy error, too keen to impress the Rankins: he missed a trick.

'Scott thinks we've got a great future together. I've just had another few lines, it's the best of gear,' said Craig, 'I don't know how you managed it, Benny, you've only been out a week and you get hold of stuff that good. You must've some good contacts.'

'Let's put it this way—if you need it, Craig, I'll get you it.'

Chapter 43

Dorsey had a night from hell. His bruised ribs made it impossible for him to lie on his side, and he hated sleeping on his back. Breathing was bad enough but having to get up during the night to go to the toilet was agony. Hoisting himself out of bed for a second time, he was beginning to think it was more than just bruised ribs. Once in the bathroom, he washed down a double dose of painkillers with a drink of tepid water. His tired face stared back at him in the shaving mirror. If he felt the same in the morning, he would have to go to the hospital.

Exhausted, he went back to bed. After a few more moans and groans, he eventually fell asleep. There were no dreams to remember in the morning, just the darkness that engulfed his mind like a shroud.

Suddenly the alarm went off; it rang insistently before he heaved himself over to stop it. He wasn't sure how long he had been sleeping, but it felt like no more than a few hours. He tried to get up, but the pain was excruciating. Falling back onto his pillow, he could have lay like that all day, but the thought of meeting Miss Baxter forced him to get up and sit on the edge of the bed. He was determined to run the idea of immunity by her. If she was against it, then that would be that, but he had a feeling she would take a more pragmatic view of things than Knox, who was only worried how it would look in the media, especially with his promotion looming.

Gritting his teeth until the pain subsided, and now desperate for a smoke, he reached over for the cigarette packet lying on the bedside table, but the packet was empty. The craving for a cigarette gave him the urge needed to force himself out of bed. With another effort he got to his feet and made his way into the bathroom to get ready.

At the station the police van used for transporting prisoners was parked at the back entrance to the cells. Mitchell met him at the charge bar.

'What's going on, George?'

'We've got two of the Serbs here, Kovač and Nedić; the other one is still in hospital. We're waiting for the duty lawyer and an interpreter to get here before we interview them.'

'Good, but I only want them interviewed in relation to the drugs, not the two murders. We can deal with that separately; I need to speak to the Procurator Fiscal first.'

It was another hour before the lawyer turned up. Dorsey went out to the foyer to speak to him. 'My name's Inspector Dorsey, I'm in charge of this investigation.'

'Richard Liddell,' said the lawyer getting to his feet. 'Can you tell me the background?'

'DC Mitchell will fill you in,' said Dorsey, nodding in the direction of Mitchell. The lawyer lifted his briefcase and followed Mitchell into the back office. Dorsey turned to the young woman who was sitting nearby 'Are you the interpreter?'

'Yes, Anna Jakov.'

'Can you wait until Mr Liddell is informed of the charges? We'll then let you and the lawyer have a private meeting with the accused before we interview them.'

'Okay, will I just wait here?' 'Yes.'

Dorsey went back into the charge bar and spoke with the duty sergeant. 'Which cells are Kovač and Nedić in?'

'Kovač is in thirteen and the other one is in fourteen. Are

you alright, Frank? You look awful.'

'Thanks, Harry, my ribs are killing me … I'll be okay, I've taken a few painkillers.'

Dorsey made his way to the cells to see the men that half of Europe had been hunting. He lifted the cover from the spyhole and peered into one of the dimly lit cells. Kovač was lying on a thin blue mattress with his back to the cell door. He looked like a docile bear hibernating in a cave for the winter. Dorsey let the cover drop and crossed the narrow corridor. He looked into cell fourteen, where Nedić was pacing around. Nedić stopped when he realised someone was spying at him. He stared at the spy-hole, before sticking his middle finger up and cursing something in Serbian, and turning his back on the door. He looked rattled. Dorsey let the cover fall back into place and went back to the charge bar, where Mitchell, the lawyer and the interpreter were waiting for him. 'Which one do you want to see?' he asked the lawyer.

'Whichever one you want to interview first, I can only act for one of the accused. I've contacted another solicitor to act for the other one. He'll be here in twenty minutes.'

It was another half hour before Kovač was brought to the interview room under armed guard. Before the interview began he asked for a cigarette, which was refused.

'We're not allowed to smoke in this building or any public building for that matter,' said Dorsey, who would have been quite happy to give Kovač a cigarette, only the lawyer was present. Being a lawyer, he might challenge the interview later, arguing that the cigarette was some kind of inducement. Dorsey had always hated the smoking ban; it was just the politicians being 'goody two shoes' to win votes from the non-smoking majority, but being a police officer, he had no choice but to comply with it, all be it, with a few exceptions. Even so, it was one thing giving the likes of

Massimo Tamburini a couple of cigarettes during an off-the-record interview; this was too serious to take any chances. Kovač just shrugged his shoulders and folded his arms.

'Mr Kovač, we understand you can speak pretty good English, but as is your right, we have an interpreter here to make sure you are fully aware of what's going on. Mr Liddell, the duty lawyer, is also here to give you legal advice, if and when you need it during this interview, which will be tape recorded and may be used in evidence at your trial. Do you understand?' asked Dorsey as the interpreter continued to put his words into Kovač's ear. The Serb made a facial gesture and shook his head.

'I need to know if you understand what I've just said.'

'Go to fuck.'

'I'll take that as a yes.'

'I not answer questions,' said Kovač, ignoring the interpreter and looking at the lawyer for reassurance.

'That's your right Mr Kovač, but I've to put these questions to you. It's your choice whether you answer them or not.'

'I not answer questions.'

Dorsey nodded to Mitchell, who pressed the record button. The overwhelming evidence was put to Kovač, who declined to say anything in response. Dorsey had conducted hundreds of interviews like this, and simply carried on putting questions in spite of the Serb's silence. After twenty minutes of this, Kovač was formally charged with twenty-two charges in connection with the substantial drugs haul, the six firearms, and the numerous false passports, driving licences and credit cards recovered. When each charge was read to him, Kovač was asked if he wished to comment, but he showed no emotion and said nothing.

Once Kovač was returned to his cell, Dorsey went

through the same procedure with Nedić, who also followed his lawyer's advice and declined to answer any questions. The only difference was that Nedić looked frightened.

After Nedić was taken back to the cell, Dorsey sat back in his chair and put his hands through his hair. Even without any admissions by the accused, he knew he had enough evidence against all three Serbs to put them away from a long, long time. Now that Nedić was aware of the charges he faced, Dorsey was itching to speak to him alone about the Watson and Tucker murders, but he had to get the okay from the Procurator Fiscal before he made the Serb any offer of immunity. This time there would be no lawyer contacted. According to the information sent by Interpol, Nedić's English was not as good as Kovač's, but he would have little difficulty understanding the deal if put to him in plain language. In the meantime, it would do no harm to let him stew for a while longer. He was hopeful that once the realisation of his predicament began to sink in, Nedić would be tempted to make a deal.

'George, can you let Knox know the outcome of the interview and what we've charged these two with? I've got a meeting with the P.F.'

'Another one? I thought you met her yesterday.'

'She couldn't make it; she had a court case on. How do you think I managed to end up in Stewarton? I'll be back in a few hours.'

'Okay, Frank. If anything comes up I'll phone you.'

Miss Baxter met Dorsey at the reception and they took the lift to the second floor. The room was not the one they were in on the last occasion. There were files piled on the desk and on the floor, enough to give anyone a headache. 'You've changed office,' he said as she took her seat behind the desk.

'Yes, just for a couple of days, the other office is being refurbished. Take a seat, Inspector.'

247

'There've been developments in relation to all four murders. We've enough evidence to charge Denis Moffat with the murders of both Devlin and Sylvester. We've the murder weapon, a Beretta, found in his back garden. He's in hospital recovering from a minor stroke. We're waiting to question him and obtain a DNA sample to compare it with the DNA found on the cigar butt.'

'That sounds like a solid case against Moffat, especially if the DNA is his. What about the other two murders?'

'As you know, the Serbs we arrested yesterday for the drugs and firearms charges are the prime suspects in both the Watson and Tucker murders. But the little evidence we have, only relates to them being caught on CCTV going into the car park in front of the block of flats where Tucker's body was found. Professor Jenkins has confirmed the *M.O.* of both murders is the same and estimates the time of death of Tucker was near to the time the Serbs were caught on CCTV.'

'Is that all you've got on them?'

'That's it, and I'm all too aware that it's not even enough to charge any of them with either murder, but they're the only suspects we have.'

'What would've been their motive?'

'Drugs … They were obviously trying to take over Moffat's territory. Moffat must've thought it was McGowan, which gives Moffat the motive for killing two of McGowan's dealers.'

'Are any of the Serbians likely to give more than a no comment interview?'

'No, I've already interviewed and charged two of them in connection with the drugs and weapons. They declined to comment. The other one is still in Crosshouse Hospital under armed guard.'

'Where *you* put him.'

'You could say that.'

'How're you today? Have you recovered from your ordeal?'

'I'm fine, ribs are still a bit of a problem,' he said, 'but there's nothing to worry about.'

'Good. Is there any possibility that one of them might take a deal?'

Dorsey smiled. He was relieved that she brought up what he was trying to work his way towards. She looked at him and waited for an answer, wondering why he was smiling.

'A deal?' he said finally.

'Well, what's so funny, Inspector? Did I say something silly?'

'No, the complete opposite, I was going to ask if you thought a deal would be something the Crown Office would consider. I wasn't expecting you to bring it up; that's why I smiled.'

'Well, I'm glad to see that I can get you to smile so easily. So, you think one of them might be willing to take a deal?'

'There's only one thing we can offer and that's immunity. Anything less will be a waste of time.'

'If one's prepared to give evidence against the other two for both murders then I think the Crown Office would be willing to give you the authority to make such an offer, but only if the evidence is unequivocal and is likely to lead to the conviction of the other two.'

'Have I got the green light to sound them out?'

'Yes, but don't offer the deal to Kovač. I've read his file. He's the brains and the most dangerous of these three men.'

'I wasn't planning to offer Kovač anything; I don't think Petrović will go for a deal. He's Kovač's nephew. Nedić may be willing to testify. He has a wife and two sons back in Bosnia. Even if we drop the charges there're always the outstanding Bosnian warrants, we can just send him back to them after the trial of the others. I'm sure he'd rather be in a Bosnian prison, near his family, than stuck in a Scottish prison for the next fifteen years. So, I can speak to him when I get back to the station?'

'No, not yet,' she said, reconsidering things, 'just to be on the safe side, wait 'til I get the Crown Office to agree to it first. I'll speak to the Lord Advocate.'

'I'll be waiting to hear from you, Miss Baxter. I guess I better get off and let you get on with your work, you look like you've got a lot on,' said Dorsey, getting to his feet rather too quickly. The sudden movement caused the pain that had been dormant during their chat, to come back. He let out a groan as he grabbed the front of the desk to steady himself. The blood drained from his face.

'Are you alright, Inspector?'

'It's my ribs; it'll pass in a minute.'

'Is there anything I can do?' she asked, getting to her feet.

'No, it's okay, I've got some painkillers,' he said, rummaging through his coat pockets.

Miss Baxter handed him the bottle of mineral water from her desk and he took the tablets with a gulp. 'I'm sorry,' he said, handing her back the bottle.

'Don't be silly, you must be in a lot of pain. Most people wouldn't even be at work in your condition. Here take that with you to take your painkillers,' she said handing him the bottle back. 'Maybe you should go to the hospital.'

'No, I'm okay, it's only bruised ribs. It was good to meet you again. I'll wait for your call.'

Dorsey was still trying to get used to various buttons and knobs on his new BMW dashboard. Although it had all the latest gadgets, he still preferred his old car. His ribs were still hurting, and he sat for about ten minutes until the pain eased off a little. He then drove slowly back to the station, every bump in the road causing his sides to hurt that little bit more. Not wanting to go through the awkward manoeuvring to get into his usual space in the car park he pulled up in the side street next to the station. He was just about to get out of the car when his mobile buzzed. He tried three pockets before finding it in his inside jacket pocket. 'Inspector Dorsey, Police Scotland.'

'Hello again, Inspector. It's Liz Baxter here.'

'Hello, Miss Baxter, didn't expect to hear from you so soon.'

'I phoned Edinburgh just after you left and spoke to the Crown Office. They've agreed to offer immunity to Nedić so long as it's conditional on him turning Queen's evidence, not only for the murders but for all the charges the Serbians already face, and that he agrees to be extradited on the Interpol warrant without a fuss.'

'Good … I'll let you know how I get on.'

Chapter 44

Nedić was taken to a holding cell while Dorsey and Mitchell discussed the best way to sell the deal to him. They decided to let him see the video of the van entering the car park and then the one at the petrol station to see his reaction. Mitchell set up the video player before bringing Nedić into the interview room where Dorsey was waiting with an ashtray on the table. He offered the Serb a cigarette, which he took in one of his cuffed hands.

'Nikola,' began Dorsey, 'I know you speak a little English and I'll make this as straight forward as I can. You don't have to say anything, but listen to what I've to say, it may be in your interest.' Nedić exhaled a plume of smoke. 'You've been charged with very serious offences today, and in spite of what your lawyer may've told you, you're looking at ten to fifteen years in prison. Do you understand what I'm saying?'

The Serbian showed no emotion and simply took another draw from the cigarette. Dorsey looked at Mitchell, who shrugged his shoulders.

'I'm in a position to drop all those charges if you're prepared to give evidence against Kovač and Petrović.' Dorsey got his first reaction, which sounded like a curse. *At least he understands English*, thought Dorsey, edging towards what he was prepared to offer. 'You've a family in Bosnia,' said Dorsey, taking the photograph of Nedić with his wife and two sons from the file. He moved the picture towards Nedić, who stared down at it like a holy relic. Dorsey then turned and switched on the video player and said nothing as Nedić looked from the picture to the small monitor on the table. They watched in silence as the white van appeared and entered the car park. Dorsey fast forwarded the video to show them leaving. He then played the video of Kovač at the petrol station, but there was still no reaction as Mitchell stood with his notebook and pen in hand. 'What were you and the others doing that night?'

There was no answer as Nedić's gaze went back to the picture on the table. Dorsey removed the picture and handed it to Mitchell, before producing the mortuary still of both Watson and Tucker. The Serb looked at the pictures and then at Dorsey, his expression was one of bewilderment.

'Look at them,' insisted Mitchell, when Nedić looked down at his handcuffed hands and bowed his head.

'Look at them!'

'We believe that you and your two comrades murdered both these men to take over the drugs trade in the East End of Glasgow. I've the authority to give you immunity from prosecution if you confess to your part in these murders and you're also prepared to give evidence against Kovač and Petrović. Do you understand?'

'Mr Policeman, we've not murdered anyone in your country. These pictures prove nothing,' said Nedić, his English better than Dorsey had expected.

'But you've murdered plenty of women and children in Bosnia, you fucker,' interrupted Mitchell.

'George, go and take some fresh air,' said Dorsey, more than a little annoyed at Mitchell's outburst, just when he had the Serb talking. Mitchell left his notebook and pen on the table and left without saying another word.

'You show me a picture of my family and you expect me to betray my comrades. What kind of man do you think I am, Mr Policeman?'

'Your children will be middle-aged by the time you get

out of prison and your wife …'

'My wife and my children are dead. They were killed during the war. So you cannot blackmail me. I've no reason to want to go back to Bosnia. I've no fear of going to prison in Scotland, so you are wasting your time. But I'll tell you this; you're looking in the wrong direction. We've not killed anyone. We did not have to.'

'But why were you at these apartments on the night this man was murdered there?' asked Dorsey, pushing forward the photograph of Tucker.

'What apartments, we were not at any apartments. This is ridiculous. If you're finished trying to bribe me then I'd like to go back to my cell.'

'This van went into this car park and stayed there for around ten minutes before it was caught on video leaving. We believe that this man was killed during that time,' said Dorsey tapping the morgue photograph of Tucker with his fingers, to emphasize his point. 'So, why were you there?'

'Coincidence, Mr Policeman. We were lost and had to look up a map to find where we were. That's all. We did not murder anyone, and this proves nothing.'

'Okay,' said Dorsey, 'do you want to keep this?' he asked taking the photograph from Mitchell's abandoned notebook and placing it in the Serb's cuffed hands.

'Thank you. We did not kill anyone, Mr Policeman. That's all I can tell you. I have no reason to lie.'

Once Nedić was returned to his cell, Dorsey went in search of Mitchell, who he found still standing at the front of the building in the freezing cold without a coat on. 'Is this your fucking penance, George? What the hell was that all about?'

'I'm sorry, boss, I looked up the Bosnian War on the internet last night. Some of the things those bastards did was barbaric.'

'George, you're a professional police officer, if that was a formal taped recorded interview where the fuck would that leave us?'

'But that's it, Frank. It wasn't formal or tape recorded, it was a seedy deal to let that bastard off completely.'

'Damn it, George, don't let it happen again. Anyway, there's no damage done. There isn't going to be any deal. He denies any knowledge of the murders, maybe we've been barking up the wrong tree.'

'What about the white van being there that night?'

'Maybe, like Nedić said, it's nothing but a coincidence.'

'And you believe him?'

'George, I'm just not so sure anymore. We tried to bribe him with the photograph of his wife and kids, using them as a carrot to get a deal. Some fucking carrot, they were all killed during the Bosnian War.'

'Shit,' said Mitchell as he followed Dorsey back into the station.

'George, can you check with the hospital and see if Moffat is well enough to be interviewed. The way our luck is going, he's probably kicked the bucket.'

After a quick coffee, Dorsey went back into his own office to think things over; he decided there was no point in phoning Liz Baxter with an update until they had interviewed the other Serb who was still in hospital. Now the gift of offering immunity was in his hands he was not going to throw it away until it had become totally useless. His ribs were hurting again, and he was tempted to take a nip of whisky, but the pain subsided a little and so did the urge. The phone on the table began to ring. He lifted the receiver. 'Sir, you need to come down to the cells, one of the Serbs has cut his throat!'

Dorsey rushed down to the cells; this was the last thing he needed. The duty sergeant was flushed faced and his hand was shaking as he handed Dorsey the picture of Nedić and his young family. 'That was lying beside him. How the hell did he get that and a Stanley knife into the cells? How do I explain this to Knox?'

Dorsey said nothing; he was rooted to the spot, staring at the photograph.

Chapter 45

Denis Moffat was desperately looking for the remote control to change the television channel. 'Which one of you old bastards had the fucking thing,' he demanded, before noticing the doctor and nurse standing at the open, ward door.

'You've made a remarkable recovery, Mr Moffat,' said the doctor. 'But I think you should get back into your bed. The nurse will change the channel for you.'

'Okay, doctor … *Rio Grande* is on at half-three, it's one of my favourite films. I'm going to miss the start.'

'But does anyone else wish to watch it?' asked the nurse, lifting the remote from the windowsill, where Denis had forgotten he had left it. With no response from the three other patients, she turned the channel as the credits for the film appeared.

The doctor gave Denis a cursory examination, apart from stiffness to the left side of his body he looked in pretty good shape. 'You'll be glad to know that you're well enough to go home tomorrow, Mr Moffat.'

'Tomorrow,' repeated Denis, with one eye on the film.

'Yes, you have been very lucky. You had a transient ischemic attack.'

'What's that? I thought I'd a stroke?'

'It's similar to a stroke, but not as serious. You should rest for a few weeks when you get home. You've been given a warning and the next time you might not be so fortunate,' said the doctor, removing his stethoscope from his distracted patient's chest and buttoning up the pyjama top. 'If your wife hadn't called the ambulance when she did, you might've been left with permanent paralysis to your left side. You must also stop smoking or you will have a stroke.'

'Sure, doctor,' said Denis, who was already looking forward to the cigar he was planning to smoke as soon as he was discharged.

Once the doctor had gone Denis watched the rest of the film until John Wayne finally rode off through the Nevada desert, and into the sunset. Now feeling tired, he struggled to watch the news programme that followed. He was about to close his eyes, but suddenly became alert when the newsreader confirmed that a gang of Serbians were arrested on serious drug and firearms charges. He took the mobile phone from under his pillow that Irene had left behind and pressed the redial.

'Benny, I'm getting out tomorrow. The doctor said there's fuck-all up with me. Can you pick me up?'

'That's great news, Dad. Of course I'll pick you up, what time?'

'Be here about eight … Have ye seen the evening news?'

'No, what's wrong?'

'A bunch of Serbians have been arrested with a boot full of cocaine and guns.'

'Aye, what's that to do with us?'

'It said they had links to East End gangs. It must've been them and no' the Romanians that were trying to move into our patch and take over. But who the fuck did they've links with?'

'I don't think they were trying to move in on our patch.'

'What else were they trying to do?'

'If they were caught with cocaine, then the last place they'd try and sell it is in the East End. Coke is sold in the clubs and bars in the city centre, not in the schemes.'

'Do you think Watson and Tucker were working for them?'

'No way, Watson and Tucker would never get past the bouncers to sell anything in the clubs. They were only selling tenner bags to smackheads. Dad, let me put it this way, the Serbs were here to sell in bulk to anyone with the money to buy it.'

'How do you know what they were doing?'

'Dad, I'll let you know what I know when I pick you up tomorrow.'

'Before you go, did you do what I asked you to do?'

'Aye, don't worry; it's as clean as a whistle. I'll see you tomorrow.'

Denis put the phone back under his pillow. He felt that things were happening around him and that he was the last one to know. Was he just getting old? He wiped some spit from the side of his mouth and lamented his youth.

Chapter 46

There was a feeling of despair in the station. The police surgeon had already confirmed that Nedić had severed his carotid artery and would have died very quickly. The body was stripped and removed to the morgue in a black body bag. Dorsey watched one of the turnkeys mopping up the pool of blood from the cell floor as he tried to understand why Nedić would do such a thing. Kovač was shouting from his cell demanding to know what had happened, but his concerns were ignored.

'Knox is going to hit the roof when he hears about this,' said Mitchell, following Dorsey back into the main office. 'Where is he anyway?'

'He's at HQ; he'd a meeting with Cullen and the Justice Minister.'

Dorsey went to the charge bar where the deceased's clothes were being searched. The sergeant shrugged his shoulders and shook his head. He was at a loss as to how Nedić had managed to smuggle the Stanley blade into his cell. Dorsey went behind the charge bar and viewed the CCTV of the Serb's search. It seemed thorough enough.

Kovač was immediately removed from his cell and strip searched. There was nothing sinister found. The knowledge that his friend had committed suicide had subdued him. 'I want to speak to someone,' said Kovač, as he was handed a white paper suit to wear.

Dorsey closed the interview room door behind Kovač, who looked less sure of himself. There was silence as they sat opposite each other. It was the Serb who spoke first.

'Why did my friend kill himself?'

'I don't know, I thought you might be able to tell me?'

'Did you threaten him?'

'We don't threaten anyone. We only ask questions. He knew that he was facing a long time in prison, maybe it was that that made him take his life. I don't know. We know he spoke to you in Serbian when he was led back to his cell. What did he say?'

'He told me you were accusing us of two murders. What murders?'

'We've evidence that you and your comrades were seen in the car park of a block of apartments where the body of a local drug dealer was found. His friend was also murdered on the same night with the same murder weapon.'

'What are you talking about? We have not murdered anyone. Where is your proof?'

Dorsey pressed the play button on the video recorder. He was not expecting to have this conversation with Kovač and was already on thin ice for not taping the Nedić interview with a corroboration officer present. Now he was taking an even greater risk with Kovač as Mitchell stood in the corridor to warn him if Knox suddenly appeared in the office. They watched the monitor in silence. Dorsey studied the same bemused look from Kovač that he saw on Nedić's face earlier. When he pressed the stop button, Kovač sat back in his seat and shook his head. 'What is any of this to do with murder?'

'You tell me,' said Dorsey rather hopefully.

'I have nothing to tell you.'

'A young man, by the name of William Tucker, was murdered around midnight in one of the flats.'

'And you think we killed him?'

'Yes, and killed his friend, Norman Watson the same night?'

'This is not true. I know I am going to prison, maybe for the rest of my life, but we did not kill anyone.'

'So why were you there?'

'What do I get if I tell you? I know you offered Nedić something.'

Dorsey sat back. Was this the time to get Mitchell back in and get the tape on or was Kovač simply playing games? He could not offer him immunity; Miss Baxter had made that all too clear. Anything the Serb said at the moment was off the record and of absolutely no value as evidence. He could feel the thin ice under his feet begin to crack.

'There's nothing I can offer you that'll get you out of the drug charges you're facing, but if you're prepared to tell me that you and your comrades were responsible for these murders, then I'll speak to the prosecutors. They may be prepared to offer you something. What do you want?'

'I want absolutely nothing. You tried the same thing with Nikola. We did not murder anyone, but to stop you from making a fool of yourself I tell you why we were there.'

'Go on,' said Dorsey, trying to remain calm, as his heart began to race ahead of itself.

'We were looking for someone in connection with the drugs. Nikola got lost and we turned off the road to check the directions.'

'Who were you meeting that night?'

'Who we were meeting doesn't matter. He was merely the go between. They wanted to test the cocaine before they made arrangements to buy it. That's why we were there that night. We were lost.'

'Who wanted to buy the drugs?'

'That I cannot tell you.'

262

'Was it someone by the name of Moffat?'

'What do you take me for? I thought you were only interested in these murders. You wanted to know why we were there that night, and I've told you. If you don't believe me then that's your problem. We had not killed these two men. I've nothing more to say.'

Dorsey got to his feet and opened the door. Mitchell looked at him expectantly. 'George, take him back to his cell.'

With Kovač gone, Dorsey sat back down in the interview room and tried to make sense of what the Serb had told him. It was the same as what Nedić had said. Did he believe them? Had he got it so wrong? There was nothing else to link them with the murders. Did they really have a motive to kill two of Moffat's heroin dealers if they were selling large quantities of cocaine wholesale? While he was pondering the possibilities Mitchell returned. 'You're taking a big gamble, Frank; you know we can't use anything he said in court.'

'I know, but he didn't admit to the murders anyway.'

'So we're back to square one.'

'It looks that way. We don't have enough to charge him or Petrović with either murder.'

'I take it Knox isn't back yet?'

'No, he phoned earlier to get someone to go and pick him up. Harper went to get him about ten minutes ago. He should be here shortly.'

Dorsey got to his feet, and walked passed Mitchell and into the main office, still trying to make up his mind which way the investigation should go.

'Right, everyone, gather 'round,' he shouted, in his no mood for nonsense voice. 'You all know that Nikola Nedić, one of the Serbians has committed suicide in the cells. What you may not know is that I interviewed him only half an hour earlier and offered him immunity if he was willing to give evidence against the other two. He refused. He denied that any of them were involved in the murders of Watson and Tucker. He was also adamant that he'd no reason to lie. I also questioned Kovač, who gave the same reason why they were at the Lomond flats that night. He insists they were merely looking to meet someone in connection with a drug deal and that they got lost. Who they were looking for was a go-between. If they were in that area looking to offload drugs, it was probably someone connected with the Moffats. With the amount of drugs they were trying to offload, it would have to be someone reasonably high up in the Moffat clan. I am no longer certain that the Serbs had anything to do with these murders. There is nothing other than the van being in the car park for around ten minutes on the same night of the murders. We've no forensics to confirm that they were ever in Tucker's flat that night, and there's absolutely nothing to link them with Watson.'

'What about the McGowans? I still think they're behind this.'

'Okay, Charlie, let me finish. The Serbs were not looking to peddle tenner bags of heroin, but large quantities of cocaine, so why would they've an interest in these two? They're not even in the same league. Like Nedić said, it was just a coincidence the white van was there that night. We have to widen this investigation and check over everything that we have already to see if we've missed anything … Any questions?'

'What about the McGowans?' repeated Strachan, still a little aggrieved at the earlier rebuke, but not wanting the others to know that it annoyed him. 'I think we should at least put them under surveillance to see what they're up to.'

'Okay, Charlie, you can get the surveillance procedure up and running tonight.'

'Do any of you have anything to say?' There was no response. 'Well, let's get back to work.'

After his address to the squad, Dorsey went upstairs to his office to prepare himself for Knox's imminent return from HQ. The bottle of whisky was tempting him from the bottom drawer. He got up and looked out the window. It was a miserable day. He looked down the road to where the bulldozers had demolished some of the slums that had been lying empty for years. He then thought about Nedić being taken to the morgue. He could see the suicide all over the newspaper in the morning and there was very little spin he could put on it. Nedić was in custody and should never have been in possession of a blade. What if he had used it to try and escape? The thought that he or Mitchell could have been slashed across the face during the interview suddenly made him succumb to the bottle in the bottom drawer.

When Knox arrived back at the station, the duty sergeant asked to speak with him in private. No doubt, hoping to mitigate his responsibility for what had happened as much as possible. The idea of it being a private chat was soon blown away. Even Dorsey, in his first floor office, could hear Knox's tirade of abuse at the unlucky sergeant. Dorsey put the bottle back in the drawer and locked the filling cabinet. He then waited for the hurricane that was Andrew Knox, whenever his career prospects were in jeopardy. Something like this could sink his promotion, and Knox knew it as soon as he received the call from Strachan. Everyone was on edge as the superintendent went from one part of the station to another, looking for someone to blame. 'Where's Inspector Dorsey?' he demanded when he entered the subdued operations room.

'He's upstairs in his office,' replied Strachan.

Dorsey could hear Knox climbing up the stairs, each step echoing up the stairwell and along the corridor. He knew he was coming for him, guns blazing. Dorsey looked up at the clock on the wall opposite, it was only seconds away from six o'clock, not exactly high noon, but as both hands reached a perfect posture, Dorsey sat back and drew breath. The door opened without the courtesy of a knock.

'Frank, what the fuck's been going on here?'

'Sit down before you blow a gasket, Andrew.'

'How the hell did he get a blade into the cells area?'

'We don't know.'

'What do you mean you don't know, was he searched or not?'

'Of course he was searched, but he wasn't strip searched. There didn't seem any need to at the time. He must've had it stashed down his bollocks.'

'Fuck … Why'd you interview him again after his lawyer left?'

'I guess Strachan told you that.'

'What does it matter who told me, why'd you interview him without his lawyer present?'

'I offered him an immunity deal to turn Queen's evidence against the other two Serbs for the murders of Watson and Tucker.'

'So, while I'm meeting with Cullen and the Justice Minister, you're here going against what I said this morning and offering immunity … Where'd you get the right to make such an offer without Cullen agreeing to it?'

'From the Procurator Fiscal, she got the green light from the Lord Advocate to offer immunity.'

'So, Frank, you not only went over my head, but you went over Cullen's head and went to the bloody Lord Advocate.'
'No, you're wrong, Andrew; it was Miss Baxter, who suggested it during our meeting. It was you who wanted me to update her about the investigation. You weren't here when I got back, so I offered Nedić the deal, but he wasn't interested. He was obviously making his own plans for his

future.'

'What do I say to Cullen?'

'Just tell him the truth. If you want to blame anyone just blame Nedić, he was going to kill himself one way or another, it's just unfortunate that he did it here and not in Barlinnie.'

'Why'd it have to happen now?'

'It'll blow over long before your promotion comes up.' 'I bloody hope so.'

'It's just one of these things, Andrew. Yesterday you had a good press conference, tomorrow maybe not so good.'

'Are you mocking me, Frank?'

'No, but that's what this job's been like since the day I joined: one day good, the next shit. We just have to deal with the good and bad, because like yin and yang they're part of the whole set-up and go hand-in-hand.'

'Have you been drinking?'

'It's after six and we're both off duty, you may as well have a drink with me.'

Dorsey got up and brought out the bottle from the bottom drawer for the third time that day. He poured Knox and himself a decent glass. 'There, Andrew, get that down you. We can't change what happened, we just have to deal with it and get on with our jobs.'

'How do we explain it to the Press?' asked Knox, taking the glass of whisky.

'We've just had the biggest drug haul in years and we've stopped a gang of Serbian war criminals from flooding the streets of Glasgow with 22 kilos of cocaine. Concentrate on the positive, Andrew. The fact that Nedić took his own life was his decision. You've a whole team of spin doctors; make them earn their big salaries.'

By now, with another sip of whisky, Dorsey was beginning

to convince himself that the whole thing would blow over in a few days and he would be reading about Nedić's suicide through grease and vinegar stains when he bought his next fish supper out of Giuseppe's chip shop. Whisky had that way with it. The phone suddenly rang on his desk. Knox nodded for him to take the call.

'Tomorrow, what time? Okay, thanks Nancy,' said Dorsey, before putting down the receiver. 'The hospital has just confirmed that Moffat is being discharged tomorrow morning. We'll have him brought in for questioning as soon as he's out of his pyjamas.'

'Well, that's something. Don't go too hard on him, we have enough evidence to nail him already. I don't want him having a relapse and dropping dead in the cells on us.'

'Don't worry, Andrew. All I need is his DNA sample.'

'I better go and get my train, my wife has got yoga classes tonight,' said Knox, the whisky making his mood a little more mellow. 'I guess you're right, Frank. We'll just have to deal with it as best we can … yin and yang, what the hell does that mean, anyway?'

'Haven't a clue,' said Dorsey as he watched Knox get up and take his leave with none of the drama of his arrival.

Chapter 47

After a few drinks in the pub Dorsey took a taxi home and was soon fast asleep on the living room couch with the television still on and a can of beer overturned on the carpet. He dreamed of happier times when he was able to sit down at a table with his wife and son and have dinner. But those dreams were becoming few and far between. This illusion of domestic bliss was suddenly usurped by the lifeless body of Nedić; the blood still spouting from the Serb's lacerated neck. Dorsey tried to waken, but his mind was too heavy to get itself out of the unfolding horror that made him call out. There was no one in the flat to hear him and he continued to shout and swear until the spell of nightmare finally broke.

He only woke when his phone started buzzing. He sat up holding his ribs, before putting his bare feet on the wet carpet where the beer was spilled earlier. Somehow he had managed to get the bottom half of his clothes off and was sitting in his underpants with his shirt and tie still on. The mobile phone stopped ringing. He lifted the upturned can of lager, now empty, and put it on the coffee table with the rest of the rubbish that had accumulated there. The phone began buzzing again and he lifted his jacket from the floor. It was Mitchell.

'What's it, George?' he asked with his usual laconic brevity.

'I'm sitting outside. Remember we have Moffat to

interview this morning.'

'I'll be down in ten minutes.'

Mitchell could smell the drink from Dorsey when he got into the car but said nothing. What was the point? He was now worried that his boss was drinking himself into an early grave. They headed for the station in silence. At least Knox was at a fatal accident enquiry that morning, but it would only be a matter of time before Dorsey's luck ran out.

It was a miserable day and the sky was threatening to off load a deluge. Mitchell parked in the lane at the back of the station and followed Dorsey into the operations room.

'Is there someone at the hospital to bring Moffat in?' shouted Dorsey.

'Harper and Cooper, sir,' replied one of the clerical staff, who was busy typing up statements. 'They went there first thing this morning.'

'Thanks Nancy, sorry for shouting … Can you get me a coffee?'

It was another hour before Denis Moffat arrived in handcuffs. Some in the station stopped what they were doing to go and have a look at the man they had all heard about, but few had actually been up this close to. Moffat had not lost his power to intimidate, and he turned to look at his audience with his dark, defiant eyes. 'What the fuck are you lot looking at? Have you never seen an innocent man being framed before?'

'Right you lot, back to work,' shouted Dorsey when he entered the cells area from another door.

'Is this your doing, Inspector? Arresting an innocent man from his hospital bed?'

'Harry, contact his lawyer as soon as possible. Tell him his client is being interviewed this morning,' said Dorsey, ignoring Moffat, before returning to the main ground floor office, where Mitchell was trying to make sense of the incident boards, which were now crowded with photographs. It was twenty minutes later when Moffat's solicitor arrived out of breath and a little agitated-looking. It was not Phillip Stanton, the solicitor that Moffat demanded, but one of the firm's assistants, who was clearly out of his depth. He was immediately told by Dorsey the nature of the allegations and then taken to the cells to have a private consultation with his client. What normally took ten minutes lasted half an hour, and Moffat and the young lawyer could be heard arguing with each other in the cell.

'Harry, you better go and rescue the lawyer before Denis knocks his lights out,' said Dorsey, 'and bring them into the interview room once Moffat has calmed down. George, can you go to the productions room and bring up the Beretta and the cigar butt?'

Mitchell returned with the productions just as the lawyer and Moffat were brought into the interview room where Dorsey was already sitting waiting, silently going over the questions he intended to ask. 'Sit down, Mr Moffat. You're here to be asked questions in relation to two murders.'

'Listen, Dorsey, this is a lot of fucking bullshit and you know it.'

'Mr Moffat, remember what I said,' interrupted the lawyer.

'Just be quiet, son,' said Denis, 'I'm talking to the Inspector.' The lawyer shook his head but said nothing more.

'You'll get your chance to say your piece in a minute,' said Dorsey nodding towards Mitchell to switch the tape on.

After completing the preliminary procedure, Dorsey began the interview in earnest.

'Mr Moffat, you were arrested at 9:15 this morning. Is that correct?'

'You forgot to mention I was still in my hospital bed when you lot turned up.'

'Okay, you were arrested at the Royal Infirmary after you were discharged by the hospital … is that correct?'

'If you say so.'

'I intend to question you about two murders. The first being that of Robert Devlin and the second being that of James Sylvester, did you know either of these persons prior to their deaths?'

'No, never heard of either of them. Like everybody else, I only read about them in the newspapers. It's got nothing to do with me.'

'What's got nothing to do with you?'

'Who ever killed these guys, it was no' me … why would I? I'm a respectable businessman.'

'Mr Moffat we've evidence that you murdered both Robert Devlin and James Sylvester.'

'What evidence?'

Dorsey turned towards Mitchell, who handed him the production bag containing the Beretta, which Dorsey put on the table in front of Moffat. 'This gun was recovered from your back garden, concealed in a bin liner under a slab in your patio. It has been forensically tested with the two bullets found at both crime scenes and the ballistic examinations have confirmed that they were fired by this gun.'

'Is that all you've got, Inspector? That's not my gun. Someone's planted it in my back garden to frame me. If you can't see that then the two of you are fucking blind or in on it. My QC will blow this out of the water and you know it, so can I go now? I've got a wife waiting for me at home.'

'Sit where you are, Mr Moffat,' insisted Dorsey as Mitchell handed him the smaller of the two production bags. 'This was found at the locus where Sylvester was murdered.

It's a cigar butt. Both bodies had post-mortem burns on them from a similar size cigar.'

'And you think that's my cigar?'

'We don't know if it's your cigar, but if you provide a DNA swab then we can check it with your own DNA,' said Dorsey; sure he would refuse to provide a sample. 'If you don't, your refusal can be used in evidence that may make a jury believe it is your cigar butt. That, along with the Beretta, would almost certainly result in your conviction for both murders.'

'Inspector, it's no' my gun and it's no' my cigar butt. I'll give you a DNA sample, no problem.'

'Mr Moffat, you don't have to provide a sample,' said the lawyer, 'they can't force you to.'

'I've got nothing to hide.'

'My colleague will take a sample and it will only take a few minutes,' said Dorsey, sitting back to let Mitchell take the samples from Denis Moffat's mouth. The procedure took no more than five minutes as the swabs were bagged and signed before the accused and the lawyer. 'Mr Moffat, these swabs will be taken to the forensic lab straight away and we should've the results back within a couple of hours. We'll stop this interview now and resume it when we've the results of the DNA tests. In the meantime, you're still under detention and will be returned to your cell.'

While Mitchell took the saliva samples to forensics to have the DNA analysed, Dorsey got on the phone to the lab, insisting that they treat the DNA sample with the utmost urgency. The phone call did the trick and he went downstairs to study the incident boards to keep himself occupied until the results came back. He took a deep breath when he noticed that someone had put up the picture of Nedić with his young family. Would Nedić have killed himself if he had not been shown that photograph? Dorsey knew that was one question

273

he would never get an answer to. He took the photograph down and put it back in the folder on Mitchell's desk.

It was well into the afternoon before Mitchell returned with the forensic report, duly signed and corroborated. It confirmed that the DNA on the cigar butt belonged to Denis Moffat. Dorsey let out a huge sigh of relief. 'Okay, George, bring him out and let's get him charged.'

Chapter 48

Thursday 29th December

Considering the sullen man he dropped off the previous evening, Mitchell was surprised how well Dorsey looked the following morning; it was as though a weight had been lifted from his shoulders. He was even wearing a decent suit, and a tie that looked like it just had the tag removed.

Denis Moffat was taken to the sheriff court for his petition hearing. Dorsey and Mitchell stood in the yard at the back of the station and watched Moffat, head bowed and silent, being taking into the prisoner transfer van.

'He doesn't look so tough now,' said Mitchell.

'I still wouldn't like to meet him in a dark alley,' replied Dorsey, throwing his cigarette butt into a tin bucket at the back door.

'Did you stay long in the pub last night?'

'No, George, a couple of pints that's all. I've decided to give up the drink and cigarettes in the New Year.'

'You're not serious?'

'You'll make a good detective one day George. No, I'm not serious.'

'You should really think about cutting down the drinking, Frank.'

'Shut up, George, this conversation is at an end. Go and put the kettle on, sometimes it's like talking to my mother when you start all that crap.'

The fact that one of Glasgow's most notorious gangsters was going through court caused a stir in the lawyer's common room, and some lawyers, who had no business in the petition court, went down to the basement anyway, to see if they could catch a glimpse of Denis Moffat and his equally well-known QC, Marcus Hepburn.

It was no surprise to the QC or his instructing solicitor, Philip Stanton, that bail was being opposed by the Crown, mainly on the grounds of the serious nature of charges. Both men attended the cells area to have a chat with their client in order to extract from him any information that might persuade the sheriff that, in spite of the nature of the alleged crimes, there was no good reason for the accused to be in prison pending his trial.

Denis Moffat look haggard when he was brought to the interview room. His face was pale, and he had a stoop that seemed to have developed during his long night in the police cells. He handed the QC a copy of the petition. 'You've got to get me out of here, Marcus,' he said as his counsel looked at the charges, circling the parts that were of interest to him before looking back at the client.

'I'll do my best to get you bail, but you have to be realistic, Denis, you're facing not just one murder charge but two, and, not surprisingly, the Crown has already confirmed they're opposing your bail.'

'But I didn't do either of them; someone is trying to frame me. I just got discharged from hospital yesterday, after a stroke … I'm not a well man.'

Stanton listened and took notes. He was surprised how broken Moffat looked and sounded. Stanton would have normally dealt with this type of hearing himself, but he knew having a QC like Hepburn involved at an early stage would reassure the client that he had the best defence team in Scotland working for him. The publicity attached to defending the likes of Denis Moffat was enormous, and, if he could get his client off, then police stations all over Glasgow would be echoing with the demanding voices of Glasgow's criminal fraternity, 'Get me, Stanton.' However, he had to get him bail first, and that was no easy task, even with Hepburn pleading the case.

Outside the petition court, Irene Moffat and her daughter waited anxiously for the lawyers to re-emerge. The basement corridor was busy with other relatives and friends, all eager to hear if their loved ones were getting out for the New Year. Holding on to her mother's arm with a look of dread on her face, the waiting was excruciating for Ashley. Any attempt to hide the nature of the charges from her was futile; she was at the hospital when her father was taken away in handcuffs protesting his innocence. The fact that her father was now facing two murder charges made her feel sick, how could she go back to University and face the other law students, who would see her now as the daughter of a Glasgow gangster? She could hear all the Mafia jokes, that she had often heard at school, but then she could ignore them, now she couldn't. With notebook in hand, Barney Collins seized his moment and approached his prey with his questions already formulated in his mind. 'Mrs Moffat, my name is Mr. Collins, from *The Daily Record*. Your husband has been charged with two murders. Do you think he will get bail?'

Irene stared at the reporter as though he had just crawled out from under a stone. 'How, the hell do you know what he's charged with?'

'I'm allowed to see the charges, it's standard to let the press see the petition. So, do you think your husband will get bail?'

Before he could get an answer, he was pulled abruptly by the lapel of his coat. 'Take a walk short arse,' demanded Benny, who had just arrived with the twins in tow. 'Print anything about my dad and I'll kill you.'

'Alright, let go,' squirmed Collins, before scurrying along the corridor to lick his wounds.

Chapter 49

Dorsey was on his third cup of coffee and sifting through the mass of paperwork on his desk. He hated form filing, but it had to be done. Just when he was making some progress, the phone rang. He reluctantly picked up the receiver.

'Sir, Miss Baxter's on the line.'

'Put her through, Nancy,' said Dorsey, straightening his tie as though she was about to walk in through the door.

'Hello, Inspector.'

'Hello … Miss Baxter.' He was tempted for a moment to call her Liz but managed to stop himself just in time. 'How can I help you?'

'I thought you should hear it from me first. I was in the petition court earlier dealing with the Denis Moffat case … his bail was refused.'

'Thank fuck … sorry for the language.'

'That's okay, don't apologise, I nearly said the same thing in court when the Sheriff finally refused the motion. Moffat had a very determined QC and the hearing lasted over an hour, the longest bail application I've ever had to deal with. Moffat played the sick man card and Hepburn said he was concerned that remanding his client in custody would likely bring on another, perhaps more serious stroke. He laid it on thick, virtually telling the sheriff: *send him to prison, but if he dies of a massive stroke then that will be on your head.* Hepburn did not use those exact words, but that's what he meant. Thankfully, it was Sheriff Hammond on the bench, and he wasn't in the least intimidated by the QC's veiled threats.'

'Well he's all yours now. We'll get the rest of the statements and productions over to your office in the next few days.'

'Thanks. I'll have to get this case ready as soon as possible. I've already been told that the Lord Advocate is going to take this one on. At least we'll have a QC who is as good, if not better than Hepburn. There's going to be a lot of publicity around the trial, and the last thing we want to end up with is another not-proven verdict.'

'With the DNA on the cigar butt and the Beretta recovered from his garden, it should be an easy case to prosecute. He might even plead guilty.'

'Maybe … Oh, I read about Nedić. That must've been awful.'

'Yes, it was a disaster, but if someone is going to kill himself, how can you stop it? If it wasn't here, then it would have happened in Barlinnie.'

'I guess there's no point in offering Petrović the deal?'

'We can offer it, but I don't think he'll take it. I'm not even convinced the Serbs had anything to do with Watson and Tucker's murders. Apart from them going into the car park at the locus that night, we've absolutely nothing to link them to either killing.'

'Where does that leave you if it wasn't the Serbs?'

'God knows. We are now concentrating on the text messages and the McGowans. We've got the father and two sons under twenty-four-hour surveillance. But we still don't have a shred of evidence against them. BT have only managed to confirm that the text messages were sent from somewhere in the Bishopbriggs area, they need it to be used again to get a more precise location. They are also arranging for one of their technicians to examine Tamburini's phone.

Who knows what that'll throw up.'

'At least we've got Moffat in custody ... well, for a week at least. He'll be back down next week for his full committal. He'll have another chance to try and get bail then.'

'He's not likely to get it ... is he?'

'No, I can't see any sheriff granting him bail ... Are you working over the New Year?' she suddenly asked, changing the subject dramatically.

'No, no, I'm off for a few days ... unless something major comes up,' he replied, aware of the awkwardness in his own voice.

'Some of us are going into town on Friday ... do you fancy joining us for a few drinks?'

'Friday?'

'Yes, about six.'

'Where're you going?' he asked, with a nervous cough.

'The Regent, just off Buchanan Street, do you know it?'

'No, but I'll find it.'

'It's on the ground floor. See you about six then.'

'Okay,' said Dorsey, putting the receiver back down just as Mitchell came into the office.

'Why the smile, boss, you look like you've just won the lottery?'

'Am I no' allowed to smile sometimes ... What do you want?'

'That's better; you sound more like your old grumpy self. Just wondering what you're doing for the new year. Claire's parents are taking the kids for the night. Do you fancy coming over to see in the bells with us?'

'Thanks, George, but I have already made arrangements.'

'Sorry to interrupt, sir,' said Harper, sticking her head around the half-open door, and looking more than a little pleased with herself. 'BT has finally got a fix on the phone. Someone is using it in the Trongate. I've got it on my computer. The signal is moving west from Glasgow Cross towards Stockwell Street.'

'At last … George, let's find out who this fucker is.'

The race was on to get to the Trongate before the signal stopped. Mitchell maintained radio contact with Harper as Dorsey drove onto London Road and sped towards Glasgow Cross. It was still daylight, but only just.

When the got to the Trongate, Dorsey bumped the car onto the pavement outside the Tollbooth bar. 'Fuck,' he groaned as he forced himself out of the driver's seat, his ribs were still hurting.

'Frank!' shouted Mitchell, holding his hand to his radio earpiece. 'Kate's just confirmed that the person has just crossed over Glassford Street and is stationary at the corner with Argyle Street, outside Marks and Spencer.'

Dorsey did not wait for Mitchell to get out the car and began running along the busy Trongate with his open coat flapping behind him. He moved onto the road to avoid bumping into pedestrians. Every other one he looked at had a phone in their hands. He crossed to the other side of the road when the traffic slowed down at the lights. All the late nights in the pub, drinking and smoking, had taken their toll on his fitness as Mitchell overtook him with embarrassing ease. He began to feel a burning in his throat as he tried to catch up, but he eventually had to slow to a quick walking pace.

'Fuck, George, I need to start going to the gym,' groaned Dorsey, still trying to catch his breath as he reached Mitchell, who immediately told him that he had just received confirmation from Harper that the phone was no longer emitting a signal.

'Fucking typical. What now?'

'Kate thinks whoever used the phone has gone into Marks, but there's probably a couple of hundred people in there,' explained Mitchell, constantly shifting his gaze from the front doors on Argyle Street and the side door on Glassford Street.

Dorsey pulled up his coat collar as it started to rain. In spite of the look of astonishment from Mitchell, he lit a cigarette. 'We'll just have to wait and see if the signal comes back on.'

'Mate, can ye spare a fag?'

Dorsey turned to see a youth with a face only a mother could love staring at him. 'I don't carry spares, son.'

'Fuck, give us a fucking fag, mate … are you cops?'

Dorsey looked at Mitchell, were they that obvious?

'Here, there's a couple, now fuck off.'

'Look!' said Mitchell. 'Is that not one of McGowan's dealers?'

Dorsey turned away from the youth and looked towards the front doors of Marks and Spencer, where a man in his thirties was sheltering from the sudden downpour.

'Let's check him out,' said Dorsey.

Before they even got across the road, the man abruptly pushed a customer aside to get back into the shop.

'George, get the side door!'

Once in the department store, Dorsey simply followed the trail of overturned clothes racks and stunned customers to the side door, where Mitchell had already managed to get the man wrestled to the ground.

'Why'd you run when you saw us?' asked Dorsey as the man continued to struggle.

'Why the fuck dae think! Let me up … he's breaking ma fucking arm!'

283

'What's going on here?' demanded a flustered floor manager.

'Police,' said Dorsey, showing his warrant card. 'Is there anywhere in here where we can speak to him?'

'Yes, of course, my office.'

By now Mitchell had managed to handcuff the man's hands behind his back and was getting him to his feet. They frogmarched the protesting suspect through to the floor-manager's office.

The small room they entered was more of a storeroom than an office. The floor-manager wasn't sure if she should remain, but Dorsey was, and held the door open for her. 'Can you please wait outside? I'll call you if we need you.'

'Stand there,' demanded Mitchell. 'Do you have any sharps on you?'

'No.'

'What's this?' asked Mitchell, feeling a bulge when he padded down the man's upper torso. He unzipped the jacket and removed a plastic bag.

'It's only a fucking pair o' jogging bottoms.'

'Do you have a mobile phone on you?' Dorsey asked, as Mitchell took the jogging bottoms out of the bag and placed them on the rung of a ladder lying against a battered-looking filing cabinet.

'Aye, it's mine, Ah only fucking nicked the joggers, the phone's legit.'

Mitchell took the phone out of the man's jacket pocket and handed it to his boss.

Dorsey switched the power on, which immediately prompted a request for a pin number. 'What's your pin?'

'What the fuck! Ah'm no' telling ye.'

'If you don't tell me your pin number then we'll charge

you with theft and resisting arrest.'

'Resisting arrest ... Fuck off, he fucking assaulted me. All Ah've done is nick a pair o' jogging bottoms. This is all a bit mental. The last time Ah got done for shoplifting Ah got a £60 fixed penalty: none o' this shit. You're no' getting ma fucking pin number, no way!'

'What's your name?'

'Gerry ... Gerry Tolland.'

'Do you work for the McGowans?'

'Who the fuck are the McGowans?'

'What's your address?'

'240 Allison Street, Govanhill.'

'Here's the deal, Gerry, you give us your pin number and if we don't find what we're looking for, then we let you go ... no charges. If you don't, then we'll charge you with theft, resisting arrest and keep your phone as a potential production. You won't get it back for months.'

'Oh, fuck. Ye can't keep ma phone ... Okay, if I give you ma pin, Ah walk out o' here ... No charges ... Can I keep the joggers?'

'No you can't keep the joggers ... So, what's your pin?'

'25-05-67'

Dorsey, who was already doubtful about finding the texts messages, typed in the pin number with more hope than expectation. With Mitchell and Tolland looking, he began to scroll through the messages, only slowing down when he reached those sent in October.

'Has he got anything else on him?'

'Just a set of keys and a few pound coins.'

'Okay, take the cuffs off and let him go.'

As soon as the grinning shoplifter left the office, the floor-manager came in looking somewhat bemused. 'You let

285

him go?'

'Yes, a case of mistaken identity,' explained Dorsey. 'By the way, he returned those jogging bottoms. They were too small for him.'

Chapter 50

It was after 3pm before Moffat was taken from the court to the packed prison bus. Apart from a couple of periods on remand in the early eighties, he was unaccustomed to being behind bars. Those cons that knew him immediately paid homage and made sure that the other, younger hotheads gave him peace. The driver had never known a bus full of prisoners to be so quiet.

Dumbstruck, Denis was still trying to come to terms with the fact that he was now facing the prospect of the rest of his life in prison. The last week had become surreal to him. The stroke seemed to have marked a line in the sand between his old, secure, comfortable life and a new one of uncertainty. He began to wonder if some of his memory had been wiped out. The Beretta looked identical to the one he had put in the strong box in the lockup. The DNA on the cigar butt was even more perplexing to him. How could that be? Could he have murdered two men and completely erased them from his mind? The tablets the doctor had given him in the cells that morning were beginning to wear off and he could feel a slight numbness to the side of his face. He turned to look at the other prisoners, most of whom were young men, who saw prison as a retreat from their normal life of deprivation. The reality of his situation became acute when he saw the Victorian facade of Barlinnie Prison coming into view. He suddenly began to feel unwell.

Chapter 51

With New Year just a few days away, the majority of the detectives in the station were busy collating all the evidence that had accumulated over the two intense weeks of the multiple murder investigation. Dorsey had spent the shift double-checking everything that was being sent to the Crown Office. He had learned from experience how easy   it was to overlook something that later turned out to be   an important piece of evidence. With the Serbs and Denis Moffat in custody, there was a feeling of achievement among the murder squad detectives. There was still plenty of detective work to do, but for the moment even Knox was in a good mood.

'Frank, it's nearly four o'clock. The lads are heading to The Logan for a few pints, you coming?'

'I've got all this paperwork to get through.' 'That can wait. It's time to take a break.'

'Well, I guess I won't get this done today anyway, so let's go before Knox gets back and we have to invite him.'

The Logan Bar was only a ten-minute walk from the police station, and a favourite haunt for the murder squad when they had a get together. It was a typical old man's pub, but at least it had a small lounge where the officers could drink in relative peace away from the locals, who preferred the chaos of the bar. It was not the kind of pub you would

288

take your girlfriend to, or even your wife for that matter, unless you were trying to hasten divorce proceedings. Feeling generous and wanting to thank the diligent work of his team, Dorsey bought the first round, knowing fine well that he would not be around for the eight rounds it would take to get his money's worth.

The atmosphere was jovial and there were soon more drinks on the table as pints were consumed with undue haste; the New Year celebrations had started early. Dorsey was feeling relaxed and optimistic; the invitation from Miss Baxter to join her and her colleagues was unexpected and held promise. He was the only one nursing a pint; he had to pace himself.

Mitchell noticed his boss clock-watching when he returned with a tray laden with drinks. 'Are you sure you don't want one?'

'No, I've got to go soon.'

'Help yourselves,' said Mitchell, carefully placing the tray in the middle of the table, before lifting his own pint and sitting back down beside Dorsey. 'I guess you're going around early.'

'What?'

'To Helen's.'

'Oh … No, I've to meet someone in town.'

'Business or pleasure?'

'George, sometimes you ask too many questions,' snapped Dorsey, clearly irritated.

'Sometimes you're so touchy it's hard to have a conversation with you.'

'Sorry George, I've got a lot on my mind.'

'Haven't we all.'

Cooper was at the bar when he got an unexpected call from his wife. Harper knew immediately something was wrong when his face turned deathly pale and his eyes glazed over. 'What's wrong, Sandy?'

'That was Rebecca at the hospital, Hannah has … Sorry, Kate, but I better go.'

'What's happened to Hannah?' insisted Harper, grabbing him by the arm.

'God has finally taken her from us.'

Harper let his arm go, and was about to say something, but he rushed out the pub before the words reached her lips. The others turned when the door banged closed. 'What's wrong with Sandy?' asked Dorsey, getting to his feet to put on his coat.

'It's his daughter … she's finally passed away.'

The mood in the lounge suddenly changed, and the smiles and laughter were replaced with sullen faces and silence. Dorsey took his coat off and went to the bar and ordered himself a large whisky.

Chapter 52

After his second pint and third double whisky, Dorsey made his excuses and left when he realised the time. His determination to remain sober was redundant, and he felt himself staggering across the road to flag down a taxi. The death of Hannah Cooper was playing on his mind. He thought about losing Daniel and how he would feel if he was in Sandy's position.

The taxi dropped him off on Saint Vincent Street, from where he walked down the busy pedestrian thoroughfare of Buchanan Street.

The Regent was packed and he had to push through the throngs of office workers to get to the bar, where he ordered a whisky, all the while looking around for Liz Baxter. There was no sign of her.

As time passed, the prospect of drinking all night on his own was making him melancholy. He drank the whisky with a grimace and took another cursory glance around the bar. It was not his kind of pub, too bright and sterile. The chatter of drunken voices was drowning out the music in the background and he could only just make himself heard above the noise when he ordered another whisky.

'Hello, Inspector. I didn't think you were going to turn up,' said Liz, startling Dorsey out of his stupor as he turned to see her standing beside him.

'Hello, something came up ... Call me, Frank; I don't want everyone knowing what I do for a living. It might clear the bar. What should I call you, now you're off duty?'

291

'It's Liz; Miss Baxter makes me sound like an old spinster.'

'You're hardly old. I didn't see you when I came in.'
'That's because I wasn't here. We waited until half seven.

I tried to phone but it just went straight to your answering machine. The others wanted to move on to another bar just around the corner. This place was getting a bit too noisy. I only popped back to see if you were here,' she explained, over the incessant noise. 'Why don't you join us for a few drinks?'

'Okay,' said Dorsey, ignoring the whisky that the barman had placed on the counter, before following her out of the bar.

Outside the cold air was bracing. They walked to the other bar without talking. Now he had the chance to speak to her, he could think of nothing to say. The whisky, instead of loosening his tongue had turned him mute.

The Horseshoe Bar was a city landmark, an old Glasgow pub with an atmosphere the trendy new pubs lacked. It was busy, but the bar was big enough to move around without having to push past people. They joined a table on the far side of the bar where a half dozen of Glasgow's prosecutors were drinking and arguing over the pros and cons of Scottish independence. Liz introduced him and he shook hands, each name going in one ear and out the other.

Dorsey noticed that most of the glasses on the table were nearly empty and he offered to buy a round of drinks. Two of the older female fiscals immediately declined as they got up and put their coats on. They had a train to catch and no amount of coercion was going to stop them as they said their goodbyes and left. That left three males and a young timid looking female. The males did not need much persuasion and were only too happy to accept Dorsey's offer.

'Three bottles of lager, that makes it easy,' he said turning to the girl, who merely said she would have whatever Liz was having.

'A gin and tonic,' said Liz, with a smile. 'I'll give you a hand.'

'Sorry, I'm useless with names, what was the girl's name?' he asked before ordering the round at the bar.

'That's Lucy, she's still a trainee. Brian is the one with the scarf on, he's Lucy's boyfriend.'

Dorsey turned back to make a mental note of who was who. He had assumed straight away they were a couple; they just looked like they had been paired up by a very experienced matchmaker.

'The one doing all the talking is Duncan, he's a senior depute. Tony is the other guy. Tony hates doing trials and gets a lot of stick from Duncan for hiding in the office when something difficult comes up. He shouldn't be a fiscal. Some people are just too nice to do this job.'

When they returned to the table, Duncan was bragging about a sheriff and jury trial in which he had recently secured a conviction for armed robbery. Dorsey showed an interest at first, but he hated anyone blowing their own trumpet, and Duncan had more hot air in him that most.

He noticed that Liz, Claire and Brian were engrossed with Duncan's courtroom antics, while Tony looked withdrawn and forlorn. Dorsey listened for nearly ten minutes before irritation and boredom set in and his mind began to wander. Is this all they talk about, their work? He had nearly finished his pint and had barely said a word since he sat down. With the story nowhere near a conclusion, it didn't look like anyone was going to buy him a drink. They all looked happy just to sip and nurse their drinks like students.

'Excuse me,' he finally said and went back to the bar to order a whisky.

As he waited to be served, Liz came up beside him. 'I'm sorry, this must be boring for you, let me buy you a drink,' she said. 'It's my round.'

'Okay, I'll have a whisky and ice,' said Dorsey, his humour restored as they exchanged a smile. The smile did not last long. Dorsey had not noticed Helen coming into the bar and was not aware of her presence until he turned to see her standing with a much younger man at the other end of the bar. She turned and hurried out the bar with the man following in her wake.

'Who was that?' asked Liz.

'That was my wife,' said Dorsey, still tying to take in that she was with another man.

'Oh … She didn't look too happy.'

'No, she never is these days. I better go, say goodbye to your friends for me.'

There was no sign of Helen in the lane outside. He phoned her, but the number just rang out. When he tried a second time, a voice message confirmed that her phone was switched off. It was freezing, but he could not feel the cold, and walked up one street and down another with the wind tearing at his face and the whisky blackening his thoughts. *Who the fuck was that with her?* he continually repeated to himself. He went into a few bars in the lanes just off Buchanan Street, all packed. He drank his way through another few bars until he eventually found them in Sloans, sitting outside.

'Is it no' a bit cold to be sitting out here?' he shouted, making his way through the crowded tables, ignoring the complaints of those he pushed aside. 'I thought you'd given up smoking.'

'Frank, you're drunk,' she said, in a strained whisper, stumping out the cigarette.

'Who's your boyfriend?' he sneered, before stumbling down on the bench opposite.

'He's not my boyfriend, so can you please just go.'

'Hi, Mr Dorsey, I'm your wife's lawyer … '

'Her fucking lawyer!' exclaimed Dorsey with a forced laugh and ignoring the lawyer's outstretched hand. 'Is this not a bit unethical … screwing my fucking wife?'

'For God's sake, Frank, please go!'

'You've got this all wrong, Mr … '

'No, you've got it all fucking wrong!' shouted Dorsey, getting to his feet. 'You can have your fucking divorce. I've had enough of this shit, and I don't want that fucker sending me any more of his fucking letters either.'

Dorsey pushed his way back through the complaining customers and went into the bar. He ordered a double whisky and stared at himself in the mirror opposite. He drank the whisky, which barely touched his lips and for a moment was tempted to smash the mirror with the empty glass. 'Another whisky, son.'

'Sorry, I can't serve you. The manager thinks you've had enough to drink.'

'Fuck the manager, another whisky.'

'I'm going to have to ask you to leave,' said the barman, nodding to the bouncer at the door.

'Okay, son, you're only doing your job. I'm going.'

When he got back out to the courtyard, there was another couple at the table where his wife and the lawyer had been sitting. He suddenly felt cold and his body began to shiver under his damp coat. With little chance of getting a taxi, he began the long walk home.

Chapter 53

Saturday 31ˢᵗ December

It was late in the afternoon before Dorsey woke. He could not remember undressing and going to bed, but somehow he had managed. The central heating had been on all night and the room was too hot. He got up and staggered into the kitchen and switched off the boiler, which shuddered to a stop like an old locomotive. He took a drink of cold water and a couple of painkillers to subdue his hangover. The hunger that he had suppressed came back, only this time he needed to eat something to satisfy it. He looked in the fridge: there was a lump of mouldy cheese and some bacon that looked like it had turned to leather. Still feeling a little drunk, he sat at the kitchen table and reached for his packet of cigarettes. As he lifted the cigarette to his lips a sudden impulse came to him. He crushed it between his fingers as though he was taking revenge on it for his troubles. He then turned to the few that were left in the packet and did the same, before throwing the lot into the rubbish bin with a sense of purpose.

What had started with an impulse quickly became a mission and he went around the flat emptying ashtrays and lifting dirty plates. He threw a half-eaten pizza into the bin and poured what was left in the bottle of whisky down the sink. He then began filling black bin liners with all the other detritus that he was soon collecting around the flat. It wasn't a bin he needed, but a skip as the bags of rubbish pilled up in the hall.

For the next couple of hours he cleaned the flat from the top to bottom, even washing the windows for the first time since he moved in. When he was satisfied he had restored the flat to some semblance of tidiness, he went down to the local shop, and bought enough groceries to keep him going for the rest of the week. During his zeal to make the flat look the way it should, he had made up his mind. He would sign the papers that had been lying on the hall table for over a month, and Helen could have her divorce, the house and everything in it. She already had it anyway. From now on he would only meet Daniel if *Daniel* wanted to meet him. He was old enough to make up his own mind if he wanted to be with his father or with his friends. With these thoughts replaying in his mind, Dorsey made himself a fry-up that had more calories in it than he had eaten in the previous month. It was only when he was halfway through his breakfast that he remembered Sandy's daughter had died the night before. The sudden memory put him off finishing what was left on the plate. He picked up his phone, trying to think what anyone could say to a man who had just lost his only child to a drug overdose. Sandy's number rang out a couple of times and he reluctantly left his condolences on the voice mail. He suddenly had an urge to phone Daniel, but he was feeling too fragile to suffer any more feelings of rejection and put the phone back on the coffee table. He needed a cigarette and could not think of anything else to do to keep his mind off the temptation to go back out and buy a packet. It was going to be a long day.

To kill some time, he decided to watch the boxset of *Game of Thrones* someone bought him one Christmas, and until now never had the time to get into. After the first few episodes, he found it difficult to concentrate much longer on this fantasy world and his mind drifted back to the pubs of Glasgow, where he imagined Helen gearing up to bring in the Bells with her lawyer boyfriend. The light gradually disappeared outside, and he finally switched off the television and lay in the darkness.

Dorsey woke early on New Year's morning glad he had managed to sleep through the Bells and all the usual nostalgic Hogmanay rubbish on television. His craving for a cigarette was gnawing at him again. Laying in the dark, with only a slither of light coming through the closed curtains he wondered how he was going to spend another full day on his own.

With some effort he finally forced himself out of bed and lay facedown on the floor. 'One … Two … Three … ' His arms were soon aching with the increasing struggle to lift his upper body off the floor. He stopped after only ten press-ups. Exhausted, he lay on the floor, breathing heavily. A couple of years earlier he could have done fifty and not broken sweat. He lay there with the alcohol slowly sweating out of his pores and the little energy left draining from his body. 'No pain no gain,' he muttered, using what strength was left in his aching arms to do at least another ten. 'One … Two … Three … '

Dorsey knew it would take more than a few press-ups to get rid of the extra stone in weight he was carrying. After a few minutes to recover some feeling in his arms, he put on an old tracksuit, which had not seen the light of day for years, and went out for a run. The first couple of hundred yards were easy enough, but soon the back of his legs began to ache even more than his arms did. After forcing a couple of miles out of his tired limbs, he walked back to the flat soaking in sweat in spite of the bitter January wind.

Instead of a fry-up, he made a bowl of porridge and forced it down against his stomach's reluctance to accept it. A long shower left him feeling better than he had in months. Restored to life, he fancied a walk in the park to keep his mind occupied and to dispel the temptation of the pub.

Just before he reached the park gate, his phone began buzzing. He tried to ignore it but the temptation was too strong. *It might be Daniel,* he reasoned as he took it out of his pocket to see who was calling. It was George.

'What's the matter?'

'I'm sorry to call you, Frank, but I'm sure you'd want to know straight away.'

'I spoke to Harper this morning to see if there was anything new from BT about the phone.'

'And?'

'Well, she hadn't heard anything.'

'George, you're worse than Ronnie Corbett sometimes. Get to the point,' complained Dorsey, making has way across the road towards the park entrance.

'You're not going to believe this … Kovač's just made a confession to the two murders.'

'What!' exclaimed Dorsey, stopping in the middle of the road as a car swerved to avoid him. 'Confessed to who?'

'To Strachan.'

Dorsey was dumfounded as another car touted at him before he managed to get to the other side of the road.

'Frank, are you still there?'

'Aye, George. How did he manage that?'

'He saw him in Barlinnie with Harper this morning. That's all I know.'

'George, I'll speak to you later.'

'Frank, before you hang up, the funeral's on Thursday at ten.'

'I'm not looking forward to that.'

'I don't think anyone is.'

Dorsey stood at the park gate; the notion of going for a brisk walk had worn off. He was having difficulty thinking straight. That's that then, all four murders were now sewn up. He should have been elated, but he could not understand why Kovač had suddenly decided to confess. He could not imagine Kovač being someone who would be suffering from pangs of guilt. Dorsey was tempted to flag down a taxi and go into the station to speak to Strachan, but quickly changed his mind. He had interviewed Kovač and Nedić and came away with the belief that the Serbs were not involved in the killings. He was slightly embarrassed when he recalled addressing the whole squad in the muster; he had all but exonerated the Serbs from the murder inquiries. *How had he got it so wrong?*

He needed a cigarette, and if there was a shop open nearby he would have bought a packet, but there wasn't. He could now take that couple of weeks off he had been putting back. George had been banging on at him for months to use his holiday apartment in Tenerife. Maybe this was the time to take up his offer. He walked back to the flat.

Chapter 54

The next three days dragged on, and Dorsey had to stop himself from going into the station each morning to find out what Strachan was up to. The cravings for nicotine and alcohol still tempted him in spite of his new exercise regime. With not much else to keep him occupied he continued watching episode after episode of *Game of Thrones,* until it finally came to a disappointing end just before midnight on the Wednesday. Aware that he had to be up early the next morning to attend Hannah's funeral, he finally went to bed around 1am.

It could not have been a more dismal day. The skies were heavy and threatened rain. Dorsey drove slowly behind the funeral cortege towards the cemetery. He cast his eyes towards the passenger seat and Hannah's memorial card, eighteen years of age, dead before she had a chance to live. The service that morning had been at the Reformed Evangelic Church, on the outskirts of the city. The whole squad, including Knox and Cullen, attended to offer their condolences to the grieving parents. Rebecca was distraught as she listened to a heartfelt eulogy read by one of Hannah's college friends. In contrast to his wife, Sandy showed no outward emotion and had the look of a man who was in another world as he carried his daughter's coffin from the church.

The cortege turned into the cemetery and Dorsey

301

parked behind Mitchell, who had both Cullen and Knox as passengers. It was bitterly cold, and he turned up his collar before following Mitchell and his two bosses to the graveside, where they stood at a respectful distance from the grieving family. The minister was already standing over the open grave; his unruly grey hair blowing in the wind that swept across the exposed graveyard. Dorsey watched as the coffin was set down by the pallbearers onto a small wooden trellis at the side of the grave. The minister began reading from his Bible: the words of redemption and salvation drowned out by the cries of anguish and despair as the coffin was slowly lowered into the ground.

After offering his condolences to Sandy and Rebecca, Dorsey hurried back to his car as the skies finally opened up. He was not in the mood to speak with either Knox or Cullen, who were still waiting for an opportunity to speak to the grieving family.

Once in the station Dorsey took Kovač's file from Strachan's desk and read the confession. It was all there. They had killed Watson and Tucker to take over the drugs scene in the East End. Kovač had disposed of the Browning pistol somewhere in the Fenwick Moors, where, he could not say. Dorsey knew that those already out searching for the weapon had no chance of finding it in such a vast area of bog land. It all tied up nicely.

'Bit of a result, Frank,' said Mitchell as he came up beside him. 'The Fiscal's already issued a petition warrant. They're bringing him down from Barlinnie today.'

'Why did he suddenly confess?'

'Kovač wanted a deal to get his nephew off with the drug and firearms charges.'

Dorsey just smiled and handed Mitchell the file. 'Where's Knox?'

'I dropped him off with Cullen. They've a meeting in

the city chambers ... That was the saddest funeral I've ever been to.'

'Aye, what a waste of a young life ... '

'He looks a mean bastard,' said Mitchell, looking at the picture of Kovač, before placing it in a box. 'An indictment could be served by the end of the week—game set and match. What's the matter?'

'I don't know; everything has gone too easily. It makes me worry.'

'Frank, we'd have more to worry about if we still didn't know who committed these murders. It at least gets Knox off our backs for a while.'

'I guess so ... I was thinking of having a couple of weeks off. I'm owed about six weeks holiday as it is. The Moffat trial won't be for another couple of months. Is your apartment in Tenerife still up for grabs?'

'Sure, you can have it for as long as you like. When do you want to go?'

'The sooner, the better.'

'Are Helen and Daniel going with you?'

'No, just, me ... I just want a quiet break on my own.'

'It's a decent size, be great for the three of you to ... '

'For fuck's sake, George ... My marriage is fucking finished; it has been since I moved out. She wants a divorce and that's the fucking end of it ... '

'Sorry. Frank, but I thought you were both ... never mind.'

'I didn't even spend Christmas with them, I was too embarrassed to tell you ... let's just leave it at that.'

303

Chapter 55

It was another cold, dark morning. Ice had even formed on the inside of the window pane. Dorsey looked at his watch when he heard the taxi pulling up in the street and checked his jacket again to make sure he had his passport and wallet before leaving the flat. He had gone nearly two weeks without a drink or a smoke and felt better for it. The daily exercises had helped him to lose nearly half a stone and he was hoping to shed the other half in Tenerife.

'Going anywhere nice?' asked the driver, before he had even put the car into gear.

'Tenerife,' was Dorsey's laconic response.

'I was there a couple of years ago wi' the wife. Absolutely loved it, whereabouts are ye staying?'

'Puerto de Santiago.'

'That's where we stayed … There's a great wee bar on the front, Costa de … fuck … Ah can't remember the name. It was full of Brits and had a great karaoke night at the weekend. One guy got up and did a few Elvis songs, absolutely brilliant. Ye'll love it. How long are ye going for?'

'Two weeks.'

'We were there for three weeks. I think two weeks is long enough. Ye can get a bit bored after a couple o' weeks … '

In spite of the cold, Dorsey rolled down the window and let the driver ramble on; his mind was elsewhere. He watched landing lights of an incoming plane through the early morning darkness as the taxi finally took the slip road from the motorway.

After checking in, Dorsey settled down in a quiet corner of the waiting lounge to read *The Papers of Tony Veitch*. He only got to the end of chapter three before he began to feel tired and stopped reading to rest his eyes for a while. His mind began to wander back to the last time he spoke to Helen after finally returning the divorce papers. The realisation that he was prepared to give her all she wanted suddenly changed her attitude towards him. She even seemed a little jealous that he was going to Tenerife and asked, with a hint of anxiety in her voice, who he was going with. She was taken back a little when told it was none of her business. With that, the spell had been broken, and Dorsey went back to his own flat that day and threw out all his old clothes from the time they were together, especially those things she had bought him. The few photographs he still had of her also ended up in the bin. The suitcase he checked in had nothing but new clothes in it, most still with the price tags on them. This was going to be the start of a new life for him. The past was in the past and it could remain there.

He looked at his watch; still had another hour to kill. A few weeks before, he would have been in and out of the building, puffing up to half a dozen cigarettes to pass the time. Not now, it was coffee and a breakfast that he had on his mind as he made his way to the café at the back of the lounge. Before he got there, he felt the phone in his jacket buzzing. It was George Mitchell.

'I'm sorry, Frank, Knox told me to phone you. There's been another murder. He wants you back here!'

'Why can't Strachan deal with it?'

'It's another one of Moffat's dealers, same *M.O.* as the other two. He was murdered when we had the Serbs in

305

custody.'

'How the fuck can that be? Shit, my suitcase … Okay, I'll get a taxi.'

'Don't bother. I'm already on my way to pick you up.'

Dorsey went to the checkout and managed to get his suitcase returned without much of a fuss. 'Fuck it,' he mumbled to himself before going to the kiosk on the ground floor and buying a packet of cigarettes.

Chapter 56

Uniformed officers had already secured the derelict tenements where the body was found. To the side of the building was a large crane with a wrecking ball attached; now standing idle. The workers were all milling around the half-demolished building, smoking and talking amongst themselves about what was found inside.

Not wanting to disturb things before the forensic team got there, Dorsey and Mitchell stood at the living room door. The unfortunate Mr Welsh was lying on his side with his brains splattered across the linoleum covered floor. It had the hallmarks of a professional killing. Dorsey looked around the room for clues. Welsh had obviously been using the flat as a squat. There were still a few odd bits of furniture in the room, including a tatty old sofa and Formica table. There was no actual bed, only a mattress with some filthy looking bedclothes heaped on it. Beside the makeshift bed there was a syringe in a small tin basin and a rubber band that he must have used as a tourniquet.

'Get out of my way,' shouted Jenkins, coming up the stairs with his usual sense of importance and disregard for the uniformed officer guarding the locus. He was followed by a team of forensic investigators, dressed in their white jumpsuits and rubber boots. The two officers stood aside to let them do their job. Jenkins waited in the hallway until everything around the corpse was checked, photographed and labelled.

'This must be the busiest few months I've had in a long time,' said Jenkins. 'It looks like he's only been dead a few days—three, maybe four at most. Thought you had the murderer in custody, Frank?'

'So did I ... I don't know what to think anymore,' said Dorsey, turning to the scenes of crime team who were painstakingly searching the room on their hands and knees.

'If you find anything let me see it before logging it.'

Before the body was removed to the morgue for a more thorough examination, Jenkins carried out a rudimentary assessment. 'The bullet wound looks like it was caused by the same or a similar weapon as in the Tucker and Watson killings. It also looks like he put up a bit of a struggle before he was killed,' said Jenkins, pointing to the scuff marks on the linoleum floor and the broken chair in the corner. 'He has a fracture to the side of his jaw, but apart from that it's identical to Watson and Tucker. There are no other injuries that I can see at the moment, but he has needle marks on has arms. It's the same MO, and I'm certain it's the same killer, Frank, or I'm a horse's arse.'

Dorsey exchanged a look at Mitchell and they both turned back to Jenkins. 'How can that be, if Kovač confessed to the other two?' asked Dorsey.

'How should I know? I only give you my opinion on the causes of death. What it means to the investigation is a matter for you, Inspector, unless you want me to do your job for you?'

'No, just do your own, you cheeky old bugger. I need the ballistic test done as soon as possible.'

'Twenty pounds says it's from the same gun,' said Jenkins, who had now retrieved the bullet from a cavity in the wall.

'The same make, maybe?'

'No, it's from the same gun.'

308

'I won't take your money off you, Professor. It can't be. That gun is still buried somewhere in the Fenwick Moors.'

'I know, I read the file, but the bet still stands. Twenty pounds it's the same gun that was used in both Watson and Tucker's murders.'

'Okay, you're on.'

'Sir,' interrupted one of the scenes of crime officers, holding an old Nokia mobile phone. 'I found this under the mattress.'

Mitchell put on a pair of latex gloves and took the phone. He switched on the power. It seemed to take forever, but the dated phone finally opened at the rudimentary function window without the need of a pin number. He went into the messages and scrolled down. He showed it to Dorsey. 'It's the same message the others got.'

'Bag it.' said Dorsey.

'That's as much as I can do here,' said the Professor, getting to his feet, and lifting his briefcase. 'I better get back to the morgue; I guess you'll want this post-mortem done straight away?'

As they drove back to the station, Dorsey was still trying to make sense of things. 'What do you think, George?'

'It looks like Kovač only confessed to get the drugs and firearms charges dropped against his nephew. It's the only thing that makes any sense. What did he have to lose?'

'When is Petrović to be released?'

'Sometime today, I think … He had already agreed to be deported to Bosnia.'

'Fuck,' shouted Dorsey, frantically looking for his mobile phone, which he could never find in a hurry without a complete body search. When he finally retrieved it from one of his coat pockets, he began dialling Barlinnie Prison while tapping his fingers nervously on the dashboard. He waited impatiently as the recorded message went through a list of options before he was at last put through to the records department. 'Hello, my name is Inspector Frank Dorsey. I need to know if a prisoner by the name of Miloš Petrović is still in custody ... No, I don't know his prison number or his date of birth. You can't have many people in Barlinnie with that name ... Okay, I'll hold.' He put the phone on speaker mode as the annoying classical music droned on.

The whole investigation was unravelling in Dorsey's mind. Had Kovač been smart enough to dupe them? Had they all been so gullible in the pursuit of a conviction not to be able to see the wood from the trees? Why had he given up on the text messages so easily? The receptionist at Barlinnie came back on the line. 'He was released this morning at 7 am into the custody of immigration officers. He was booked on the 9:30 am flight to Sarajevo.'

Dorsey looked at his watch. It was 9:05 am. 'Who is he flying with and what is the flight number?'

'I'm sorry, I don't have that information. You should contact immigration.'

'Okay, thanks for your help,' said Dorsey, before dialling the operator and asking to be put through to Glasgow Airport. To add to his frustration, the phone immediately went on to another recorded message, he turned to Mitchell. 'George, put your foot down and let's see if we can get to the airport before his plane takes off.'

Mitchell drove to the limit of his ability with the siren screaming at the cars in front to move aside. Dorsey was being passed from pillar to post trying to speak to someone at the airport who had the power to stop a plane from taking off on the basis of a phone call. He hung up on the last person he had been transferred to after being told that the request had to be emailed with a copy of the warrant. As they took the slip road off the motorway, they could see the terminal up ahead. It was now 9:20 am. They still had time to stop the plane.

The last boarding call had already gone out as Petrović was escorted across the tarmac by the two immigration officers charged with making sure he got on the plane. When he made his way up the stairs two Bosnian plainclothes officers took custody of him. Once the boarding stairs were removed and the doors closed, Petrović watched the two immigration officers returning to the terminal. After the usual safety routine by the air stewardess, the plane began to taxi onto the runway as the pilot welcomed the passengers aboard their three-hour flight to Sarajevo. Petrović was clearly relieved to be leaving Glasgow and the certainty of a long prison sentence. He would take his chances in a Bosnian court. The engines roared for take-off. He smiled at the stewardess as she checked he was wearing his seat belt.

Mitchell ignored the strict security restrictions and parked in front of the main terminal. They rushed through the internal security checks and ran to the departure gate as startled travellers moved to get out of their way.

The flight coordinator was adamant that they would not reopen the door to allow them onto the tarmac, but she agreed to radio the cabin crew. The two detectives waited anxiously as the captain's voice responded. 'We've already been given the all clear to take off ... Do they have a warrant for his arrest?'

'Do you have a warrant, Inspector?'

Dorsey looked at Mitchell for a moment, and was tempted to lie, but he shook his head.

'They don't have a warrant, Captain,' said the flight coordinator. 'You are free to take off.'

Demoralised, they watched the plane lift from the runway. That was Petrović gone and there was nothing they could do about it. Dorsey was pretty sure that the court would not grant an international warrant for Petrović's arrest when he arrived in Sarajevo. The Procurator Fiscal had already dropped the charges. They had nothing to legally hold him on.

When they arrived at the station they were met by Knox in the foyer, 'I heard what's happened ... How's that possible when we have all the suspects for these killings accounted for?'

'You tell me.'

'I'm asking you, Frank; you're in charge of this investigation. So what's going on?'

'How come you're in charge when things are going well, but as soon as there's a fuck up, I'm suddenly in fucking charge? We'll just have to get the ballistic result before we can say it's the same killer. Anything else, sir?' Dorsey sneered, walking past a dumfounded Knox.

That afternoon a provisional forensic report was emailed to Dorsey. He read it, feeling sick when it confirmed that the bullet recovered at the locus had been fired from a Browning 9mm pistol. The barrel marks on the bullet were from the same gun that was used in the Watson and Tucker murders. He retrieved a copy of Kovač's signed confession from the filing cabinet in the main office. Kovač's signature was at the bottom of each page along with Strachan's and Harper's corroborating signatures. The confession was handwritten by Strachan, but that was not unusual when a person was in prison and interviewed without access to recording equipment. He then read the detailed admissions that only the murderer could have known.

'Where's Strachan and Harper?' he shouted when noticing that neither were at their desks.

'They've gone back out,' replied Mitchell.

'Where to?'

'They didn't say.'

'George, you better put all the evidence of the Watson and Tucker murders back up on the boards, along with what we've got on Welsh.'

Chapter 57

After reading the report for a second time, Dorsey left the station without letting anyone know where he was going and drove to the city morgue. It was a dismal evening, and the rain was lashing off the windscreen making visibility poor. Only for Mitchell's phone call he would be in Tenerife, resting from the most stressful few months of his career. It wasn't so much that Knox needed him back to lead the investigation, but it was more likely that he needed him to take the blame for anything that went wrong, and right now it looked like a major cock-up had happened that would cause a public outcry once the press got wind of the deal with Kovač. He pulled up outside the morgue and smoked a cigarette before going in.

Jenkins looked pleased with himself and put the twenty pounds into his wallet with a smile that came from years of being right about almost everything.

'Stop gloating,' said Dorsey, following Jenkins into the cold storage chamber. Jenkins pulled one of the freezer drawers open where the body of Ian Welsh was deposited.

'It seems that I was right about Mr Welsh, unlike Watson and Tucker, he put up a bit of a struggle before he was killed. I found both skin tissue and blood under his nails. Whoever killed him must've quite noticeable scratches, probably on his face. We should've a DNA profile in a few days. If he's on your database then you've got your killer.'

'So you're certain that the same person killed all three of them?'

'I've no doubt; Mr Kovač was not the killer. How could he be? Your murderer is still out there, Inspector. And clearly not finished whatever it is he's trying to achieve. Come with me.'

Dorsey followed the Professor into the main dissection area, where there was one body still lying on a slab with a sheet over it. Jenkins put his hand on the top of the deceased's shroud and after a moment's hesitation, pulled away the sheet and stood back on his heels as though he had just performed a great feat of magic. It was no illusion. Dorsey stared down at the lifeless face of Denis Moffat, still recognisable even with the top of the head removed.

'For fuck's sake, why's no one told me about this?'

'Language, Inspector. No one told you because he was only brought in an hour ago from Barlinnie.'

'As you can see, I've removed the brain,' said Jenkins turning to lift a metal tray from the work surface behind him and presenting Dorsey with the partially dissected frontal lobe. 'As the doctors at Barlinnie suspected, he died of a massive brain haemorrhage, but he also had a small tumour on the cerebral cortex. With the pressure that would've caused on this part of the brain, Mr Moffat would've been having hallucinations and memory blackouts in the last year or so of his life. It is quite possible the surprise he exhibited during his interview when confronted with the Beretta and the results of the DNA was quite genuine. His mind might've wiped out any memory of Devlin's and Sylvester's murders.'

'Thanks, Professor, that's put my mind at rest a little.

With what's happened with Kovač, I was beginning to have my doubts that Moffat was guilty.'

Dorsey returned to the station feeling a little cheated that Moffat had escaped justice once again, even if his escape was not one the old gangster would have planned. He was also not looking forward to advising Knox of the contents of the post-mortem and ballistics reports on the Welsh murder, but he could not put it off any longer.

The news of Moffat's demise had beaten him back to the station. The atmosphere was mixed, some felt like Dorsey, but others were just happy that he was dead, and they would not have to deal with the stress of giving evidence in the High Court, where even formal evidence would come under the pedantic cross-examination of Marcus Hepburn Q.C. Dorsey immediately made his way to Knox's office.

'Can I have word?'

'Frank, I'm busy. I have to see Cullen this morning and explain what the hell's going on. Can't it wait?'

'Well, you should've a look at these before you speak to Cullen,' said Dorsey, placing the reports in front of Knox, and taking a seat opposite. Dorsey said nothing; the reports would speak for themselves. He watched in silence as the contours of Knox's face turned from curiosity to anger.

'Does this mean what I think it means?' 'It depends what you think it means.'

'Don't play games, Frank; this is too serious to fuck about with. Has Kovač provided a false confession to get Petrović off with the drug and firearms charges?'

'Yes, a special knowledge confession he couldn't have possibly made unless he was made privy to the information we had on file.'

'Strachan!' shouted Knox, getting to his feet. 'Frank, I should never have trusted that bastard.'

'How were you to know he was going to do this?'

'He's got a lot to answer for. This is a fucking disaster!'

'I think we should speak to Harper first. Find out how Kovač made the statement.'

'Right, get her up here … I'll need to cancel my meeting with Cullen until we get to the bottom of this.'

Harper was ashen faced when she timidly chapped the door, before wiping her sweaty palms on her trousers. Knox barked at her to come in.

'Take a seat, DC Harper,' said Knox. 'Inspector Dorsey and I are going to ask you a few questions … think very carefully before you answer.'

'Yes, sir … Questions about what, sir?'

Dorsey opened the file in front of him and placed a copy of Kovač's confession in front of Harper, who looked at is a though it was a snake about to sink its poisonous fangs into her. 'You know what this is?' asked Dorsey.

Harper nodded.

'And this is your signature at the bottom of each page?'

Again, Harper nodded.

'You were the corroborating officer to this interview, which was carried out by DS Strachan at Barlinnie prison.'

Harper looked as if she had been in the company of vampires the night before. Her face was now completely drained of blood. She nodded again.

'Answer the bloody questions,' bellowed Knox, which brought a look of rebuke from Dorsey.

'Yes, sir I was the corroborating officer,' said Harper, her voice dry and barely audible.

'Stefan Kovač made a statement, which you signed and that we now know to be untrue. He stated that he, acting along with Nikola Nedić, murdered both Norman Watson and William Tucker. There are details in that statement he couldn't have known about unless he was involved in both murders. Did you hear Mr Kovač say everything that is in this statement, which you and DS Strachan signed to be a true and accurate?'

Harper coughed to clear her throat and looked from Dorsey to Knox and back again. 'No, sir.'

This was too much for Knox and he got to his feet again. 'No!! You signed a statement that the witness never even made ... Dear God. This was a bloody murder enquiry!'

'Sit, down ... sir,' said Dorsey, forgetting for a moment that he was speaking to a senior officer. 'Please ... '

Harper began to swoon. She could see her career as a detective swirl down the proverbial plughole. The room seemed to close in on her as she waited for Dorsey to ask his next question.

'How did that happen?'

'Well, sir, we were informed by Kovač's solicitor that his client wished to make a confession and that he did not want his lawyer present.'

'He waived his right to have a lawyer present?' 'Yes, sir.'

'Go on.'

'Well, sir. I went with DS Strachan to Barlinnie to interview him. DS Strachan began to question him and wrote down the answers on a witness statement form. Kovač was a bit hesitant in what he was prepared to say. After a few minutes, DS Strachan asked me to go back to the office and bring him a copy of both autopsy reports.'

'During an interview he asked you to go back to the office?' interrupted Knox, in a tone that was a little more levelled than the last time.

'Yes, sir, I assumed the interview was being suspended until I got back.'

'So you went back and got the autopsy reports. What happened when you got back to Barlinnie?' asked Dorsey in a controlled voice.

'DS Strachan took the autopsy reports and put them in his folder. He told me that Kovač had already given a full statement and that he was going to read it over to him to confirm that he made the statement and that he accepted

318

what was in it.'

'And did he?'

'Yes, sir. DS Strachan read it over twice. Kovač agreed that it was his statement and it was true and accurate. He then signed it.'

'And Strachan signed it as the officer taking the statement and you signed it as corroborating officer,' reaffirmed Dorsey.

'Yes, sir.'

'Did you hear Strachan, at any time, give or correct Kovač in the making of this statement?' asked Knox.

'No, sir.'

'That's because you weren't there when the statement was actually noted by Strachan, is that correct?' asked Dorsey.

'Yes, sir.'

'DC Harper, I want you to go back to work, and not mention this chat we've had with anyone,' said Dorsey. 'The next time you conduct an interview, you only corroborate a statement that you actually hear the witness making, not what is read over to him by another officer, even if it's a superior officer.'

'Yes, sir … it won't happen again.'

'It fucking better not!' bellowed Knox. 'Ask DS Strachan to come up, and remember, you're in enough trouble, so don't tell him what we want to speak to him about.'

'Yes. sir, I mean no, sir,' said Harper, trying to work out just how much trouble she was really in. The fact that Dorsey mentioned a *next time* was like being thrown a lifeline in a treacherous sea of uncertainty that was her future. Her hands were trembling as she opened the door and went downstairs. Dorsey had already made up his mind that Harper was not directly involved in the production of Kovač's false confession. The statement, however, was damning in the extreme as far as Strachan was concerned. He was wondering

319

whether Strachan had the least idea what was facing him when Knox broke his silence.

'What are we going to do with her?'

'She is honest enough, just a little too keen to please superior officers by going along with what she is asked to do rather than what she should do. I think you should put her on probation for six months and send her on a weekend training course on interview techniques. She's young, she'll learn.'

'That bastard Strachan, he's finished.'

'Let's see what he has to say for himself first.'

When he took a seat in front of his two superiors, Strachan showed none of the fear that gripped Harper. Knox turned his back on him and looked out the window as Dorsey began the interview.

'Was it you who obtained a full confession from Kovač in Barlinnie Prison that he and Nikola Novak murdered both Watson and Tucker?'

'What the fuck is this? You know I did.'

'In return for the charges being dropped against his nephew, is that correct?'

'I was given the okay by the Super to make the offer.'

'But not to make up a fucking confession,' shouted Knox, unable to contain his anger.

'I never made up anything. He confessed and signed it in front of me and Harper!'

'During the interview you sent DC Harper back to the office to get the forensic reports into the case, is that correct?' asked Dorsey, while watching the beads of sweat starting to roll down Strachan's forehead.

'So what?'

'And is it correct that when she came back Kovač had already made a full confession, which you read over to him twice before getting him to sign it?'

'Yes, so what?'

'So what!' Knox shouted. 'We've enough evidence to charge you with attempting to pervert the course of justice!'

'What evidence?'

'The statement that Kovač gave was special knowledge, he could only have given it if he was the murderer or he was told what was in the forensic reports … ' explained Dorsey, ignoring Knox, who was never known for his interview techniques.

'Or he was told about them by *you*, when *you* interviewed him without a corroboration officer present,' retaliated Strachan, with a contemptuous sneer. 'I'm not answering any more of your fucking questions. You're both trying to cover your own fucking backs for this fucked up investigation that *you* were both in charge of. If you want to speak to me again, I want my lawyer present. Can I get back to my work?'

'You'll need more than a lawyer to get out of this,' said Knox. 'I trusted you, Strachan, but you're the lowest of the low. I've heard enough. There'll be a formal investigation by internal affairs into your conduct. For the moment you're suspended from duty, forthwith. Now get out of my sight.'

'Right, I've had enough of this fucking farce,' shouted Strachan, getting to his feet and throwing his warrant card at Dorsey. 'You'll be hearing from my lawyer!'

After the door was slammed, Dorsey turned to Knox. 'I guess we'll have to let Crown Office know of this as soon as possible. Do you want me to call them?'

'No … leave it just now, I'll call Cullen first … And there's no way we can get Petrović back here to stand trial for the drugs?'

'The Crown dropped the charges, but even if they re-raised them, the Bosnians might not be too keen to return him. It will be up to the Lord Advocate what happens next on that score.'

'You were right about this fucking job, Frank ... yin and fucking yang.'

Chapter 58

It was a bitter winter's morning, but it did not deter the crowds from gathering outside Denis Moffat's house and along the streets leading to the local church. Irene was determined to do her husband proud and in spite of Denis Moffat's lack of religious belief, he was a proud Protestant and would be buried accordingly.

While the curious and the hacks for the tabloid media gathered, limousine after limousine pulled up and parked outside the church as the 'cream' of Glasgow's underworld came to pay their respects to a man that many were glad to see the back of. Hughie McGowan greeted Irene on the steps of the church with a firm handshake and words of condolence that brought a smile to her face. His eldest son, Rory placed a wreath beside the large floral tribute that had grown throughout the morning. Francis McGowan shook hands with Benny and exchanged words as though their enmity was also being buried that morning.

A suntanned Jackie Dempsey joined the mourners, his healthy, smiling face out of place in the dull morning, and the grey, sombre expressions of the Moffat family. Dempsey had returned to Glasgow early that morning, determined to be at the graveside of a man he had once thought to be immortal. He was also back in Glasgow to take care of business, and to assess the opportunities now that the head of the Moffat clan was finally dead. He was still not sure about Benny Moffat as they shook hands and exchanged a few words; good looking and self-confident: but was he able to fill his father's shoes? Time would tell. Dempsey saw the change of circumstances as an opportunity to broker a marriage alliance between Benny and his daughter, totally unaware that Benny had already drank from that cup in his youth and had satisfied any desires in that direction.

The service was short, the minister less than comfortable with the words that Irene had asked him to say about her dead husband. A pillar of the community, a man of integrity: was this the same Denis Moffat who acquired his wealth from money lending, extortion and murder? To add to the illusion of respectability Benny gave a passionate eulogy about a father he genuinely loved and respected.

While the mourners listened to Denis Moffat's life achievements, the fact that he died while on remand for a double murder was conveniently overlooked.

At the back of the church, Barney Collins was making mental notes of the proceedings, itching to get back to his laptop to write an obituary of Denis Moffat that most in Glasgow would recognise as the true history of the man and his life of crime. He has already noted down the heading and opening paragraph: 'Death of Glasgow's Godfather'. *Today, the most notorious gangster in Scotland was laid to rest in true Mafia style. He was a brutal man who would go to any lengths to maintain his empire of crime that was a nefarious blight on the lives of ordinary Glaswegians in the East End of the city.* Barney had already looked at his old notes and press cuttings that morning of the murders of Bert 'The Badger' Milligan and Freddy 'The Fence' Wilson in the seventies. Both trials ended with Denis being acquitted when the Crown's essential witnesses suddenly went back on their evidence in the witness box. Very few at the time mourned the demise of Milligan, a local loan shark and extortionist, who was happy to lend a few pounds to the needy in hard times in exchange for exorbitant rates of interest that turned a hundred pounds loan into a debt for life. There was some sympathy for Freddy, a pawn broker who had convictions for handling stolen goods, and who had been forced to make Moffat a business partner in his two pawn shops after getting an offer he could not refuse. Being a business partner with Moffat was never going to last.

There was also a litany of other crimes that Moffat was suspected of but never charged, and Collins was now free to write about with little restraint. He could not wait to get back to the office, but he still wanted to enjoy what was left of the funeral and its unashamed hypocrisy.

With the eulogy done and with the tears running down his face, Benny returned to his seat beside his mother and his siblings. The minister then led the congregation in a hurried rendition of *Abide with Me* as Benny and the twins took their places beside the coffin. It was only when she saw the coffin being lifted by her sons and Denis's three younger brothers that Irene Moffat showed any emotion. She grabbed hold of her daughter's arm to steady herself as she cried out his name. With tears running down her face, she followed the coffin out of the church to the waiting crowds of onlookers and the flashing cameras of the media.

Chapter 59

Dorsey was tempted to go to the funeral that morning to see just who turned up, but there was already a half dozen CID surveillance officers doing that job, and he was afraid he would be recognised and draw attention to what was an important fact gathering operation into organised crime. He spent the morning sifting through the evidence of the three unsolved murders. What had they missed?

'Sir, that's Miss Baxter on the phone for you,' interrupted Nancy. 'Do you want to take it in here?'

'No, I'll take it in my office,' replied Dorsey, getting to his feet and hurrying upstairs. He closed the door and lifted the phone. 'Inspector Dorsey, here,' he said in a formal tone. 'It's Liz Baxter, Inspector. The Crown Office was on at me this morning about the Kovač case. They're demanding answers. The defence is now intending to lodge an appeal on the grounds that Kovač only pled guilty because he was given an inducement and put under duress, and then told what to say in his statement by police officers.'

'I understood that Superintendent Knox explained everything to your office.'

'I haven't spoken to the superintendent, and neither has the Lord Advocate. What's going on?'

'In a nutshell, Kovač lied in his statement to get his nephew off the drugs charges. It's as simple as that. DS Strachan's been suspended pending an inquiry into how he conducted the interview.'

'So we let a guilty man go and Kovač pled guilty to a

double murder we now know he didn't commit.'

'Something like that … I don't know what you want me to say. It was a deal sanctioned by the Crown Office, but it seems that Strachan over-stepped the line during the interview.'

'Over-stepped the line? He did more than that. He helped Kovač pervert the course of justice and got Petrović released from extremely serious drug charges.'

'Kovač not only conned us, but he also lied to his own lawyer when he insisted on pleading guilty to the murders by way of a Section 76 notice.'

'The Press are going to have field day with this. We'll have to drop any opposition to the defence's appeal. It's going to make us all look incompetent, if not corrupt.'

'You have to do what you have to do. I've still got a murderer to find.'

'Well, I guess you're right, we'll just have to get on with it,' she said with a sigh in her voice. There was a silence. She was expecting him to speak. When there was no response. She quickly changed the subject. 'Anyway; I heard you were on holiday when you got the call to come back.'

'Not quite, I was still at Glasgow Airport waiting for a flight to Tenerife.'

'You should've switched your phone off.'

'I'll remember that the next time.'

'Have you any leads on the Welsh murder?'

'No, we're still going through the evidence.'

'Let me know if anything comes up … maybe you and your wife will finally get a holiday when you solve these murders. I'll speak to you again, bye.'

Dorsey did not say goodbye. He listened to the phone go silent, before getting up and going over to the window to clear his head. Should he have told her the marriage was

327

over? Would she be even interested?

There was a knock at the door that brought him out of his thoughts. It was Mitchell back from the funeral.

'Well, that's Moffat well and truly planted.'

'Good … Let's hope he doesn't come back to haunt us.'

Chapter 60

The Victoria Hotel was used to holding funeral receptions, but none as big as the spread that Irene had put on for her dead husband. The function suite was able to hold two hundred and fifty guests, and every corner was utilised to capacity. She had ordered a menu that she knew her late husband would have approved of, and no expense was spared as the waiters diligently refilled glasses with expensive wine.

After the main course of roast beef and Yorkshire pudding, some of the guests began to make their excuses to leave, offering further condolences to Benny, who was now seen by all as the head of the Moffat clan. Irene watched Jackie Dempsey, a man she never liked, almost bend the knee to Benny before making his way out of the hotel with a swagger that had not altered with age.

'What did he want?' she asked.

'Nothing … Business.'

'Business? It's your father's funeral and you're talking business with that weasel?'

'Leave it out, Mum, I'm not arguing with you today,' said Benny turning to another associate of his father, who was also offering his hand and allegiance. Benny made the same plaudits as he had to the others that had come to his table. Today he would honour his father by being accommodating to the men who his father had dealings with in the past, but he had already made his mind up; they were out. None of those that had been his father's business associates were right for what he was planning. He saw his future with the

Rankin brothers; they knew how to turn a coin, and it was not running brothels and supplying heroin to street junkies. The old days were gone and he was glad to see the back of them. Cocaine was different class, for a different clientele, who had the money to pay for what they wanted. He had already seen his father's will, and with the exception of the family home and a hundred thousand pounds in shares bequeathed to his mother and sister, Benny had been left everything else. Billy and Eric were still in the dark about the contents of the will, and Benny was in no hurry to tell them. He hoped to placate the twins with the deeds to one of the pubs and a couple of brothels; the rest he intended to sell and reinvest in his own nightclub.

Chapter 61

Sergeant Ferguson only discovered the mistake that morning by chance. He was hoping not to have to tell Knox, but with Sandy Cooper now off for a second week, he could not ignore the fact that the DC had not returned his firearm. The lack of any response from Cooper's phone was making the sergeant increasingly worried. Not prepared to cover for him any longer, he took the firearms logbook, and made his way to Knox's office like a school boy heading towards the headmaster's room.

Knox had enough on his mind preparing for his upcoming interview for the Assistant Deputy Chief Constable's job in a week's time, and he lost his temper before the sergeant could finish speaking. 'He's had it for nearly two fucking weeks! Both of you will be on a disciplinary report for this! Have you checked his locker?'

'No … '

'Well, go down and check it, for God's sake. Have I got to think of everything in this place… And where the hell's Dorsey?'

'Don't know sir, he went out about an hour ago. He didn't say where he was going.'

'Typical … Go and check Cooper's locker and I hope it's there for both of your sakes.'

Chapter 62

There was a half empty bottle of whisky on the coffee table beside a framed picture of Hannah that had been taken only that summer. Apart from the ticking of the clock on the mantelpiece, the room was in silence. It had been still since Rebecca was taken back into hospital, leaving Sandy to retreat into his own tormented mind. He wanted to be strong and make every effort to help her recover from the severe depression that had overwhelmed her after Hannah's funeral, but with every hour that passed he was also losing his own battle with the will to live. With Hannah gone, all their hopes and joy for the future had died with her, and nothing was going to bring her back. What was the point anymore? Even his strong religious convictions left him bewildered. *Why would God do such a thing?*

He lifted the open Bible from the coffee table and read the passage again:

The Lord, the God of the spirits of the Prophets, has sent his angel to show his servants what must soon take place. And behold, I am coming soon.

He poured himself another whisky to fortify his nerve. This time he was determined to put an end to it.

He put down the empty glass and raised the pistol to his mouth and closed his eyes. The metallic taste of the barrel soured with the bile rising from his stomach as he held the cold nozzle of the gun between his teeth. The gun suddenly felt heavy and brutal, and he could not muster the mental strength to pull the trigger. He was no nearer pulling it than he had been on the two earlier attempts since Rebecca was taken away in her fit of madness. He took the gun from his mouth and let out a deep sigh. He began to sob.

There was a sudden knock at the front door. Cooper had forgotten that he had phoned the station earlier. He could not stand the worry any longer, not on top of everything else, but the thought of having to confess to Dorsey made him suicidal again. He looked at the gun in his hand as though he had come out of a trance and was surprised to be holding it. He tried to clear his mind from the stupor it had been in for the last two days. There was another knock at the door. He got up and put the gun into the dresser drawer and looked at himself for a moment in the mirror. Was that old, haggard man really him? He put the bottle of whisky behind the settee and closed over the Bible. There was another knock. 'I'm coming … hold your horses,' he shouted as he staggered down the narrow hall.

Chapter 63

Dorsey was about to leave when he heard Cooper's voice. He sounded drunk. When the door opened he was taken aback at the dishevelled appearance of Cooper, who looked like he had slept in his clothes for a week. Dorsey immediately noticed the bruise above his left eye, and the strong smell of whisky.

'Hi, Sandy, you wanted to speak to me … I'm sorry I didn't get a chance to speak to you or Rebecca after the funeral,' said Dorsey, feeling a little awkward when there was no response. 'I bought these for Rebecca,' he continued, handing a bunch of flowers to Cooper, who took them and stepped aside.

'You better come in,' he finally said with little enthusiasm. Dorsey followed the smell of whisky into the living room, where Sandy put the flowers on the coffee table before retrieving the whisky bottle from behind the couch.

'Will ye have a drink with me, Frank?'

'I can't, Sandy, I'm still on duty.'

'Sorry, well I'm not, and I need a drink.'

'Of course, go ahead,' said Dorsey. 'What happened to your face?'

'Rebecca … She's lost it again. This time she hit me with the heel of her shoe while I was sleeping.'

'Why the hell would she do that, for God's sake?'

'There's no why to it. She became unwell again after the funeral. I don't know if her medication was making her worse, but it wasn't helping. She was seeing things and going from being morose one minute to hysterical the next. They took her back in yesterday. She's been sectioned again … Are you sure you won't have a drink with me, Frank?'

'Go on then, just the one. What's it you want to speak to me about?'

Dorsey could feel his mobile phone vibrating in his pocket but decided to ignore it as he listened to Sandy pouring his heart out about his daughter. Dorsey sensed that Sandy was on the verge of telling something that was troubling him, but he would get there in his own good time.

'I don't think Rebecca will ever get back out of that place. I've never seen her so bad.'

'Of course she will, it will take time,' said Dorsey, taking another sip of the whisky.

'She's been ill for years, Frank … What happened to Hannah just tipped her over the edge … I've got nothing left to live for.'

'Sandy, don't drink any more. Rebecca needs you more now than ever. You can't bring Hannah back, but you're a good police officer and we need you back.'

'Am I? A good police officer? I don't think I'll be going back to work, Frank. I can't do it anymore. It's doesn't matter how many drug dealers we arrest, there's always someone else to take their place … I didn't even know she was using heroin … ' He began sobbing.

Dorsey reached over and placed his hand on Sandy's shoulder, but he was never very good at dealing with other people's emotions. He could feel the phone in his pocket vibrating again as Cooper sobbed in his arms like a child.

'I've got to get something off my chest, Frank, but I'm not sure if I can tell you,' said Cooper, getting up and going over to the dresser. He opened the drawer and stared at the gun.

Chapter 64

'He's not answering,' said Mitchell, turning to look at Harper, who was placing a mobile phone recovered from Cooper's locker into a production bag. 'Frank for fuck's sake answer your phone … You better go and tell Knox what we've found here,' he said turning to Sergeant Ferguson, who was looking ashen faced. 'And tell him that Dorsey went to see him.'

'Fuck,' was all Ferguson could think to say as he went back upstairs to inform Knox. This time he felt more like a condemned man making his way to the gallows.

'Why don't you send him a text message,' suggested Harper. 'It will be at least twenty minutes before we get there … He might read it before then.'

Mitchell could feel his hands shake as he typed the text. *Frank, we found the phone in Cooper's locker. It has the text messages on it. He must have sent them to Watson and Tucker. He's the murderer. He's armed. Phone me when you get this message!!!*

'Let's go, knowing him he'll not check this either,' said Mitchell, putting on his body armour and checking the magazine in his pistol.

En route, Harper relayed the details over the radio to the armed response team that Knox had ordered as backup. Not wanting to spook Cooper, Mitchell turned off the police siren when they were within a couple of miles of the address, but he drove as though it was still on. Mitchell shouted at the cars in front to get out of his way and reactivated the siren.

Harper could feel her stomach churning as the car swerved in and out of traffic at high speed. She counted at least three speed cameras flashing as they raced along the dual carriage way, before turning into a cul-de-sac, where Mitchell slowed the car down to check the descending house numbers.

'Fuck,' shouted Mitchell, as he bumped the car onto the pavement and undid his seat belt. There was an ambulance parked in the driveway of one of the end terraced-houses. Its back doors were lying open.

'Look,' said Harper. 'It's the Inspector.' They both got out as Dorsey walked down the garden path towards the ambulance.

'Fuck, Frank, are you alright?' asked Mitchell, when he saw the blood on Dorsey's coat.

'It's not mine, it belongs to Sandy,' replied Dorsey, nodding back towards the ambulance. 'He was drunk and slipped and cracked his head,' said Dorsey, as the backup police cars finally arrived in a cacophony of sirens and flashing lights. 'Kate, tell them it was a false alarm and get them out of here.'

'Frank, did you get my text, about the gun?' asked Mitchell, while looking towards the ambulance where two paramedics were carefully lifting Cooper into the back.

'Aye, a couple of minutes ago … He gave me the gun to log in a few weeks ago. I forgot all about it. It's in my locker,' said Dorsey, thinking on his feet with Cooper's gun weighing down the left side of his coat.

'What about the messages he was sending?'

'It wasn't Sandy that was sending them. It was his wife. He only found out a few weeks ago. He took the phone she was using and kept it in his locker. That's what he wanted to talk to me about. He didn't tell us before because he was trying to protect her.'

'So, Sandy didn't send them … he's not the murderer … ?' puzzled Mitchell.

'No, the text messages have got nothing to do with it. Rebecca got the numbers from Sandy's computer and started sending the messages a few months after Hannah overdosed. Sandy was just unlucky that a few of those that got them ended up dead,' explained Dorsey, keeping the bruised right hand that knocked out Cooper in his coat pocket. 'I'll go to the hospital with Sandy, you can let Knox know that everything's under control. You know what he's like.'

Chapter 65

Jackie Dempsey waited in the car for the warehouse shutters to be opened. It had been a glass making factory in its prime. The building had been derelict for nearly a decade before he bought it for next to nothing. Dempsey had imported over a thousand pairs of shoes and ladies' handbags to sell in the shop he had bought in the Trongate. They were made from cheap Spanish leather. It was only a front for his real business—drugs. With Denis Moffat dead, he was now in a position to flood the East End of Glasgow with heroin. Sitting beside him was the man that had made this possible. Ricardo Santos was a heavy-set man in his mid-thirties, whose brother, Miguel, ran a similar operation in Malaga. Once the gate was open, the car was driven into the warehouse. In the far corner, hundreds of cardboard boxes were stacked on top of one another. Dempsey smiled.

He ordered his driver to stay in the car as he and the Spaniard got out and shook hands with the man waiting to meet them.

'Is everything here?' he asked, as Santos began looking through one of the boxes of shoes.

'Everything is here, Mr Dempsey. It arrived yesterday,' said T-Bone.

'Okay, where is it?'

Dempsey and Santos followed T-Bone to a small office at the back of the warehouse, which was lit by a single bare light bulb. There was another man waiting there, and more boxes. The nervous man snuffed out his cigarette when

T-Bone nodded to him to stand aside. He took a pen knife from his pocket and cut the masking tape along one of the boxes. It was full of handbags. He put his hand deep into the box and lifted out a heavily wrapped parcel about the size of a bag of sugar, slitting the top of the plastic bag with the knife. T-Bone nodded to the other man, who placed a small silver tray on a camping stove at his feet. The stove was quickly lit, and T-Bone took a spoonful of the heroin from the bag. He put it onto the tray. The other man then produced a leather pouch from his pocket and placed it on the ground. The pouch contained his heroin kit. He mixed the heroin in the tray until he was satisfied it was ready. Trying to hide his feelings of disgust, Dempsey watched the man inject the heroin into his arm. He began to swoon a little and his dark eyes lit up as if a bolt of electricity had surged through his veins. He nodded his approval.

The rest of the boxes were opened and thirty similar, tightly wrapped parcels were removed and placed in one box. With thirty kilos of heroin, and his main competitors running scared, Dempsey stood to make a fortune on the streets of Glasgow from this shipment alone.

'Follow me, there's two boxes in the boot of my car. Bring them in,' he said to T-Bone. 'I want this cut today, and you can start getting it on the streets tonight.'

Once the boxes were taken into the warehouse, Dempsey turned to the Spaniard. 'Here,' he said, taking a holdall from the boot of the car. 'Your brother will get the rest when I get back to Malaga.'

'Sure, Mr Dempsey, he knows that,' replied Santos, who opened it, to make sure it contained the 100,000 Euros he was expecting.

'You don't have to count it. It's all there … Let's get out of here,' shouted Dempsey to his driver, who was on edge ever since he picked up the Spaniard on the way to the warehouse.

'You drop me off in the city centre,' said Santos, getting into the car without waiting for an answer. 'I have some unfinished business.'

It began to snow, making Dempsey glad to be heading back to Malaga.

As soon as Dempsey left, T-Bone and his sidekick got busy cutting the heroin with baking soda, and re-bagging it in smaller bags. A two-band police radio crackled in the background and they laughed and joked about how much more they would make working for Dempsey. It was over a year since T-Bone agreed to run the operation in Scotland and had no regrets about betraying Denis Moffat, a man he had grown to hate.

'Here, stupid, you're not putting enough in that,' criticised T-Bone, making sure the cut was going to be big enough to boost his own share. 'Shush, what's that?'

'Ah never heard anything.'

'There it's again,' said T-Bone, taking a gun from his shoulder holster. 'Go and see what it is.'

'Why me?'

'Because ah fucking told ye tae.'

'Fuck,' moaned Massimo Tamburini, climbing a metal staircase and peering through a small window that gave a good view of the road leading up to the estate. 'There's nothing out there but fucking snow.'

'Well, get yer arse down here and get some of this shit bagged. We've got a few punters tae see tonight.'

Chapter 66

Knox looked at Mitchell and back at Dorsey. 'Where does this leave us?'

'Back where we started,' said Dorsey.

'This is beginning to mess with my head,' said Knox, getting to his feet. 'Frank, why the fuck did you not remember you had Cooper's gun in your locker for nearly two weeks?'

'It was buried under my own stuff. What else do you want me to say? I had a lot on my mind when he asked me to take it.'

'And his wife sent the text messages? Can this investigation get any more fucked up?'

'Andrew, his wife was mentally ill at the time. She's now back in Leverndale and might never get back out. Maybe, like the messages said, they were just sent to warn them of the evil of drug dealing. It's not a crime. Remember her daughter was in a coma after taking heroin. The Coopers were very religious, but Sandy kept it to himself. There was a Bible in the house, that's where she got the quote from. The page was dog-eared.'

'Okay, but Cooper knew we were wasting time on them.'

'We didn't waste that much time on them. They were at best a distraction.'

'Well, I've no option but to put Cooper on a report when he's fit to come back to work. He should've come clean about those text messages as soon as he knew about them.'

'I'd rather you didn't, Andrew. What would you have done in his shoes?' said Dorsey. 'Sandy's a good cop. He's gone through enough.'

'Frank, get to the bottom of these murders and I'll give Sandy a break. I don't want him to suffer any more than he has already. If he still had the firearm it would've been a different matter.'

'There's an urgent call for you, Inspector,' shouted Nancy.

'Go ahead, take it,' said Knox, running his fingers through his thinning, grey hair.

Dorsey listened for a few minutes before speaking.

'Where? Okay, I'll be there in ten minutes … That was DS Fleming. He's dealing with a fatal car crash on the M8. Jackie Dempsey was a passenger in one of the vehicles. He's been killed outright along with his driver.'

'Shit, I only saw him at Moffat's funeral this morning,' said Mitchell, getting to his feet.

'There's a third man in the car. He's badly injured. They found a Browning pistol on him and a holdall full of money between his legs. George, let's go. This might be the bit of luck we've waiting for.'

'Hold on, I'm coming with you,' said Knox.

Chapter 67

The M8 was backed up for almost ten miles. Mitchell drove along the hard shoulder with the siren screaming. The motorway around the accident was illuminated with the flashing blue lights of three ambulances, four fire engines and half a dozen police cars that had raced to the scene through a heavy snow fall. Mitchell began to slow down as the reached the police cordon.

It was clearly a major incident. The wreckage of a Jaguar car lay crushed under a jack-knifed tanker. Now that the victims had been removed to the ambulances, the whole area around the crash was being foam-sprayed by the fire brigade to try and prevent any sparks igniting the petrol that was pouring onto the motorway from the car's ruptured tank. If the petrol ignited then the tanker and its highly inflammable liquid would immediately turn what was a serious accident in to a major disaster. With their lives in great danger, a team of chemical specialists began the procedure of transferring the dangerous liquid into another tanker. Dorsey got out of the car. 'Wait here,' he said, forgetting that Knox was in the back seat.

'I'm your senior officer; don't tell me to bloody wait in the car!'

'Sorry, sir, I forgot you were there,' replied Dorsey, causing Mitchell to suppress a smile, while Dorsey walked on with Knox trying to follow without slipping on the fresh snow.

DS Fleming was ensuring that the uniformed officers had moved the exclusion zone back to a safe distance recommended by the Chief Fire Officer when he saw Dorsey walking towards him.

'How did it happen, Gus?' asked Dorsey.

'It looks like the lorry went into a skid on the snow, jack-knifed and pushed the car into the crash barrier.'

'Are you sure it's Dempsey?'

'Yes, sir, it's definitely him,' Fleming replied in a formal tone when he saw Knox appear behind Dorsey. 'I found his passport and return flight ticket to Malaga in his coat pocket. He must have been on his way to the airport when this happened. The driver is James Quigley, from Shettleston. He had his driving licence on him. The other guy had a Spanish passport. His name is Ricardo Santos. One of the paramedics found the gun in a holster under his coat when he was being removed from the car. He's in a bad way, might not make it.'

'Where's the gun and the money?' asked Knox.

'They're in the boot of my car.'

'Well, get them, I don't want them going missing in all this chaos. We'll take them back to the station … if that's alright with you, DS Fleming,' added Knox with intended sarcasm, when he saw Fleming looking instinctively to Dorsey for approval.

'Of course, sir, follow me.'

Chapter 68

Professor Jenkins was not happy at all at being called in to work at such an hour; especially when he had not long settled down to dinner. He took a sip from his glass of red wine and reluctantly put it back on the table as his wife returned his half-eaten dinner to the oven to keep warm. He put on his coat and hat with the same reluctance when he saw the wind blowing the snow past his window, promising his wife he would be back within the hour.

It was over two hours before he was able to put his coat back on and hand the preliminary forensic report to Dorsey. 'It's the murder weapon alright, and his DNA matches that taken from under Welsh's fingernails. You finally have your killer. But before you start celebrating, there's more. Because of your doubts about Denis Moffat, I also checked the Spaniard's prints with the partial thumbprint found on the black bin-liner. It's a perfect match. This character killed all five of your victims. So much for detective work! It was lucky that the tanker got into a skid when it did, otherwise he would be back in Spain drinking sangria and watching the sun go down.'

'So Moffat was set up, after all?'

'Yes, but he got away with so many murders in the past: I wouldn't lose any sleep over it, Frank. I told you all along we were dealing with a professional killer. Not a two-bob gangster like Moffat.'

'He's hardly that.'

'Anyway, the Spaniard could've got the cigar butt easy

enough. Moffat, as we know, smoked them like cigarettes. It wouldn't be difficult to pick up one of his butts outside a pub. Moffat, like everyone else, had to go outside to have a smoke. The Spaniard could've waited outside one of Moffats' pubs and lifted the butt after Moffat threw it in the street, as most of you with that filthy habit seem to do.'

'So it looks like Jackie Dempsey was behind this all the time. He must've been planning to take over the whole of the East End. This guy must've been sent to clear the way by starting a feud between the Moffats and the McGowans.' 'Well, I'll leave the details for you to work out. I've got a wife waiting and a dinner that's no doubt already in the dog. Goodnight, Frank.'

Once back in his office, Dorsey read the report for a second time. Jenkins was right again, only for the accident the Spaniard would have disappeared without a trace. Only for fate, he would have committed not just one perfect crime, but five of the most serious possible. He was glad that Knox had already gone home. He put a copy of the report, marked for his eyes only, in the Super's inbox. He would deal with Knox's pointless questions in the morning. He went down to the main office to address the squad about the contents of the forensic report, before heading home.

This time there were no vitriolic outburst, just tired faces taking in the fact that the largest investigation that any of them had ever been involved in was now almost at an end. All that remained was to collate the evidence gathered and pass it on to the Procurator Fiscal's office. The Spaniard would be interviewed when he was fit to be arrested, but that was now just icing on the cake. The evidence they had against him was already overwhelming.

'Sir, before you go,' said Harper, with her usual smile when she had something of interest to impart to her boss. 'I checked the Satnav from the car, sir. It confirms that they had been to Rosslea Street in Dalmarnock twenty minutes

347

before the accident. I've looked it up on Google, there's nothing there but an industrial estate that's earmarked to be demolished in a few years time to make way for redevelopment.' She explained, zooming into the 3D map. 'I checked the title deeds with the online council site. This one was bought by Jackie Dempsey last year and is registered as a store for stock under a company he's the director of, called *Spanish Leather*. It trades in shoes and handbags. It's probably a front for drugs.'

'Well done, Kate,' said Dorsey, before turning to all the detectives, who had by now gathered around Harper's computer screen. 'Right, everyone get ready, if there's anyone in this warehouse they'll likely be armed. So, everyone keep radio silence and no sirens. We don't want them slipping through our fingers ... Kate, contact Knox, let him know we need armed backup and aerial surveillance right away.'

Chapter 69

Snow had been falling for hours and the warehouse was now covered in a thick white shroud that hid the years of rust and decay. Even the tracks of Dempsey's earlier presence had been smothered.

Dorsey stood outside his car with Mitchell and had a cigarette as the building was quickly surrounded by armed officers. There was a constant whir coming from a police helicopter hovering over the corrugated roof, spraying snow in every direction. Its search light concentrated on the main shutter at the front of the building where a unit of armed officers were putting on gas masks and waiting for the signal to storm the building.

'Do you think there's anyone in there?' asked Mitchell, staring, with some apprehension, at the silhouetted figures preparing themselves for whatever lay beyond those shutters. 'We'll soon find out,' he said, as the heavily armed unit received their orders to move in. It only took seconds for a door next to the metal shutter to be forced open, and a CS gas canister to be fired in. It immediately exploded. The armed officers entered in quick succession as the gas seeped back out from the building.

The sound of gunfire cracked repeatedly over the drone from the helicopter. Dorsey threw his cigarette into the snow and look anxiously at Mitchell. 'What the fuck's happening in there?'

There was another burst of gunfire.

Radio silence was suddenly broken. 'All clear … all

clear … ' relayed the unit commander as the main shutter suddenly opened and a plume of gas raced out to crystallise in the freezing air.

Mitchell put a hand to his mouth and nose and followed Dorsey into the building with other plainclothes officers not far behind.

'Fuck,' shouted Dorsey, the residue of the gas catching his throat. His eyes began to water, but he was able to see two men facedown on the ground and handcuffed from behind. Two armed officers stood over them as other officers tore open cardboard boxes that were full of handbags and shoes. 'They're all yours, Dorsey,' said the unit commander, removing his gasmask and lighting a cigarette. 'They were lying on the ground shitting themselves as soon as we fired a couple of rounds of blanks. They couldn't wait to get the fucking handcuffs on.'

'Blanks?'

'Works every time, well, so far. Your hunch was right, Frank. There's fair bit of smack back there. I'll be outside if you need me.'

'Thanks for you help, Ben,' said Dorsey as he and Mitchell made their way over to the two men lying on the ground next to a stack of plastic bags containing white and brown powder.

If he was more than a little surprised to see Tommy Bone, he was shocked to see Massimo Tamburini, and shook his head. 'I thought you were still in hospital, Tamburini.'

'I wish to fuck I was,' groaned Massimo.

Chapter 70

Monday 22nd May

Dorsey was not very comfortable travelling to Tulliallan to receive his commendation. Only for the insistence of both Knox and Cullen he would happily have went to The Barkley for a couple of pints instead. 'This is not just about you, it's for the whole division,' persisted Cullen as Dorsey finally relented. It now seemed a long time since he drove the Serbian's car off the road. The fact he knew that the Serbians were armed was the main reason given by Knox to the Chief Constable to support his recommendation.

He was up early and took a cold shower to shake off his tiredness and reluctance before getting dressed in a suit bought that weekend on the insistence of Knox, who had long since got over the disappointment of not getting the Assistant Deputy Chief Constable's job that he coveted so much. The fact that Cullen failed to get the Chief Constable's job clearly placated him a little. He had convinced himself that it was all Cullen's fault for not being good enough for the top job.

Daniel had become even more distant since his parent's divorce and was going through one of his moods when asked by his mother if he wanted to go with his father to the ceremony, claming he could not take any time off school.

'I'm sorry, Frank; he's been like this for weeks. He spends all his time in his room and I hardly get two words out of him. How are you, anyway?'

351

'I'm fine. Don't worry about Daniel. He'll soon grow out of it. If it was up to me, I wouldn't be going either … I'll take him out somewhere at the weekend … I better go.'

It was a bright sunny morning and he began to relax a little, it would be over soon enough he assured himself. He had not been at Tulliallan since he took his final exams for detective and began to look forward to the novelty of being there again as he drove over Kincardine Bridge and looked over the wide expanse of the River Forth below. His job had been relatively quiet since they concluded the interviews of both Tommy Bone and Massimo Tamburini and sent all the case papers to the Crown Office. The interviews of both Bone and Tamburini, if they were not so serious, were almost comical. Both were looking at long sentences, and were not only prepared to incriminate each other, but everyone else involved, including Dempsey and the Spaniard. When they were told Dempsey was dead, they both thought it was a trick until they were shown a copy of a morning newspaper. The Spaniard was a different matter; he denied everything and insisted he was innocent. That all changed a few days before the trial when the weight of the evidence against him finally broke his stoicism and he tendered pleas of guilty to all five murders and a string of other charges relating to firearms and drugs. Both Bone and Tamburini made deals that reduced their sentences to five years. The only fly in the ointment was the deal that let Petrović leave the country without facing the drug and firearms charges that would have seen him with a similar lengthy sentence as Kovač. The fact that he received a ten-year sentence for crimes committed in Bosnia was of some consolation.

Dorsey pulled up outside the main entrance to the training college, and was met by Knox, who was in his full-dress uniform. 'I was beginning to think you were not going to turn up,' said Knox.

'Did I have any option?'

'No … at least you managed to get yourself a decent suit but try and smile for God's sake.'

Dorsey gave a forced smile, before following Knox into the main foyer area where he was introduced to a number of senior officers and the leader of Glasgow City Council, who felt he had some reason to be there.

'Oh,' said Knox, 'there's someone else I think you should meet … Miss Baxter, can we have a minute?'

The roof of Dorsey's mouth suddenly became dry as he turned to see Liz approaching.

'Liz, you two know each other. Can you keep him here for a few minutes while I go and speak to Cullen?' said Knox, when he saw the Deputy Chief Constable checking in at the reception.

'Hello, Frank … your big day at last?'

'Not really, seems a complete waste of time. Why are you here?'

'I give a lecture to budding detectives on criminal law once a month … Did you ever manage to get on holiday with your wife … ?'

'No, we were too busy getting divorced.'

'Oh, I'm sorry … '

'No need to be, it was finished a long time ago … When's your lecture, do you have time for a coffee?'

'No, it's at ten, maybe some other time. I need to go. It was nice to see you again.'

The awards ceremony was not as bad as Dorsey had expected. There were enough other officers picking up awards to help direct some of the attention away from him. Once he received the framed commendation from Cullen and suffered a few forced smiles for the cameras, he left. He had no intention of sitting through a formal lunch with Knox and Cullen.

Dorsey was already over the Kincardine Bridge when Knox phoned for a second time. He ignored it and put his foot down on the accelerator. He was back in Glasgow when the phone rang for a third time. He pressed the accept button and slowed down.

'Hi, I'm sorry about the coffee.'

'That's alright, like you said, maybe some other time.'

'What about this evening?'

'Coffee?'

'No, for a drink.'

'Okay, where?'

'I can meet you in The Horseshoe Bar at seven, if you like?'

'Okay.'

'You're a man of few words,' she said with a laugh in her voice.

When she hung up, Dorsey smiled the first genuine smile he had made all day.

THE END

Acknowledgments

I am grateful for the support and encouragement I received from family and friends who read early drafts of this novel and provided valuable constructive criticism, in particular my partner, Lesley Walker.

My gratitude is also extended to everyone at Ringwood Publishing for their continued support and belief that my work is worth the expense and effort to publish.

Finally, this novel was greatly improved by the valuable input of my editor, George Alexander, and his assistant editor, Rowan Groat.

About the Author

Charles P. Sharkey has worked for nearly 30 years as a criminal lawyer in Glasgow.

Clutching at Straws is his fourth novel, all published by Ringwood Publishing. His successful debut novel, *Dark Loch*, was followed by *The Volunteer* and then *Memoirs of Franz Schreiber*.

Somewhat of a renaissance man, he has also had concurrent careers, as a landscape gardener and as a singer-songwriter. He has had a number of his songs recorded by other artists. His first studio album 'Strange Hotel' has been well received, with more to follow.

Other Titles from Ringwood

All titles are available from the Ringwood website in both print and ebook format, as well as from usual outlets.

www.ringwoodpublishing.com

mail@ringwoodpublishing.com

Memoirs of Franz Schreiber

Charles P. Sharkey

Memoirs of Franz Schreiber gives a unique perspective on the trials and turmoil of life in Germany during the First World War and the lead-up to the Second World War. When Franz and his mother get the news that his beloved father would not be returning to their home in Berlin from battle-fields of the First World War, their lives changed in unimaginable ways. Following Franz as he grows into a man, the effects of war are endless, and the story of his life is littered with love, tragedy and danger.

ISBN: 978-1-901514-64-3
£9.99

The Volunteer

Charles P Sharkey

The Volunteer is a powerful and thought-provoking examination of the Troubles that plagued Northern Ireland for almost three decades. It follows the struggles of two Belfast families from opposite sides of the sectarian divide.

This revealing novel will lead the reader to a greater understanding of the events that led from the Civil Rights marches in the late Sixties, through the years of unbridled violence that followed, until the Good Friday Agreement of the late Nineties.

ISBN: 978-1-901514-36-0
£9.99

Dark Loch

Charles P Sharkey

Dark Loch is an epic tale of the effects of the First World War on the lives of the residents of a small Scottish rural community.

The crofters live a harsh existence in harmony with the land and the changing seasons, unaware of the devastating war that is soon to engulf the continent of Europe.

The book vividly and dramatically explores the impact of that war on all the main characters and how their lives are drastically altered forever

ISBN: 978-1-901514-14-8
£9.99

Murder at the Mela

Leela Soma

Newly appointed as Glasgow's first Asian DI, Alok Patel's first assignment is the investigation of the brutal murder of Nadia, an Asian woman. Her body was discovered in the aftermath of the Mela festival in Kelvingrove Park. During the Mela, a small fight erupted between a BNP group and an Asian gang, but was quickly quelled by police.

This novel peels away the layers of Glasgow's Asian communities, while exploring the complicated relationships between Asian people and the city.

ISBN: 978-1-901514-90-2
£9.99

Not the Life Imagined

Anne Pettigrew

A darkly humorous, thought-provoking story of Scottish medical students in the sixties, a time of changing social and sexual mores. None of the teenagers starting at Glasgow University in 1967 live the life they imagine.

In *Not the Life Imagined,* retired medic Anne Pettigrew has written a tale of ambition and prejudice laced with sharp observations, irony and powerful perceptions that provide a humorous and compelling insight into the complex dynamics of the NHS fifty years ago.

ISBN: 978-1-901514-70-4

£9.99

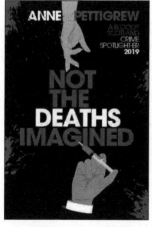

ISBN: 978-1-901514-80-3

£9.99

Not the Deaths Imagined

Anne Pettigrew

It's here, the medical noir novel you've been waiting for! The sequel to Anne Pettigrew's acclaimed debut, *Not the Life Imagined.*

In *Not the Deaths Imagined* we again follow Beth Semple, now a dedicated GP and mother in Milngavie, as she aims to navigate Glasgow's busy medical scene.

But when she starts asking questions about a series of local deaths, Beth finds her life – and that of her family – is about to be turned upside down.

Cuddies Strip

Rob McInroy

Cuddies Strip is based on a true crime and faithfully follows the investigation and subsequent trial but it also examines the mores of the times and the insensitive treatment of women in a male-dominated society.

It is a highly absorbing period piece from 1930s Scotland, with strong contemporary resonances: both about the nature and responsiveness of police services and the ingrained misogyny of the whole criminal justice system.

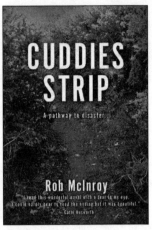

ISBN: 978-1-901514-88-9
£9.99

ISBN: 978-1-901514-43-8
£9.99

The Ten Percent

Simon McLean

An often hilarious, sometimes scary, always fascinating journey through the ranks of the Scottish police from his spell as a rookie constable in the hills and lochs of Argyll, through his career in Rothesay and to his ultimate goal: The Serious Crime Squad in Glasgow.

We get a unique glimpse of the turmoil caused when the rules are stretched to the limit, when the gloves come off and when some of their number decide that enough is enough. A very rare insight into the world of our plain clothes officers who infiltrate and suppress the very worst among us.